Two Out of Three

A Meagan Maloney Mystery

M.M. Silva

authorHOUSE®

AuthorHouse™
1663 Liberty Drive
Bloomington, IN 47403
www.authorhouse.com
Phone: 1-800-839-8640

First published by AuthorHouse   10/26/2011

ISBN: 978-1-4634-4295-8 (sc)
ISBN: 978-1-4634-4297-2 (hc)
ISBN: 978-1-4634-4296-5 (ebk)

Library of Congress Control Number: 2011913171

Printed in the United States of America

Any people depicted in stock imagery provided by Thinkstock are models, and such images are being used for illustrative purposes only.
Certain stock imagery © Thinkstock.

This book is printed on acid-free paper.

Two Out of Three is a work of fiction. Names, characters, places, and incidents are products of the author's imagination or are used fictitiously. Any resemblance to actual events, locales, or persons, living or dead, is entirely coincidental.

Book design by Carl Graves

Author picture by John Silva - location was Pleasant Valley Country Club in Sutton, MA

To My Family

PROLOGUE

It was well after midnight, and the waves were crashing along the shore of the Santa Barbara coastline. The storm that had been building pressure all evening was finally unleashing its wrath, but the house high on the cliff was protected from the deafening water below.

Despite the torrential thunder and lightning, the man alone in the bed was sleeping soundly. He had chosen this location for safety, but he would soon learn that he wasn't safe. He would never understand why, not even as he took his last breath.

Something undefined suddenly jerked him into consciousness, his heart pounding as he opened his eyes and waited for them to adjust to the darkness. When they did, he could see the storm raging outside the floor-to-ceiling windows. The branches in the trees were swaying in a fast, rickety cadence, and the shadows danced around the room like ghouls. He took a few deep breaths, telling himself that he was simply on edge and to stop acting childish. There were no monsters, it was just some wind and rain.

However, in the next flash of lightning, he saw a silhouette in the bedroom doorway. Was that possible? The man blinked several times, hoping that his eyes were playing tricks on him. But the figure remained, unmoving and ominous. The man realized he wasn't being childish after all, and the terror that swept through him was overpowering. He started to tremble.

From the darkened doorway, the figure switched on the bedroom light. The man in bed squinted in the room's sudden brightness and automatically raised his hands to cover his face.

When nothing happened, he cautiously peered at the person in the raincoat, and his eyes grew wide. "What are *you* doing here?"

"Two out of three," the killer replied and fired.

CHAPTER 1
SATURDAY, MARCH 1ˢᵀ

I'm an addict. I've heard that the first step in overcoming a problem is to admit to it, so I've done that much. However, I *like* being an addict, so what's to overcome? I wonder if admitting to the issue and then ignoring it is worse than never admitting to it in the first place. Hmmmm.

To be honest, I'm making this sound a good deal worse than it is. My addiction is not crack cocaine, alcohol, or any type of weird sexual perversion. It's nothing overly nefarious or scandalous. It's simply *caffeine*. Specifically, a certain overpriced caramel latte that has whipped something-or-other at the top and smells like warm heaven. My daily love affair with this concoction begins around eight o'clock in the morning, at one of those national chains located in the heart of downtown Boston.

My name is Meagan Maloney, and I'm a Beantown girl through and through. I've got the accent, the attitude, the parking tickets, and the road rage to prove it. In my defense, a map of Boston city streets looks like a handful of toothpicks that have been dropped to the floor. I defy anyone to stay sane on those roads. I'm a Red Sox fan, a Patriots fan, and I order chowdah and lobstah without the r's, like any native New Englander.

I grew up on the south side of Boston along with a bazillion other Irish families. Our family was a little strange, though. Instead of having a ton of kids like all of the other nice Irish families, my mom and pop had only two—my younger sister, Moira, and me. I think that they decided on *no more children* about the time that I was three years old. Just a coincidence, I'm sure.

Moira and I are grown now, and we live together in a pretty great apartment on Commonwealth Avenue. I can thank her for the swanky address, as she's a bigshot corporate attorney who also happens to be drop-dead gorgeous. I'd hate her if she wasn't my sister. She's the apple of Pop's eye, my mom thinks that she hung the moon, and even I have to admit she's pretty special.

But back to my addiction, which is really the staging for the whole story. Hand-in-hand with my addictive personality, I have an overactive imagination, and I sometimes obsess over things. And people. Well, one person, to be accurate. I don't obsess over him in a stalker way, but in a wow-I-would-like-to-get-to-know-him type of way. But I've never done anything about it. The part of my life where I used to act on my little crushes has been put on hold for quite some time. I'll get to that later.

Anyway, this obsession of mine has about a six-foot-four-inch frame, wavy black hair, deep brown eyes and preppy, square, designer glasses with dark frames. He gets coffee nearly every morning around eight fifteen, and I swoon from my table and then generally drool in my coffee. On occasion, he'll sit down to glance at a newspaper, but he's usually in and out. Sadly, it's often the highlight of my day.

A few days ago the highlight became a blockbuster hit, as my mini-obsession headed right for my table, looking like he was on a mission. I turned my head to see if he was meeting someone sitting behind me, but there was no one else. *Gulp.*

"Hi, my name is David Fontana. Do you mind if I sit down for a minute?" He smiled and held out his hand.

I nearly fell out of my chair. After a quick handshake, I gestured to the chair across from me and managed, "Um, sure. I'm Meagan." I couldn't remember my last name.

"Yes, I know. The people at the counter said you're a private investigator."

My balloon somewhat burst. He hadn't come over to propose marriage or invite me to Paris for the weekend. It was a business encounter. But actually, that was fine. It was good to know that my business cards and word-of-mouth campaign were still working. Clearly my peeps at the coffee shop were taking care of me.

"That's right, I am. Are you in the market?"

"Well, I think so," he sighed. "I need to find a missing person."

I cocked my head and waited for him to continue. I've generally found that if I shut up, the other person talks. Even if he didn't talk, I was fully prepared to just sit and look at him for, let's say, ten, twelve hours, so I was all set.

"If I hire you, is what we talk about confidential?"

"Like attorney-client privilege?" I asked, and he nodded. "Not exactly. I mean, I won't run to the police if someone ran a red light, but if it's something hinky or illegal, then that's different. I'd be obligated to tell the authorities."

He seemed concerned, and I didn't want him to saunter out of my life with his hair, his eyes, and his glasses. On the other hand, I wasn't going to help him with money laundering if that's what it came to, either. I did have *some* standards, thank you very much.

"At this point, David, we're just talking. If you hire me and I find something shady going on, you've got my word that I'll let you know as soon as I can. Fair enough?"

He nodded. "Yes, that's fair." He paused for a moment, and then asked, "So what do we do now?"

Several completely inappropriate suggestions came to mind. "Tell me what you know, and we'll go from there."

"Okay," he said, looking down and stirring his coffee. "I got this Fed Ex delivery late yesterday afternoon, and it's got me very worried. It was from my brother, actually my stepbrother, Darrin, with a note telling me to put it in a safe place and that he'd call me when he could. Of course, I tried to reach him right away, but I learned that his home phone's been disconnected, and his cell is going straight to voicemail. I didn't sleep all night. I just kept calling and calling, but he never answered."

I smiled sympathetically. "I'd be worried as well. Do you mind if I jump in with some questions?"

"Not at all. I'd like to bounce some ideas off you," he replied, seemingly relieved.

"Okay, good. So what was in the delivery?"

"It was a laptop case."

I held his gaze and waited for more, but he didn't say anything further. "With a *laptop* inside of it?" I inquired.

"I can't really say right now," he said quietly. "I'd just prefer to focus on finding my brother."

I studied him, trying to figure out his reluctance to tell me about the contents of the case. Despite my aforementioned obsession, I wasn't

3

a pushover and certainly wasn't satisfied with his answer. Taking a deep breath, I silently counted to five. I don't have the patience to count to ten.

"David, I'm trying to respect how you feel. However, I need you to see this from my point of view for a second. You and I've just met, so I'm not trying to be offensive, but what's in the case probably matters. And if it contains body parts or blood or anything to do with little kids—"

His eyes widened, and he put up his hands in the universal sign to stop. "Whoa whoa whoa!" He shook his head quickly. "Meagan, I'm sure my hesitation seems odd from where you're sitting. Rest assured, if I'd opened that case and there'd been something illegal in it, the police would already be involved. I promise that we can discuss it if we need to, but right now, I don't want to focus on that. I just need to find Darrin. I don't know what's going on, but I have a bad feeling."

This time I forced myself to count to ten. "I'll make you a deal. *If* we move forward with this, and *if* I decide that I need to know what's in the case, then you need to give me your word that you'll tell me. The contents could have *everything* to do with why Darrin is missing. I won't ask you again unless I need to know, but the very next time that I ask, you're going to have to tell me."

"Done," David said with conviction.

I still didn't like it but decided to back off the subject. For the moment. "Good, then that's settled. Now, why don't you tell me about your brother, um, stepbrother?"

He looked sheepish. "I'm kind of embarrassed to say that I don't see him or talk to him more than a couple of times a year. We weren't part of the same household until he was twelve and I was fifteen, so it's not like we really grew up together. I guess our relationship probably isn't what you'd call normal."

"I don't know any family that's *normal* anymore," I said, smiling. I wanted him to feel comfortable.

He nodded and seemed to relax a little. "Yeah, I know what you mean."

"Why don't you tell me whatever you can about him?"

"Well, when my dad and his mom got married we became a ready-made family. I'd always been kind of a book nerd and a pretty good student, and Darrin was a lot different from me, sort of wild. He didn't have the best grades and messed around with drugs a little bit in high school. He graduated and then tried community college, but it didn't really suit him, and he dropped out before his first year was over. Since then, he's been out in Los Angeles doing some odd jobs, a little modeling, some bartending, acting, all the crap people do in L.A."

I nodded encouragingly and took a sip of my coffee. It was amazing how much better my addiction tasted with my obsession sitting mere inches from me.

"So anyway, he gets by but never has any extra money as far as I know. I spotted him a few bucks a couple of years ago, and I never saw it again, but no big deal. You know what they say about lending money to family or friends." He rolled his eyes, and I sensed something behind those dark lashes. Meagan Maloney, Mighty-Mind-Reader-Extraordinaire.

"Do you like him?" I wanted to get a sense of their relationship before I dove into this.

He took a minute, seemingly weighing his words before saying anything. This was a new phenomenon for me. Most of the people I associate with, including myself, speak and then think. Sometimes the thinking part doesn't happen at all. He seemed to be doing the opposite. Thinking before speaking. What a wonderful, strange being, this David Fontana.

"Yes, I do like him, and I really like his mom. I was pretty young when my mother died, and I didn't know if my dad would ever get over her. But eventually he met Darrin's mom, and it was great to see him move on with a nice lady who treated him well. In the same vein, she'd had a heck of a time with her ex-husband, and she seemed grateful to be with someone stable like my dad."

"What was the deal with the ex?" I didn't know if that had anything to do with anything, but I wanted to get as much information as possible.

"I don't know many of the details, but I guess that Darrin's dad was some type of mess. He was really heavy into booze and drugs and wasn't exactly a model parent. At one point when the marriage was ending, he actually kidnapped Darrin for several months one summer. Jean, his mom, had no idea where they'd gone, and she spent all of her time and money looking for Darrin. One day she was notified that her husband had been arrested and was told that Darrin had been asking for her. She got full custody, obviously, and then came to Boston to start over. It was a pretty bad scene, I think. It's probably where Darrin got his wild side."

I nodded. "Yeah, that makes sense."

"So anyway, our age difference didn't really have us in the same circles, and we basically put up with each other. No ugliness, really, just regular brother stuff. Now I see him around the holidays, and we email off and on. That's about it."

None of this sounded too weird, but I still had a few questions. "Is there any chance he's hooked up with his dad?"

He scrunched up his mouth a little bit and knitted his eyebrows. "I doubt it. I don't think Darrin's heard from him since his dad went to jail, and that was a long time ago."

I mulled that over. "Do you have *any* idea as to what might have happened to Darrin? Any suspicion at all?"

He shrugged and shook his head. "No, sorry. I'm just really worried and have a bad feeling about all of it."

I cocked my head at him, curiosity getting the best of me. "Is part of your worry due to what was in that laptop case?"

He smiled. "Maybe. Will you help me? You'll probably need to go to L.A. for a few days."

"I *think* I'd be able to rearrange my schedule," I said slowly, as if pondering the many things I had going on at work. He didn't need to know that my schedule was currently a blank slate. "I do have a couple other questions before I decide, though."

He must have caught the wariness in my voice, because he looked at me with apprehension. "Go ahead," he said tentatively.

"Why aren't *you* going out there?"

He nodded in understanding. "It's a couple of things, really. I'm a CPA and own a small accounting firm not too far from here. Since it's March, tax day is fast approaching, and I can't just take off. Also, I'm hoping that it's just something silly that doesn't need my involvement. Don't get me wrong, if you get out there and uncover a mess, then I'll do whatever I can to help. I guess that I just need you to do the initial legwork for me."

"Makes sense. Final question," I said. "Why aren't you hiring someone out there? It would save you the expense of a plane ticket and a hotel."

He didn't hesitate. "Because I can't look them in the eye and have a cup of coffee with them. I want to know who I'm working with, so the money is worth it to me."

"Fair enough," I responded and waited a beat. "I'm in."

We spent the next few minutes talking about my fees and exchanging contact information. I accepted an initial deposit and told David that I'd email him a contract later in the day. He, in turn, said that he'd send me a picture of Darrin, along with my flight arrangements. *He* was going to make *my* flight arrangements! I was officially digging him. I memorized his cell number and hoped that someday I might use it for something other than business. But time would tell on that one. I didn't know if my heart was ready again anyway.

CHAPTER 2

I got back to the apartment and walked in to find Doobie, our neighbor, sitting on the couch, television blaring and stereo blaring even louder. Doobie has a key to our apartment, ostensibly to help us if we ever find ourselves locked out, but he routinely makes himself at home. He viewed the giving-of-our-key as if he was a rock star who was awarded the key to a city, and we've never had the heart to tell him otherwise. Plus, he often helps out with our Springer Spaniel, Sampson, so we cut Doobie a lot of slack.

It was nearly nine thirty in the morning, and I was fairly shocked to see Doobie up among the living. He keeps some odd hours and was in typical form today. Disheveled hair, bloodshot red eyes, and a gray tee shirt so thin and faded that I couldn't even read it. It looked to have something to do with Beavis and Butthead. There was a tear in one of the shoulder sleeves that revealed a patch of white, freckled skin. A pair of mismatched socks, with holes in one of them, and brownish sweatpants topped off his getup, and his laptop was where it belonged, in his lap. With Doobie, his computer is a natural appendage. Breakfast, which was a bag of half-eaten Fritos, was beside him on Moira's Thomasville leather couch. I turned down the television and stereo and then barked at him.

"Doob, get the food off the couch! Moira would kill you if she saw that."

"Jeez, chill out, Meg. Nice to see you, too," he whined and slowly placed the Fritos on the floor.

"Oh, that's much better, Doob," I said sarcastically and propped a television tray in front of him. He reluctantly picked up the bag of chips and placed them on the tray. He kept the laptop in his lap and pouted.

"Well then, I came over here to show you something. But I guess you don't care to see what I stayed up all night working on."

I was definitely intrigued, but I wouldn't admit it. "Fine by me. When's the last time you slept?"

He shrugged and looked at his wrist, trying to find a watch that wasn't there. He then swerved his head slowly around the room, evidently looking for a clock. "What day is it?"

I rolled my eyes. "It's Saturday, Doob, all day."

He nodded a few times as if that solved everything. "I slept a few hours on Wednesday or Thursday afternoon, I think."

"You want some coffee?"

"I'd like some eggs and bacon, please," he replied.

"Coffee, Diet Coke, or bottled water, those are your options," I said testily.

"Coffee." His pout grew exponentially.

I have an emergency stash of some decent coffee in the apartment, for days when I can't get to the super-wonderful-land-of-Oz-coffee-shop on Boylston Street. Those times are few and far between, believe me. I started the coffee maker, and Doobie gave it one last effort.

"You have any pancakes or anything?"

I thought about smacking him upside the head, but he was looking really pathetic. "Doob, when's the last time you had something to eat?"

He shrugged again and twisted his mouth. This was taking way too long. He held up the Fritos. "Do these count?"

"No!"

"I don't know then," he finally said.

"Good grief." I rummaged around the cupboards and found a box of blueberry muffin mix, probably dating back to pre-World War II era. We usually have a reasonable amount of food on hand, but neither Moira nor I had found time to hit the grocery store in the past couple of weeks. Doobie saw me heading for the oven, and his eyes lit up.

"Pancake mix?"

"Blueberry muffins, take it or leave it."

"Cool."

I preheated the oven and then mixed up the eggs, milk, and muffin powder. After dropping the gobs of goo into the mini-paper things, I plopped them into the oven. Look out Martha Stewart. From the tiny kitchen area, I glanced through the built in pass-through into the living room and saw that Doobie was sound asleep on the couch, sitting straight up, his computer still resting on his lap. I tiptoed over and slowly slid the laptop off of him. Then I covered him with a blanket that would undoubtedly need fumigating after his nap.

It goes without saying that Doobie is an odd duck, but he leads a fairly charmed life. He's a computer whiz and also a trust fund baby. He spends his days and nights hacking into all sorts of websites, just for the fun of it, to hear him tell it. He says he's never caused any damage (that he's aware of) and that he likes to hack into places just to see if he can. I don't understand that for one second, but then again, I don't need to. Plenty of people probably wonder why I'm a P.I. as well.

Doob's originally from the Midwest. Iowa, to be precise. Doob's parents were in their mid-40s when his mom found out she was pregnant with Doobie. They'd never planned on having children, but they did their best with him, and he had a nice, quiet upbringing. He did well in school and got hooked on computers when he was pretty young.

I don't know the particulars, but when Doob was in junior high school, his dad came up with some type of generic fertilizer or pesticide that he could market for less than half of what the big-time brands were charging farmers. He developed the product and then sold it off to a huge conglomerate, making an absolute fortune in the process. Once Doob headed off to college, his parents headed off to Europe, and he sees them once or twice a year, in various cities across the globe. They don't know that he never graduated from college, and I'm not sure they'd mind. He gets his monthly stipend from them, and he just keeps hacking away, day and night, night and day. He is also suspected to smoke a bit of something now and then, hence his nickname, but I've truly never seen him with any illegal substances. His lifestyle seems to work for him, and the Doobster is a good guy to have around, so who am I to judge?

The buzzer went off, indicating that the muffins were done, and Doobie woke up and looked like he had no idea where he was. He shook his head quickly, trying to shake the cobwebs loose.

"How many do you want?" I asked, leaning my head through the pass-through.

"How many what?"

"Muffins, Doob, muffins!"

"Oh, you made muffins? Cool. What kind?"

I didn't bother with an answer. I put three muffins and a hunk of butter on a plate and walked into the eating area adjacent to the living room. After setting the food on Moira's round, antique table, I gave Doob his instructions. "At the table, Fritos Boy. No more food on the couch." He rose and shuffled over to the table.

"Do I smell coffee?"

"Doob, we had this whole conversation fifteen minutes ago."

He pondered that for a second. "Cool."

I set a mug of coffee in front of him and retreated to my bedroom. After digging a large suitcase out from under my bed, I shouted out to the living room. "Hey Doob, can you take me to the airport tomorrow?"

"Which one?"

I thought about that. I assumed that David would have me fly out of Boston, but sometimes flights were cheaper out of Providence, Rhode Island. I wasn't sure. I yelled back to him. "I don't know."

"What time?" He'd yelled with a mouthful of food and starting coughing like crazy. I went back out to the living room to make sure that he wasn't choking to death.

"Don't know that, either," I said. Somehow I knew it wouldn't matter. In Doob's world, destinations and times of departure were of no consequence.

"Yep, I can do that," he coughed. "Where are you going?"

"Sunny Los Angeles," I replied. "And it's for a missing person case, thank you very much."

"Wow, your first big-girl gig! Congrats, Meg, that's awesome."

I smiled modestly and said, "Aw, shucks."

"Have you told Norman about it?"

"He's on vacation, I thought I told you that. It's his and Jacqueline's twenty-fifth anniversary, and she convinced him to be a snowbird for a couple of months. They're in Aruba living large."

"God help the firm," Doob said with another mouthful of muffin.

I rolled my eyes but couldn't help agree with him just a little bit.

Norman is the principal in our P.I. firm, which means he's in charge of basically everything. He generally handles all of the heavy lifting and leaves me to the easier jobs, although he'd never admit to that.

To date, my sleuthing activities can be placed into two categories. The first is spying on some unsavory spouses, generally men, and it's always depressing. My second activity has been to take pictures of supposedly injured people who are committing insurance fraud. The latter doesn't bother me as much as the cheating spouses and is sometimes kind of entertaining.

My favorite had been a guy with a doctor's note, claiming he had only ten percent usage of his left arm, due to an accident at his job involving a mutant copy machine. I followed this guy to a golf course one afternoon, and it didn't look like he had a foursome, so I grabbed my clubs out of the back of my car. Albeit cliché, my motto has always been—*have clubs, will travel*. Sure enough, we were both singles and got paired up with another twosome for eighteen holes. The "injured" man shot three over par for the day and took a total of twenty-three dollars from the rest of the group. I hope he saved it because it cost him over fifty thousand in disability money once my pictures made their way to his insurance company. It turned out that his doctor also happened to be his college roommate from back in the day, and they'd been number one and two on their collegiate golf team. I think the doc got in some hot water as well. At least I hope so.

Doob shook me out of my reverie. "So Norman obviously didn't set you up with this one. How did you get the case?"

"The client is that guy at the coffee shop I've told you about. For whatever reason, the ladies behind the counter knew that he needed a private investigator, and they told him about me."

Doob raised his eyebrows. "It's not *theeeee* guy, is it?" Doob is such a girlfriend sometimes.

I smiled mischievously. "It is *theeee* guy, yes. I forgot my last name and nearly fell out of my chair, but he probably didn't notice."

Doob nodded his head approvingly. "Smooth, Meg."

"I'm pretty excited. I just hope that everything goes well."

"Can I come?"

I looked at him to see if he was serious. He blinked at me and waited for an answer. Yep, he was serious.

"Well, it's for work, Doob, so I don't know that there'll be much free time."

He blinked at me again and looked thoroughly confused. A piece of muffin fell out of his mouth. "Yeah, but *I* won't be working."

He had a point there. Doobie never had, and probably never would, actually work. I had to get him off topic.

"Speaking of work, what's the project you were talking about earlier?"

"Hunh?"

"When you were pouting earlier, you said you weren't going to tell me about your all night endeavor."

"Oh yeah! Well, as of four o'clock this morning, I've completed my goal of getting into all fifty states DMV websites."

I was incredulous. "As in the Department of Motor Vehicles?"

He smiled like a Cheshire cat. "Yes, ma'am."

"Don't call me ma'am, Doob. You know better."

"Sure thing, ma'am." His smile widened.

"You're aware that what you're doing is totally illegal?"

Doob rolled his eyes. "Meg, it's what I do. I'm not going to *use* the information. I just wanted to see if I could get into all fifty systems before Easter."

"You've got some interesting goals in life, my friend. What happens if you get caught?"

He shrugged. "That's doubtful, but if it happens, then I guess it's a good thing I know a great lawyer."

"That isn't Moira's type of law."

"Meg, stop yammering. I know you're just trying to get me to forget about going to L.A. Are you going to let me go or not?"

"Well, I'm only going to be gone a few days, and Moira will probably need some help with Sampson, so it would be better if you stayed here." As if on cue, the black-and-white Springer Spaniel entered from stage right, appearing a bit groggy from his morning nap. His curly haired ears were drooping, and his eyes were still half closed. There's nothing quite like the appearance of his adorable freckled face to brighten my day, and he's one of the best things about my life. I'd throw most of my friends in a volcano for this dog, and he absolutely knows it.

Sampson generally stays on Moira's side of the apartment, but occasionally he'll come slumming over to my side of the tracks. I can't say that I blame him, though. Moira has a massive bedroom, and she had an up-and-coming designer from Manhattan create a four-poster doggy bed for Sampson that matched her own antique bedroom set. Yes, it has a mattress, and yes, it has a little two-step mahogany stool so that Sampson can easily enter and depart his royal bed. Moira has three sets of four-hundred-thread-count sheets that she rotates every few days for Sampson's comfort, and his ensemble is completed with several fluffy pillows and a stuffed dog that he humps regularly. Moira and Sampson also have matching eye masks in several different colors, but Sampson has eaten most of his. He lives a more luxurious lifestyle than most people in five-star hotels. It won't surprise me if I come home someday to find

Sampson and a bunch of doggy hookers eating caviar and smoking cigars on his four poster bed. The dog has it absolutely made. I'll admit it, I'm a little jealous. But since it's him, I can get over it.

Sampson walked over to the table and gave Doobie a snooty little sniff. For once, I was grateful that he couldn't talk, but he did give off a fairly pathetic whine. Sampson then walked over to his Canine Café, which is a dark wooden box that elevates his food and water bowls so that he'll never have to bend his precious head too far. Sampson took a very small sip of water and then looked up at me like I was a dumbass. He actually sighed.

I walked over to his bowl and looked at him. "What's wrong, boy?" I gave his ears a scratch, but he kept looking at me expectantly.

Doob said something completely unintelligible. I glanced at him, and crumbs were shooting out his mouth.

"Is there *any* chance that you could wait to speak until your mouth is empty?"

Doob smiled, which caused more crumbs to spill out. "He wants ice."

I looked down at Sampson. "What are you talking about?"

"He likes it if someone puts ice in his water before he gets up from his morning nap. That way it's nice and cold for him."

"Oh, good grief, you've got to be kidding me! When did this start?"

Doobie shrugged. "I put some ice in there a week or so ago, after I took him out for a walk. Now he doesn't really want any water unless it's super cold."

I put my hand in the doggy water and flicked it in Sampson's face. He licked at the air, as if he might catch a few drops. "No way, Mr. Fancy Dog, you drink it as is. We aren't going to have someone putting ice in your bowl on a regular basis." Sampson lifted his paw.

I cocked my head at him. "Did you just flip me off?"

Sampson cocked his head back at me, and damned if it wasn't about the cutest thing I'd ever seen. I sighed and grabbed a glass to fill with ice cubes to put in his majesty's bowl.

"Doob, I swear this dog owns *us*." As it should be really, but I had to at least *act* disgusted.

Doob agreed. "Of course he owns you. You walk around the city picking up his shit. Who are you kidding?"

"Don't single me out, Muffin Man. You pick up as much shit as either Moira or me. Probably more."

15

"I don't mind. It's not like he can do it for himself."

True. "But the ice? Are we going too far with this?"

"Nah. Why should we be the only ones who get to enjoy cold beverages? Sampson has rights, too. I'm here all the time anyway."

I walked into the living room and perched my free hand on my hip. "Sampson has rights?"

Muffin continued to rocket out of Doob's mouth. "It's a free country Meg." It came out sounding like, "Shis a fwee cudry Meh."

I rolled my eyes. "You don't sleep, you don't eat, you don't know what day it is, your socks don't match, but you want to keep a dog in a constant supply of chilled water? I've heard it all."

"Whatever," Doob replied after he swallowed. "He might get dehydrated."

I tried a tough-girl-glare that I knew didn't work on anyone, especially Doob, and then stomped into the kitchen to dump the ice into Sampson's bowl. He gazed up at me and didn't move.

I put both hands on my hips and bent down, getting nose to nose with Sampson. "What? The ice came from the tap? Not good enough?"

Sampson looked into my eyes for a moment and then licked my nose. He knows how to temper my sarcasm. I smiled grudgingly and then ruffled his ears. The dog should run for office.

With Sampson happily slurping and Doob full of muffins, I went back to my bedroom to pack. Today Boston, tomorrow L.A. Woo hoo!

CHAPTER 3
SUNDAY, MARCH 2ND

The next morning Doob and I departed for Boston Logan around five o'clock. Doob drove like an old lady, and neither of us did much more than grunt during the short trek to the airport. I'd doubled up my coffee and wondered how fishermen and other early risers did it day-in and day-out. This hour of the morning was absurd. I gave Doob a quick hug as I got out of the car and hoped he didn't fall asleep sitting curbside. TSA would lock him up in a heartbeat.

Until I'd arrived at the airport, I hadn't noticed that David had booked me a first-class ticket. Loved him! The nearly six-hour flight was uneventful, and due to the time change, I arrived in sunny California around nine thirty in the morning. After waiting forever for my luggage, I proceeded to the car rental counter. I was scheduled to stay for five days, but the warm air that greeted me as I walked to my rental made me wish that it was five months.

David had sent me Darrin's address the night before, and I'd brought my indispensible GPS to get me from the airport to the apartment in Valencia. When I hopped in the car and programmed the navigation system, it indicated about a forty-five minute drive. That time would change drastically if there was traffic. And one thing I knew for certain—there's *always* traffic in L.A. I wished I'd had the foresight to bring a book on tape.

The drive was scenic, the sun was bright, and I was tired and wired at the same time. I stopped at a convenience store to grab my beloved caffeine in the form of two Diet Cokes and hit the road with renewed vigor. Traffic wasn't too bad, and I arrived at my destination just before eleven.

The apartment complex was about a mile off Interstate 5, and the street address was Magic Mountain Parkway. I half expected to be greeted by Disney characters and fairies, but no such luck. I found Darrin's building midway through the twists and turns of the chic complex. The whole place looked like a luxury resort, and it seemed very much like a place where young, pretty people would come to chase their dreams. I parked the rental and guzzled the remainder of my second soda.

I walked through a massive, beautiful brick archway into Darrin's building and trooped up four flights of winding stairs that made me dizzy. While vowing to shed five pounds, I proceeded through an ornate wooden door that led into the hallway to Darrin's apartment. I knocked on his door several times, but no one answered. Yes, I did try the doorknob to see if it was unlocked, but I'm not that lucky. Frustrated, I looked up and down the hall, hoping that Darrin would suddenly appear. After all, it was Magic Mountain Parkway.

On the long flight from Boston, I'd basically concluded that Darrin didn't live on Magic Mountain any longer. His phone was disconnected, he wasn't listed under a new number, and his cell was going straight to voicemail. David knew a couple of Darrin's friends, by first names only, so there wasn't anyone I could track down to ask some questions. I didn't exactly have squat, but I didn't have a lot, either. The neighbors closest to Darrin's apartment were either not home, or they weren't answering their doors. I meandered around the apartment building for a little bit, hoping that I'd run into someone who knew Darrin, but the few people I questioned either didn't know him or eyed *me* suspiciously. The nerve. If I was stalking Darrin, I'd be a little less obvious about it.

As I saw it, the two remaining possibilities on Magic Mountain were the rental office and the maintenance crew. I found a very friendly—too friendly—maintenance worker, and the only thing I learned from him was that he didn't have dinner plans that night. I politely declined his advances and scooted towards the rental office, feeling his eyes on my ass as I walked away.

I inwardly groaned when I saw a young couple sitting at the desk with the lone rental worker, and there were two others in line in front of me. One was a huge, bald man in a tank top, who resembled a professional wrestler, and the other was an extremely thin man who was barely over five feet tall and wearing a pink boa and tiara. No way was I waiting in line with those two.

I'd spent just over an hour of time with nothing to show for it, so I opted for a plan, a nap, and a shower. I went back to the car, punched the hotel address into my GPS and hoped to check in a little early. I would rest up, clean up, and then head back to Darrin's apartment, just to double check. If there was still no one home, I would go back to the rental office.

I arrived at my hotel around twelve forty-five and overdid my sweet-girl act to get into my room early. The overweight young lady behind the counter was very friendly and said that she'd see what she could do. She started clicking away on her computer keyboard, while a fancy lady in line behind me obviously wanted some assistance *immediately*. Her arms were folded, and she was tapping her expensive high heels and sighing every couple of seconds. She was clearly put-out, but I couldn't have cared less. I'm from Boston—you don't get anymore put-out than we do.

With a huge smile, the accommodating young lady produced a keycard to my room, told me that the elevators were to my left, and that there would be a free continental breakfast from five thirty to nine the next morning. I asked if they would have my caramel whipped something-or-other concoction, and she looked at me as if I had two heads. I guess not.

I got to my room, propped the door open with my suitcase and then proceeded to check the closet, shower, and under the bed for fugitives, rapists and/or murderers. I always do this. I often wonder how I'd react if I did find one of them peering out at me from under the bed. I'd probably faint. What I never really stopped to contemplate was the fact that the bad guys might enter my room via the open door while I was, in fact, searching for one of them. That would be the ultimate in irony.

Satisfied that no boogeymen were on the premises, I shut the door, and set the alarm clock for two fifteen. I checked it about ten times to make sure that I had correctly set it for P.M. and then fell asleep, completely decked out in the clothes I'd worn on the plane.

It felt like the alarm went off five minutes later, and I erupted from my sleep with a very bad four-letter word. My head felt like a squashed watermelon, my tongue the size of a state-fair-winning potato. I needed caffeine. I shuffled down the hall, paid way too much for a soda, and then padded back to my room for a shower. I didn't bother to check for the fugitives who might have broken into my room during the ninety seconds I'd been gone.

I stood in the shower for at least twenty minutes and gave myself a blast of cold water at the end, which had the desired effect of getting my brain in gear. Then I went through the motions of drying my hair, which is always a chore because it is so thick. Nonetheless, I managed to pile my unruly brown locks into some semblance of a ponytail. I then moved on to the makeup routine, complete with a couple coats of mascara and some foundation that I use in an attempt to hide my freckles. It never works, but I keep trying. Sometimes it's such a pain in the ass being a girl. Although I'd never be mistaken for a supermodel, I wasn't exactly chopped liver, either. And I consider my average appearance a big plus in my profession. Some lip gloss topped off my effort, and I was back in the hotel parking lot by three o'clock.

Forty minutes later, I was back at Darrin's apartment complex, and two minutes after that I was again walking away from his unopened door.

I decided to check the rental office again and smiled at the worker in the now-empty area. She looked to be in her early twenties and was all things California. A blue-eyed blonde, she had perfectly straight, shiny long hair, and a great tan. Her smile revealed a set of even white teeth. She had no freckles, and she had two magic mountains of her own. I immediately felt inadequate and thrust my own B-cups into full attention. I told her that I was a private investigator and wondered if she'd answer a few questions about Darrin.

What I gleaned from this pretty girl was as follows: 1) her name was Cally, 2) she wasn't kidding about that, 3) her roommate, Tatia, had had a crush on Darrin for months, 4) Darrin had a male friend who'd been staying with him for a while, 5) the friend had died, 6) after a late evening out that previous weekend, Tatia had seen Darrin moving out around three o'clock in the morning, 7) he was getting help from a tall, thin girl with a brunette ponytail, 8) Tatia immediately wanted to assault the girl, and 9) Tatia said the girl was wearing a long white glove on one hand.

"Hunh?" I asked.

Cally shrugged. "That's what she said."

Hmmmm. "Maybe she did the white glove test to check that the apartment was clean after he moved out?" I suggested. Meagan Maloney, Mighty-Comic-Extraordinaire.

"She did *what*?" Cally wrinkled her pert little nose and looked thoroughly confused. Evidently the white glove test had not worked its way into Cally's era.

"Never mind. Do you know how Darrin's friend died?"

She hunched her shoulders a little and said, "I figured that's why you're here."

"What do you mean?"

"Well, since he was shot and everything."

"Who was shot?"

"Darrin's roommate. Isn't that why you're here?"

"Uh, no."

She narrowed her pretty eyes, and her mouth tightened. I didn't want to lose her.

"I'm sorry if you thought that, Cally. I didn't mean to mislead you. The reason I'm here is because Darrin's brother, David, is trying to find him. He hasn't heard from Darrin for a while and is quite worried. Darrin's phone has been disconnected, and he hasn't returned any of the messages that David has left on his cell phone." I decided to leave out the part about the mystery delivery. "From what you've told me, it sounds like David does have cause for concern. Do you know what happened exactly?"

She frowned a bit and shook her head. "I've been on vacation and just got back yesterday. Tatia filled me in on everything when I got home. She said there'd been cops asking questions around the apartment building and that she'd heard that Darrin's roommate had been killed."

"Was he killed here at the complex?"

Cally's blue eyes widened to the size of pie pans. "God, no! It happened up in Santa Barbara, or somewhere like that. I really don't know the details, but I'm sure I'll hear more about it once I talk to some of the neighbors. Tatia was more upset about the fact that Darrin had moved out." She grimaced. "That's pretty insensitive, isn't it?"

I didn't bother with an answer. "Do you know what Darrin's roommate's name was?" I was thinking that Doob could do some digging for me and probably get some answers from the online newspaper articles fairly quickly.

"It was Bobby, but I don't know his last name. I'm not being much help, am I?"

"Oh my gosh, please don't think that. I know much more than I did when I got here. Is there anything else that you can tell me about Darrin? Did he belong to a gym or a church? Did he have a hobby or anything like that? If you could suggest anyone else to talk to, I'd really appreciate it. His brother is very worried." I gave my best pleading-combined-with-sincerity-face, and it worked.

Cally brightened and suddenly looked as eager as a puppy. As it turned out, Tatia had joined the same gym as Darrin, hoping to catch his eye there, with no luck. Tatia had even stalked him to his part-time job at a grocery store, and Cally gave me that information. Cally personally knew that Darrin took an acting class on Tuesday nights because Cally was taking the same class. She was being much more helpful than she realized.

After a little coaxing, she dug out his rental application, and it showed a temp agency that he'd worked for when he first started renting at the complex. She didn't know if he was still temping or not. The paperwork didn't reveal anything about the bar and restaurant where he was currently working, so he must have gotten the bartending job after he'd been in L.A. for a while.

"Thanks so much, Cally, you've been great. If you would, please take my business card and call me if you think of anything that might be helpful. Nothing is too insignificant, so call me anytime. Or, in the unlikely event that Darrin ever comes back, please give him my information and ask him to call me." I started to walk out and then turned around.

"Come to think of it, Cally, if anyone at all is looking for information about Bobby or Darrin, please have them call me directly. My cell number is on my card, or you can tell them that I'm staying at the Courtyard in Culver City if they'd like to contact me there." I gave her the number I'd memorized from the Courtyard with my magic memory.

Cally nodded enthusiastically, and her glistening hair followed the curve of her shoulders as she placed my card in the top drawer of the desk. "Sure thing," she said with a smile. "Do you want me to give your number to just the cops or to anyone at all?"

"Anyone at all, cops, detectives, whoever. Please have them call me, and I'll take it from there. Thanks, Cally."

Bobby's shooting probably should have made me a little cautious about handing out my number to just anyone, but I'd been hired to do a job. One roommate's murder, a mysterious delivery from the other roommate—and his subsequent disappearing act—had to be related. I needed to know what was in that laptop case.

I shook Cally's hand and smiled as I left. Something told me that she wouldn't be stuck in a rental office much longer. Gals like her did well in L.A.

"Good luck," Cally called after me. I hoped I didn't need it, but something told me I might. Dead roommates and three A.M. move-outs didn't sound too promising to me.

CHAPTER 4

Cally had looked up the address for the gym that Darrin belonged to, so I went and spoke to the manager, but he wasn't much help. He hadn't seen Darrin lately but said that he'd call me if Darrin stopped in. Something told me that I wouldn't hear from him.

I spent the next couple of hours poking around the other places Cally had mentioned. The manager and a few clerks at the grocery store all spoke highly of Darrin, but no one seemed to know where he might be. I got the same result at the acting school, which really wasn't a school at all, but rather a rented space in an old warehouse. I called the temp agency, but it was closed, so I left a message with my contact information.

After spreading business cards far and wide, my stomach expressed its unhappiness by growling like a saber tooth tiger. I took heed and decided it was time for some chow.

Around seven, I pulled into Sunny's Steak and Seafood Grill, which David had said was Darrin's last known place of employment. On the drive to the restaurant, I drove through sections of town that ranged from extremely ritzy, to mildly ritzy, to quite nice, to nice, to mildly old but well kept, to definitely old and just a smidgen rundown. I envisioned that another mile down the road was probably crackhouse-central, and I was glad the restaurant wasn't farther along on the map.

I parked my rental and noticed a late model, red Chevy Impala pull in a few spots over from me. My car had Florida plates on it, and I noticed that the red car had Florida plates on it as well. Two cars very far from home.

The restaurant turned out to be a great, casual place and boasted a few awards for being one of the top local bar and grills in that county for a few years running. Pretty impressive. I hoped that the food would live up to the hype.

Since Darrin had disappeared from his apartment and wasn't picking up his cell phone, then it was likely that he wasn't working, either, but I had to try. I thought someone here might be able to help me track him down. Heck, maybe he would even be here, grabbing a sandwich and watching some sports. I'd sidle up and introduce myself, he'd explain his situation to my satisfaction, we'd have a good laugh, I'd fly home, ask his brother out, and call it a day. Sigh.

I took a seat at the bar, and about twenty seconds later, a thin girl with a shiny brunette ponytail came around the corner and started stocking bottles. She hadn't seen me, and I didn't want to interrupt her. She was having trouble with the box of bottles, and I noticed that she had a cast on her left arm. To a faraway drunk at three o'clock in the morning, her cast would have definitely passed for a long, white glove. Bingo.

"What happened to your arm?"

She cast me a sideways glance. "Car accident. I'll be with you in just a second."

"Oh jeez, I'm sorry. No rush."

She gave me a tight smile and emptied her box. In the meantime, a bartender named Bill took my order that included a large margarita, chips and salsa, and a burger. Screw those five pounds.

Bill delivered the margarita in record time, and I casually asked him if Darrin was working. Hopefully Bill wasn't an aspiring actor, because his face registered panic and his ears turned bright red. "Uh, you'd have to ask Melanie about that," he stammered and walked away.

The skinny, brunette girl resurfaced, and I took a shot. "Melanie?"

"Yeah?"

I reached my hand across the bar, and she tentatively shook it with her good arm. "I'm Meagan Maloney, from Boston. I'm a friend of Darrin's brother, David, and I was just wondering if he's working tonight?"

"No."

I waited for her to say something more. She didn't.

"Well, do you know if he'll be working tomorrow? I told David I'd look him up while I'm in town."

I saw a tiny squint at the corners of her eyes and knew she was sizing me up. "I'm not sure if he's still working here anymore, to be honest with you."

Yeah, right. "Oh, well who would know that? I can speak to them." I smiled my fake-earnest smile to show her that I'm just a friendly gal looking for some information.

She sighed. "Look, why don't you give me your name and number, and if I see him, I'll pass it along."

She was protecting him. Part of me admired her, and part of me wanted to break her other arm. But she was my only link at this point. I rummaged around in my purse and couldn't find a business card, so I grabbed a cocktail napkin and scribbled the hotel name and number on it. When she reached for the napkin, I didn't let go, rather I pulled her towards me using it as a tiny tug-of-war item.

I lowered my voice and spoke gently. "Listen, Melanie, I'm a friend, I promise you. Tell Darrin to call David or me. David's worried and Darrin owes him an explanation."

She stared at the napkin and puffed out her cheeks. "Like I said, if I see him, I'll pass it along." She walked away from me and then stopped to retrieve her cell phone from a backpack underneath the bar. With that, she disappeared into the kitchen. I would have bet good money she was calling Darrin.

I got caught up in some pre-March Madness basketball games, but after less than an hour, my head started bobbing, and I realized I was falling asleep in my drink. I probably looked like some type of booze-hound to anyone paying attention. While I was only on my first margarita, the jet lag and time change was kicking my fanny. It felt like Doob had dropped me off at Logan a lifetime ago, and I was in dire need of a pillow. Even my beloved caffeine wouldn't help me at this point. I paid the bill, left a large tip, and told Melanie not to forget about me. On the way out, I grabbed a business card from the hostess stand. The manager's name was on it, and I knew that I might have to talk to him in the next couple of days as well.

The fresh air hit me when I stepped outside of the restaurant, and I desperately wanted to get my second wind and do something productive. There were a couple of large, wrought iron benches just outside of Sunny's, and there were huge vases of dark purple petunias on each side of them. It was very simple, yet lovely, and the smell was fantastic. I plopped down on one of the benches and decided to enlist some help from my favorite computer hacker. I dug my cell phone out of my pocketbook and called Doob's apartment. It rang about twenty times, and no one answered, and no answering machine picked up. Doob had to be the only twenty-something on earth without voicemail.

I hung up and huffed in frustration when some remnants of common sense kicked in. I then dialed my own apartment number and quickly did the time change mathematics in my head. It was after eleven in Moira Land, and I hoped she wouldn't be answering the phone if she had an early morning planned.

"Hello? Sampson, Moira and Meagan's house, this is Sampson speaking." Then Doob giggled like a school girl.

"Doob, it's me. What are you doing?"

"Hey Meg. I saw the caller ID. How's it going?"

"I dunno, not much to report just yet. I was wondering if you could help me out with something, please?"

"What's the temperature?" Doob obviously would get around to assisting me only after a weather report. I wet my finger and stuck it in the air, like I knew what I was doing.

"Seventy-two degrees, Doob. Listen, I have an idea, and I was wondering—"

"What time is it there?"

Good grief. "It's a little after eight, Doob. Anyway, I was wondering—"

"Have you seen any movie stars?"

"Doobie, no! I'm out here *working*. Are you going to help me or not?"

"If you continue in that tone, Meagan, I'm going to have to terminate the call."

That shut me up for a second, and I didn't know if he was serious. Doob was a tough one to read sometimes, especially over the phone.

"Okay Doob, I apologize. But I'm jetlagged and bitchy, and I'm not making much progress, so I'm hoping that you'd be willing to help me with a little project."

"Will you bring me a souvenir if I do?"

"Of course, Doob, of course." Saying it twice seemed to make it more meaningful. I filled Doob in on the info that I'd received from Cally. "I need you to look up an address for me, please. You can use 411.com or that other service Norman and I pay for. I put it in your *Favorites* on your laptop."

"Yep, I got it. Just give me a name."

Oh boy. "Melanie."

"Very funny, Meg. How about a last name?"

"Don't have one."

"That's extremely helpful. Shall I pull a monkey out of my ass as well?"

"But Doob, you're the master!"

"Don't kiss my butt, Meg, it's very transparent."

"She has a broken arm."

"Well, why didn't you say so sooner? I will find Melanie-the-girl-with-the-broken-arm-in-California in no time." Heavy sarcasm.

"Doob, of all people, can't you do something with a first name?"

"With just her first name, I could probably have something to you within the next three months."

"What I do know is that she works at Sunny's Steak and Seafood Grill. Does that help?"

"Maybe. It could still take some time."

I had an idea that I should have thought of before calling him. I definitely needed sleep. "Doob, I'll call you back in a few minutes."

"I'll be waiting." I heard a click, and Doob was gone. I stared at my phone and made a face.

I fished out the manager's card and dialed the number for Sunny's. It was weird calling a restaurant that I was sitting right outside of. I could see the young girl at the hostess stand reach for the phone, and then her cheery voice greeted me over the airwaves.

"Sunny's Steak and Seafood, how may I help you?"

I projected my best confused voice. "Um, hi. I was wondering if I could speak with Melanie Jones, please?"

I could see the girl's puzzled face. "Who?"

"Melanie, in the bar. I think that her last name is Jones or something like that?"

"Oh, you mean Melanie Summers. Hang on just a minute, please." She put me on hold, and I hung up. I dialed the apartment, and Doob answered immediately.

"Hey Doob. I've got a last name. Melanie Summers."

"S-o-m-m-e-r-s or S-u-m-m-e-r-s?"

"Don't know."

"Good God, Meagan."

"Go with the second one, like the season. If that doesn't work, then try the other one."

"Okay, I'll call you back in about ten." The line went dead again, and I made another face at my phone. Doob was definitely pouting. We were going to have to have a pow-wow over Fritos when I returned to Boston.

I settled into my bench and inhaled the beautiful scent and the crisp

California air. I could see why people loved the West Coast, but my heart would always be in Beantown. Ten minutes later my phone chirped.

Doob started talking before I could say anything. "We've got a bit of a problem."

"You're not just trying to sabotage this, are you?"

"Meg, please. I would if I thought that I'd ever hear the end of it, but I know better."

"Okay, so what's up?"

"Well, Melanie's most recent address is in Nevada. I haven't been able to find anything to show where she lives in California. I can keep digging, but it might take some time."

I thought about that. "She looks pretty young, so maybe she just got out of school. The Nevada address could be her parents' house."

"Yeah, or she might be staying with a friend or something. I don't want to bum you out, but there might not be any record of her out in California. I will keep trying, though."

I had a thought. "Doob, could you find out what she drives?"

Silence. And then exponential sarcasm. "Gee, how in the world would I do that? Can I find that on 411.com? Is there a website called whatdopeopledrive.com? Or maybe that fancy service you and Norman subscribe to includes vehicles?"

"Ummmm. Actually, I think it does." But I was reaching. Some of the information on that service was pretty outdated.

"Well then, I'm at a dead-end here, Meg. Unless you have some suggestion for me?"

He was going to make me say it. "Well, I'm thinking about *you*, Doob. I mean, obviously I want you to try the service that Norman and I typically use. But if that doesn't work, it seems to me you'd hate to have that whole DMV project go to waste. I know how long it took you to get into all fifty states, which, if I haven't already mentioned it, was so incredibly impressive—"

"Again, don't kiss my butt, Meg. If I didn't know better, I would think that you were almost *encouraging* me to hack into the DMV for you."

"Doob, I would never actually *ask* you to do something illegal. I really don't want to know your methods."

"Sure thing, Meg. I'll legally get the information and call you back." The line went dead again. He had to be setting some type of record for hanging up on me. After another fifteen minutes of people watching, my phone chirped.

"Talk to me, Doob."

"Old, tan Toyota Camry. Four door." He told me that it was a Nevada plate and gave me the number.

"Okay, bear with me," I said as I trotted to where my rental was parked. I started it and began driving around, looking for Melanie's car.

"Meg, are you there?"

"Yeah, Doob. I'm going to cruise around the restaurant and see what I can find. I'm guessing there's probably more than one old Camry here tonight."

"It's a popular make, but check towards the back. Employees usually have to park in an out-of-the-way location."

I smiled. "And you know this from some previous work experience, Doob?"

"I'm happy to hang up again, Meg."

"I'm kidding! Okay, I'm getting back there right now, so just hang on a second. I'm going by a dumpster and coming up on a lot of beat up cars."

"Definitely the employee section."

I didn't see the car after a couple of circles through the lot and was thoroughly irritated, a sentiment I shared with Doob.

"Maybe she isn't driving because of her arm?" Doob suggested. "Or maybe she drove in with one of the other workers?"

"Yeah, maybe. But I need to know for sure."

"So what's the plan Detectress?"

"I'm just going to take a cat nap in my car and then follow Melanie when she gets done with her shift."

There was another beat of silence. "Is there some reason you can't *cat nap* in your hotel room, Meagan?"

Uh oh. "As a matter of fact, there is. She's probably going to be off work in a couple of hours, and I don't want to be driving back and forth. I'm going to hunker down in the back seat and set my phone alarm, and then I'll follow her home when she leaves work."

Nothing. Had he hung up yet again?

"Doob?"

"I'm here. I'm just trying to decide how I'm going to break this to Moira."

"Doobie!"

"Well, it's stupid, Meg. I'm sure if you give me enough time that I'll find Melanie's address, and then you can go check it out tomorrow in the daylight."

"Doob, I'm sorry, but even *you* might not be able to find that address if it isn't on record anywhere. Plus, if I follow her tonight, I have a much-improved chance of not being seen. I just need a little shut-eye and I'll be good as new when she gets done with her shift."

"When is that?"

I fished out the manager's card again. "The restaurant closes at eleven tonight. I'll catch a few winks between now and then, and I'll be good as new when Melanie is off work."

"Or you could just go to your hotel and get some sleep and then find her place tomorrow. I really think I can find that address."

"Doob, what if Darrin is at her house, and what if they are planning another middle-of-the-night move? Or maybe I'll get lucky and he'll pick her up? Or it's possible that she'll catch a ride with someone and that he'll meet her at the front door. Which reminds me, why don't you try to look up his license plate info as well? Then I can be on the lookout for his car, too. I wouldn't be able to face David if I didn't try to get as much information as soon as possible."

"Whatever you say, Meg. But this is a terrible idea, and I don't want to have to tell Moira that you got chopped up in your car and I could have stopped you."

"Good grief, Doob! I'm in a public area, and I'm going to lightly rest. I might not even fall asleep because of all of this excitement. No one is getting chopped up."

"Just promise you'll be careful."

"I will, promise."

"Why don't you call me once you get back to the hotel?"

"That could be four or five in the morning in Boston. I'll just talk with you tomorrow."

"Meg! I mean it. If you don't call me by five Boston time, I'm calling the cops in L.A."

I laughed. Doob was the biggest worrywart I'd ever seen. "Fine. I will call you when I get back to the hotel. Give Moira and Sampson hugs for me."

I hung up and steered the rental to a somewhat covert location towards the far corner of the parking lot. The lighting was sparse in that section, thanks to a broken overhead light, and I parked right below it. I'm one of those people who need one hundred percent darkness in order to get some shut-eye. I set the alarm on my phone to go off at ten thirty so that I'd be alert and ready once Melanie finished her shift. I cracked open all four windows just a little bit and then snuggled up in the backseat of the car. I wondered about this glamorous life that I was leading, sleeping in rental vehicles in strange cities. Then I smiled to myself and realized that there was nothing else I'd rather be doing. Shutting my eyes, I quickly drifted off to dreams of caramel coffee.

CHAPTER 5

It felt like two seconds later when I woke to someone knocking on the back window of my car. I shot up as if I'd been goosed and realized that a light rain had started. I shook my head quickly a few times, trying to get my bearings. Okay, backseat of my rental at Sunny's, waiting for my alarm to go off, going to follow Melanie home, strange man at my window. *Strange man at my window?!*

Maybe he was just checking to make sure that I was okay. Maybe Doob had called the cops, as promised. I looked around the darkened parking lot and didn't see a police cruiser, though. I didn't think this guy had identified himself as a cop, either. So who was he? I had no intention of flopping over to the front seat to lower the window any further, nor was I getting out of the car. I resorted to yelling at him through the slightly lowered backseat window.

"I'm okay, just sleeping it off! Thank you!" I used hand gestures to shoo him away, but he wasn't having it. As my eyes adjusted to the darkness and the rain, I noticed that he filled up a lot of space out there. He was a big guy, and he evidently wasn't going anywhere. It looked like he had some type of bandana on his head, and he seemed more like a kid than a man. A man-child. A big gorilla-man-child who was basically as wide as the car window.

He yelled back at me, "I need to talk with you!"

Oh boy. Talk with me in the middle of the night? In a dark parking lot? But then I had a thought. What if this was Darrin? Maybe Melanie had tipped him off.

"Who are you?" I had grabbed my purse and was digging frantically for my cell phone. I knew that it would light up if I called 911, but I didn't really care.

"It don't matter who I am. We just want to talk and take you on a little ride."

We? I turned and squinted to see in the darkness. The rain was falling heavier now, but I could see what looked like a huge car parked directly behind me. I squinted at it some more, then my eyes bulged as I realized it was a hearse. *A hearse?!* And it was directly behind my car. I had to buy some time.

"Are you a mortician?"

"A what?"

Clearly he wasn't a Mensa member. "You know, the guy who takes care of dead bodies. That is a hearse that you're driving, isn't it?"

"I ain't never done shit with no dead bodies, but that doesn't mean I wouldn't try it sometime. What do you have in mind?" I saw him gesture towards the hearse with some type of gang yo-yo-yo arm movement.

"I have nothing in mind. If you'd just kindly move that, uh . . ." I couldn't say *piece of shit,* but that's all that my brain was coming up with. "I'll just be on my way once you move along." I again shooed him away with my hands, but I'm sure he couldn't see it. If he could have seen it, he probably would have laughed out loud.

He motioned his head towards his aforementioned piece of shit. "That there is my sweet ride. It gives me street cred, and it lets all the punk ass bitches know they better stay out of my way, or they'll end up riding in the back of that mo fo."

"Well, it makes quite a statement," I yelled.

"That it do, be-atch. Now quit running your mouth. Me and my homies want to give you a sweet ride of our own. So get your ass outta the car, and you better have some coin. We ain't cheap dates." He then grabbed his crotch.

Oh shit. There was no way I could get my rental around the hearse, and that's when I noticed that there were no other cars in the parking lot. What the hell time was it? Why hadn't my alarm gone off?

The man-child banged on my window again, this time with much more force. "Get out of the car, ho-bag bitch! I don't want to do this the hard way."

The hard way? Ho-bag bitch? This jackass had clearly watched too many straight-to-video movies. But still, I didn't want to find out what he meant by the hard way. Especially if it had anything to do with his crotch.

Part of my brain did not seem to be keeping up with this situation.

A few times in my life, generally after watching true-crime television, I'd wondered what I'd do if someone ever tried to abduct me. I'd always pictured myself fighting off the bad guys with some sweet kung fu moves, of which, of course, I have none. But they'd come to me in the heat of the moment. After stomping some major ass with my limber kicks and lightning quick hands, I'd rescue an innocent bystander and would end the ordeal by handing a daisy to a small child before walking off into the sunset. My silhouette would be doing kicks and spins in the waning light, and there'd be soft music playing in the background. All would be right with the world.

Unfortunately, my delusional little fantasy world did not involve the backseat of a car, a dark, rainy parking lot, a strange city, or a hulking man-child and his overgrown death-vehicle blocking my way.

"Listen, you little bitch, get outta the fucking car or I'm putting my fist through this window and dragging you by your hair to my rig!"

The "b" word always manages to tick me off, and he was using it far too much. His threat of dragging me through the rain unwillingly didn't sit too well with me, either. Fortunately, the fear-combined-with-anger adrenaline was exactly what I needed at that particular moment, because my brain woke up and kicked into overdrive.

First, I quickly surmised that this gorilla-man-child was an asshole. Second, when dealing with any asshole, my strict policy is that I must always win. It is a policy that has served me well since I knocked Skippy Maldonado on his fat ass back in the second grade. This man-child was simply an overgrown Skippy, and I had to get the better of him. That or probably die, but I wasn't going to let my thoughts run away with that possibility. Third, he had mentioned putting his fist through the window. My hope was that meant he didn't have a gun to shoot through the window instead. I was banking on that because of what I was going to do next.

As if in surrender, I held up my hands and yelled that I was getting out of the car. I knew he couldn't see me any better than I could see him. I hooked my purse around my arm and scooched to the back door opposite the man-child. I had the car keys in my hand and clicked on the key fob to unlock the doors. In the next second I jerked the back door open and took off like an Olympic athlete. The dome light had come on when the door opened, and I could hear the guy screaming at me. I bolted into the night as fast as I could and didn't look back. The rain was coming down hard now, and I told myself that might work to my advantage. The property line at the back of the restaurant had extremely tall bushes lining it, and my intent was to squeeze through those to freedom, but I found that there was a wooden fence behind the bushes that was allowing passage to exactly nowhere. I took a hard left and headed towards the main road, hoping that I would lose them or find someone to help me before the hearse ran me down. Getting killed by a hearse seemed like another ironic way to go.

I didn't know if anyone was chasing me on foot, but if they were all the size of the first guy, then my money was on me. I hoped they were all overgrown man-children with too much baby fat and not much speed.

I heard some more yelling and then car doors slamming. The area that I was running in brightened as the hearse headlights locked in on me. I risked a look back at the vehicle that was now gaining speed and tried to calculate if I'd get to the road before they got to me. An irrational wish that I'd paid more attention in physics class crossed my mind and then vanished.

I looked to my left and to my right and silently thanked the heavens when I saw lit-up convenience stores in both directions. One was on the same side of the street as me, and to the right, but it looked to be about two blocks away. The other was across the street and down about a block to my left. I chose the one to my left because of its closer proximity and sprinted with all of my might, keeping my eye on the glass door and praying that it was an all-night establishment.

Nearly weeping when the door to the store opened, I shouted at the clerk to call 911. He seemed more than happy to oblige, and I realized I must have looked like a lunatic. I was soaked to the bone but very happy to be alive and un-abducted.

I crouched behind a stand of Twinkies and other assorted goodies and popped my head up just enough to spot the hearse. If it pulled in, then I would be out the back door lickety-split. While waiting for the hell mobile, I quickly checked my watch and couldn't believe that it was after one in the morning. Why hadn't my alarm gone off when it was supposed to? I'd worry about that when I wasn't in fear for my life. I stood behind the Twinkies stand for about a minute and figured they'd gone the wrong way or had simply given up.

Just as the thought crossed my mind, I suddenly saw headlights on the street, and then the old model, wet body of the hearse appeared in the rain. It was moving very slowly and came to a full stop in the middle of the road in front of the convenience store. I held my breath, wondering if it would pull in or if someone with a semi-automatic something would hop out. Either way, it didn't look promising. I looked to the back of the store and quickly devised a plan B for getting the hell out of there. Grabbing the clerk en route would probably be difficult, but I'd have to do it to make sure that he didn't get hurt. I was raised Catholic, and the guilt of getting someone killed on my behalf would have me in the loony bin by the end of the week.

After about ten seconds of holding my breath, I was surprised to see the hearse quickly pull away. As the road brightened with what looked like strobe lights, I realized what happened. A police cruiser pulled up to the front of the store, and two officers rushed out of the vehicle.

The officer who had been driving was a large, white man who looked to be in his mid-40s and evidently didn't miss much time at the gym. He wasn't muscle-head gross but very solid and fit. Kind of yummy in a hot-uncle sort of way. His partner was a slight, black woman, and her dark hair was done up in a severe bun just below the brim of her hat. Her face rivaled any super model that I'd ever seen, and I wondered what in the heck provoked her career decision. She was gorgeous.

I met them at the door, and they looked at me as if I might be the perpetrator. In rapid fire, I told them about the events of my evening, and they didn't seem too impressed with my general appearance or the fact that I'd been sleeping in the backseat of the rental. The male officer went over to speak with the clerk while his partner stayed with me. She reviewed the notes that she'd been taking in a little blue spiral notebook, and I was dying to see what she'd written. I tried to peek at the page, and she gave me a look that backed me up a full two feet. It was like a force field. She was kind of scary.

"So, Meagan, did you happen to get the license plate number on this—uh—hearse?" She arched a perfect eyebrow at me when she asked the question. I decided that I didn't care for her eyebrow, her notebook, or her attitude. But she was a cop, and that merited my respect, so I did my best to stay polite. Somewhat.

"Not while I was running for my life, no. To be honest, it didn't even cross my mind. I just wanted to get away from them as fast as I could."

She nodded and made another note in her little book. "And when you saw the hearse driving very slowly and then stop in the street? Did it cross your mind then?"

Being a crack detective, I picked up on the slightest hint of condescension in her voice. I tried to give her a scary look of my own, but she didn't flinch. I trudged on.

"Officer, it was raining quite steadily when they stopped in front of the store. They stayed out on the road, so I could only see the side of the hearse, not the front or the back of it. Since it didn't pull in here, I didn't have a chance to get the plate."

"I see," she said tightly. This time my well honed skills definitely picked up some blatant condescension, mixed with disbelief in her voice, and my face heated up.

"Come to think of it," I said sarcastically, "the hearse was pulling away from here just as *you* were pulling in. Did you or your partner happen to get the plate number?"

She narrowed her eyes at me, and I defiantly stared right back. She scribbled a note and walked off towards her partner and the clerk. She spoke to the other officer for a moment, and then they glanced over at me. Both of them headed my way, and the male officer was the first to speak.

"Miss Maloney, we do have a camera mounted in the police car. You're sure that this hearse was leaving right as we pulled in?"

"I'm positive. I actually think you scared them off. You didn't see it?" I was incredulous.

They both stared at me. I guess they didn't see it.

The male officer spoke again. "I need to go out to the vehicle for a little while and look into this. Officer Jackson will stay with you in the event that you want to change your statement."

I'm not sure what he meant by that, but I was hoping they'd be a little less cynical when they saw the hearse on tape. After about five minutes of uncomfortable silence with Officer Jackson, I grabbed two packages of Twinkies, a small bag of Doritos, and two Diet Cokes. Before going to the register, I gave Officer Jackson my best beauty pageant smile. Of course, the beauty pageant would have to include day-old, wet, smelly clothes that had been slept in, combined with rain soaked hair that rivaled Medusa, but those types of pageants probably exist somewhere.

"Would you like anything? I'm buying."

She didn't smile back. I made a mental note to not invite her to my pageant. She looked at my items with disdain and sniffed. "No, thank you."

Fine. At least I asked. I paid the clerk and was happily chowing on my junk food when the other officer came back in, a stern look on his face. His eyes narrowed further when he saw what I was eating, and he looked at his partner as if to ask if I was for real. She shook her head slightly as if to say that I wasn't worth the effort.

"Miss Maloney, you were right. I was able to retrieve the plate off of the hearse, and the vehicle is registered to a well-known street thug who has a very long rap sheet. He's been arrested several times for selling drugs. You wouldn't know anything about that, would you?"

My eyes grew wide. "Of course not! As I've already told you, I'm out here from Boston working on a case. I'm certainly not looking to buy drugs from some street hoodlums, if that's what you think."

The male cop made a couple of notes while Officer Jackson continued to stare at me. Somehow I felt like I'd actually done something wrong, so I continued to blabber.

"Look, I don't know who those guys were, and I don't know why they bothered me. All I did was fall asleep in a car after a really long day and after *one* margarita. I woke up to a guy knocking on my window, who then threatened to harm me, and I feel lucky that I got away. End of story."

Officer Jackson gave me a smile with no humor behind it. "Miss Maloney, do you even have a license as a private investigator in the state of California?"

Gulp. "Uh, well, I assumed that there was some type of reciprocal arrangement." Norman would have my ass.

She rolled her eyes, and the other policeman took his turn. "Miss Maloney, clearly you're out of your league here in more ways than one. These are not men that young ladies like you want to be associated with. If you think of anything additional you'd like to share with us, here is my card, and Officer Jackson will give you hers as well. I would strongly recommend that you be on the first plane back to Boston. We wouldn't want to have any problems with an unlicensed P.I. getting herself hurt out here."

My cheeks flushed, and I was suddenly back in the second grade, getting scolded by people with much more authority than me. They both handed me their business cards, and I mumbled a quiet thank-you to them for their help. Then I realized I had to get back to my car.

"Uh, Officers, would you mind following me back to my car at the restaurant? I don't want to replay what I just went through." They did better than that and gave me a ride in the backseat of their cruiser. It was pretty cool, but I momentarily wondered if they would just haul me off to the station and lock me up for being out of my jurisdiction. They didn't.

When we got to the restaurant parking lot, Officer Jackson let me out of the backseat, and I hopped into my rental and let out a big sigh.

The police cruiser followed me out of the parking lot and stayed behind me for a few blocks. I'd admitted to having a margarita. Were they going to let me go, only to follow me and arrest me for drunk driving? Could one margarita from six hours ago count?

As I was thinking this, I rummaged through my purse with my free hand, again wondering why the alarm hadn't gone off on my phone. I found it and discovered that the battery was dead. I didn't have a car charger in the rental, either. Duh.

I looked into the rearview mirror and saw the cruiser turn onto a side street. I shuddered a little bit, realizing that I was now just a lone driver in a strange city at one thirty in the morning.

CHAPTER 6
MONDAY, MARCH 3RD

When I got back to the hotel, I was bone tired. After parking, I blew out a deep breath and thanked the heavens I was safe and sound. What a night. Despite my exhaustion, I surprised myself by noticing a late model, red Chevy Impala with Florida plates. Hmmmmm. I was probably being paranoid, but it definitely got my attention. Were they the same plates? I hadn't memorized the numbers; I'd only noticed that the vehicle was from Florida. Even if it was the same car, it was certainly possible there were people at this hotel who also went to eat at Sunny's. After all, it was an award winning restaurant. Plus, who knew I was here, and why would they follow me? I dismissed it.

When I got to my hotel room, I did a half-hearted boogeyman search. It seemed futile since I'd already had a run-in with a boogeyman-child hours before. I mean, really, what were the odds?

After checking the shower and closet, I plugged my phone into the wall charger and willed it back to life. I then pulled the comforter down and called Doob from the hotel phone. After hearing that I was safely back at the hotel, he launched into a tirade of expletives that will probably go unmatched until well into the next millennium. He blasted me about calling my cell close to a billion times, saying that it had gone straight to voicemail with each and every dial. He'd planned on calling the police five minutes later if I hadn't called him, and I thought about telling him that I was already on a first name basis with two of L.A.'s finest, but I opted to leave that little tidbit to myself. I simply said a silent prayer of thanks that I'd reached Doobie before he'd contacted the police. I apologized profusely and said that I'd fallen asleep and my cell battery had died. I told him that

I didn't even have the chance to follow Melanie home, but I neglected to mention the running-for-my-life episode. It wouldn't have been good for Doob's system. He sounded so tired, and he'd obviously been up all night worrying about me.

"Doob, I'm beat, and I know you are too. Thanks so much for your help tonight. And again, I'm really sorry I worried you."

"I'll be going gray before my time because of you, Meg, but you're welcome. And by the way, I never did find Melanie's California address. She must be living with a friend, or maybe she's subletting the place, because nothing is in her name. There's not a lot of background info on her, but she does have a debit card through a national bank. Do you want me to keep looking?"

Even though I was still dressed, I'd shut off the nightstand light while Doob had been yelling at me, and I simply didn't have the energy to turn it on again to write anything down. "I don't know, Doob. I'm too tired to move right now. If I decide tomorrow that she's somehow involved, I'll let you know. Til then, it can wait."

"Sounds good. Get some sleep, Sherlocka."

After hanging up with Doob, I mentally ran through a list of the various people I'd given business cards to throughout the day, but the names and faces were blurring together. Had one of them unleashed the bad guys on me? Or maybe Darrin had been at the restaurant incognito, and he'd turned the bad guys on me. Or maybe the Magic Mountain magically told the bad guys that I was sleeping in the parking lot. Or maybe my rental was a talking car like in *Knight Rider*, and it had tattled my whereabouts to the bad guys. My exhaustion was evident as my ideas got dumber by the second. It was probably just some asshole thugs doing what they do, and I was in the wrong place at the wrong time. I gave up on figuring it out and didn't even bother to change into my pajamas before falling asleep.

The digital readout on the clock showed 4:39 A.M. when the ringing started. I blurted out the requisite four-letter word while groping for the phone on the unfamiliar nightstand. I finally found it and sat up in bed.

"Yeah?" I didn't even recognize my own voice because it was so scratchy.

"Is this Meagan?"

"Who's this?" For some reason, I was picturing the man outside of my car window and had a flutter of panic.

"This is Darrin. I heard that you've been looking for me."

CHAPTER 7

My sticky goo-covered-sleep-eyes shot wide open, and I reached for the light and switched it on. I tried to sound casual, wide-awake, and not too desperate. "Hey Darrin, I'm glad you called. Your brother is really worried about you." *Also, did you know it's forty thirty in the effing morning?*

"Yeah, I heard. Sorry about that."

"Did you call him?"

"No, not yet."

"Why not?"

"I'd really rather not explain things over the phone."

Well now, that sounded fairly covert. Maybe he really was in trouble. "Okay, let's meet tomorrow. You tell me when and where."

There was a long pause, and I thought he might have hung up.

"Are you there?" I panicked, shouting into the phone.

"Jeez, give me a minute," he said, exasperated. "Boston native, hunh?"

That made me smile. "South side, born and raised," I said proudly.

"I can tell," he said, and I took that as a compliment. "Meet me at the Magic Mountain Park tomorrow morning at eleven. Plant yourself on a bench by the center fountain, and I'll find you. How will I recognize you?"

"I'll wear a Red Sox hat and have the whitest legs in a ten-mile radius."

He chuckled softly. "See you tomorrow."

The next day was absolutely gorgeous and, after getting directions from the hotel lobby, I stopped by the gift shop and bought two magazines. I stuck the grainy picture of Darrin inside of one of them in case I needed to reference it later.

After finding the park, I meandered around a bit before heading towards the fountain. Toddlers were taking first wobbly steps, dogs were catching Frisbees, and there was a sweet old couple walking hand in hand. Someday I hoped to be half of an old couple walking hand in hand.

I finally made my way to the fountain and found a bench. My sunglasses allowed me to covertly appreciate some of the male joggers making the circuit. One in particular was easy on the eyes. I surreptitiously pulled the grainy photo of Darrin out of my magazine and tried to determine if he was one of the circling runners. Before I could analyze it, the easy-on-the-eyes jogger arrived at the other end of my bench and began to do some leg stretches.

"Meagan?"

The sound of my name startled me, but I managed to keep my cool. I pretended to read my magazine.

"That's me. Enjoying your jog?"

"Not in the slightest, but I wanted to make sure I wasn't being followed."

Good grief. "And?"

"And I think we're okay," he said and settled himself at the other end of the bench.

As I studied him, it was odd to think of him and David as brothers, albeit stepbrothers. They were polar opposites, but they were both very good looking. David was tall, dark and handsome, and Darrin was average height for a male, with a deep tan, blonde hair, and killer blue eyes. While David's build was lean, Darrin looked to be chiseled out of stone. I reminded myself that I was here on business.

"So, what's up?" He asked this very nonchalantly, as if I'd just dropped by California for no apparent reason. Since patience will never, ever, be one of my virtues, my bull-in-the-china-shop routine started before I could stop myself.

"What's *up*?! Are you shitting me, what's up? Let's see." I tapped my finger near my mouth and pretended to think. "Well, for starters, your brother is very concerned about your little mystery delivery and subsequent disappearing act. I flew way the fuck across the country and had a very long night thanks to some gorilla-man-child who attempted to run me down in his hearse. You certainly wouldn't know anything about that, now would you?" I looked at him accusingly.

Darrin looked stunned. "*Gorilla* man? What are you talking about?"

"I just find it odd that I spend a few hours around town, asking questions about *you*," I pointed at him for emphasis. "And then suddenly,

I'm facing a street thug who wants to give me a ride in his death mobile and then chases me into a convenience store where I was forced to turn to junk food to quash my fears and hysteria."

Darrin studied me for a moment, and I figured the junk food comment probably had him questioning my ability, sanity, or possibly both.

His eyes narrowed. "I'm not sure if you're accusing me of something, but if you are, then you're way off base. And that would also make you kind of an asshole, just for the record. I didn't know anything about you until Melanie got home and gave me your information. You had the hotel phone number wrong, by the way. It's a good thing you wrote down the name, or I wouldn't have found you."

I sniffed in indignation. So much for Meagan's-Magic-Memory. "I'm *not* an asshole, for the record. It just seems a little coincidental that I'm nearly run down only a few hours after beginning my search for you, don't you think?"

"I have no idea. But I certainly didn't send anybody after you. Like I said, I didn't even know you were coming here." He glared at me for a moment, and I glared back. But David was paying me to find his brother, not argue with him, so I got back on topic.

I held up my hands in supplication. "Okay, fine. The bottom line is you're here, and you seem to be okay, and your brother is worried sick. He's been thinking the worst since he received that delivery."

Darrin looked sheepish for a moment. "Yeah, I'm sorry about that, but I didn't know that he'd flip out. David is Mr. Calm, Cool and Collected, so I thought he'd chill. It's not like we're kids anymore."

As an older sibling, I felt my nostrils flare. If I ever made it to eighty-five years of age, Moira would be a spry eighty-three, and I'd worry about her until the day I died.

"Quite frankly, Darrin, you should be glad he gives a shit. Turn it around. What would you think if David put you in this situation? Jesus Christ!" I heard my mother's voice saying, *"Language!"* in my head, and I said a quick prayer of apology to the baby Jesus.

"To be honest, I'd think it was kind of cool," he said, and my glare reignited. He leaned his head to the side and said, "But yeah, I can see where he's coming from."

"That's big of you," I said sarcastically. "So what's going on? And I'll tell you upfront if you did something wrong or illegal, you might not want to answer that question. I'm not going to help a criminal."

He scowled and pantomimed what I'd just said, moving his head from side to side. "Thanks, Mrs. High Horse, I'll bear that in mind. And the jury is *definitely* still out on you being an asshole, by the way. You seem convinced that I did something wrong. So I will state in no uncertain terms—that money was given to me. But it's complicated."

That money? Hunh. So that's what was in the laptop case. How much? Was it cash? If so, why in the hell would he have sent cash through the overnight mail? Think, think, think!

"Well, the money was actually secondary in David's mind. He was worried about you first and foremost. But you have to admit, that delivery was pretty unusual." I held my breath.

He nodded in agreement. "I suppose that amount of money in a FedEx would kind of weird a guy out."

"You think?" I then tried my staying silent routine, but it didn't work. This kid was going up my keester sideways.

"Darrin, don't make me kick your ass in front of all these children and dogs."

He laughed out loud as he looked me up and down. "You wish."

"Fill me in!"

He held up his hands. "Okay, okay, take it easy. The money was given to me by a friend. His name was Bobby McBride, and we knew each other from way back. We both came from Roxbury, which I don't have to tell you is *not* the nicest section of Boston. Bobby definitely came from the school of hard knocks.

"We were childhood friends. We became buddies in third grade when I smacked around some kids giving him a hard time at the bus stop, and we always palled around after that. But I moved out of the area when my mom married David's dad, so Bobby and I kind of lost touch. We'd see each other around occasionally, and his mom and my mom always exchanged Christmas cards, but we basically grew apart as we got older."

"So how'd you reconnect after all this time?"

"I'm getting there. Bobby's dad left when he was pretty young; I think he went to jail for something. That wasn't uncommon for some of us. Anyway, as soon as Bobby graduated from high school, he and his mom moved down to Florida. He got a decent job, was a wonder with anything that had an engine. He could build an Escalade with just this park bench and a motor." Darrin's thoughts seemed to drift away for a moment, but then he continued.

"Anyway, they lived down there with no problems for about nine years, and then wham! In a span of less than two weeks, Bobby's mom died in a house fire, he found out that his wife was cheating on him, and he was diagnosed with an inoperable brain tumor. Twenty-seven years old."

"My God," I murmured.

"Yeah, no kidding. Anyway, when he and Carol got married several years back, Bobby had purchased a life insurance policy to take care of her in case anything ever happened to him. It was for a *ton* of money, too, a million bucks. It didn't cost him a lot, because he was so young. He went through the physical and all the stuff you need to do for that large of a policy, and he passed with flying colors. He went through the whole thing because he didn't want Carol to ever be short on money the way he and his mom had been their whole lives.

"So after the shit hit the fan, Bobby was determined that Carol wasn't going to make one red cent off his death. He spoke to the agent who'd sold him the policy, and he told Bobby about viatical insurance policies."

Darrin paused, as if I might know what in the world he was talking about, which I didn't. "*What* insurance policies?"

"Viatical."

"Start at the beginning. Insurance 101, please."

He nodded. "Okay, let's say that Person X has an existing life insurance policy and is then diagnosed with a terminal illness. Person X can then sell their policy for a certain cash value."

"You mean they can cash in their policy for the accrued value?" I asked.

"No, no, not at all. That would simply be cashing in the policy. This is totally different. With a viatical situation, they actually *sell* their policy to an investor, for some agreed upon amount."

"Hunh? What do you mean?"

"Let's say Person X has a $500,000 life insurance policy and then finds out that they're terminal. Maybe they've got a year—maximum—to live. Let's say they want to try some experimental drugs that insurance doesn't cover, or maybe they just want to travel the world before they check out, or maybe they want to eat in a five-star restaurant every night of the week until their time is up. To do any of those things, they'd obviously need money. You with me?"

"Yep."

"Okay, so Person X needs money, and they have this life insurance policy. That's when a broker enters the picture."

"Good grief." I needed some caffeine. Why would a terminally ill person need a broker? This was confusing.

"We're almost there. The broker does what brokers do. He or she has a buyer, who is willing to give Person X money for their $500,000 life insurance policy. Maybe they'd buy it for $300,000 or $350,000 or whatever the calculation ends up being. That part of it is kind of over my head."

"Why would someone do that?"

"Just like everything in this country, it boils down to money. The sick person gets the $300k, the broker gets a commission, and the buyer takes over the payments on the life insurance policy and essentially waits for Person X to die."

The fog was lifting a little, and I was pretty sure that I was disgusted. "Okay, so the sick person gets $300,000 to do with whatever they want?"

"Correct."

"And the person that bought the policy makes the payments and keeps the policy up-to-date?"

"Correct."

"And when the sick person dies, the buyer gets the $500,000 in life insurance money?"

"You got it."

I pondered that for a minute and decided I was definitely disgusted. "So essentially, the buyer is rooting for the sick person to die as soon as possible? That way, they get a bigger return on their investment."

He pointed at me. "Precisely. Say the buyer in my example only had to wait six months for the sick person to die. He shelled out $300,000, paid a few months of premium and some other minor fees, and then got $500,000 six months later. Not a bad return on his investment."

I recoiled. I couldn't speak for a moment, and the beautiful day seemed utterly tainted. I finally found my voice, and it sounded very small. "It seems morbid and wrong."

"I felt the same way when I first learned about it. Is this a capitalistic society or what?

"But the thing is, it's perfectly legal. And it doesn't always work out like my example. Sometimes the investor gets burnt. In the 1980s, a lot of investors bought viatical policies on people who were diagnosed with AIDS, and the investors were licking their chops, waiting for a whole bunch of people to die. Some did, but others didn't. There were investors who paid the upfront money and then paid years and years of premium. In the end, they may have actually realized a loss. Some of the AIDS patients actually outlived their investors."

"Good," I said emphatically.

"And you've got to remember, the sick person makes the choice to take the cash. They basically profit from their own impending death."

I snarled, and he held up both his hands, palms facing me.

"So I'm not the most sensitive guy, I'm sorry. All I'm saying is the sick person gets to spend some dough they might otherwise never have had. It's their choice. Bobby liked the idea because he wanted to do some good with the money, and he also wanted to make sure his cheating-bitch-of-a-wife wouldn't get a cent."

I let that sink in for a minute or two, and Darrin didn't seem to mind the silence. Then something hit me.

"Wouldn't the beneficiary on the policy have to give Person X permission to sell it?"

He smiled as if I'd just figured out a secret. "Yes."

"So explain this. I am assuming that Bobby's wife, Carol, was the beneficiary?"

"Initially she was, yes."

"Okay, so if she, Carol, was the beneficiary, why in the world would she let him sell the policy? She would have to know it would leave her with nothing."

"You're a sharp little cookie. David did all right by hiring you."

"Thanks." I smiled and felt myself blush. Other people's opinions of me have such a huge effect on my self-esteem. I know it's ridiculous, but it's the truth.

"Anyway, I had the same question, and it's a bunch of technical mumbo jumbo, but I'll try to remember it correctly." He took a breath and forged ahead. "Florida isn't a community property state. Because of that, and since Bobby was the owner of what's called a revocable policy, he was able to change the beneficiary without her consent. That's when he showed up on my doorstep."

"For what?"

"As we talked about, all this viatical stuff is done through a broker. And like you just figured out, Bobby had to have the beneficiary's consent before he could sell his policy. That's when Bobby thought of me, for a few different reasons. For one, I lived across the country from Carol, and he wouldn't have to be anywhere near her. He packed up a couple of suitcases and just left, no divorce, nothing. Two, Bobby and I hadn't talked in a long time, and I'd never met Carol, so she wouldn't even know where to start looking for Bobby. And three—"

It all clicked for me, and I interrupted him. "And three, he knew he could ask you to become the new beneficiary. Then you would sign off that he could sell the policy and get his money through this viatical thing?"

"You got it. I became the beneficiary, signed off my permission, and, voila, Bobby got his money. I'm guessing it was a shitload of money at that. Probably $600,000 or $700,000, I'm not really sure."

I whistled under my breath. "That much?"

"From the little that I know about these viatical things, the key factor in determining the amount of dough that will be paid is the life expectancy of the person who's dying. The longer it is, the smaller the offer. Which is why I think Bobby got quite a chunk of change."

"He didn't have long to go?" I asked quietly.

Darrin shook his head sadly. "Nope, it was down to a matter of months, really. But he made the best of it. He had a great time out here, met some nice girls, tried a few experimental drugs for the tumor, and then it was over."

I scooted down the bench towards him a little. "Was it terribly hard at the end?"

"Unbelievably hard, but not like you'd think."

"What do you mean?" From what Cally had told me, I had a sense of what was coming.

He picked a rock off the ground and threw it in the bushes on the other side of the running path. I didn't think he was going to answer me, but then he did. "Bobby was murdered."

"I'm sorry," I said quietly.

Darrin looked disgusted. "It happened up in Santa Barbara, where he'd gone to be safe." He scoffed. "That's a crock of shit. The guy snuck into the house in the middle of the night and shot Bobby three times in the chest while he was in bed. The cops said he was awake, though, so he must have seen it coming. What a fucking nightmare."

"That's terrible."

"Beyond terrible. And the really weird thing was that he had a thousand dollars shoved in his mouth."

"*What?*"

"Yep. Ten one-hundred dollar bills rolled up in his mouth."

It took me almost a minute for that to sink in, and then I had a million questions. "Did they find the person who did it?"

"Well, they think so. It's kind of an odd scenario."

"How so?"

"Well, the guy who supposedly did it was this drifter dude and a major druggie. He'd been in and out of jail all over the country his entire life. What bugs the cops is that there doesn't appear to be any connection between him and Bobby at all."

"So why do they think he did it? It couldn't have been a robbery if the guy left a thousand dollars. What an odd, and expensive, calling card."

"The police concluded that it was him because he was dead inside of his rental car, outside of the house where he'd shot Bobby. He'd also left a note saying that he did it." Darrin gave me a look, as if to ask if things could be anymore obvious.

I lobbed my head from shoulder to shoulder. "Yep, that might make him a prime suspect."

"According to the cops, the dude died of an overdose but had a gun in his lap. It was the gun that killed Bobby. There were also lock picks in his backseat that had been used to break into the house. And the note basically sealed the deal. The guy was supposedly Bobby's killer, so the cops closed the case pretty quickly." He shook his head slightly.

"What do you mean by *supposedly*?"

"It just doesn't really add up. It was all too contrived and easy to solve. As far as I know, Bobby didn't know the guy. If he was really some drifter dude, I just don't see the connection between the two."

"So he's a mystery man?"

"The cops figure there's some connection we just haven't figured out yet. I have no idea who this guy was, but I guess that doesn't mean much because Bobby just came back into the scene about eight months ago. Obviously I don't know everyone from his past."

"You said Bobby had gone to Santa Barbara to be safe. Had he been threatened or something?"

"That's a long story. He hadn't really been threatened directly, but he'd gotten a tip that he might be in danger."

"A tip? Explain, please."

"Well, the company or the guy or whoever owned Bobby's policy obviously wanted him dead. The tip Bobby got made it sound like they'd murdered before, so he was just trying to lay low. My thinking is they hired this thug to get rid of Bobby."

"Why kill a kid who was going to die anyway?"

"Well, maybe the owner needed him dead sooner rather than later. I don't know."

I raised an eyebrow. "Well, assuming that they got away with murder, would they still get the money?"

"What do you mean? Why wouldn't they?"

"Well, if Bobby was deliberately killed, I thought it might negate the policy or something?"

"No, they'd get the money no matter how he died. He didn't need to die of the disease, if that's what you mean."

"That is what I meant." I pondered this new twist a little further. "So I guess it goes without saying you've talked with the police about this possibility?"

"Yeah, but so far nothing. They haven't been able to tie this drifter guy to the owner of the policy. Evidently, the investment company that bought the policy is headed up by this scumbag drug dealer who's worth about a zillion bucks. From the little I've heard, he has an airtight alibi. In my book that doesn't mean shit. I've called the police every day, but they don't have any other leads, and they've got to focus on new cases. And don't get me wrong, I know they work their asses off, and I'm not trying to bust their balls. I just want to know what happened to my friend."

"I don't blame you. Even if the owner of the policy had an alibi, you're right, that means squat. A guy with his resources would obviously hire someone. It's just a matter of finding the connection."

"Well, one cop is really cool, and I know he's doing some research on his own time. In the meantime, it's the waiting game."

"How frustrating." It seemed logical that the guy who bought the viatical policy was behind the murder, but suspecting it and proving it were two very different things.

"Yeah, it's been pretty awful. Bobby was suddenly gone. His disease was bad enough, but I had sort of come to terms with that. His death seemed imminent, but his being murdered wasn't the way it was supposed to happen."

I nodded. "He got cheated out of the short time he had left."

"That's exactly it. Anyway, Bobby wanted to be buried by his mom, so they flew his body back to Florida, and that was it. It's almost like he was never even here." Darrin's chin started to wobble, and I had the decency to look away. After a minute, I slid further down the bench, still a little closer to him.

"I'm sorry," I said softly.

Darrin reached into his pocket and handed me a folded piece of paper. I opened it and immediately noticed that the handwritten note was signed by Bobby. I didn't want to intrude and looked up to protest.

But Darrin cut me off before I said a word. "Go ahead, it was in a laptop case he told me to open after he died."

Darrin - if you're reading this, then I've got to believe I'm in a better place. Thanks for being a friend up until the end, it had to be hard on you. I've got things all set up with a lawyer, and he'll see to it that everything is taken care of. I gave some of my dough to one of the animal shelters in Valencia, some more to a school for underprivileged kids, and a little more to a shelter for single moms. There's a chunk of it going to The Jimmy Fund back in Boston, and I even set up an account with a few bucks for my dad, if he ever gets out of the joint. I want you to take what's in here and do something nice for yourself. You stuck up for me a long time ago at a bus stop, and I told you that someday I'd pay you back. Now I finally got my chance. Be good to your family, and have a beer for me the next time the Sox make the playoffs. Your friend - Bobby

I swiped a tear from my face, for a young man from Roxbury whom I'd never known. I suddenly missed home.

"When did you find this?"

"Well, about a month after Bobby did the viatical settlement, he told me he'd left a note in the case and made me promise that I wouldn't read it until he was gone. I promised and basically forgot about it. He kept it under his bed at our apartment, so out of sight, out of mind, I guess."

"You never looked at it?"

"Not once. I respected what he'd asked me to do. I mean, I was kind of curious about it, but I'd pretty much assumed that he was leaving me his laptop. When I remembered what he'd told me, I got the case out from under the bed, but there wasn't a computer in it. There was just a huge envelope that was stuffed to the max. When I opened it, I was stunned. It was the fifty grand that I ended up sending to David."

Fifty grand?! "I see," I murmured, trying to act like I'd known about the money all along.

"Yeah, it was bizarre. First of all, I didn't want it. It felt dirty. Then from a practical standpoint, who the hell would leave that in an apartment, anyway? We had people in and out of there quite a bit. Anyone could have found it, but I guess that no one did."

"That had to be awful—getting all of that money because he died." I didn't know Darrin well enough to know if he thought it was awful or not, but *I* certainly felt that way.

"You have no idea," he said quietly.

We sat in silence for a little bit, and I let everything sink in. My brain was putting things into little compartments, and there was something I simply had to ask him.

"Darrin, this is probably going to piss you off, but do the cops know about the money you found?"

He stiffened. "Why do you ask?"

"I would think it's obvious. Cases like these are usually a follow-the-money scenario. Some people might consider fifty thousand dollars a pretty attractive motive."

He glared at me. "Are you one of those people?"

I sighed. "The honest answer is yes, I am. That sounds insensitive, but I don't know you. What I do know is that certain people might do some really bad things for fifty grand."

He sat in silence and stared straight ahead.

"Darrin?"

He slapped his hands on the top of his legs, and I thought he was going to stand up. Instead, he surprised me.

"No, the cops don't know about the money. I was one of the first people they spoke with after Bobby was murdered, and they weren't giving me any type of preferential treatment. Thankfully, I was at Melanie's the night of the murder, so she was my alibi."

When I'd met Melanie, I'd sensed that she was protecting him, but I hadn't guessed that they were an item. I must have missed it. "You two are involved?"

Darrin looked startled. "No, not at all. We're buddies, we just work together. We'd watched a movie that night, and I was super tired, so I just crashed on her couch."

"And that's what she told the police?"

"Yeah."

"And they were satisfied with that?" I wasn't sure I was.

He shrugged. "I guess so. Plus, when the bullets taken from Bobby's body matched the dead guy's gun, they felt they had their man. And then there was the note."

"So why would the guy kill himself?" I asked.

"No idea," Darrin responded.

I winced. "Again, devil's advocate. *You* could have hired that guy."

"And then drugged him to make it look like a suicide? Jeez, Meagan. I know you don't know me, but I've spent countless hours with the police, and I've done everything I can to help them solve this. If they somehow find out about the money," he said while looking at me pointedly, "then I won't lie about it. But I didn't know what I would gain by telling them about it because then they would focus on me. And that would be a complete waste of time, because I didn't do this. I did not kill my friend." He looked away and shook his head slowly.

Part of me wanted to believe him, and the other part of me wondered how good an actor he really was. I needed to get us off this emotional roller coaster and on to business.

"Okay, so for the sake of argument, let's say you didn't know about the fifty grand. Then why all the secrecy? Why did you mail the money to David? Why not just leave it in the bank? And why in God's name did you send cash?"

"Did you hear what I just said?"

"I did."

"If I'd suddenly deposited fifty g's in my bank account, the cops would have quickly stumbled onto it. Again, they would have suspected me, and they wouldn't have been focusing their efforts on the real killer."

I raised an eyebrow at him.

He smiled sadly. "I sound like O.J. don't I?"

I smiled back. "Yeah, you do, but I'll give you the benefit of the doubt for now. So you decided a bank was out of the question. Why Fed Ex?"

"Well, I wanted to get the money into good hands. I knew David wouldn't spend it, but I wanted to know he could use it if something happened to me."

That didn't sound too promising. "Such as?"

"Such as something not good." His eyes were cast downward, and I knew he was hiding something.

"Spill it, Darrin."

He sighed. "I've got a pretty big problem on my hands. The guy who Bobby's wife is having an affair with is a cop, and he's out here following me around. He's threatened me verbally, my tires were slashed a couple of days ago, and he trashed my apartment."

I felt a chill despite the warmth of the California air. This wasn't good. "Can you prove any of that?"

"Not a word."

"Beautiful. Those are pretty big accusations against a cop."

"I know, but he's not the good sort of cop."

"Would anyone else be trying to scare you for some reason?"

"No, I know it was him. Bobby was killed on a Wednesday. I didn't open the laptop case until the following Wednesday night. I'd been so bummed out and wired that I totally forgot about it. Then when I opened it, I found the cash. I was amazed that it could all fit into that big envelope. Anyway, I was a little freaked out and decided that I'd do something with it the next morning. I slept with the case beside me all night.

"As they say, timing is everything. The next morning the laptop case and I got out of bed and left the apartment to get a safety deposit box at a new bank. Evidently by that time, Carol had learned of Bobby's death, because this Neanderthal guy was waiting by my car when I got outside. He flashed me a badge, said that he was a Florida policeman who had friends out this way and then said I better get the million to Carol, *or else*."

I briefly wondered if a Florida policeman had any jurisdiction in California and decided he probably didn't. "The million?! I thought you said that Bobby got $600,000 or $700,000?"

"Well, this dude obviously didn't know Bobby had sold the policy, and Carol must have told him she had a cool million coming."

"Oh, yeah. This is confusing. So what'd you do?"

"I told him I didn't know what the hell he was talking about and that he definitely had the wrong guy. Call me crazy, but I didn't think he'd be interested on a lecture on viatical insurance policies. In the meantime, I was shitting my pants because I had fifty thousand right there in my hands. It wasn't a million, but I'm sure he'd have accepted it as a down-payment."

"Did he believe you?"

"Not for a second. He said I shouldn't insult his intelligence, which probably wouldn't have taken much, by the way. I don't know how he tracked me down, but he was on a mission. He got right up in my face and said he'd be thrilled to make life very difficult for me. Then he said he'd be thrilled to make life end for me, if that's what it took. I believed him. He looked like a steroid freak, real crazy like. I told him to stay the hell away from me and literally sprinted to my car and took off."

"Did you happen to see what type of car he was driving?"

Darrin looked confused. "What?"

"Do you know what he was driving?"

"Hell, no. We didn't exactly kick tires while he was threatening me. What does it matter?"

"Never mind, I'll get to that. So, get back on track. You ran to your car, and then what?"

"I drove like a maniac to the nearest bank, and I thought my heart was going to explode. But then it hit me that there'd be a bunch of paperwork in order to get a safety deposit box, and I really didn't want to draw attention to myself. But I also knew I couldn't keep the money on me, not with that freak on my tail.

"So I sat in the bank parking lot for about ten minutes, trying to decide what to do, and that's when I noticed a FedEx office directly across the street. I walked in and overnighted the laptop case to David. I tried not to think about the fact that packages sometimes get lost. I just did it on autopilot."

His voice was getting shaky. "Thank God I did it, because when I got back to my apartment, it was completely trashed. All the cupboards were open, most of the glasses were broken, the cushions were slashed, the beds flipped over, and food was everywhere. It was a friggin' disaster. If I had walked in on him, he probably would have killed me.

"Anyway, that's when I started staying at Melanie's place, and the next night, she got about twenty phone calls, and the person hung up every time she answered."

"Does she have caller ID?"

"Yep, but the number was blocked. I had been there less than a day and knew it had to be him. She'd never had that happen until I showed up.

"I don't know what type of friends this guy has, but he's a cop and probably has connections, right? I'm worried that he'll somehow track down my mom or stepdad or David. That's why I didn't call David, and that's why I didn't convert the cash to a check. This freak might have threatened or paid someone at the bank, and they might have talked. Or he might know someone at the phone company who could have found David if I'd called him. My mom took her husband's last name, so no family member in Boston has the same last name as me. They're all Fontanas, and my last name is Hood, like my father's. I just don't want to bring this shit down on them. I need to fix this on my own, and I need to make sure this money never gets back to Carol. I owe at least that much to Bobby."

Despite my reservations about his story, my heart went out to this kid. "I hate to tell you, but I think this guy already knows all about you and your family, pal."

He frowned. "Why do you say that?"

I gave him the brief rundown of my antics with the hearse earlier that morning, as well as my two sightings of the red Impala. "I don't know if they're related or not, but I'd rather not find out."

"What did the red Impala guy look like?"

"I saw the car twice, but I never saw the driver. So maybe it's the same guy, maybe not, but it looks like someone knows what I'm up to, and I've been in town for less than twenty-four hours. I think you're dealing with pros here, Darrin."

"Shit." He ran his hands through his hair. "Here I thought I was being so clever."

"Listen Darrin, David is already worried, so you can't avoid that anymore. He paid good money to send me out here to see if you're okay, and it doesn't sound like you are."

"I know."

"You'd be better off fighting this guy with some backup."

"Well, you seem to think you can kick my ass, so you must be a pretty tough broad. Are you up for playing bodyguard? Bonnie and Clyde style?"

I barked out a laugh. "Well, let's review my credentials. I weigh about a hundred and twenty pounds soaking wet, and my courage is somewhere in the neighborhood of the lion from *The Wizard of Oz*. So I think I'm up for the job."

"We're screwed."

"On our own, that's probably true. This guy doesn't exactly sound like a lightweight."

"He isn't."

"And it sounds like he isn't going to let up."

"I doubt it."

"Then, as I see it, it boils down to one question."

"Yeah? And what's that?"

"If we get a U-Haul *right now,* load you up, and drive cross-country, will you provide the caffeine for the whole trip?"

He shook his head like I was cuckoo. "You're crazy. That's exactly what I *don't* want him to do. Follow me to Boston so he can get close to my family."

"He's made it pretty clear he's going to follow you no matter what. At least in Boston, you're on your home turf."

"You've gotta point there. To tell you the truth, I've actually been thinking about going back for a while now. Maybe you coming here was a sign or something."

I smiled. "Is that a yes?"

He sighed and looked around, taking in the park, the sun, and the beautiful day. "It's just gotten so complicated out here," he said softly.

"Is that a yes?" I asked a little more forcefully this time.

He blew out a big breath of air. "Beantown, here we come. No country music."

CHAPTER 8

I breathed out a sigh of relief. "First things first. You need to call your assigned detective at the police department and see if there is a problem with you leaving town. If not, give them all of your contact information so it doesn't look like you're trying to disappear. Got it?"

"Got it. I'll call them right now." He pulled out his cell phone and punched a button. He must have programmed the number for the police on his speed dial. I heard him ask for the detective on the case, and my thoughts wandered as he was on hold. I shut my eyes and let my head fall back over the top of the bench. For a few frightful seconds, I wondered if I was helping a fugitive drive across the country and get away with murder. But I was going with my gut, and this kid didn't seem like a murderer. Right?

"Meagan?"

His voice startled me. I didn't even know he'd hung up. "Hunh? Sorry, I was spacing off." *I was just wondering if you were going to chop me up on the drive to Boston.*

"The detective didn't seem too happy about it but said he couldn't stop me from leaving. I'm supposed to touch base with him a few times a week."

I pulled the brim of my hat down sharply. "So let's do this."

In a matter of hours, we'd picked up a U-Haul, sold Darrin's tire-slashed-car to a friend of a friend in the wholesale auto business, and also dropped my rental car back at the airport. We took a cab back to Melanie's and then conducted a covert operation just after dark to load up his belongings. It struck me that this was the second time they'd done this in a matter of days.

In between boxes, I pulled out the policeman's card from my purse and dialed the number. To my surprise, he picked up.

"Officer Simonetta? This is Meagan Maloney. We met last night at the convenience store?"

I thought I heard him chuckle. "Yes, Meagan, how are you?"

"I'm fine, thanks. I just wanted to let you know that I've solved my case and that I'll be getting out of your lovely state soon."

"Well, thanks for letting me know. I hope you have a nice trip back to Boston." There was silence for a moment. "Is that all, Meagan?"

"Well, no, not exactly. I'm sure you're very busy, but I just wanted to tell you about a related case that the Santa Barbara police recently closed."

"I'm all ears."

I told him about Bobby and the fact that Darrin wasn't convinced that solving the murder was as simple as it had seemed. He said he obviously couldn't reopen a closed case outside of his jurisdiction, but he told me about some type of internal computer program that lets surrounding venues talk to each other. He said he would make some notes in the computer file and request that any additional information on the case be routed to him, in addition to the assigned detectives. I was a little disappointed he couldn't do more, but he seemed sincere, and I liked him for it.

After the brief phone call, I helped Darrin load up a small amount of furniture, and what remained were some boxes of personal items. Because of her cast, Melanie gave us moral support and lemonade, but that wasn't cutting it, and our stomachs were letting us hear it.

"DiMicci's?" Darrin asked suddenly. "I'll buy if you fly."

I looked at Melanie to see if she knew what he was talking about.

"I'm in," Melanie said.

"Meagan, you're the guest, so you get to pick the pizza toppings."

Ohhhhhh, now this was right up my alley. But I wanted to choose wisely. "Is there anything you two don't like on your pizza?"

Melanie shrugged as if to say it didn't really matter to her, and Darrin said he didn't really like pineapple. Something about fruit and pizza not mixing.

"Okay, then," I said. "I'm going with pepperoni and onion. You guys decide on the crust."

"DiMicci's only does thin crust, and it's the best in the world. Unbelievable sauce, too." Darrin looked like a kid at Christmas. "So call in the order and get over there pronto!"

I smiled and looked around at the remaining boxes. "I'm sold. But don't they deliver?"

Melanie smirked and Darrin shook his head, like I was the ignorant pupil and they the seasoned DiMicci's experts.

"DiMicci's definitely doesn't deliver. They don't have to." Darrin's voice was reverent.

I smiled knowingly. "Ah, if-they-build-it-you-will-come type of thing?"

"So you've watched *Field of Dreams*?" Darrin asked.

"Only a couple zillion times. My neighbor is from Iowa."

"Sorry to hear that," Melanie quipped.

I scowled. "It's a nice place," I said, my defense of Doob and his homeland never wavering.

"Have you ever been there?"

Was she challenging me? "We're going to be going through there on our cross-country trip," I responded. I thought it was a clever way of avoiding her question, because I actually had never been to Iowa. But if Iowa produced Doob, then Iowa was two thumbs-up in my book.

Darrin intervened. "All right, Mel, you dial in the pizza, and throw in an order of breadsticks with extra sauce, too. By the time you two get there, it should be ready to go."

You two? I assumed I'd be helping with the final boxes and really didn't want to be traipsing around with the anti-Iowa Melanie.

I tried to sound light when I asked, "Do we both need to go? I can help with the last of these boxes."

Melanie jumped in. "DiMicci's is jammed into a very small space at this strip mall where parking is a nightmare, so I'll drive around while you run inside and get the food. Plus, their large pizzas are huge, not to mention the breadsticks, and I can't carry things around very easily right now." She gestured at her cast.

I acquiesced. "Okay, no problem. Let me grab my pocketbook, and we'll hit the road."

Darrin handed me some money on the way out the door, and Melanie and I hopped in her car. It smelled great, producing that new car smell none of my cars have ever had.

I whistled lightly as I buckled my seatbelt. "This is a nice ride. Is it new?"

"Nah, it's a rental," Melanie said. "The little fender bender that did this to my arm did a lot worse to my car. It's in the shop for a while."

"Oh, that sucks."

She nodded. She seemed content to not say anything as we drove along, but I am the non-content type when it comes to silence in a vehicle.

We didn't even have the radio on, for goodness sake. Actually, she'd been pretty quiet throughout the evening, and I wondered if she'd hoped her friendship with Darrin would eventually blossom into something more. Darrin had invited her to pack up and head out with us, but she'd declined, saying it was too short notice. She'd subletted the house she was in for a year, and she had work and other obligations that grown-ups tend to have. Still, she seemed bothered that he was leaving, and I felt a little bad for her.

"Well Melanie, you'll have to come visit us once Darrin gets settled in."

She nodded again. "I'll definitely do that. I actually have some relatives around the Boston area, but I haven't been to that part of the country since I was a baby."

I thought about that and smiled. "I've never been anywhere *besides* Boston since I was a baby. I'll admit I've led a sheltered life, but we Bostonians are homers. It's tough to get us to admit that anywhere on earth is as good as our little slice of the world. I guess we just feel that there's no place like home."

Melanie shrugged. "I wouldn't know."

I wasn't sure how to take that, but I took a stab. "So I guess you moved around a lot as a kid?

"You could say that," she replied.

"Where do your parents live?"

"I was adopted, and my adopted parents died when I was little. Then I got bounced around the southwest while I was growing up. I guess that's why I'll probably always be on the move. I don't really have roots anywhere."

I couldn't relate to that at all. "Do you have any brothers or sisters?"

"I had a brother, but he died, too."

Ugh. I didn't want to ask about any more family, as it didn't seem like her family tree was growing. I decided to change the subject. "So what brought you out here?"

"It's a long story."

I spread my hands out. "I've got all night."

She sighed deeply. "Well, the short version is that I was running away from a guy who wasn't too nice. Let's just say we had a difference of opinion as to whether I owed him some money or not. So I got in my car and ended up here and started fresh."

I was intrigued. "What's the long version of that story?"

She cast a quick sideways glance my way and then her eyes returned to the road. I figured she was going to tell me to mind my own friggin' business, but she surprised me by smiling slightly.

"Why do you care?"

I shrugged. "I'm just curious, I guess. It's what I do for a living. I'm also hoping the not-so-nice guy didn't catch up with you."

"It took him some time, but he did."

"And?"

"By the time he found me, I had my head on straight and sent him packing. I haven't heard from him since."

I nodded. "And what about the money?"

"I didn't owe him a cent, and I didn't give him a cent." She kept her eyes on the road, and it was apparent that we'd come to the end of the conversation.

"Well, good for you. I hope you don't hear from him again."

She didn't respond, and I gave up on small talk. Melanie wasn't the chattiest person I'd ever met, and we drove the rest of the way in silence.

The parking lot where DiMicci's was located was completely jammed, as promised, and the smell of the place was heavenly. The young man at the take-out counter handed me a huge plastic bag that had grease on the bottom of it. The grease had evidently already soaked through the bottom of the pizza box, and I immediately knew I was going to love their food.

It was all I could do to not rip the bag open during the drive back to Melanie's house. She and I managed a little bit of chitchat on the drive back but nothing of real substance. After pulling into her driveway, I literally ran up the steps to her front door. Darrin must have been as eager as I was, because he opened the door before I got to the top step.

"Let's eat, ladies!" The three of us attacked the food with reckless abandon and inhaled pizza, breadsticks, complete with the extra sauce, without saying a word. Then we all settled into food comas. After watching about an hour of nonsensical television, Melanie said she was going to bed. Darrin offered me the couch that he'd been staying on, and Melanie gave him an extra blanket for his night on the floor. I fell asleep within seconds of lights-out and dreamt of policemen arriving at Melanie's door.

CHAPTER 9

TUESDAY, MARCH 4TH-WEDNESDAY, MARCH 5TH

The alarm was absolutely torturous at four thirty the next morning, but we forced ourselves to get moving. After thanking Melanie for her hospitality, Darrin and I hit the road and were headed east by five.

During the first couple of days, we were a little jumpy that Steroid-Neanderthal-Man might be following us, but by the end of the second day we'd relaxed. Maybe we were just getting punchy from seeing so much highway. You don't realize how big our country is until you road-trip from one coast to the other in less than a week.

We were somewhere in middle-America, Doob country, when Darrin asked, "So Meagan, how did a girl like you decide to become a private investigator?"

There it was. The question. The one that always made my heart hurt. The one that made my stomach twist every single time. I wasn't comfortable enough to tell him the truth. I wasn't sure there was enough interstate left to delve into that part of my life. So I took the easy way out and threw the question back in his face.

"A girl like me? I'm not sure what that's supposed to mean."

He shrugged. "It doesn't mean anything. I just don't know any P.I.'s and wondered what made you decide to do it for a living?"

I opted for the mundane answer I always give at cocktail parties because it's so much easier than the truth. "Well, I tried to follow the normal path, if you will." I made quotation marks with my fingers when I said the word *normal* and then rolled my eyes. "I finished college, even went on to get my master's degree, mainly because I wanted to avoid the so-called real world for another two years. But, even after that schooling, and let's not forget the additional student loans, cha-ching, the grand scheme for my life still eluded me."

Darrin nodded while staring down the road. "Yeah, I know that feeling."

"The only thing I had figured out was that life wasn't waiting, and bills had to be paid, so I found myself schlepping away at an entry level position with an investment brokerage for a few years after graduate school."

"That sounds awful."

I nodded. "It sucked. I hated every minute of it and knew I had to have a job that did more than deliver a paycheck."

"So you just up and decided to become a P.I.?"

I shrugged and again opted for the path of least resistance. "Sort of. The idea came to me one night a few years back when my sister Moira and I shared one, two, possibly three, bottles of pinot grigio. I basically had an epiphany about changing careers, and the alcohol glow gave me the belief that I could actually do it." I held my hands up over my head, as if my name were in lights. "Meagan Maloney, Private Investigator. I told Moira my idea, but she brushed it off."

"How come?"

"Well, I've come up with all kinds of ideas while drinking pinot."

He smirked. "Care to share?"

I blew out a deep breath. "I've made plans to become a rock star, an astronaut, a forensic scientist, a hair stylist to the stars, a dog whisperer, a ferret whisperer, a professional golfer, a professional golf caddy, a guard at a women's prison, a snake charmer, a jockey, a camera person for ESPN, an Olympic luge competitor, a Feng Shui decorator, and a host of other things."

"The luge?"

I laughed. "I friggin' love watching that event. And it really doesn't look like it would involve all that much training. I'd just turn my toes in and be on my way. Screaming the entire time, of course."

Darrin smiled. "So Moira thought this was just another harebrained scheme?"

"Pretty much. I think that she planned on becoming an attorney from the moment she was conceived. I've just never had that type of single-mindedness. I envy it, but I think she envies me a little, too. At the very least, I entertain her."

"So what did your parents have to say about it?"

I grimaced. "Let's just say that it didn't go so well. Pop walked out of the room and straight to his not-so-hidden bottle of scotch, and my mom burst out crying."

"Oh jeez. That sucks."

"Yeah, the whole disappointment thing, which is a million times worse than if they would have screamed at me. But I was optimistic. It felt right, and it was something I knew I could do. And I hoped that, in time, the folks would be singing my praises, and I'd have a Perfect Daughter Plaque up on the mantle by Moira's collection." I sighed. "A girl can dream."

"So then what, you just opened shop? Did you have to get a permit or something?"

"Well, after the folks, I had another hurdle to clear. I didn't realize the steps involved in becoming a private investigator, nor did I realize that I didn't have the qualifications to become one, but my mind was made up. A man named Norman Switzer, a lifelong friend of my uncle, had been a Boston policeman for over twenty-five years, and Norman qualified for a P.I.'s license. After hearing my pitch, he agreed to become the principal private investigator for the yet-to-be-formed firm. What that meant was he'd be held responsible for the licensing, bonding, compliance, and other rules and regs of the Commonwealth until I'd gained the experience to do so on my own. The firm was founded on my dream, but Norman had a twinkle in his eye on the day that our office opened, and I knew he was going to have some fun doing a little sleuthing on his own. Norman's faith in me made me even more determined to make the whole thing work.

"So it took some time, money, and a whole lot of insurance, but before long, everything was formed, and I was approved to be what a layman would call an assistant private investigator in the Commonwealth of Massachusetts."

"Have you ever had to shoot anyone?"

I smiled. "Everyone asks me that. To this day, I haven't shot at anyone. My hope is that all of my investigating will be of the non-shooting variety. Norman can be in charge of the gun stuff."

"Don't you think that's a little naïve?"

"Totally."

"Are you a good shot?"

"Yep," I said.

"Modest, too," he said with a grin.

I blushed. "Sorry, just honest. I am a pretty darn good shot, though."

His smile widened. "You tired?"

"Yep."

"Why don't you get some sleep, and I'll get us a few more hours down the road."

"You sure?"

"Absolutely. You've driven more than I have, and I'm wide awake. I'll wake you if we get to the world's largest ball of twine before dark."

I leaned my head back and closed my eyes. Darrin's innocent questions as to why I'd become a private investigator had churned up a lot of memories and feelings that were always lurking near the surface.

As I tried to doze off, my thoughts drifted back to a beautiful morning in July several years before. I'd been just a few short hours away from marrying the man I loved. But a phone call from his mother telling me that he'd been murdered early that morning shattered my life in an instant. The fact that his murder was still unsolved haunted me every single day.

CHAPTER 10
THURSDAY, MARCH 6TH-FRIDAY, MARCH 7TH

As each day went by, Darrin and I got used to being road warriors. We talked, we sang, we ate junk food, we slept, and we counted down the miles to Beantown every couple of hours or so.

We spent a great night in Chicago with some friends of mine from college, Anne and Dino. They brought along some friends of their own, Shane, Candy, and Brent, and we convened at a pub close to Wrigley Field. Dino had just purchased a fabulous new condo, and after an evening full of food and cocktails, we all headed to his place to crash for the night. Thankfully, Candy had volunteered to be the designated driver. She, Darrin and Brent commandeered the U-Haul while the rest of us piled in a cab bound for Dino's new pad on the Gold Coast, a historic section of Chicago near Lake Shore Drive.

Dino's cat, Little Elvis, greeted us at the door like a dog, and even though I'm usually anti-cat, I liked him immediately. The feeling seemed to be mutual, as the fat, orange feline spent the night on the floor right beside my sleeping bag. I have to admit it was a strange comfort. If there was ever such a thing as a guard cat, then Little Elvis fit the bill. Dino had rescued him from the streets of Terre Haute, Indiana, several months before, and the cat had made up for lost time and meals. He weighed at least twenty pounds and snored louder than any human I've ever heard.

After bidding our Windy City friends farewell very early the next morning, we hit the road with a vengeance. By the time we crossed the Massachusetts border, I was ninety percent sure that Darrin wasn't capable of murder. Lucky for me. It was just that other ten percent that kept niggling away at my little brain.

We'd called ahead to let David know we'd be arriving in Boston late that Friday night, and true to our word, we illegally parked in front of David's building at eleven thirty. We hadn't told him about the U-Haul, and I couldn't completely gauge his reaction when he learned his stepbrother was home for good. He looked to be something between surprised and wary.

Darrin gestured to the U-Haul and explained. "I hope this is okay, David. It'll just be until I get a job and find a place of my own. Plus, I know you're short on some furniture now that Jocelyn is gone."

Whoa! Just one minute, here. Who was Jocelyn? Why had she left? Was she insane? As long as she was gone, why did I care? Good riddance, Jocelyn, you dumb bitch.

"Sure, no problem, it's good to have you back. I'm hoping you have a toaster in there somewhere?" David smiled good-naturedly, but I couldn't stop wondering about this toaster-taking Jocelyn.

"At your service, a four-slicer to boot," Darrin responded.

"Then how could I refuse? Let's get you unloaded and crack open a bottle of whatever Jocelyn left of the wine selection. Probably cooking sherry."

We spent about an hour unloading Darrin's things, and I was trying to find a way to inquire about Jocelyn the entire time, but the opportunity never seemed to present itself. That had really never stopped me before, but I couldn't casually work someone into the conversation who I didn't even know. I would have to put my sleuthing skills to work another time.

After the manual labor, we found what we hoped was a legal parking space for the U-Haul, not an easy task in Boston. The three of us then walked back to David's condo, and I actually enjoyed the cold air on my face. Darrin went upstairs while David and I waited at the front of his building for my cab. When my ride pulled up, David hugged me. My God. It had been a really long time since I'd been held by a yummy man.

"Meagan, thank you for everything. It'll mean the world to his mom that Darrin's back."

"How about you?"

"What do you mean?"

"Well, I saw your face when you realized that he was moving in, and it didn't seem like you were jumping for joy. Are you okay with all of this?"

"Yeah, sure. I was just surprised you guys didn't mention it, but it'll be nice having him around."

I wasn't sure I believed him, but I also wasn't up for debating it at this hour of the night. "Well, I don't want to get the cabbie mad, so I better head out."

"Thanks again, Meagan. I don't think he would have done this if it hadn't been for you pushing him."

I smiled but couldn't take credit. "He would have, eventually. I'm not sure California was everything he'd hoped it would be."

"I'll see you in the morning then?"

"The morning?"

"At the coffee place."

"Oh, of course. I'll be there around ten or so. I need to catch up on some z's."

"See you then, Meagan." David put my suitcase in the cab, and I fell asleep immediately after giving the driver my address.

CHAPTER 11
SATURDAY, MARCH 8TH

When I got to the coffee shop later that morning, I saw David waving at me from my usual spot. My foggy brain processed that two coffees were on the table.

"I hope I got this right," he said. "*With* the whipped cream, correct? At least that's what the girls at the counter told me."

"Perfect, thank you," I said, and my grogginess vanished.

"So, Darrin and I have been up all night talking about everything he's been through," David said.

I found it hard to believe he could look so incredible after being up all night. The puffy dark circles under my eyes resembled little sausage links.

"And?"

"Well, it's all a little hard to digest. What do you think?"

I shrugged a shoulder. "I've got to admit I'd never heard of this viatical thing before meeting Darrin. To be honest, it seems pretty disgusting to me. I mean, poor Bobby died, got murdered no less, and somebody profited from it. It just doesn't seem right."

He tilted his head to the side. "Yeah, I know what you mean. But at least this way, Bobby was calling the shots at the end. I'm sure he would have felt worse knowing all the money would be going to his wife."

"I guess, but it still seems so sad and wrong. Not to mention the murder still doesn't make sense to me. The police never connected the dots between Bobby and his alleged murderer. At least that's what Darrin told me." I raised an eyebrow at him, hoping that he might speculate, but he didn't.

David nodded his in agreement. "Without a doubt, it doesn't sound like Bobby ever caught much of a break."

"Did you know him?"

"I didn't. When Darrin and his mom moved across the city to live with me and my dad, it sounds like he and Bobby lost touch. Darrin speaks highly of him, though. It sounds like he had some fun towards the end, and he definitely did some great things with the money. I hope that Darrin uses his portion wisely."

I smiled and lifted my Styrofoam cup in a toast. "Spoken like a true older brother."

He tipped his coffee towards mine, and we both drank to our younger siblings. And then I couldn't resist. "David, why were you so reluctant to tell me about the fifty thousand in that laptop case? You had to know that the money and Darrin's disappearance were related."

He didn't answer for a moment and then rubbed his face with both hands. "I didn't tell you about the money because I didn't know it was there."

Didn't see that one coming. "Hunh?"

"Darrin's note was sticking out of a zippered compartment in the laptop case when I opened up the FedEx box. I read the note first, and after reading it, I got nervous about what might be inside, so I didn't open it. I put it in a safe place like he'd told me and then tried to contact him."

I raised an eyebrow. "I think that you lied to me, Mr. Fontana. You said nothing illegal was in the case. But you didn't know that for certain."

He held up a finger. "Meagan, you wanted to know what was in the case. 'I can't really say right now' were the exact words I used because I *didn't* want to lie to you. And I wasn't lying. I couldn't tell you because I didn't know."

"Seriously? That's your argument? You also told me that you'd have taken it to the cops if it had been illegal."

"I told you that if I'd *opened* it and discovered something illegal that I would have involved the police. But I hadn't opened it, so I had no need for the police."

I glowered at him. "You played me. You carefully twisted your words and led me to believe that nothing illegal was inside that case. And now you're splitting hairs."

"To split a final hair, then, I must say that having possession of fifty thousand legitimate dollars in-and-of-itself isn't illegal. Right? And that's what was in the case."

I growled, and he smiled at his own glib attempt to circumvent the issue.

"I'm sorry, Meagan. But if the situation had been reversed, your top priority would have been finding your sister. Nothing else would have mattered. If I'd needed to, I would have opened that case eventually, but it turns out that I didn't need to. All's well that ends well. Case closed." He thought about that for a second. "No pun intended."

I rolled my eyes and grinned in spite of myself. David and I went on to talk about some current events and the outlook for the upcoming Red Sox season, and I was sad to see him go when we said good-bye. How could I have known that by month's end I'd regret the day we met?

CHAPTER 12
SUNDAY, MARCH 9ᵀᴴ

Like everyone, my beloved mother's birthday falls on a Sunday every so often, and this was one of those years. My mother does not exercise much power over Moira and me anymore, but if we are not seated by Ma and Pop at Mass on her birthday morning, then hell and damnation, in the form of a four-foot eleven, red-headed, freckled Irish woman, will reign supreme. She says that it's *her day* and if she wants the family at church together on *her day*, then the least we can do is oblige.

My Uncle Larry, who is one of my father's older brothers, is in attendance for nearly every holiday or family event that we ever have. He's a lifelong bachelor and probably won't ever change that status, now that he's in his late-sixties. Larry, who I generally refer to as Uncle Lare, is basically a professional gambler and spends most of his time at one of the casinos in Connecticut, either Foxwoods or Mohegan Sun. It depends on whose tables are treating him better that week.

One year, Uncle Lare was brave enough—or maybe just stupid enough—to skip Ma's Sunday birthday. According to him, the craps table had been hot, and he just couldn't tear himself away. Plus, he'd been drinking for twenty-seven hours straight and thought it wouldn't have been safe to drive back to Boston. My mother hadn't spoken to him until Thanksgiving of that same year. She only caved in then because he'd brought a date to dinner, and Ma wanted to be hospitable. That night, Pop and Uncle Larry had gotten completely drunk and had started talking politics, or should I say, started *screaming* politics. Hours had passed before Larry realized his date had called a cab and gone home. It's such a shocker he's still single.

The thing about old Lare, though, is that he's almost always laughing, always the life of the party, and he used to bring me a present even on Moira's birthday, so he won me over early-on in life. With Larry, there's love, spontaneity, and no judging, which results in a huge thumbs-up in my book.

Nowadays Larry lives in a three-family house over in Southie that I affectionately refer to as the geriatric frat house. There are a total of eight men who live there, and the youngest of them is sixty-seven, the oldest is eighty-eight. They have varying backgrounds, some never married, some divorced, some widowed, and I have my suspicions the seventy-nine-year-old might be gay. One of the guys who lives there owns the house, and the others pay him a pittance for rent, and they all seem to get along swimmingly. It's the damndest thing I've ever seen, but I've been welcomed like a celebrity on the few occasions that I've been there, so what the heck. It works, they're happy, God Bless.

This birthday Sunday we all dutifully showed up at the church on time, Ma, Pop, Moira, Lare, and me. Pop had on a suit that I'll call vintage, and Ma had a new yellow hat that was the size of a small satellite dish. Moira was dewy and glowing in an ivory outfit that would have looked terrible on anyone larger than a size 4, and her hair was swept into some type of soft chignon with a small flower tucked behind one ear. One of us simply had to be adopted. Uncle Lare had managed to shave and didn't smell of whiskey, so he was batting a thousand. I had on a white blouse and a pair of khaki pants that had fit when I'd purchased them at the end of last summer.

We survived Mass and even survived brunch back at my parents' house without my dad or Larry fighting at the dinner table. A birthday celebration to remember.

Just as we were finishing up dessert, my mom asked how my trip to California had been. I hadn't told her, and I shot Moira a dirty look. Her eyes were suddenly glued to her chocolate cake.

"It was fine," I responded crisply. "More birthday cake, anyone?"

Pop raised his hand like a school boy, and I scampered off to the kitchen. I hoped my West Coast travels would be forgotten by the time I returned. No such luck.

"California?!" Larry boomed as I reentered the dining room. "What were you doing there?"

Good grief. "I was on my first big out-of-town case, Uncle Lare, just for a few days. I didn't even get to enjoy the weather."

Pop took over. "What case? You have big cases that take you to California? What is the time difference over there, anyway?"

"Three hours, Pop. And I shouldn't have said it was a big case because it was really no big deal. A client was looking for someone, I found him, the end."

My father scowled. "Someone paid you for *that?* It must not have been too hard if you were only out there a few days. Sounds stupid to me."

"Yes Pop, it was all very stupid, which is why we don't need to talk about it."

Enter friggin' Moira. "What we *should* be talking about is the client. A certain someone who is six-four and very good looking. And someone who has actually managed to catch my older sister's attention."

My eyes bulged, and I thought about javelin tossing my fork at her jugular, but with my luck, I'd probably hit it.

Ma's voice suddenly went up ten notches. "Oh, *really?*" She looked like a puppy who was about to get filet mignon for dinner.

"Good God, Ma."

"Language, please," she responded. But she continued to stare at me expectantly. It had been so long since there'd been a man in my life, and I knew my parents worried about me.

"Yes, my client, emphasis on *client*, is quite handsome, but I am a professional, and my work with him is over."

"Which is why you can ask him out now," Moira chimed in. I am bigger than she is, so I could not understand this continued idiocy on her part.

Pop's hand smacked the table. "No girl of mine is asking some pretty boy who can't travel on his own out on a date. I will not allow it!"

Time to start clearing the dishes. "I'm not asking anyone out," I said testily. "My love life is non-existent. Besides, Moira has been seeing *Porter* for several months, now. Why isn't anyone grilling her?"

I rolled my eyes when I said Porter's name, mainly because I don't think he's the best fit for my baby sister. That might be a tiny understatement. If pushed, I would go so far to say that he's a stuffed shirt who I can't stomach. If pushed further, I would have to admit that I can't stand the little prick, and I'd gladly run him over with a bus and then get a great lawyer to help me plead self-defense, temporary insanity, whatever. Porter and I have absolutely nothing in common, but we've always managed to coexist in a mildly-tolerant bubble, probably because of both of our feelings for Moira.

That all changed when Porter took Pop golfing one day and afterwards spent forty minutes at our apartment, telling Moira how embarrassing it had been. Evidently Pop hadn't measured up to his blueblood country club standards. Moira should have kneed him in his undoubtedly tiny genitalia and dumped him on the spot. She didn't. That disappointed me.

And then I disappointed her. I told Porter that he better not show his fat-fuck-of-a-face in our apartment ever again or I'd get my gun out and shoot him. It's been a sore spot for Moira and me ever since, and she's consequently away from the apartment a lot. I miss her, but I guess I hate Porter more than I miss my sister.

"Porter is fine, but he's old news," Moira chirped. "We're much more interested in Mr. Tall, Dark and Handsome."

"No, we are most certainly not," I said, glaring at her. I had a vision of Frisbee-spinning a plate at her head.

Ever the mediator, Ma intervened. "So what's his name, Meagan?"

"As a professional private investigator, my client's identities are confidential, Ma. I can't discuss—"

"David Fontana," Moira blurted. She had just crossed the line.

"Jesus, Moira, that is totally confidential! You absolutely know better. Nice friggin' attorney!"

My mother's jowls started shaking. "Meagan! Language, please."

Moira glared at me. "You pay me a dollar a year for my lawyerly advice, so I have access to your cases, remember? His name just accidentally slipped out, and it's not like Ma is going to tell anyone. Don't have a conniption!"

One of Pop's bushy eyebrows shot up into the stratosphere. Moira and I had both inherited the eyebrow trick from him, but we'd never reach the heights his bushy eyebrows could climb. "Fontana! Is that Cuban or Italian?"

I lifted my hands that were both full of dishes by now. "Oh, here we go. Pop, I don't know his nationality, and it doesn't matter. God forbid if he doesn't have blue eyes and freckles."

Pop wailed. "Why the hell can't you girls settle down with a hardworking Irishman? Someone who can fly to California on his own, for Christ's sake."

"Language, please."

Pop grabbed his beer bottle, and headed towards the living room, where he would sit and watch sports for the rest of the day. Before disappearing into his Man-Cave, he turned back towards the dining room with a pained look on his face. He raised his arms above his head, nearly dumping the beer in his hair.

"What is wrong with our people? Why must you contribute to the end of the Irish race?"

End of the Irish race? I wasn't going to touch it.

Uncle Larry grabbed a few items off the table and looked at me. "Meg, do you like this guy?"

Moira evidently thought that her name was now Meagan, because she continued blabbing. "It was love at first sight. At the coffee shop, no less. She's been obsessing about him for months."

"Holy shit, Moira, I can't tell you anything!"

"Language, please. Girls, stop fighting, it's my birthday!" Now Ma was completely frazzled.

"We're not fighting. Moira is simply being an asshole."

"Meagan Marie!" Ma was now fanning herself and had invoked my middle name, so I had to disappear quickly. I snarled at Moira and headed towards the kitchen with a precarious load of glasses and plates in my arms. Uncle Lare followed me into the kitchen with some of the remaining dishes and silverware.

I filled the sink with hot water, and Lare and I started doing the dishes in companionable silence. I washed, he dried. Thankfully Ma and Moira stayed in the dining room. Moira was undoubtedly sharing all of my secrets from the third grade forward to my mother.

Uncle Larry broke the silence. "For what it's worth, Kiddo, you should give him a call if you like him."

I almost groaned, but his intentions were good, and I could never tell Larry to butt out. "I can't. I'd be mortified if he turned me down."

He frowned. "Is he blind or stupid?"

I smiled. "He's neither."

"Well, then what's the problem?"

"He's just not as biased as you when it comes to me. I couldn't deal with him turning me down."

He thought about it for a minute. "Has he paid you yet?"

"He paid me an upfront amount, but I still need to send him his remaining balance. It's in the neighborhood of a few hundred bucks. I haven't totaled everything up yet."

Larry's eyes lit up. "There you go, call him to verify his billing address, and then see what it leads to."

"That might be a little obvious. I could always verify his address at the coffee shop when I see him. Or some people even use this thing called a telephone book or an even more outdated thing called the internet to look up addresses."

He clonked me on the head with a spoon. "You're over-thinking it, as usual. Just skip the coffee shop for a day or two, and then call him. Tell him you've been very busy and that you just need to make sure you have his correct address."

"I can't miss my coffee!"

"Go a little later, then."

"What do I say when I call him?"

"Just see how the conversation goes. If it's all business, then thank him, hang up, and he'll never be the wiser. But if it's going well, then just bite the bullet and ask him to dinner. He'd be crazy to say no, and I'm not just saying that because you're my niece."

Of course he was, but I loved him for it anyway.

"I'm telling you, Meggie. It's a real turn-on when some of these gals call me. Someday when you're a little older, I'll share some of their secrets with you."

Gross! I lightly covered my ears with soapy hands. "Jesus Lare, I'm thirty years old. But please save it. I can't deal with hearing about how your lady friends seduce you."

Ma bellowed from the other room. "Language, please!"

Larry's eyes grew wide, but I wasn't surprised. "She has bionic ears."

Larry looked around the kitchen conspiratorially. "I think she has the place bugged."

I laughed and continued washing. We managed about a full minute of silence before Larry started in again.

"So you'll call him?"

I sighed. "Maybe. I guess that I don't know if I'm ready—"

Out of nowhere, my eyes welled up. After Tom died, it took me almost two years to even admit another man was cute. And now, here I was, telling Uncle Lare about my stupid school girl crush. And I felt bad about it. Guilt blows.

Fortunately, Uncle Larry is a mind reader. He grabbed my shoulders and turned me into him and gave me a huge bear hug. Then he held me at arm's length and stared at me intently. "Tom Sullivan would want you to be happy. That boy was all about living life to the fullest. You need to quit apologizing to his ghost and get on with your life, Meg."

I nodded and blinked away tears. "I know. I'm trying."

Larry ruffled my hair. "So you'll call this Fontana chap?"

I took a deep breath. "I will call him tomorrow."

Larry smiled his crooked smile. "Good. He's a lucky fellow, that one. Let me know how it goes."

I kissed Uncle Lare on the cheek and we finished the dishes without another word. Tomorrow then.

CHAPTER 13
Monday, March 10th

I'd decided that ten thirty the next morning would be the best time to call David. It wasn't so early that it screamed how badly I wanted to talk to him, plus I didn't want to look hard up for his remaining balance. It wasn't so late that he'd be dying to leave for the day, either. Although I don't think accountants leave the office very early during tax season anyway.

I dialed the phone and then panicked when it started to ring. My mouth suddenly felt like the Sahara, my confidence over the dishes the day before absolutely vanished. What had I been thinking? I had resorted to love-life advice from a lifelong bachelor. I made the decision to hang up when I heard his voice.

"Hello, this is David Fontana."

Oh God. What now? Did he have caller ID? Should I hang up and chance it? He wouldn't call me back anyway. Would he?

"Hello? Is anyone there?"

"Oh hi, David, this is Meagan Maloney. Sorry about that, I was just taking a sip of coffee." Okay, that was believable.

"Hey Meagan, I didn't see you at the coffee shop today."

He'd noticed. Yippee! Maybe Uncle Lare was on to something after all. Okay, *breathe*. Think of a safe topic. "So how are things working out with Darrin?"

"So far, so good. He's already got a couple of interviews for bartending jobs lined up, and I'm relieved about that. I was worried that he'd decide on a life of leisure now that he's got some cash to play with."

"That's good, you'll have to tell me where he ends up, and I'll pay him a visit." *Translation: you and I should go have dinner and drinks at Darrin's new place of employment.*

"I'm sure he'd like that. Actually, Meagan, I'm glad you called because I needed to call you anyway."

He was going to call *me*? Well, well, now things were getting interesting. I felt my heart speed up.

"Oh yeah, what's up?"

"Well, I have a client who might be interested in hiring you for a job. The truth is, he's a little bit of a strange one, so I thought I'd run it by you to see if you'd be interested."

Ugh. Another job. You'd think I'd be excited at the prospect of building my client base and paying some bills, but I was really more interested in dinner with David.

"What do you mean by strange?"

"Well, he's normal for the most part, at least as far as I can tell. He's been a client for over five years, and I've never had a problem with him. The strange part is that he's trying to find out if his ex-wife is cheating on her current boyfriend."

"His ex-wife? Why would he care?"

David let out a sigh. "I'm sure I don't need to tell you that in your line of work, you're eventually going to run into some situations you might not like and might not personally agree with. But in some of those situations, you might end up taking the job because at the end of the day, it's just that, a job."

"Okay?" I said this very slowly, hoping to give the impression that I had no idea where he was going with this.

"The thing is, the guy feels like he's paying his ex-wife too much in alimony. He makes a good deal of money, it's not like he can't afford it. But they never had children, and when she caught him cheating, she left him and received a nice little monthly stipend for herself." He paused briefly.

"Okay?" Again, no idea in hell what he was getting at.

"Well, his ex-wife has been living with some guy for a few years, but she's never married him. My client said she never will marry him, either, because she doesn't want to lose her alimony. It drives him nuts to think that a chunk of their nice lifestyle is due to his money. So when he received some information that led him to believe that she's cheating on her new man, he decided to look into it."

Even with David, this was getting tedious. "Which leads me back to the question: *why would he care?*"

"He wants to blackmail her with the evidence."

"I'm sorry?"

"He wants evidence of her infidelity, and then he's going to go to her and threaten to spill everything if she doesn't agree to waive her right to alimony."

"Good grief."

"You said it."

"He sounds like an asshole."

"Like I said, I wanted to run it by you before I set something up between you two."

"Let me think about it, okay?" Something about the story made me feel like the guy probably deserved everything he got, but a paying client is a paying client. Still. Maybe Uncle Lare would have some pearls of wisdom for this one. However, the fact that Uncle Larry was becoming the voice of reason in my life was something I was going to have to evaluate in the very near future.

"Sure, no problem, just let me know."

"Okay, thanks David. I'll let you know in a day or two, probably at the coffee shop."

"Sounds good, see you then."

"Okay, bye." I hung up before realizing I hadn't even done my phony address check for his remaining balance. I wondered if he'd noticed. Did he think I had just called to shoot the shit? If so, was he okay with that? I am terrible at this stuff.

I ran a few errands and didn't get back to the apartment until about eleven thirty. The homestead was a little quieter than usual, and I found a note from Doobie on the kitchen table.

Meagan, Sampson is with me. I took him to the saloon. See you later.

Saloon? A bar? Drinking establishments for canines? This could get interesting. Leave it to Moira to find a place for Sampson to get hammered, but even I wasn't buying this one. If Moira were to support his drinking habits, I doubt she'd approve of him tipping a few back at this time of day. Sampson would have a strict policy of not consuming alcohol before noon. I dialed Doobie's cell number, and it rang six times before he picked up, probably due to all of the background noise at the bar. Maybe there was a band made up of sheep and cats.

"Hello?" Doobie drug out the solo word with some effort, and it sounded like I woke him up. Only Doobie could sleep at a place with a bunch of drunken dogs.

"Doob, it's me."

"Hey Meg, I left you a note."

"I saw it, thanks. But where exactly are you?"

"We're at the pet salon on Newbury Street. Some shee-shee-foo-foo place that Moira found. She's not taking him to that other place because they nicked his paw, remember?"

Jeez, how could I forget The Wound? Sampson had been propped up on pillows for two days after the episode. Moira had even bought one of those doggy-lampshade-things that the poor dog had to wear around his neck so he wouldn't lick The Wound. I think the dog lost, in total, two miniscule drops of blood as a result of The Wound, but Moira damn near sued the place. No doubt about it, she loves that dog.

"Thanks, Doob, just making sure."

"Didn't you see my note? I told you where we'd be."

"Yes, Doob, I read it, but your spelling sucks. You said you had Sampson at the saloon, not the salon."

A beat of silence. "Cool."

"Later, Doob, I've got to go."

"*Is* there a pet saloon around here?" Doob sounded like he'd actually perked up, a rarity for Doob.

"Good *bye*, Doob." I hung up.

My cell phone rang the second I hung up, and I assumed Doob was calling back, looking for directions to the elusive Pet Saloon. I didn't even look at the caller ID before answering.

"What Doob?"

"SONS OF BITCHES!!!!"

Oh boy. This was not Doobie. My friend Kayla generally uses curse words in everyday conversation, but it was her volume that caught my attention immediately. She was clearly in some dire straits.

"*Ma*?" I couldn't resist. Kayla ignored me.

"The sons of bitches called me in and had the nerve to tell me they're going to fuck over my entire team. Well, I'm not going to put up with it!"

"Yes, I can hear that," I said, hoping to the heavens she wasn't still at work.

"When can you meet me for margaritas?"

Oh, God help me. If this was a margarita-situation, then this was beyond trouble. However, I had known this day of reckoning was coming, and I was in for the long haul. Maybe later we could meet up with Doobie and Sampson at the pet saloon.

The shit-storm-countdown had started ticking a few months ago when the insurance company Kayla worked for had been bought out. It had been pins and needles ever since. She'd been employed there for just over eight years and had attained a management position in sales. Her team was tops in the company, and they loved her. And it was a two-way street; she'd go through fire for each one of them.

Obviously she'd received some bad news today and was now going to handle it in the most immature way possible. I was pledged to be there by her side.

"You say when and where, I'll be there." Meagan Maloney, friend to the end, ready at a moment's notice. I imagined myself fashioning some type of super-hero-friendship-cape.

"Cactus Grill, I'm already there."

I cocked an eyebrow at that one. "Hunh? Kayla, it's eleven thirty in the morning."

"Thanks, Mother Timex, I know what fucking time it is. But after my reaction to the you're-getting-porked-news, they suggested I take the rest of the day off. And they further suggested I take tomorrow as a vacation day."

Oh boy. "I'm on my way," I said. "Where's your car?"

"I left it at the office and took a cab straight here. I'm not driving, so don't worry your curly little head. Just get down here now!"

The line went dead. Good grief. Disaster was looming, and I was going where I had boldly, stupidly, gone before. The last time Kayla and I had gone out for a night of serious margaritas had ended, let's just say, poorly.

We'd started at Cactus Grill on Maverick Square, and my memory gets a little fuzzy after that. I remember several cab rides, a couple of hitchhiking adventures with complete strangers, and finally there was a railroad train Kayla and I ended up hopping on, pretending we were hobos off to a new life. We'd immediately passed out and then woken up hours later, with no idea what day it was or where we were. For a minute, it was hilarious and liberating, but in the following minute it wasn't so funny. The good news was that we'd woken up because the train had been lurching to a stop, and a few seconds later we'd gotten the hell off the hobo-railway.

By the grace of God, we'd both maintained control of our purses and cell phones. We found out it was about ten o'clock on Saturday morning and also discovered we were in Buffalo, New York, only about a seven-hour jaunt from Boston. I'd called Moira to apologize that I hadn't come home and told her I was at Kayla's. I'd been completely incapable of telling her the truth. I don't know what that says about our relationship, but I just wasn't able to do it.

Kayla had called her roommate, Kristi, with the whole story, and Kristi had called us back about ten minutes later. She'd prepaid two bus tickets for us and had then given Kayla the address for the bus station in Buffalo.

We'd proceeded to befriend an elderly female worker at the railroad yard, who was understanding and even seemed to envy us a little bit. She'd called her daughter to come get us, and the eight-month pregnant daughter had driven like a maniac to get us to the bus station with seven minutes to spare. We gave her our last thirty-two dollars as a thank you and then piled on the bus for the long ride home.

I never told anyone about my impromptu train ride to New York, and I don't think that Kayla has ever told anyone besides Kristi. It was undoubtedly one of the most idiotic things I've ever done in my life. Still, I can't help but smile a little bit when I think back on it. If I ever have children, I'll do my best to remember the days back when I was a dumbass.

Entering the Cactus Grill, I heard Kayla before I saw her. My hope was that airport security would stop us if we got any ideas about going overseas.

I found Kayla belly-up to the bar, with a full margarita in front of her. Her gray business suit was wrinkled, and she had a long run in her nylons. One of her shoes was on the floor, and the other was dangling precariously from her foot. Her long hair was sort of pulled back in a ponytail, but there were unruly blonde wisps shooting out of it, and they completely contrasted with her flushed complexion. She was leaning over the bar and pointing her finger menacingly at a fifty-something man across the way, who was overweight and wearing a Yankees cap. The latter was undoubtedly causing a problem.

"—so why don't you just shut your mouth and we'll see who has better pitching during the playoffs?" She was slurring and spitting, and it looked like she would fall off her bar stool at any moment.

She noticed me and gave me a big, drunken smile. "Meg!" She seemed a little surprised, and I wondered if she even remembered calling me.

"Hey Sweety, how are you doing?"

"What type of dip-shit question is that?" She spewed margarita, and I had to wipe a good amount of spittle from my face.

"Okay, okay, stupid question," I admitted.

"No shit. I am rip-roaring pissed, and I'm taking it out on *New York* tourists," she yelled, nudging her head towards the man across the bar. I winced as I saw him paying his bill and getting ready to leave. He paused and flipped us the bird, and Kayla and I shot four middle fingers right back at him. It seemed the tone had been set for the afternoon.

I held up both my hands and pushed them towards my drunken friend. "I'm *not* going to sit down until I say something."

Kayla sucked on a lime and looked at me suspiciously. "Let's hear it."

"I absolutely *will not* be leaving the state of Massachusetts today or tonight. I will drink with you, listen to you, commiserate with you, but I *am* going to wake up in my own bed tomorrow morning."

Kayla shrugged and plopped her used up lime back in her margarita. "We'll see."

"Kayla!"

"Okay, okay. Just sit down and get caught up with me." She motioned to the bartender for two more drinks. "I won't seem so obnoxious if you've had a few, too."

"Doubtful."

Her head fell backwards and she groaned. "I know, I'm being a total slob. But I feel so unappreciated. I'm just another number at that place." She paused briefly and wrinkled her turned up nose. "My God, I'm a cliché."

I cocked my head and made a sympathetic face at her. "You're not a cliché. Tell me what happened."

"Well, Dickerson and this human resource asshole called me in to review the new pay plan and goals. The HR prick was all puffed up and proud of himself as he handed both Dickerson and me these laminated sheets, complete with bright colors and a pie graph and some other shit." She paused to take a big slurp of margarita before continuing. "The bottom line is that if my team *grows* our book of business by ten percent in the next quarter, they'll all make about three thousand *less* than the same quarter last year. That's if we *grow* the business! Can you imagine?"

A few heads were now looking our way, but I didn't dare shush her. That would be tantamount to disaster. I reached over and tucked a loose hair behind her ear and asked, "What are you going to do?"

"The short term plan is to just drink." She smiled sadly.

"Okay. How about the long term plan?" I took a swig of my margarita, and it was very, very good. Oh boy.

She sighed. "I don't know. I'll probably start looking for a different job. It's so weird to even think about. I thought I was in it for the long haul."

I tried to think of something profound to say. "Well, it might be a little unsettling, but this will probably be the best thing that ever happened to you. You will land on your feet and find a wonderful job that will pay you well and appreciate you for who you are." I felt like I should have some pom poms in addition to my friendship cape.

Kayla thought about that for a minute, and her face lit up. Clearly my vast knowledge and good advice had gotten through to her. "We should get tattoos!"

"Not on your life."

"Please, please, please! Sugar on top."

"Quit acting like a three-year-old. You will thank me tomorrow."

Kayla looked down and used her straw to swirl around her lime in her bottomless margarita glass. She looked at me through bleary eyes and then busted out with the refrain from 'You Don't Bring Me Flowers Anymore'. It would have made Streisand proud. We were both cracking up and would undoubtedly be thrown out soon, but it was good to see her laughing.

I put my hand on top of hers. "You will be fine, Sweety, I know it."

She nodded grudgingly. "I've just gotta figure out what I want to do when I grow up."

I nodded and remembered how hollow I felt working for the investment firm. "I know how you feel."

She erupted. "That's right! I talked to Moira when you were gone. How did your first big case go? Did you do any *real* private investigating? More importantly, did you see anyone's privates?"

I smiled and realized I was proud to tell her my news. "Actually, I just finished up that case the other day. It involved some investigating and no privates, but I met some cool people, had some fun, and made some money. I really enjoyed it."

She gave me a big hug and seemed genuinely happy for me. I loved her for being so excited despite her crappy day. She excused herself to go to the restroom, and I glanced out the restaurant window and saw traffic backed up on the busy street. I was startled to see a red Impala sitting amongst the cars. I stared for a few moments and then disregarded it. Besides, no one was going to mess with me with Kayla at my side. She arrived back at the bar, and the two of us proceeded to enjoy many more margaritas and laughs over the course of the afternoon and into the night. We didn't even discuss going to the airport. Clearly we'd matured.

CHAPTER 14
TUESDAY, MARCH 11TH

The ringing phone woke me up around five the following morning, and I immediately assumed someone was dead. No one in their right mind would ever call Moira or me before six thirty, it was simply asking for trouble. Once I came to my senses, I felt horrible, thanks to tequila maximus the night before. At least I was in Massachusetts. I would search for a tattoo on my person later.

Okay, so who was dead? My head was pounding like I couldn't believe. Maybe *I* was the one who was dead? Maybe this was some bizarro-afterworld I was going to have to endure. It would be like the movie *The Sixth Sense*, and I would roam around thinking I was alive.

I lifted the receiver and heard Moira's voice, as she had already picked up the other line from her bedroom.

"Hello?" I croaked and didn't recognize my own voice.

"—slow down, Uncle Larry, I can't understand you," Moira was saying. She didn't acknowledge me. Oh my God, I *was* dead. I was going to be doomed to wander the earth with a permanent hangover due to my night of drunken debauchery.

"Hello!" I screamed. *I'm here, I'm here! Please say that you can hear me.*

"Meagan, shut up, Larry is trying to talk!"

Okay, so I was alive, good deal. However, I didn't need Moira yelling at me this early in the morning. She sounded panicked, and Uncle Larry calling us at this hour was definitely out of the ordinary. Then my heart almost leapt out of my chest.

"What's happened?" I demanded. "Are Ma and Pop okay?"

Uncle Larry coughed for about ten seconds before answering. "Yes, they're fine. Who am I talking to?" He was slurring his words, which made his thick Irish brogue even harder to understand than usual.

Moira jumped in. "We're both on the phone. Are you drunk?"

"Yes, I probably still am," I replied.

"I'm not talking to you Meagan! Larry, are *you* drunk? Is everyone drunk?" Moira's simply a witch before seven.

"No, no, not drunk. I just had a few with dinner is all," he explained.

Just talking about drinks was making me dry heave. "Larry, dinner was eleven hours ago. What is going on? Are you sure Ma and Pop are okay?"

"Fine, they're fine, I already told you." Now Larry sounded pissed. He calls us at five in the morning, and he's pissed? Some nerve.

Moira chimed in again. "Larry, as much as we enjoy talking with you, either tell us what you need, or we're going to have to hang up. Some of us have to *work* in a few hours."

Moira has always received excellent marks in sarcasm. For as far back as I can remember, Larry has never much believed in work. He'd had some questionable "jobs" when we were little, and they were rumored to involve the Irish mob when they'd still had a stronghold in Southie. I've never confirmed that, nor did I ever really want to know. All my mother had once said on the subject was that we needed to say a lot of rosaries for Uncle Larry.

Larry's voice brought me back to the conversation at hand. "I just got in a little bit ago, won eighteen hundred bucks on blackjack, by the way."

"The *point*, Uncle Larry?" Moira was fed up.

"Okay! Anyway, I was listening to the scanner and heard about a break-in at some office complex not too far from you girls." Larry and his cronies pass some of their free time listening to a police scanner. God knows how they got it, but who cares? It's a source of entertainment for a bunch of old guys who wish they were still out there in the thick of it.

"We're fine, Uncle Larry," I assured him. It had been nice of him to call, though.

"I know *you're* fine. Let me finish, please! You girls interrupt worse than your father. The reason I'm calling is that the office is a CPA firm owned by some guy named Fontana, and I remembered us talking about a guy named Fontana on your mother's birthday, so I just thought—"

I was out of bed and throwing on clothes before he could finish. Brushing my teeth while simultaneously putting my hair in a ponytail, I saw Moira walk in, shielding her eyes from the bright light in my bathroom. Her pretty, sleepy face was pinched, and I could tell there was more bad news.

"What?" I demanded with a mouthful of toothpaste.

She took a deep sigh. "He said it sounded like someone might have been hurt. He doesn't know how seriously, but an ambulance was called, and the office was a pretty big mess. This is your guy?"

Yes, David was my guy, yes he certainly was. "I think so," I responded and wiped my mouth with a towel. "I've got to find out for sure."

"Call me as soon as you know something. I hope he's all right."

I got a lump in my throat. "Me too."

Moira looked at me imploringly. "There's no way you could just call him?"

I frowned at her. "Not a chance."

She sighed again. "Please be careful. I'm starting to hate this job of yours."

"I'm sorry." That reminded me of something. "Do me a favor, and call Larry back. Tell him not to call Ma and Pop with this. I don't want them worrying, and I could do without a lecture this morning."

She nodded. "I'll call him. I can worry enough for all of us." I gave her a quick hug and dashed out to face the early morning air.

CHAPTER 15

I hit the pavement at a full sprint, and there was a light, cold mist in the air that chilled me to the bone. David's office was about three city blocks from my apartment, and I quickly began cursing those extra five pounds again. However, they were forgotten as soon as I rounded the corner and saw the ambulance pulling away from David's office building, sirens blaring and the rotating lights swirling round and round. My heart leapt to my throat, and I ran for all I was worth until I arrived at the front of the building.

I hadn't brought my P.I. license or even my driver's license or anything at all. When I finally stopped, I approached an officer who was speaking into a walkie-talkie gizmo and tried, unsuccessfully, to get my breathing under control.

I pointed at the building and panted. "My name is Meagan Maloney, and I'm a friend of David Fontana, who owns the CPA firm that was burglarized. Can you tell me if he is okay?"

The officer looked at me skeptically. Undoubtedly my hair had frizzed into something resembling a small haystack, and I sounded like I would need an oxygen tank momentarily.

"And how did you know that there'd been a burglary, Miss, uh, Moroney?"

I scowled. "It's Maloney, and you can call me Meagan." I purposely didn't answer his question, realizing just a moment too late that I didn't want to sell out Uncle Larry, and I couldn't think up a plausible lie this early in the morning.

"And *how* did you come by this information, Miss Maloney?" His tone had gone up a notch, and he hadn't used my first name. Evidently we weren't going to be exchanging Christmas cards. His loss.

"I was, uh, out jogging, and I saw the ambulance and got worried?" It was more a question than a statement, and he didn't buy it.

"You're a jogger, are you, Miss Maloney?" He was sneering.

"Well, yes, I've actually just started. I want to run the marathon next year. It's been a goal of mine ever since I was a little girl."

He looked me up and down. "That was probably a long time ago."

I've been thirty for a while, thank you very much, so wise cracks from a cop with acne don't exactly work for me. First, there was Officer Jackson in California and now this guy. I gritted my teeth and reminded myself that I love the police, so I tried for some common ground. "Do you happen to know Norman Switzer?"

"No," he said flatly. "Why?"

"I work with him at our P.I. firm, and I thought you might have heard of him. He was a policeman here in the city for over twenty years."

"That's nice."

I sighed loudly. "Anyway, would you *please* tell me if Mr. Fontana is okay?" I thought that using "mister" might give me a bit of credibility. Not likely, but I was desperate.

"And what's your relationship with Mr. Fontana?"

"I lust after him, and he paid me to go to California."

The officer's eyebrows almost touched when he frowned. He was clearly not amused. I braced myself for the handcuffs and wondered how bad my mug shot would look. I also dreaded having to call Moira. Maybe Uncle Larry would be interested in bailing me out, but he'd probably just end up in the cell next to mine.

"Meagan!" David's voice came from the top of the stone steps that led to the office building. He waved to me urgently, signaling I should come up.

I turned to the officer and almost stuck my tongue out at him. "May I?"

"Move it," he said testily. He yelled after me. "I'll be interested in hearing about how you knew of the break-in before you leave."

I hightailed it to the top of the brownstone's steps and gave David such a huge hug that he lost his balance and almost fell back into the doorway.

"Oh my gosh, I'm so sorry!" I shrieked as I helped him recover his footing. "I'm just so glad to see you, I was very worried!"

He shook his head slightly and looked amused. I immediately became self-conscious and assumed that he was smirking at any number of things: my hair, my sweatpants with holes, the fact that I was still out of breath, the sleep goo stuck in the corners of my eyes, the list was endless. I probably had a newly formed zit as well. I suddenly realized how Doobie must feel on a daily basis, the difference being that Doob doesn't care.

"Meagan, how in the world did you hear about this? You were only about five minutes behind the ambulance, for God's sake!"

"What happened? Who was hurt?" I still didn't want to sell out Uncle Larry, even to David.

He rubbed his forehead with one hand and shook his head again. "A kid that I met a couple of years ago, his name is Manny Cordeiro, great guy. He's going to Suffolk University to get his degree in Accounting, and he's interned for me during the past two summers. Hardest working kid I've ever met. He and his family are from Providence, and he commutes in a rickety old car every day. They don't have a pot to piss in, and he works so many odd jobs to make extra money that I can't even keep count of them.

"Anyway, my office isn't big enough to hire a regular janitorial service, so Manny comes in every single morning to empty our trash, make sure our water cooler is full, throw out old shit in the frig, keep the paper towels stocked, just some general stuff. It doesn't even take him an hour, probably a half hour at the most. I think he might sleep on the couch occasionally, if he has an early morning class."

David's face turned red, and I suspected that Manny probably slept in his office most nights and that it was perfectly fine with him. The more I learned about this David Fontana, the more I liked. He continued.

"Anyway, I throw him a few bucks at the end of every week, all on the up-and-up, of course. I know the money helps, and I'm hoping he'll come work with me full time when he gets out of college."

David stopped talking abruptly, and his chin started to wobble. He covered his eyes with his hand, and I told myself to keep it together for him.

"He's going to be okay, isn't he?"

David sniffled and shrugged. "God, I hope so. But somebody hit him on the head really hard. He was lying in the entryway to the office and was out cold when I got here. I called the ambulance from my cell phone and held him until they arrived. He kind of came to and managed to say he was sorry." David paused again for a minute, and his beautiful brown eyes teared up.

"Sorry for what?"

David shrugged. "Who knows? The alarm wasn't set, so I'm guessing he was cleaning and someone snuck in and cracked him when his back was turned."

"Poor kid," I said sympathetically. "Are you going to the hospital?"

"I wanted to ride in the ambulance, but they wouldn't let me. Plus, they have to take a statement about the break-in, and I need to try to determine if anything was taken. It's a disaster up there. I just can't believe this happened. Why would anyone want to break into my office? It's crazy. There's no money, there's no fancy furniture or equipment. There's nothing but files and tax returns, and that's another nightmare."

"What do you mean?"

"Well, I'm going to have to notify ten years of clients that their information has possibly been compromised."

"Oh my God. You have to?"

"Absolutely, there is so much personal information in there that it's scary."

"Speaking of scary, I don't think whoever did this was looking for your client information."

"What then?"

I frowned a bit, because I knew he was smarter than that. Then again, his friend was just conked over the head, and his office was demolished. I decided to cut him some slack.

"David, don't you find it just a bit coincidental that this happened shortly after you received fifty thousand in cash and just days after your brother got back to town?"

It was his turn to frown. "The guy who threatened Darrin in L.A.? You think?"

"I think."

"Oh, shit."

"Yes, shit." I lifted my shoulders and heaved a big sigh. I then clapped my hands together and did my best imitation of a coach right before game time. "So here's the deal. You head up to your office and make your statements, do whatever you need to do with the police. I head to the coffee shop *immediately* and get double our normal orders. I come back and we consume our beverages at mock speed. We'll stay in touch with the hospital all day to see how Manny is doing. Provided he is all right, we'll clean up the office and then draft a letter to your clients. I'm even thinking that you could offer to pay for a year of online credit monitoring so your clients will be notified if anything strange is going on in their credit bureaus, something like that."

His smile had broadened during my diatribe, and he was nodding his head. "That sounds great, Meagan, I really appreciate all of this."

"No sweat," I said. "I'm happy to help." Happy to wash your car, happy to stare at you all day, happy to go to dinner . . .

David started up the stairs to his office and said, "I don't need a double order, though, just the regular is fine with me. Thanks Meagan, see you in a little bit."

I immediately thought about upgrading mine to a triple, when something struck me. "David?"

He turned to face me from the top of the stairwell. "Yeah?"

I felt like an idiot, but I'd left the house in a flurry of panic and worry. "I need some money." How embarrassing. He reached for his billfold and pulled out a twenty. I thanked him and scampered away.

As I got to the bottom of the stairs outside of David's building, I caught the slightest glimpse of a red Impala going around the corner. I couldn't see the license plate, but it gave me pause. I stood there for a minute and then disregarded it. Yet again. There had to be thousands of them from coast-to-coast.

CHAPTER 16

After dismissing the red Impala, I half-jogged to the coffee shop, the thought of caffeine driving my every step. I caught sight of my reflection in a storefront window and realized I looked like the bride of Frankenstein. I was downright beastly, but I hadn't exactly had time to freshen up while in my panic. The fact that David had seen me like this was something I chose not to dwell on. It wouldn't change anything anyway.

It was almost six o'clock by the time I arrived at caffeine heaven, and I was shocked at how many people were up at this ridiculous hour of the day. It reaffirmed my decision to never rejoin the real world.

I ordered David's coffee, ordered two for myself and then asked for a cardboard carrying tray for the trek back to David's office. I jammed the tray with some napkins and rotated around to head out the door.

That's when karma came a-calling. I have a mental list of people who I absolutely *do not* want to run into when I look like dog shit. That said, I am *completely* convinced there is some law of the universe that dictates that a person who is out-and-about and who looks, and vaguely smells, like dog shit is destined to run into at least one of those people on that list, possibly more.

As I spun around, I nearly collided with Miss Snob of the Century, Gina Giovanni. She was stunning with her long, shiny black hair, her huge brown eyes, and her peaches and cream skin. She had on a business suit that melded to her size nothing frame perfectly, and it somehow looked professional despite the fact that it was three inches above her knee.

"Meagan?" Gina pulled her chin into her chest and held up her hand, basically warding me off. She looked like she was about to vomit.

I did my best to take this encounter in stride. "Gina, how are you?"

"Well, better than you, it would seem!" Gina barked out a laugh and looked at me as if waiting for an explanation.

I straightened up and tossed my head in an attempt to throw a lock of fuzzy hair out of my eye. "And why is that?"

"Well, my God," the word came out *Gawd*, "you're a mess! What happened to you?"

"Nothing's happened to me, Gina, it's just that I can leave the house without having to lacquer for two hours like you do." I moved past her and walked very quickly for about three blocks, cursing the day I met Gina Giovanni every step of the way.

Gina and I had gone to graduate school together, and she was every stereotype about a rich kid you've ever heard. A beautiful rich kid who was born with a silver spoon up her perfectly rounded ass. Her family owned several parking garages and some office buildings in downtown Boston, which is basically the equivalent of winning the lottery every minute of every hour of every day. Gina never had to sacrifice or scrimp or save for anything in her entire pampered life.

Back in the day, Gina and I were both working on our master's in finance. She'd constantly complained about school, but evidently *Daddy* wanted her to have the degree on the wall, so she suffered through and usually paid people to do her assignments for her. We had a lot of the same classes, and I always went to class, no matter what. Early mornings, bad professors, hangovers, snowstorms, whatever the case, I was always there. Gina, on the other hand, made it to class about half of the time. She probably thought that eventually she'd just be able to buy herself an MBA with *Daddy's* money.

In January of our first year, we both took an elective that was a website design class. The professor was great, and it was actually the first class in my adult life that had caught my eye and made me think I might belong somewhere out there in the real world. About two months into the class, our professor told us that he knew of a paid summer internship at one of the web companies in downtown Boston. I'd been ecstatic for the opportunity, along with a couple of the other students. Gina, of course, had been uninterested. I'd desperately needed a summer job and thought the internship might even give me some direction in my wayward life.

The interviews had been scheduled after class the following week, and three of us had been competing for the position. Five minutes before the class ended, a perfect looking blonde man had entered the room. He'd had on an impeccable black Armani suit, a huge gold pinky ring, and he'd been extremely tan for that time of year. He'd looked to be in his mid-twenties and had a smug, self-satisfied look about him.

Gina had suddenly become very interested in the job and gave the professor some song and dance about how she'd forgotten to sign up for the interview the previous week. She pouted and sniffled, and of course, she was granted an interview. And of course, she'd been awarded the job. A job that she hadn't even wanted, certainly hadn't needed, but she'd wanted to meet Mr. Goldilocks.

It sounds silly now, but at the time, I'd been very upset. It had been the Titanic all over again, and I was the Irish girl who'd drowned because I'd been in steerage. She'd been escorted to a lifeboat with no effort whatsoever.

Gina and Mr. Goldilocks were engaged by the end of that summer, and she was Mrs. Goldilocks before Christmas of that year. She never finished her master's degree. I spent that summer sweating my ass off at a local ice cream shop, as well as working at an outlet mall in my "free time", but I got the degree. As it turned out, she got an ex-husband. Mr. Goldilocks had recently been found sleeping in someone else's bed.

While I walked back to David's office, I decided that Gina Giovanni wasn't going to ruin my day. Just because I looked a fright didn't mean I couldn't face the world. All the same, I made sure not to catch my reflection in any storefront windows. The world could deal with me, but I couldn't deal with myself.

After I got back to his office, I spent the next few hours helping David clean up, and we put together a professional letter to his clients. He called the hospital every thirty minutes and finally learned that Manny was out of the woods. I'd never seen someone look so relieved.

"Meagan, I want to get to the hospital to spend some time with Manny. I can't thank you enough for all of your help today. You're a gem."

I felt myself blush. "No problem. I'm really glad he's going to be okay."

"Do you want to come with me?"

It was a nice gesture, but I didn't know Manny and thought it would be inappropriate to intrude. Plus, with the state of my hair and my general dishevelment, I didn't want to scare the kid into a coma. "Thanks, but you two should spend some quality time. Please let me know how he's doing, though."

We made small talk on our way outside, and then I put David into a cab and watched it drive off. I started my walk back to the apartment and wished I'd taken the opportunity to ask him to get together sometime.

While lost in my thoughts, I glanced up to see a red Impala rounding a corner just a block in front of me. At some point, I was going to have to acknowledge the odds of that many sightings.

CHAPTER 17
WEDNESDAY, MARCH 12ᵀᴴ

Early the following morning I headed west out of Boston towards the Worcester area. It was just after seven, and I was amazed by the amount of traffic headed east on the other side of the turnpike. I couldn't imagine people driving that route day in and day out, getting stuck in traffic and paying exorbitant tolls to the Commonwealth.

My mission this morning was to meet Jim, the slimy client David had told me about a couple days before. While cleaning his office the previous day, I'd told David that I'd take Jim's case. The subsequent conversation I'd had on the phone with Jim had done nothing to win me over, but since he was going to hire someone for his dirty work, it might as well be me.

Two hours later, I had a hefty deposit in my pocket and was headed back to Boston. As suspected, Jim was in fact a jackass, but I knew going into this gig that I was going to come across a lot of those in my line of work. Meagan Maloney, P.I.-to-Jackasses-Worldwide-Extraordinaire. Bring your checkbook. I had such a bad feeling about this guy that I almost didn't accept his personal check, but his bank was the same as mine, so I decided to chance it. If it didn't clear, then I wouldn't work. Simple as that. But David had said that Jim made a lot of money, so the check would probably sail through and I'd be working for the jerk soon.

There was a branch of the bank not far from home, so I left my car in the apartment garage and hoofed it the rest of the way. I was greeted by a very perky teller, who was ecstatic to be waiting on me. She seemed way too thrilled with life in general, and I couldn't resist commenting that she didn't strike me as a local. She confirmed that she wasn't and told me she was from the Midwest. Her nametag read Sarah, and I made a mental note to tell Doob about her.

Jim's check cleared, and I wasn't sure if I was happy or sad about that. I kept forty dollars and put the rest in my savings account, irritated with myself for acting like a responsible adult. I also grabbed a brochure for first time home buyers, but I knew it would be a long time before I could afford anything in Beantown. I was strolling along the sidewalk and half-reading my brochure when I sensed someone sidle up to my right side, a little too close for comfort.

"And how was the bank, Meagan?"

I stopped and looked at the man who'd spoken to me. I didn't know him, but he immediately set off my internal alarm. He was not very tall but quite stout, and he had brownish-gray hair with a receding hairline. His complexion was awful, and his eyes were a scary light blue that seemed to be looking through me. However, the thing that held my attention was the jagged scar running along the side of his face. It started close to his mouth and ran nearly to his ear, and it looked like jutted terrain over his heavily pockmarked face. Whatever caused it had to have been terribly painful.

I stood immobile, as I certainly wasn't going to walk anywhere with this man. "I don't believe I know you," I said, trying to sound authoritative.

"No, you wouldn't," he said calmly. "But we have mutual, uh, let's say, *acquaintances.*"

I stared at him, thinking that no acquaintance of mine would be involved with this guy. He suddenly grabbed my wrist and squeezed very tightly.

"Let me cut to the chase here, Meagan. I know about you, your sister, and the big apartment on Commonwealth Avenue. I know about Moira's precious little pooch and your neighbor who always walks him. I know about your parents and your uncle in Southie. I know that Bobby somehow got the money before he died. What I *don't* know is where that fucking money is. And I really want to know, Meagan. It keeps me up at night. I'd hate to have to involve your family if I become upset."

While he'd been speaking, my heart rate had doubled, and I felt the heat rush to my face. I looked around to see if anyone was paying attention to us, but no one was looking our way. Had someone been observing us, we probably would have looked like two people just having a simple discussion on the sidewalk. It might have even appeared like we were holding hands, although he was very nearly cutting off the circulation in my wrist. No one knew that I was face to face with Steroid-Neanderthal-Man.

My throat was dry, and my voice cracked as I answered him as calmly as I could manage. "I don't have the money. This has nothing to do with me." I tried to jerk my arm away, but his grip was too strong. I wanted to yell for help, but what he'd said about my family was fresh in my mind, and I didn't want to risk pissing him off.

He tilted his head and smiled at me condescendingly. "I know *you* don't have any money, but I also know you helped Darrin get out of California. I know you've had your nose in this from the minute you landed in Los Angeles. So all I want from you is a little information, and then Mommy and Daddy Maloney can sleep well at night."

I felt my eyes narrow and realized my fear was turning to anger. This animal was going to hold me against my will and threaten my family? Over some money I didn't have? And how in the hell had he known when I arrived in Los Angeles?

I moved in as close to his face as I could without touching it, and I was pleased to see that the gesture caught him off guard. He moved his head back a little bit, but his hand remained locked on my wrist.

"I don't know who you think you are, but you better back the fuck off. My mother and father have no more to do with this than I do. If you think you're entitled to some money, then I suggest you go about it the right way instead of acting like some two-bit thug. I know you slashed Darrin's tires and trashed his apartment when you were in L.A. And I also know you followed us here in your shiny red Impala. I have the license plate number, by the way, so don't be naïve enough to think you're the only one with information, Mr. Policeman. If you think you've got some money due you, then get an attorney and make your case. Beyond that, leave my family alone and stay the fuck away from me." I spit in his disgusting face and kneed him in the groin as hard as I could. He reflexively released my wrist and doubled over with a howl.

I took off running as fast as my legs would allow and didn't look back. I sprinted the six blocks to the apartment building and ran up the three flights of stairs and down the hallway. Dashing into my apartment, I slammed and locked the door. I put my back against it, as if to stave off anything bad that might have followed me, and then bent over and burst into tears.

I was heaving in air and bawling like a baby when I felt the hand on my back. I screamed like a maniac and nearly jumped out of my skin.

But then I saw it was Doobie looking at me with a mixture of terror and concern on his face.

"Meg, what the hell?" He guided me over to the couch, and I sat down gingerly. I stayed in my coat and stared at the apartment door, rocking myself back and forth. My hands were shaking like I'd just spent the afternoon in a deep freeze. I tried taking some deep breaths to get myself under control, but it wasn't working. I used the back of my shaky hand to wipe my tears and nose several times.

Poor Doob was clearly perplexed but didn't want to push me. He got off the couch, and I heard him rummaging around for something in the kitchen. He came back with a box of tissues and a Diet Coke, and I didn't even want the soda. Obviously I was a mess.

He put his hand on my shoulder. "Meg, talk to me. What happened?"

I continued the rocking motion and kept staring at the door. Doob looked back and forth from me to the door.

"Meg, did someone follow you? Did you get mugged or something?"

"I don't know. I don't think so."

Doob's voice rose an octave. "You *don't know* if you got mugged?!" He stood up in front of me and put his hands on my shoulders and shook the shit out of me, which was exactly what I needed.

"Okay Doob, stop it!"

He stopped instantly and hugged me. "Okay, you're back. Tell me exactly what is going on, or I'm calling the police." Assertive-Doob was a new thing, and it would have been funny under different circumstances.

I spent the next ten minutes telling Doob about the man with the scar. He insisted we call the police, but I had to call my parents first, and the dread I felt was unmatched up to that point in my life.

I reached for the phone, and my hands were shaking so much that I could hardly punch in the numbers. As fate would have it, Pop answered the phone, something he's done only once since man walked on the moon.

"Who the hell is this?" he demanded.

Good grief. "It's Meagan, Pop. Is that any way to answer the phone?"

"Oh, sorry Meg. Your mother and I have been getting hang-up phone calls all day. She finally got so sick of answering that I have to answer this blasted thing. I gave the guy an earful a little bit ago and told him if he called me back that I've arranged to have the calls traced."

"Do you have any way of doing that?" I knew he didn't.

"No, but it sounded good. Who the hell would call us and hang up all day? Is this something kids are doing nowadays?"

"Pop, if it happens again, dial star-6-9. You can find out the phone number, and you can even call it back if you want to."

"Why would I want to do that?"

"Well, you wouldn't. I'm just saying—"

"Oh, save it, Meg. We're probably just going to take the phone off the hook before long. I'm not going to listen to this damn thing ringing all day."

"Well, uh, Pop, that's kind of why I'm calling. There's a man who's a little bit upset with me—"

"Who? Who is upset with you?"

"I don't know his name, Pop. But he's mad because of the case I was working on. I kind of told you about it on Ma's birthday. Anyway, I ran into him on the street today, and he sort of threatened our whole family, Sampson included."

"*Sort of threatened the family*? Meagan, what the hell are you talking about?"

"Pop, try to relax. I think he's probably just full of crap, but I want you and Ma to be extra careful for a few days. I'm going to call the police, but I just wanted to tell you to keep your eyes open." I went on to describe the guy to my dad and then had to spend a half hour on the phone with my mother, trying to calm her down. I only got her off of the phone because I told her that I had to call the police.

I then called a non-911 phone number for the police, and a couple of officers showed up at the apartment about forty-five minutes later. I described Steroid-Neanderthal-Man and told them what happened. I gave them as little information about the case as possible, and I didn't give them David or Darrin's names. They weren't too happy about that, but I told them I'd have to check with my client before I could give them any additional information. They said they'd patrol a few extra laps around our block over the next few days and urged me to call them if anything else occurred.

After that I called Moira at work. She was concerned and said she would stay at Porter's for a few nights. That made me sad. I missed our sister time. Before hanging up, she made sure that Doob was willing to stay with Sampson and me, and she told me to call her if anything happened. I felt like shit for bringing this into our family.

The only good thing that had come of this situation was that I got to call David. I dialed his cell and asked about Manny and was pleased to find out that he was doing much better. Then I told him about my street encounter, and he was stunned.

"Meagan, I can't believe this! Did you call the police?"

"I did, but I want you to know that I didn't give them yours or Darrin's information. If you want me to, then I will, but I wanted to check with you first."

"I don't care about that, Meagan. I'm just glad you're okay. I can't believe this guy probably broke into my office and is now threatening your family. He's clearly insane."

"Well, he seems hell-bent on the fact that some of that money is his. And he's clearly going to do whatever he has to in order to find it."

"Thank God it wasn't at my office. Sometimes having money is as big of a pain in the ass as not having it."

I chuckled. "I wouldn't know. I'm always on the not-having-it end of that scenario." Then something struck me. "David, there's something else. I saw this red Impala following me around in Los Angeles, and I've seen it again around here, just recently."

"Do you think it's him?"

"Yeah, I do. I told him I got his plate, but that was a lie. I'm hoping that slows him down a little bit. But what confuses me is how the hell did he know to follow me around L.A.? I'm positive I saw that car on the *first* night I was in town. Did you tell anyone you'd hired a private investigator?"

There was silence for a second. "Not that I can think of, Meagan. I don't really have anyone I would tell."

"Well, he definitely knew I was there. I'm going to sound paranoid, but I think it's possible that your office might be bugged."

"What?" David sounded incredulous.

"I just can't figure out how he knew I was in L.A. so quickly. Maybe you spoke with someone on the phone about my flight arrangements? Otherwise, it doesn't make sense."

"Meagan, I don't want to discount how you feel, but I don't remember talking to anyone about your trip. Plus, I booked it online. And I've got to ask, are you *sure* it was the same car? There are lots of red Impalas in the world."

He had a point. I'd even told myself the same thing when I was in the hotel parking lot that first night. I sighed. "I'm not positive, but the creep didn't argue when I told him I got his plate." *Although that could have been because I'd kneed him in the nuts shortly thereafter.* "But it's really freaky that I don't know this guy from Adam, yet he's following me around the minute I arrive in California? Just a few days after he scared the shit out of Darrin? He used to be a cop. Maybe he and Carol figured out that you and Darrin were related—"

"So he flew from L.A. to Boston to somehow bug my office and then flew back to L.A. to threaten Darrin? And then he started following you around when you arrived in town? And then followed you guys in his red car across the United States? And broke into my office, possibly for the second time? It seems like a long shot."

"Maybe he knows someone around here who bugged your office for him. And maybe he broke into your office to get the bug out of there or to find the money, I don't know. It sounds ridiculous, but something bad is going on. Please just be careful."

"I will, Meagan. You too."

"Will do. Also, please fill Darrin in as soon as you can. He'll definitely recognize the guy if he sees him, and he needs to be on guard."

"Of course. I'm really sorry about all of this."

"No worries, it's not your fault. I just want to make sure everyone is being extra cautious."

"I will. And let me know if you hear anything from the police. I'd feel a lot better knowing he's out of the picture."

"Me too, David. Thanks." I hung up and felt awful. Meagan Maloney, Bringing-Trouble-to-Her-Family-and-Friends-Extraordinaire.

CHAPTER 18
Thursday, March 13th

I slept terribly that night, if it could be called sleep at all. Not surprisingly, the broken dreams I had were filled with the stout man and his hideous scar. He hovered over my mother everywhere she went, but she was oblivious. He was behind her at the supermarket and followed her to church. I kept trying to get to her, but she was always just out of my reach. The man saw my frustration, and he would throw his head back in exaggerated laughter. His taunting was torture, and I felt helpless.

When I finally gave up and got out of bed, I almost stepped on a pile of blankets that turned out to be Doobie and Sampson. My protectors. They must have moved in here after I'd gone to bed, and I was extremely touched to see they'd resorted to the floor in order to be near me. It made me a little nervous that I hadn't heard them come in, though. Doob's mouth was hanging open, and Sampson's feet were twitching in his sleep, chasing rabbits in his dreams. I wanted to hug them both but didn't want to wake them.

The morning-muck-taste in my mouth always grosses me out, so I tiptoed into the bathroom and went directly for my toothbrush. Reaching for it, I immediately noticed that my wrist had turned an interesting shade of purple, and my stomach turned in disgust, with a feeling something like hate. Hate has always been a no-no in my family, and I'd always prided myself on being a live-and-let-live person, but that was before my family was threatened. I didn't want to turn into a person who understands hate, but I couldn't help it.

I was brushing my teeth and poked my head into the bedroom to check on Doobie and Sampson. Sampson was on the middle of my bed, his tail wagging at mach speed. Doob was in mid-stretch, and Morning-Doob is beyond comical.

"Hey Meg, how ya doin?"

"I'm okay. You guys didn't have to come in here. I feel bad that you slept on the floor."

Doob shrugged and reached over to rub Sampson's ears. "It was his idea."

"Yeah, right," I said, flashing a toothpaste smile at him. I finished brushing my teeth and went back into the bedroom.

"We're headed outside for morning pee pee's," Doob announced.

"I hope that you're referring to just Sampson." I gestured to the bathroom and said, "It's all yours."

"Nah, that's okay. I'll go over and use mine before Sampson and I go out. Will you be okay alone for a little bit?"

He was only being nice, but I couldn't stand being viewed as the helpless victim. "I think that I can manage for a few seconds, Doob."

"Don't get snippy, Meg. I'm not going to treat you with kid gloves, but for at least a little while, I *am* going to make sure that you're okay. So deal with it."

Assertive-Doob making yet another appearance. "You're right, Doob. I'm sorry. Would I be correct in assuming that the both of you would like some food after your walk?"

Sampson's limited English includes the word *food*, and he barked his approval. Doob and I both looked at him in amazement, as we always do when he answers a human question.

"That sounded like a yes," Doob said. "Just make sure—"

"I know. No onions! Get out of here. Breakfast will be served in twenty minutes."

By the end of the hour, Doob, Sampson and I had full bellies, and we'd all made ourselves presentable for the upcoming day. For Sampson, that involved no work whatsoever. For Doob, it involved little more. For me, it involved a ponytail and baseball hat. No makeup, no perfume, no girl stuff. I wasn't feeling very girly, considering my afternoon plans.

Doob looked across the table at me and evidently knew what I was thinking. "Are you ready to go?"

"Not really."

Doob gave me a stern look. "Meg, this is going to happen. And the sooner we get there, the sooner we leave. You promised. So buck up, Annie Oakley, and go grab your gun."

Pep-Talk-Doob was irritating. Before going to bed last night, I'd promised him that I'd go to the shooting range today. I must have been close to delusional because I'd even conceded to going three times a week until the friggin' end of time. Steroid-Neanderthal-Man was to blame for this, and I was none too happy about it. I'm a lover, not a fighter. Somehow firing bullets into a paper man at a shooting range doesn't make me feel the love.

Nonetheless, I knew that Doob would pester me incessantly until we got this over with. I went to the safe in my closet, turned the little wheel, opened the door, and pulled out my gun. It felt heavy and cold in my hand, and I felt like throwing up. My lower lip trembled, and I wondered what private investigators worldwide would think of me. I silently berated myself for being a sissy.

Closing the closet door, I crossed the room to my bureau and opened the top drawer to retrieve my gun license from its logical place, between my bras and underwear. I'd thought about telling Doob I'd lost it, but I knew he'd see right through me. Then I went into the living room and stared at him. My hope was that I looked pathetic enough for him to tell me that this could wait until another day.

He came over and hugged me. "We're doing this."

I nodded. "I know."

Doob and I drove to the shooting range in silence, and I then spent about an hour firing not-so-lovingly at a paper man. After getting warmed up, I was pleased to find I hadn't lost my touch. Norman had insisted that I get licensed before we got the P.I. firm up and running, and I'd reluctantly agreed. He'd been impressed with what he called my *natural ability*, and at the time I'd thought that had been unfortunate, mainly because I didn't plan to use that natural ability to ever kill anything. Now I wasn't so sure. I wondered how my instincts would hold up when aiming at a human being.

I was mentally and physically exhausted by the end of my hour. Doob had waited in the car and was clicking away on his laptop when I opened the passenger door. He looked concerned.

"You okay?"

I nodded and felt that stupid lip-quiver thing again.

We spent the rest of the day doing nearly nothing. We watched some old movies, played a few board games, ordered pizza for dinner, and gave Sampson a thorough brushing. I even remembered to tell Doobie about

Sarah from the bank, and he seemed a little bit interested. Getting him down there to meet her would be an act of God, but I'd figure it out.

That night, I insisted that Doob stay at his place across the hall. It wasn't because I didn't want him at my apartment, but I just had to prove to myself that I could manage a night on my own. I guess it was my equivalent of getting back up on the horse. After locking the door behind Doobie, I put my gun in the safe and then hopped into bed. The typical cricks and creaks of the apartment unnerved me, so I got up, opened the safe, and placed the gun in the nightstand drawer, within arm's reach.

CHAPTER 19
FRIDAY, MARCH 14TH

The following morning I managed to get my coffee, pay a few bills, wash and fold two loads of laundry, and clean my bedroom and bathroom all before ten o'clock. I was feeling incredibly productive when my cell phone rang.

"Meagan Maloney, Private Investigations."

A quiet voice greeted me on the other end of the line. "Uh, hello, Miss Maloney, my name is LaKeisha Jones. I live outside of Los Angeles, California."

L.A. again? "Hi LaKeisha, how can I help you?"

"I got your name and number from a policeman on the LAPD. An Officer Simonetta?"

The night of the hearse, the rain, and the two police officers quickly came to mind. "Okay?"

"He said he met you when you were out here working on a case."

"Yes, that's correct."

"I have some information that I gave to him, and he suggested that I call you as well."

I silently thanked Officer Simonetta for taking the time to make those notes in his computer. "Well, I appreciate that."

"So should I just tell you what I told him?"

I shrugged to myself. "Sure, that would be great."

"Okay, well, Darrin Hood's roommate, Bobby McBride, was a friend of my husband, Roy. They met while going to treatments at the same hospital. We were so sorry to hear when Bobby was killed."

"Yes, it sounded pretty awful. I didn't know him, but I've heard a lot of good things about him. I hope your husband is doing okay."

"He's actually doing really well, thanks."

"I'm glad to hear it." There was a moment of awkward silence. "So, what can I do for you LaKeisha?"

"See, that's the thing," LaKeisha said hesitantly. "I know that you don't know me from a hole in the wall, but I think you can help me."

"Okay. You sound worried about something?" Meagan Maloney, Intuitive-Mind-Reader-Extraordinaire.

"I am." She took a minute before going on. I managed to not butt in on her thoughts, but it took everything in me to bite my tongue. "I assume you know about all that insurance stuff with Bobby?"

"The viatical policy?"

"Exactly. When Roy and Bobby met, Bobby said that he was planning on doing a viatical settlement. It was coincidental timing, because Roy had just done one through a broker friend of ours. Roy sold his policy for quite a bit of money, and he's taking some experimental drugs that insurance doesn't cover. It seems to be helping, and we're thrilled."

"Well, that's great news," I said. I couldn't fathom why this woman was calling to tell me about her husband's treatment, but she went on.

"I encouraged him to do it. Initially he didn't want to because he was worried he wouldn't be leaving me any money, but that was ridiculous. I have a pretty good job and will be okay financially if this disease beats him. I don't want a bunch of money when he's gone; I just want him to be with me as long as he can."

I immediately thought of Tom and felt the all-too-familiar lump in my throat. I blinked several times to keep tears from forming and forced myself to plow ahead. "LaKeisha, I'm thrilled things are looking up for you, but I've got to wonder why you've called to tell me this."

"Yes, I'm sorry. It's just tough to get into. I don't want you to think that I'm crazy."

"Well, for all you know, *I* might be crazy, so let's just make the assumption that we're both half-nuts and go from there."

She giggled. "Sounds good. While I'd like your help, I don't want you to feel any undue pressure. The officer suggested that I call, but obviously you can do whatever you want with this information."

"Okay, your disclaimer is duly noted. I think you're going to feel better when you tell me."

"Probably. Okay, from what we learned of Bobby's death, they pinned it on some guy who committed suicide outside of the house that Bobby was staying at. Does that sound right?"

"That's what Darrin told me, and Officer Simonetta confirmed that, yes."

"You know how things sometimes peck at your brain but you ignore them for whatever reason?"

"Kind of like listening to that inner voice?" I asked. I loved my inner voice; it was almost always right. The thing was, I didn't always listen.

"Exactly!" She sounded relieved. "Sometimes you ignore the voice and then something else happens that makes you wonder why you hadn't listened to it in the first place." Touché.

"I'm with you so far, but I'm not sure where you're going with this."

"Well, the fact that Bobby was killed really bothered both Roy and me. It sounds selfish, but we think someone might be trying to get to Roy as well."

Something made my inner voice whisper, *Oh no.* I felt my pulse quicken a bit. "Why is that?"

"Well, have you heard the name Brenda Alvarez?"

"I don't think so," I responded.

"Well, she's the broker both Roy and Bobby used for their viatical sales. She was a good friend of mine in college, and we've grown apart since then, but I still consider her a friend. We were glad to work with her for the viatical settlement, and we referred Bobby to her as well. She's been to our house several times, for both business and personal reasons. Great girl, and quite a looker, too."

LaKeisha didn't sound envious. She seemed to be generally impressed with Brenda.

"So what does Brenda have to do with anything?" I was confused.

LaKeisha's voice dropped a notch. "Well, she was murdered recently. Her body was found in a park nearby. She was naked, and her tongue had been cut out of her mouth."

My heart started pumping a little faster. "My God, that's horrible. Do they know who did it?"

"No, but I was thinking Darrin might."

My thoughts immediately went to Steroid-Neanderthal-Man. "What makes you say that?"

"He called Roy in a panic one night and said that some freak had confronted him in his parking lot and had trashed his apartment. Evidently the guy had been there on Bobby's wife's behalf."

"I think her name is Carol."

"Yep, that's right. Anyway, this guy was snooping around, supposedly for Carol, but he wasn't exactly her lawyer."

"Yeah, I'm pretty sure I know who you're talking about." I had another flash of the psycho who'd confronted me on the street. "But why did Darrin call you? The guy wouldn't have had any claim to your money. He didn't even have any claim to Bobby's money."

"No, he definitely wouldn't have had any business bothering us. But he might have tried to find Bobby's money through us."

"How would he have even known about you?"

"Well, evidently Bobby kept a sheet of telephone numbers on the refrigerator. It had the phone number to the hospital, his doctor's pager number, and some friends' contact information, including ours. Anyway, after their apartment was broken into, Darrin noticed that the list was gone. He called as many of Bobby's friends as he could think of, warning them that some freak might be sniffing around and harassing people, trying to find a link to the money."

"Did the freak ever contact you about Bobby or his money?"

"Thankfully, no. We do have a theory, though."

"What's that?"

"Well, Brenda's name was on the list, and it wouldn't have taken too much to figure out what she did for a living. We're thinking the guy might have tracked her down and then done something to her."

"Like kill her?"

It took her a minute to answer, and I got the impression that saying the words out loud made it too real for her. When she found her voice, it came out very softly. "Yeah, that's what we think."

I started shaking, flashing back to his hold on my wrist.

"Meagan? Are you there?"

I blew out a deep breath. "Yes, I'm sorry. I'm just trying to digest all of this."

"I know. I was up all night trying to decide if I should call you or not. I would have called Darrin directly, but I don't have his cell number, and his home phone was disconnected and didn't give a forwarding number. I'm sorry to unload this on you, but I just had to tell someone."

"No, that's okay. You did the right thing."

"I appreciate it." She paused briefly. "There's something else, too."

I said good-naturedly, "I'm starting to not like you, LaKeisha."

Her laugh told me that she knew I was joking. "I wouldn't like me much either if I were you. I warned you that you might think I'm crazy."

"Unfortunately, I don't think you're crazy. I'm worried you're on to something. What's the other thing you want to tell me?"

"Well, four days after Brenda was killed, we got a package from her."

"A dead woman sent you a package?"

"Evidently, she'd told someone to mail it to us if anything happened to her. I think she was scared for her life."

"So what was in the package?"

"A few pictures of some guy. He looked like a biker dude—all dressed in leather, longish hair, a tattoo on his neck, and tough guy sunglasses."

"Do you know who he is?"

"I don't know him, but on the back of one of the pictures was the name *Vince*."

"Do you think he was the guy wreaking havoc out there?" *Who's now in my backyard?*

"I don't know. The guy looks scary, though."

Then it could definitely be Steroid-Neanderthal-Man. "Can you tell if he has a scar on his face?"

She paused for a beat. "I don't think that he had a scar, but I'm not completely sure. I don't have the pictures in front of me right now."

"Okay, what else was in the package?"

"A flash drive with some files on it."

"The little thing that you stick in computers that looks like a Bic lighter?"

I heard her chuckle. "Exactly."

"Did you look at the files?"

"We tried to, but they're encrypted, and we're not sure how to break the code."

I smiled. "If we get to that point, I have someone who can help. Was there anything else?"

"There was a note from Brenda, asking me to please get the contents of the package to Darrin. She didn't say anything about getting it to the cops, but Roy and I talked about it, and we figured that her intent was for *Darrin* to get it to the cops. Since he's not local anymore, I called LAPD and was routed to Officer Simonetta to get that ball rolling. But I also wanted to make sure I carried out Brenda's wishes and at least let Darrin know what's going on. Whoever is behind all of this needs to be stopped. My husband has enough going on."

"I absolutely agree." Then I thought about what she'd said. "Let me back up a second, LaKeisha. Brenda sent the package to *you* to get it to *Darrin*? I've got to wonder why she didn't send it directly to him? Or to her family? No offense, but you said that you two weren't that close anymore."

"That's a good point. The only thing that I can think of is that her family has got to be devastated. They're probably so wrapped up in her murder that they can barely function. Maybe she knew that I'd act quickly and pass along the information."

I mulled that over. "I guess that makes sense. She probably didn't want to burden them. There must be something in that package that only Darrin could explain to the police. But again, why not send it straight to him?"

"I wondered about that, too. I'm thinking that she was either worried about someone intercepting it, or she'd possibly learned that he'd abruptly moved out and didn't know where he was staying. She would have known my address by memory, so maybe it was just easier to send it to us, especially if she had to put it together quickly. The whole thing is scary." LaKeisha's voice grew softer. "It was awful seeing her handwriting. It felt like she was still alive."

"I'm sorry. That had to be tough." Not knowing what else to say, I got back to business. "Okay, we've got a flash drive, some pictures, and a note from Brenda. Was that it?"

"That was it."

Hmmmm. "And you said that you gave the package to the police?"

Silence.

"*LaKeisha?*"

Her voice was suddenly small. "We did."

I narrowed my eyes. "I hear a 'but' in there somewhere."

She sighed. "The whole thing was just so terrible that we were really weirded out. So, we did give the police the package, but we took copies of everything first."

Yippee! "Of all of the pictures and the flash drive thingy?"

"Yes, and the note from Brenda, too."

"And now you want to send it to Darrin?"

"Yes, that's the reason I'm trying to find him."

I debated for half a second and then lied. "I don't think that Darrin is completely settled in somewhere yet. He's bouncing around from friend to friend until he finds a place. If you want to mail the package to me, I will make sure he gets it." I would go to hell for lying, but I simply had to see what was in that package.

"That would be great, if you don't mind."

"Definitely. Also, can you give me as much information as you have about Brenda?"

"I'm really sorry, but I can't right now. I hate to cut you off, but I have to get to work."

I realized it was only seven o'clock out there, but I didn't want to hang up. "LaKeisha, do you have internet access at work?"

"Of course. Why?"

"When you get to work, please email me your contact information, and I'll respond with my home address so that you can send the package. If you wouldn't mind, would you also send me the names of any newspapers that might have printed stories about Brenda's death? I'd also like all of her phone numbers, please. I'll do a little research on this end and see what I can find out." After I gave her my email address, we hung up.

About an hour later, I was pondering the whole LaKeisha phone call when something hit me. Officer Simonetta had passed my information along to LaKeisha, and that made me wonder if anyone else had handed out my number recently. I called information and then dialed the number to the rental complex. I was pleased to hear her voice when Cally answered.

"Hi Cally, it's Meagan Maloney from Boston. I met you last week when I was looking for Darrin?"

I could hear the California smile in her voice. "Oh, hi Meagan, how did it go? I hope you found him!"

"Well, that's why I'm calling. I did find Darrin, and I wanted to call and thank you for your help. It really made all the difference."

She squealed. "Oh, that's great news!"

"And there's just one other thing. There was also a man that you spoke to about me?" I kind of half-asked, half-told her that part.

I could picture her blond hair cascading while bobbing her pretty head up and down. "Yep. He was a cop who had come by a few days before you, but I didn't know about it because I'd been on vacation. So when I was telling the girl on the shift after mine about your visit, she told me about the cop. She said that he had this huge combat scar on his face, and that he was trying to find Darrin, just like you. She'd saved his card, so I called him right away and gave him your cell number and hotel information." She paused, and I envisioned her pretty nose wrinkling as her voice got softer. "I hope that was okay?"

I smiled. "Of course, Cally. You did exactly what I asked. Do you happen to have his card nearby?"

I could hear her rummaging around and then disappointment in her voice. "Um, I'm sorry, Meagan. It was in this drawer, but someone must have done a little cleaning because it's not in here anymore."

Shit! Okay, not her fault. "That's fine, Cally. If you find it, please let me know, but I was really just calling to say thank you very much. I hope you have a great day out there, take care."

So Cally had passed along my information to Steroid-Neanderthal-Man. The good news, at least, was that David's office wasn't bugged.

CHAPTER 20

After hanging up with Cally, I immediately dialed Doobie's cell number. Interestingly enough, I could hear his phone ringing. I'd watched him go across the hall the night before and had most definitely locked the door behind him. I'd checked it three times, for heavens sake. The building walls were pretty thick, so I couldn't figure out how I was hearing his ring tone.

Doob finally picked up, and it was like hearing an echo when he greeted me.

"Doob, did you leave your apartment door open or something?"

His sleepy voice took a moment to respond. "Why? Is it open?"

I had the cordless phone, so I went to the peephole and looked across the hall at his apartment door. "No, it's not, but I could hear your phone almost as if you're in the next room."

"I *am* in the next room."

"What?!" A vision of Doob and Moira flashed through my mind, but I quickly dismissed it as absolute insanity. My bigger worry was that the essence-of-Doob was on Moira's sheets. The lawyer and her sheets were not to be toyed with, and if we ever denied Doob's being there, she would have a CSI team over in seconds to prove us wrong.

"Jeez Meg, take it easy. I'll be out later."

I threw the phone on the sofa and headed towards Moira's bedroom. I didn't have the sense to think that I might catch Doob in a compromised state. Moira's door was partially open, and I walked in to find Doob and Sampson sprawled out on Sampson's four-poster bed. I'd officially seen it all. Doob was fake-sleeping, and I was having none of it.

"Doob, what the hell are you doing? I told you to stay at your own place last night!"

He rolled over and covered his head with Sampson's dog toy. "I'm

131

trying to sleep. You're always yelling at me about not sleeping. Now I'm trying to, and you're not letting me."

He had a point, but I couldn't fathom what he was doing in Sampson's bed. However, I'd never seen Doob's bed, thank God, so it was probably a step up.

"Doob, please tell me Moira was not here last night."

"No, she called me to make sure I was going to be staying with you, and I didn't want to lie to her, so I came back over here. Sampson didn't want to sleep on your floor again, and I knew you'd be all pissy if you knew I was here, so I opted for plan B."

"Does Moira know you stayed in her room?"

Doob rolled his eyes. "Of course not. I don't have a death wish. I meant to sleep on the couch, but I was telling Sampson a story in here, and it seems I fell asleep." Doob knocked on one of the four posters on Sampson's bed. "This thing is pretty sturdy, I gotta tell you."

"That's great, Doob. Can you just get out of here, please?"

"What time is it?"

"It's after ten. I'll make breakfast if you can help me with some sleuthing."

"Cool." Doob stood up to reveal the clothes I'd seen him in a day or two before, and his hair was absolutely defying gravity. I held my nose.

"Doob."

"Hunh?"

"Shower."

"Can I use Moira's?"

"Not on your life. See you in ten minutes."

With that, Doob walked out of the room and Sampson followed behind him. "I gotta walk Sampson first. I'll see you in twenty-five."

"Perfect. That'll give me time to do my fancy egg casserole."

"No onions!" Doob yelled, as he and Sampson headed down the hall.

Within a half hour, our tummies were full and Sampson was watching *Animal Planet*. He barked each time there was a close-up of a dog, and I think he was trying to flirt. Truth be told, I'd rather find an *Animal Planet* dog in Sampson's bed instead of Doobie, but my life is what it is.

Doob drained the last bit of his coffee and cracked his knuckles. "So what are we doing today?"

As I cleared the table, I filled him in on the phone call from LaKeisha. I then plopped down on the couch and logged onto my laptop to see if she'd sent me anything, and I was pleased to see that she had. In the meantime, Doob was lounging on the chair across from me, trying to keep up with the story.

"So, let me see if I have this straight. The dude who got shot before he could die from the brain tumor was friends with the chick who sold his Viagra policy, and she also ended up dead?"

I smiled. "It's a viatical policy, Doob, not a Viagra policy. But yes, that somewhat sums it up."

Doob looked perplexed, and I could tell he wanted to say something. "Spit it out, Doob."

He scratched his head and said, "Well, it sucks and everything, but why do we care?"

"We care for a couple of reasons. Number one is Bobby's murder has technically been solved, but there's still been no connection made between him and the guy who supposedly killed him. Number two is the freak who was chasing Darrin around right after Bobby died is now wreaking havoc in Boston. Number three is that freak might have killed Brenda before he left California. Number four is that Brenda was worried enough to have a package sent to LaKeisha and Roy. She must have known she was in danger. Number five—"

Doob held up his hands in surrender. "Okay, Meg. We're not letting it go, I got it."

"There's just too much unanswered shit, and there are too many coincidences that raise my hackles."

"Hackles?"

I threw a couch pillow at him, and he didn't even try to deflect it. It hit him smack in the face without fazing him in the least.

Doob picked up the pillow. "I think I know what you're talking about. It's like Scooby sense."

"Hunh?"

"You know, in the cartoon *Scooby Dooby Doo*. When Scooby is on to something, his Scooby sense kicks in. It's never wrong."

Sometimes it's just better to not try to follow Doob's logic. "Whatever you say, Doob. Listen, can you dig around in this Brenda gal's life? Address, bank accounts, cell phone usage, car loan, boyfriends, girlfriends, where she went to school, parents, siblings, whatever you can find. I'd also like to know more about the company she worked for and how many of these viatical things she's sold. It seems like a nasty business."

"Can do," Doob said, at full attention. I'd never seen him quite so coherent. "What's her full name?"

I showed him the email LaKeisha had sent me. It had Brenda's home, work, and cell phone numbers, and it also had three articles about her death.

"Doob, this will probably take a little bit, right?"

Doob was already clicking away and simply nodded at me.

"Okay then, I need to go see Ma and Pop to make sure everything is okay in their world, and I'll probably be a few hours. You'll keep an eye on Sampson, please?"

Doob nodded again, and I grabbed my coat and headed out. As the door closed behind me, I heard Doobie shout, "Scooby Dooby Doo!"

He worries me sometimes.

I got back to the apartment about five hours later, after confirming my parents were still of somewhat sane mind and body. I fully expected to find Doobie and Sampson spooning on Sampson's bed for an afternoon nap, but to my surprise, Doobie was dutifully perched at his laptop, exactly where he'd been when I'd left him. Sampson was asleep at his feet, and it was actually kind of cute.

"Hey Doobie—"

"Please refer to me as Scooby until this case is over," Doob replied without glancing up from his computer.

Whatever. "Okay, *Scooby*, how's it going?

"Great. I got a lot of information on Brenda, but there's something I think might interest you more than that right now."

I raised my eyebrows at him. "Nothing would interest me more than Brenda right now."

He stared at me for a moment and then shrugged. "You're the boss. As far as Brenda goes, there's a lot of info on this chick, whoever she was, and she was evidently living the high life."

Something attacked my olfactory senses, and it wasn't half bad.

"Doob, are you cooking?" I was incredulous.

"It's *Scooby*, and yes, I'm making Cornish game hen, some baby potatoes, asparagus, and a small salad."

Mother of God. This new Scooby-version-of-Doobie was going to work out just fine. "Did you say Cornish game hen?"

He waved it off, as if it was something he made every day. "I had it at my apartment and decided I might as well bring it over here."

"That's awesome. Do you need help with something? I could make chocolate chip cookies."

This gave Scooby/Doobie pause, and he actually deigned to look up from his computer. "With Cornish game hen? I don't think so, Meagan." He had an air of haughtiness about him, and it was so un-Doobie-like that I laughed out loud.

"All right, Doob, how about a yellow cake with chocolate frosting?"

"Now you're talking," he said excitedly.

I went into the kitchen and started pulling out bowls and measuring cups. I grabbed a cake mix, a few eggs, some vegetable oil and mixed the ingredients into a yummy golden batter. Licking the spoon, I yelled through the pass-through to Doob, "Do you want to lick the bowl?"

"Yes! And I want to lick the twisty silver things that you stick in the mixer, too. Those are the best!"

"I didn't use a mixer, Scooby, sorry."

"You did it by *hand*?" He sounded impressed.

"Yep, the good old fashioned way. I am trying to keep up with *Cornish game hen*, after all."

"Cool."

I put the cake in the oven under Doobie's Cornish game hen, hoping the temperature was close enough to bake the cake, and then walked into the eating area where Doob was clicking away on his laptop. Setting the bowl to the side of him, I was surprised to see how quickly he discarded his laptop to attack the batter. It was like watching a four-year-old, and I enjoyed the spectacle.

"Doob, if you could come up for air at some point, I'd love to hear what you found on our girl."

He gave one last dramatic lick on my oversized spoon and then set it down. Cracking his knuckles, he took a deep breath and assumed a posture of someone delivering the evening news.

"One Brenda Alvarez. She grew up in the Los Angeles area, working-class parents, one older and one younger brother. She graduated from a local high school with decent grades and went on to get her associates degree at a community college. She didn't further her education and evidently decided she was going to make a career in insurance. She got the necessary licenses and then job-jumped to a few places before ending up at the agency she was at when she died. It seems she was their viatical specialist, whatever that means. Even though she made over six figures, she had a lot of debt and lived well beyond her means. She ate out at four and five-star restaurants several times a week, shopped on Rodeo Drive regularly, and I haven't found any evidence that she ever saved a dime." He paused for a minute, and I thought he was done.

"Okay, so we've got a young gal living beyond her means. Is that it? I thought you might have found something useful."

Doob glared at me, and I briefly wondered if he was going to take his hen and go home. "Meagan, I'm drawing a blank. Remind me again as to how much you're paying me?"

Ah, score a big one for Doobie. "Sorry, Scooby, the stage is all yours."

"That's all of the not-so-weird stuff. Then it gets interesting. Her uncle on her father's side has some pretty shady associations. The uncle's name is Pedro Alvarez, and he's some type of bodyguard/thug for a local businessman, if you want to call him that. This businessman's name is Alberto Ramirez, and he's some type of old school kingpin. He's an alleged drug smuggler and it's been said he might be into human trafficking as well."

"Yikes," I said with a wince.

"Yeah, he's evidently into some heavy stuff."

"How does this relate to Brenda?"

"Well, initially I wasn't sure if it did at all, but when I hacked into the agency's website—"

"Um," I cut in.

"Hey, you asked me to get some info on her."

"Just skip the illegal parts, please."

Doob rolled his eyes and heaped on the sarcasm. "Okay, sure thing Meg. This is all completely on the up-and-up. What I did is I entered my assigned user name and password for the intranet at the insurance agency where Brenda worked. After legally entering the site, I discovered that some of Brenda's more recent viatical sales involved a certain investment group who, when you dig through the layers, is basically Alberto Ramirez."

"The kingpin dude who her uncle works for?" I recalled Darrin telling me about Bobby's investor wanting him dead.

"You got it."

"It sounds like the uncle might have been throwing some clients her way."

"Yeah, it does. Two of her more recent viatical sales involved a certain Bobby McBride, who was Darrin's friend. The other guy was Roy Jones,

LaKeisha's husband, just like she said. The investment company in both cases is synonymous with Alberto Ramirez."

"And Bobby is dead, and Brenda is dead. Not good."

Doobie cocked his head and raised his eyebrows. "There's more."

"Good grief, now you sound like LaKeisha. What else?"

"Well, you'd mentioned Bobby's wife Carol this morning when you were giving me the background info, so I did just a little snooping in Florida."

"Good idea! My gosh, I should have thought of that yesterday. What did you find?"

"Well, last fall, Carol moved out of the apartment she'd shared with Bobby. Since then, she's been cohabitating with a certain Glenn Tremont."

"Ah, so Steroid-Neanderthal-Man now has a name. Glenn Tremont." I mulled that over for a second. "How did you find that?"

Doob pulled a face. "Um, I found that out when I *legally* entered their apartment complex's computer system to see whose names are on the lease at the new place, and both of their names showed up.

"Also, I legally reviewed Glenn's credit, and he opened an account at Zales about the time Carol moved in."

"As in the jewelry store?"

"Yep."

"Hmmmm. There must be wedding bells in their future."

"Well, not any longer. That's what I've been trying to tell you."

I wasn't listening to Doob, because I wanted to stay with my current train of thought before it evaporated into the place where lost thoughts go. I hate that place.

"If Glenn is going to propose, that would explain his extra zealous interest in the money. He thinks he's landed himself a sugar mama. Did you find anything juicy on Carol?"

"I didn't do a lot of digging on Carol yet. I focused on Glenn since he was the law enforcement dude. I did confirm he was a cop a few years back, but he was fired after a questionable episode with a sixteen-year-old girl, a whole bunch of cocaine, and a totaled police cruiser. But—"

"This Glenn continues to prove himself a real class act," I interrupted. "I just hope I don't run into him on the street again anytime soon. If I do, I'll definitely get his license plate this time around."

"Yeah, well, that's what I've been trying to tell you."

"You know something about the red Impala?"

"No, I know something about Glenn."

I threw my hands in the air. "Spit it out, Doob!"

"He's dead."

CHAPTER 21

Doobie waited for me to digest this. I blinked twice and my mouth fell open, but I was speechless. Doob took my open mouth as a request, and he handed me one of the unopened Diet Cokes. I consumed half the can in one swig.

He peered at me questioningly. "Has the caffeine hit your system yet?"

I nodded quickly and took a deep breath. "Yep. Let's hear it."

"This Glenn fellow was fished out of the harbor last night. It happened too late to hit this morning's paper, but I found it online a little bit ago." He grabbed my Diet Coke and handed it to me. "Take another swig."

I did as I was told. "Did he drown?"

"That's what it looks like. There was cocaine in his system, and his blood alcohol level was three times the legal limit. They think he might have killed himself. That, or he was so shitfaced that he stumbled into the water somehow, somewhere, and couldn't save himself. They identified him through his old cop records."

I cocked my head at him. "Doob, I highly doubt the online article told you about cocaine, alcohol, and how they identified him, now did it?"

Doob flushed. "No, the article didn't get that specific."

I thought about that for a second and then nodded knowingly. "Bonsai?"

He nodded back and smiled. When Doob had actually bothered with college, a stint that lasted only a few months, he'd attended MIT in Boston. He'd befriended a fellow student named Bonsai, who was a bit of an odd duck, just like Doob. Bonsai wasn't from the right side of the tracks. He wasn't from a rich country, nor was he from any money, nor was his surname anything recognizable, and his lineage wasn't traceable back to the Mayflower. But he'd somehow been accepted to MIT and was now revered as one of the top cancer researchers in the country. Goes to show what all of that other bullshit counts for. Fortunately for us, Bonsai had stayed in Boston and had connections at every hospital in the city.

"Let's just say that the information is accurate, Meg, and we'll leave it at that."

I envisioned a cold, dark, watery death in Boston Harbor and shuddered. "I guess I should feel bad," I said quietly, but somehow I didn't.

"No, you absolutely shouldn't, Meg. That's your good-girl Catholic upbringing talking. You don't have anything to feel bad about, and you didn't have anything to do with it. And I don't mind saying that I'm glad that we don't have to worry about him bothering you anymore."

I sighed. "I need to call the police," I said, walking over to the cordless phone.

"Why?"

"I need to tell them this was the guy who threatened me on the street."

"Why open that can of worms?"

"I don't know. I just feel like I need to let them know."

"What if they suspect you?"

"Why would they suspect me? I didn't shoot him up with cocaine and alcohol. Plus, you and I were together all day. And since you didn't listen to me and ended up staying here all night last night, you're my alibi."

"I didn't stay on your floor last night, though. I was with Sampson in the doggy boudoir on the uptown side of the apartment. You could have left when I was asleep in there."

"Doob! Are you *trying* to make the case against me?"

"No, I'm just telling you what they might think. And if they don't suspect you, then what were your folks doing last night?"

I lifted the phone out of its cradle. "Doob, do you think my five-foot nothing parents were doing cocaine and high balls with this guy? Then what? Ma distracted him with some sultry moves while Pop snuck behind him and threw him in the water? C'mon Doob, you're out of your mind."

"Fine. What about your uncle?"

That one hit home, and I hung up the phone. "Larry?" My voice came out as a squeak.

"You got any other uncles?"

"As a matter of fact, I do."

"You know who I'm talking about, Meagan. Don't be cute."

"I didn't even tell Uncle Lare."

"Gee Meg, I'm sure your dad didn't call him the exact second you hung up with them yesterday."

"Oh shit." I tried to picture smiling Uncle Larry throwing Glenn into the harbor, and it wasn't completely out of reach. Not when his family had been threatened. Not when he had friends with some questionable pasts. If Uncle Larry decided to be a guy who wanted people to disappear, then they would, and that would be that.

Doob's voice was softer when he spoke. "Why don't you take a breath or two or ten before calling the police? That'll give you some time to sort it all out, and maybe you can call Larry in the meantime. It won't even hit the papers until tomorrow, and it'll probably be a small paragraph somewhere in the middle section. This guy wasn't a local."

I nodded in agreement and went into the kitchen to check on the cake. How had my simple case with David Fontana turned into suspecting my uncle of something horrible? I needed some answers.

Doob and I finished making dinner in a bit of a fog. We went through the motions of eating some incredible cuisine in near silence. But as the food hit my system, I ruled out Uncle Larry as a suspect. There was no way he could have known what Glenn looked like. Even if he did, he wouldn't have known how to find him. Uncle Larry was not the sleuth of the family. I refused to think about it anymore. There had to be another answer, and I just needed to figure out what it was. I started drumming my nails on the table until Doob placed a hand over mine.

"Stop it, Meg."

"Sorry." My voice was very low as I stared Doob down.

His voice was soft. "What are you thinking?"

"There's absolutely no way Uncle Larry did this, Doob. I won't hear another word about it. Do you understand me?"

Doob took his hand off of mine, leaned back in his chair and crossed his arms. "Meagan, even though I probably have chocolate frosting and remnants of Cornish game hen all over my face, I'm not a child, and you don't need to speak to me like I am. If you don't want to face the possibility that Larry did this, then that's your choice. But you're not going to tell me how to think or what I can or can't talk about, because I think he very likely might have had a hand in this. And if he did, then I would stand up and applaud. I'd never sell him out, not ever."

Assertive-Doob was becoming a permanent fixture. I got a lump in my throat and thanked the heavens for my disheveled little friend. I felt my eyes tear, and Doob rolled his eyes.

"Good God, Meagan, do *not* get all misty. I just can't take it when you get emotional. I'll humor you and move forward under the assumption that Uncle Larry didn't have anything to do with this. Okay?"

"Okay. Now what?"

"Well, now you tell me what an incredible help I've been, and that you've never had such an amazing dinner, and then we'll break this thing down."

I smiled at him. "Well, first off, I really appreciate all of the hard work you've done for me, and I can't think of the last time I've had such a good dinner. Thank you from the bottom of my heart."

Doob smiled proudly, as if he hadn't known exactly what I was going to say. "You're welcome, Meg. Let's talk shop."

"Good. It appears this Glenn was Steroid-Neanderthal-Man, and he's been in Boston so he may or may not have killed Brenda. We'll probably never know that now. If he didn't kill her, then who did? And then who killed him? And was it the same person? And if it was the same person who killed them both, then he or she traveled cross-country to do so."

Doob looked perplexed. "He or *she*? Do you think it's a chick?"

"You can't rule anyone out, Doob, but it's probably a man."

The thought of Uncle Lare hung in the air, but neither of us spoke of it.

Doob said, "I'm with you." He rolled his hand towards himself, instructing me to keep the ideas coming.

A thought struck me. "I wonder if Carol was set up to get some life insurance money from this Glenn guy, should anything ever happen to him."

"They weren't married," Doob responded.

"Doob, you're so old fashioned. You don't have to be married to name someone as your beneficiary. Bobby wasn't married to Darrin, and he named Darrin as his beneficiary for the whole viatical thing."

Doob thought about that for a minute. "Cool."

I shook my head and smiled. "So, would you dig around in Carol's life, please?"

"Do you think she had something to do with all of this?"

"I don't know what I think. But two guys she was involved with are both dead. I'm trying to picture this mess from her point of view. Like Glenn, she probably didn't even know where Bobby was until his body was shipped back to Florida. At that point, he was dead, and she likely thought she was coming into some money. That is, until she spoke with the insurance company and realized that she was getting zip, zilch, nada, squat. So then she would have been pissed. Maybe she sent Glenn to California to check things out, shake things up, scare some people, whatever. Glenn might have figured out who Brenda was, but what would he have gained by killing her? And if he did kill her, who killed him? And why? Who gained by having both Brenda and Glenn dead? Was it Carol? Further, are those two deaths even related? That's what we need to figure out."

I put my head on the table and shut my eyes. Focusing on Carol seemed smart, plus I didn't want to have to think about taking on a California drug dealer and human trafficker just yet. I took a deep breath and thought I might just leave my head on the table for the remainder of the day. However, I heard a little squirting noise and looked up to see something a little startling.

Sampson was poised like a show dog at Westminster, and Doobie was lightly spraying him with Febreze furniture spray.

"Doob! What the hell? That isn't for dogs."

Doob looked like a kid who'd been caught with his hand in the cookie jar. "Well, Moira hates it if Sampson gets a doggie smell, so once a day I mist him down with a bit of Febreze. I don't do it near his face, only his hind end."

"Doob, no more Febreze on the dog, and I mean it. If he smells like a dog, I've got news for you. He *is* a dog!"

Sampson whimpered in indignation, and Doob squatted down and put both hands on Sampson's furry face. "I'm sorry buddy. Your bitchy aunt won't let me help you smell pretty anymore. She's just jealous that you smell better than she does." With that, he tromped into the kitchen and put the Febreze back in the pantry. I was constantly amazed by Doob. He showered about once a month, but he was perplexed if Sampson didn't get his daily dose of smelling pretty.

"Doob, would it be possible to get back to the case, or do you have some other pressing things to do? Maybe light some scented candles around Sampson's bed? Or put some potpourri sachets in his pillows?"

Doob came back into the living room and folded his arms across his chest. "I can manage to do all of the above."

"Well, you're quite the multi-tasker."

"Speaking of multi-tasking—"

"Yes?"

"I think I should maybe be looking at someone else as well."

"Who?"

"Darrin."

"Why?"

"Fifty thousand reasons, Meagan."

I nodded. "You're right. That was my initial reaction as well. He could be playing the part of grieving roommate when all along he knew about the fifty g's waiting inside that laptop case."

Doobie shuddered. "I'd hate to think you drove cross-country with a killer."

"I'm not too keen on the idea myself. Imagine me having to tell Norman that I'd aided and abetted a felon. He'd put me in handcuffs and turn me in himself."

"I'd visit you in the slammer."

"That's comforting, Doob, thanks. I'm hoping there's nothing to find, but yes, we've got to look at every possibility. First, please do some digging on Carol. Then sniff around Darrin's information and see if you find anything that stinks."

"Can do." Doob cracked his knuckles and started clicking away on his laptop. I began clearing the dishes off the table while Sampson placed himself at the base of the pass-through. He didn't want to miss anything good, should it present itself.

I'd just finished loading the dishwasher when Doob let out what could best be described as a yelp. I flipped off the kitchen light and went in to see what he'd uncovered.

"Not good?" I inquired.

"You might want to sit down."

I complied, and Sampson's furry head popped up when I plopped into the chair.

"Let's hear it, Doob. And it better not have anything to do with Uncle Lare."

"Carol's missing."

Sampson cocked his head and whined. They say animals know when a storm is coming, and I think Sampson had just warned me to get out of the way.

CHAPTER 22

"**W**hat do you mean Carol's missing?"

"There were two articles from about six months back in the Daytona paper. The first one says a local waitress was last seen leaving her late shift at a seedy bar—"

"Does it say *seedy bar* in the article?"

"No, but I can tell," Doob replied simply.

"Don't embellish, Doob."

Doob saluted. "Yes, ma'am. Okay, so she bid her coworkers farewell around two thirty in the morning, and she evidently drove home because her car was spotted at her apartment building later that morning."

"Who spotted it?"

"A nurse who was leaving for work early—around four o'clock—noticed it there."

"Keep going."

"Well, she didn't show up for work later that night—"

"What time was her shift?"

"It started at five. Are you going to let me finish, or are you going to keep interrupting me?"

"It's pretty likely I'll keep interrupting you."

Doob pulled a face. "So the manager called her a couple of times at home—"

"What time did he call?"

"He made three calls between five thirty and eight. No answer, so he left a couple of messages on her answering machine. One of the other waitresses called her cell number a few times, but she didn't answer that, either. Once the shift slowed down a little bit, the manager went over to her apartment—"

"What time was that?"

"Around nine thirty. He said that no one came to the door. He walked around the building for the heck of it, but nothing looked sketchy to him—"

"Did the article use the word sketchy?"

"Shut up, Meg. So the guy tried to check out her car, but it was locked. He didn't think anything looked out of the ordinary, though."

"So then what?"

"He went back to the bar and they all hashed it around a little bit and called the cops around eleven."

"When did you say this all happened?"

"It looks like late September, and there's just been this article and one follow-up story. It mentioned Glenn by name a couple of times, but according to this, he's not a person of interest." He paused. "I guess he definitely won't be now."

I again envisioned a watery death in Boston Harbor and shivered. "Did the articles say if there were any leads?"

He shook his head. "It doesn't really seem like it. The second article indicates some speculation that she just took off and started over somewhere else."

I narrowed my eyes. "With what?"

"Hunh?"

"You need money to do that. Where did she get the money?"

"Dunno. I'm just the messenger. You're the figure-outer."

"When Glenn grabbed me on the street, he said he wanted to know where the money was, but he didn't even mention Carol. Doesn't that seem odd?"

"Why?"

"Because she was his connection to the money. It certainly never had anything to do with him."

"Maybe he knows what happened to her, and it's probably nothing good."

"Meaning, he killed her?"

Doob shrugged. "It seems like no one has seen Carol, but you and Darrin have seen more than your share of this guy. Who knows? Maybe he decided he'd go after the money for himself."

I drummed my fingers on the table and pursed my lips. "So, we've got a murdered Bobby, a murdered Brenda, a dead Glenn, who's possibly a murder victim and/or a murderer, and a missing Carol. That about sum it up?"

"Yep." He paused briefly. "Can I have another piece of cake?"

"How can you continue to eat when we have dead bodies and missing people?"

Doob considered that. "Until I'm the person who is dead or missing, I'm always going to be able to eat cake."

I appreciated his honesty, so I went back into the kitchen and cut two more pieces of cake. I couldn't have him eating alone; it would be bad manners.

CHAPTER 23
SATURDAY, MARCH 15ᵀᴴ

I hadn't done much with Jim's case in the past few days and thought I'd better earn some of the money he'd fronted me. Before heading out, I called Doob and asked him to come over. When he arrived, I plopped some cereal in front of him and reviewed our plans for the day.

He responded with a mouthful of Frosted Flakes. "At your service, Boss. You're expecting that package from LaKeisha today, right?"

"Yep, that was one of the things on my list. She wrote and said that she sent it overnight-mail through the post office, so I'm going to give you my mail key. Will you check for the package later this afternoon?"

"Do I have your permission to open it?"

I rolled my eyes. "Duh, Doob. That's why I'm giving you the key."

"Okay, okay. I just think that it's a federal offense to open someone's mail without his or her permission."

"Doob! All of the places you hack into could get you for multiple federal offenses. What's one more item on that list?"

"Cool."

"Before the package gets here, I've got several things in mind. Would you do some more snooping on Carol and also on Jethro Hackett?"

"Who?"

"He's the guy they pinned Bobby's murder on. Some drifter dude evidently. I've kind of been overlooking him. Who knows? Maybe it really was an open-and-shut case."

"That would be too easy."

"Finally, would you see if you can get into Brenda's email for me? I think LaKeisha sent me Brenda's information in one of her emails."

"I can try. But it'll be useless if it's already been shut down. Are you sure you have it?"

"Pretty sure. LaKeisha has sent me about four emails. It's not very organized, but it looks like she just sends me stuff when she thinks of it."

"Did she send Brenda's work or personal email?"

I shrugged and went into the bedroom to get my paperwork from the case. I brought out the disorganized folder and sticky notes and put them on the table, scanning for LaKeisha's correspondence. When I found what I was looking for, I held it up like a trophy and then quickly skimmed it.

"It looks like she sent me Brenda's work email address, which might not be of any help. If you can find it, her personal email might be a bit more juicy."

"Well, I'll start with this one and see what comes up. Anything else?"

"Like we talked about yesterday, will you poke around in Darrin's email and finances, too?"

"And you have his email address?"

I gave him a thumbs-up. "David gave it to me the day I met him. That seems like it was two hundred years ago."

"What else?"

"Try to keep an eye open for anyone who looks shady."

"Like who?"

"Well, if someone wrote an email containing the words *contract killing* in the subject line, then that might be someone we'd like to check out."

"Your sarcasm is duly noted, Meg."

"I'm allowed. I'm the native Bostonian."

Doob cracked his knuckles. "Anything else I need to slave away at while getting paid exactly nothing?"

"Ouch! Come on Doob, you wouldn't take the money if I offered it to you. Consider it an internship."

"Scooby the Intern, at your service." He bowed his head deferentially, and it reminded me why he was the best neighbor on earth.

"Okay, so your duties as an intern involve snooping around Carol, Jethro, Brenda and Darrin to see if anything jumps out at you. Then please check for that package later on this afternoon. There's got to be something major in there. If you find anything significant, your Frito's supply is on me for a month."

"What if I don't find anything significant?"

"That will get you a two-week supply, just for the effort."

"I can eat a lot of Frito's, Meg. You might be better off paying me."

I smiled. "I'm off to follow an unsuspecting woman around all day. Call me on my cell if you find anything. Thank you!"

Six hours later, I'd followed Jim's ex-wife all over the place, with nothing to show for it except she was a professional shopper. I'd taken a quick break and gone to my car to chow on a bacon double cheeseburger in Macy's parking lot. I was parked right beside Jim's ex-wife's BMW and wondered where she got all the money to shop and drive such a nice car. I secretly hoped she was bleeding him dry.

I was mid-bite when my cell phone rang. There was a big hunk of bacon just waiting to be devoured, but nonetheless, I checked my caller ID and saw it was Doob. He was one of the few people for whom I'd delay bacon.

"Hey Doob, what's up?"

"Are you sitting down?"

"I hate it when you ask that."

"I know. But are you?"

"Yes, I'm sitting in a Macy's parking lot, half freezing my butt off."

"It's not that cold out, Meg."

"It's in the high-thirties, Doob. It's not exactly balmy." I was wasting my breath. Doob would be on this stakeout in just an orange thong. He has a permanent heater somewhere in his body, and I chalk that up to an Iowa thing.

"You're a sissy, Meg. Anyway, I got into Brenda's work email, and from that, I was able to figure out her personal email address."

"How did you do that?"

"Pretty much by luck. It looked like Brenda sometimes received jokes at work, and she forwarded some of them to her personal email address."

"Why would she do that?"

"Probably because she had all of her personal contacts in the address section of her home email. If she liked a joke she received at work, then it looked like she'd forward it to herself at home, and that would allow her to send it out to her friends and family. She probably didn't want to send it out from her business email address, being Miss Professional and all."

"Okay, that makes sense. Did you have any problems getting into the personal email?"

"Nope."

"So let's cut to the chase here, please. What did you find?"

"I found about a million emails for all kinds of sales, both online and at various malls in Los Angeles. There was also a bunch from a number of five-star restaurants and all-inclusive vacation resorts. This girl looked to be a high roller."

"Is this really why you're calling me?" The bacon was getting cold.

"Of course not. Besides all of the shopping, restaurant, and resort crap, her personal email was mostly from what looked to be her family and friends. She had close to three hundred messages in her mailbox, and there didn't seem to be anything out of the ordinary. I was getting pretty bored with the whole thing, but that's when I noticed her Drafts folder."

"Her *what* folder?"

"It's a folder people can use if they're writing an email but don't want to send it yet. For example, let's say that you're working on a really long email to your friend Tracy in Colorado. And let's say you've written a few paragraphs when the pizza man comes with a double pepperoni."

Yum. "Okay?"

"Well, you'd want to save what you'd written to that point, so you'd just hit the *Save as Draft* button, and it would go into a little file for you. Then you could pull up the file at anytime later, finish your email, and send it off to Tracy."

"Okay, I know what you're talking about. So what does this have to do with Brenda?"

"Well, I went into her Drafts folder, and I found something a little weird."

"What do you mean?"

"Well, like I said, there was an email in the folder, but it had never been sent. It had only been written and then saved."

"What does it say?"

"It says: *Info on D.H. received; claims he is in serious financial trouble. Need to discuss. Please meet at 9:00 P.M., usual location.*"

"Info on D.H. What's that?"

"Three guesses, Meg, and the first two don't count."

"Ah, Darrin Hood. Got it. But you said it was in Brenda's Drafts folder, right?"

"Yep."

"Why would she write this and then never send it off? Who was it being sent to?"

"The email address that it was going to wasn't filled in. The part I just read to you was in the body of the email. The address was blank."

"That doesn't make sense. Did you check her *sent* mail? Maybe she kept a copy in her Drafts and also sent a copy?"

"Thank God I called you, Meg. I *never* would have thought of something that tremendously obvious on my own."

"Okay, wise-ass, I'm just double checking."

"Of course I checked her sent mail. I can tell you unequivocally that this email never went out. And it was written about a week before Bobby died. So, Super Sleuth, who was the nine o'clock meeting with?"

"How the hell do I know?" I was exasperated.

"I'll keep digging." He sounded frustrated, too.

"Thanks Doob. I wouldn't want anyone else working on this. By the way, did you happen to get the package?"

"I've checked twice, but it's not here yet. I'll look again in about a half hour."

"Okay, thanks."

I spent another few minutes in the parking lot, devouring my cheeseburger. Then I went back into the mall to follow the non-cheating spouse around. I was hopeful when my cell phone rang about twenty minutes later.

"Hey Doob. Did the package arrive?"

"Um no, but I was just thinking about this draft and wanted to run something by you."

"Is it going to muddy the waters even further?"

"That's pretty likely, yeah."

"Friggin' great."

"Did you ever see the movie *Traitor*?"

"Don Cheadle and Guy Pearce?"

"Yep, that's the one."

"Nope, never saw it."

"Then how do you know who's in it?"

I thought about that and shrugged. "It's a gift. What does this have to do with anything?"

"Well, there was a way that the bad guys in the movie communicated by email without actually sending each other anything."

I rolled my eyes. "Okay?"

"They used the Drafts folder as a way to share info between two sources who were trying to remain anonymous."

"How?"

"Very simple. Let's say that Person A knows Person B's username and password and signs into their email account. Person A types up a body of an email and saves it into Person B's Drafts folder. That way, when Person B logs on, they can go into Drafts and read the email. Thus, nothing is actually ever *sent*. Get it?"

"I think. So if you knew my username and password, you could log in right now and type up a message and save it in my Drafts folder. When I get home in a few hours, I could sign in, check my Drafts, and your message would be there."

Doob chuckled. "I already did that. Easy, hunh?"

"Yeah, it sounds like it."

"Using this theory, Brenda typed this message and left it for someone who knew her information and could check it whenever they wanted."

"Okay, that makes sense. So whoever read her message was the person she was going to meet with at nine o'clock that night, whoever the hell that was. At their usual location, wherever the hell that was."

"But who and where?"

"I dunno."

"As I've said before Meg, you're the figure-outer."

"Yeah, you're just the guy who makes it more complicated."

"I can log off at anytime—"

"No! Sorry, Doob. I'm just trying to get my brain around this." I was silent for about thirty seconds as I ran all of the scenarios through my head. And suddenly an idea formed. "Doob, do you think it's possible that Brenda was working *against* Ramirez, rather than with him? If so, could this mystery person she was writing to possibly have been a fed?"

Silence.

"Doob?"

"I guess so. I'm rubbing my temples."

I smiled. "Me too. Thanks Doob."

"I'll call you when the package gets here."

"Pizza is on me tonight."

"Later, Meagan." He hung up.

I followed Jim's ex-wife out of the mall and back towards her BMW.

She was with the same two girlfriends and had about a billion shopping bags. No man, no clandestine meeting place, no affair. *Sorry Jimbo.*

My cell broke the silence yet again.

"What Doob?"

"It's in my hands."

"I'm on my way."

CHAPTER 24

Doob was staring at the package like it was a ticking time bomb when I rushed into the apartment. I was out of breath from taking the stairs two at a time.

"You didn't open it," I gushed, gasping for air.

"As much as I wanted to, I couldn't do it. It's been driving me nuts, but you should do it, Meg. This is your gig."

I seized the package and started ripping. Once I had one end open, I turned it upside down and poured out the contents. A little thing that was just bigger than a Bic lighter came out, as well as five black and white pictures. There was also a sheet of paper that looked to be a hand-written note.

Doob grabbed the pictures and started flipping through them. "Who's this?"

I grabbed one of them and studied the tough looking dude in them. I wished the picture was in color, but I did my best. The man had shaggy hair that Pop would say was a little too long, and there was a huge tattoo on his neck that disappeared under his dark tee shirt. I couldn't tell what it was, but it looked like some type of swirling snake thing. It definitely wasn't a flower or butterfly or leprechaun.

I flipped the picture over and read the name. "I guess this is Vince."

"Scary dude," Doob said quietly.

"He certainly looks it, doesn't he? And for whatever reason, Brenda wanted to get this stuff to Darrin."

"What's on the flash drive?"

I picked it up and turned it over, like that was going to do anything. After studying it for a second, I held it out to Doobie. "You're the computer guy. Take a look."

Doob took it from me eagerly and rammed it into the portal on his laptop. I watched as he started clicking away. "It's encrypted, but I can get through it."

"I can wait." While Doob started digging, I read Brenda's note.

Please get this information to Darrin. He'll know what to do with it. Please don't think poorly of me.

What the hell? Poorly of her? What had she done?

After a few minutes, Doob started making noises like "ohhh" and "ahhhh" and "hmmmm" until I almost smacked him.

"Doob!"

He jumped so high out of his chair that he almost hit the ceiling. When he landed, he actually looked surprised to see me.

"Doob, how can you get so engrossed in something in a matter of minutes? And further, how can you not tell me what's up as you're ohhhhing and ahhhing and pawing through all that stuff? What did you find?"

Doob looked a bit pleased with himself. "I know that *you* have the attention span of a fruit fly, sweet Meagan, but *my* powers of concentration are unmatched by anyone this side of the Mississippi."

I rolled my eyes. "Thanks for the Midwest reference, Doob. Now are you going to tell me what you found, or shall I beat it out of you?!"

Doob smiled and stood up. "I'd like to see that, Meg. Seriously." He kind of crouched down and put his arms out, assuming some type of wrestling move, and I laughed out loud. The University of Iowa had long been known for its wrestling program, and I think Doob had some weird fantasies about men in onesies that I didn't want to know anything about.

He gave up and plopped back down in his chair. "Well, I found a few interesting tidbits in this excel spreadsheet. The first tab at the bottom of the sheet is titled *Ramirez*. The columns list what looks to be several viatical sales to one Alberto Ramirez. Brenda has listed dates, names, and dollar amounts."

I shrugged. "Okay, that could definitely prove interesting. What else?"

Doob blew out a big puff of air. "The second tab is named *Associates* and has a bunch of names, home addresses, email addresses, home phone numbers, cell numbers and what looks to be some type of schedule."

"Hmmmmm. Maybe those are the people who work for Ramirez?"

"Could be."

"What else?"

Doob used his hands to do a mock drum roll on the table. "The third and final tab is named *Darrin*. There is only one thing on that sheet." He held up one finger, ostensibly for dramatic effect.

"Doob?"

"There is a single sentence which states that Darrin made a twenty thousand dollar deposit to his bank account about ten days before Bobby died."

"Oh shit."

CHAPTER 25

Doob and I sat looking at each other for a minute. He broke the silence. "There could be a very plausible explanation for the twenty thousand, Meg."

I raised an eyebrow. "Yeah, that's a reasonable amount of money for a twenty-something-wannabe-actor-bartender to deposit. Especially in a lump sum."

"So what are you thinking, Super Sleuth?"

I exploded. "The same thing I've been thinking since the beginning of this! It always comes back to Darrin. This whole thing started with a boatload of cash, and now there's even more. Supposedly the laptop loot came from Bobby, but where in the hell did this newfound money come from?!"

Doob started sputtering. "Ummmm, the tooth fairy, Santa, a genie, the Easter bunny, Cinderella's fairy godmother, Gazoo from the *Flintstones*, or David Copperfield."

I stared at him. "You forgot *Bewitched*."

Doob nodded. "Yep, I did. Loved that twitching nose." He raised his eyebrows twice.

"Okay, enough nonsense. What if Brenda created this spreadsheet to show Ramirez's track record with viatical deals? What if it was a payment for services rendered?"

"Meaning?"

"What I mean is, what if he paid Darrin twenty thousand to kill Bobby? What if Brenda was building a case against both of them?"

Doob shook his head. "Think about it, Meg. If Brenda or even LaKeisha thought Darrin was somehow *involved* in this, why would they send this information to you to get it to him? If he was the bad guy, or one of the bad guys, wouldn't they avoid him like the plague?"

"Okay, that's a great point. But something is still shady about Darrin getting that money. Should I start calling some of those people on the second tab?"

Doob looked at me like I'd just laid an egg. "And say what exactly? 'Hi Stranger, could you please tell me if your drug-dealing-human-trafficking-loan-shark-boss gave twenty thousand dollars to Darrin Hood so he would murder his roommate who was already dying so your aforementioned boss could get a shitload of cash which will enable him to further support his illegal and illicit activities?'"

"No good?"

Doob rolled his eyes. "Meagan, c'mon! This is so not your problem. Bobby's case has been closed by the cops, Darrin is home, David is happy, you've actually been paid, so why do you keep pushing this?"

"LaKeisha reached out to me, I didn't ask for this! But now I'm in it, and I've got to see it through," I said defensively. Then I felt my chin wobble and looked at him imploringly.

The realization hit Doob's face, and he spoke in a softer tone. "Meg, I'm sorry. And I'm not a shrink, but I know what you're doing. *None* of this is going to bring Tom back."

I wiped my nose and willed my moist eyes to dry up. "I know that, Doob. I'm not stupid. But as long as there are some loose ends, I'm going to pull. If this one can be solved, then I'm going to solve it."

Doob sighed deeply but didn't say anything. I saw him silently working through the mental gymnastics that he goes through when he's trying to make a tough decision. I felt my eyes get watery again.

He put his hand on mine and nodded slowly. "Okay, Meg. Just please lose the water works. What do you need me to do?"

"What you do best. I need you to snoop in cyber world to see if that info from Brenda leads anywhere, but you don't have to do it tonight. It's getting late, and I promised you some pizza, didn't I?"

Doob smirked. "It's late for you, Meg, but it's midday for me. I know how much you value your precious z's, Sleeposaurus. But I'll be up for hours, so I'll start digging on those names and addresses. Hopefully something will jump out and give us some direction."

I beamed. "You're the best, Doob!"

Doob nodded. "I know. And I don't need any pizza, but I do need you to bundle up and go get us some *real* coffee and donuts, like right now. I don't want that backup shit-coffee that you have around here."

I completed the caffeine and sugar run in record time and got Doob's tummy happy in less than half an hour. I curled up on the couch with an afghan and did some channel surfing while Doob was clicking away. True to form, I must have drifted off at some point because I woke up sometime later and felt a light blanket on my face. As I reached up to pull it down, I realized it wasn't a blanket at all. It was a sheet of paper that had been taped to my forehead.

As I tugged at the paper, I saw that a lamp had been left on low-beam beside the couch. Doob was nowhere to be found. I squinted at the square, decorative clock above the flat screen television and saw that it was just after four o'clock in the morning. I sat up to read the message.

In his barely legible handwriting, Doob had written the following: *Meg, you snore like a barnyard animal. Call me when you get up tomorrow. I have some scoop.*

CHAPTER 26
SUNDAY, MARCH 16TH

Although Doob kept some odd hours, I didn't think he'd want me calling at this time of night. Or this time of morning, whatever. I shuffled off to bed and set my alarm for ten. That would be a reasonable hour to call Doob, and the idea of sleeping in made me very happy.

Even though hours had passed, it felt like five minutes later when my alarm went off, and I said a very nasty word before hitting the snooze button. When the alarm sounded the second time, I turned it off and picked up the phone. It rang three times before I heard Doob's muffled voice.

"H'lo?" He sounded like he'd been in a deep sleep, and I felt bad for just a second, knowing that he rarely sleeps. But the moment passed.

"Wake up Sleeping Doobie. Breakfast is on me if you're here in less than fifteen minutes."

"What day is it?" He sounded completely disoriented.

"Sunday. A great day for brunch. The fifteen minutes start now."

I hung up the phone and grabbed my pencil and notebook from the nightstand beside my bed. Suddenly I heard keys in the door, and then I heard Doob's voice.

"With fourteen minutes and thirty-two seconds to spare!" Doob announced, groggy no more.

I jumped out of bed and went into the living room, walking towards him and shaking my head. I grabbed him by the shoulders, turned him around and ushered him back to the door.

"Toilet, toothbrush, shower, in that order. Otherwise, you're going to scare people. Be back here in fifteen minutes, not a minute sooner."

"You don't look so hot yourself, Meg."

"Doob, go."

"Don't leave without me."

Fifteen minutes later, I was freshly showered and decided to go with the all-natural look. Not my best, but I didn't care. Clean was my highest aspiration for the day.

Doob and I took Sampson out to do his business and then headed out to a yummy schmummy cafe on Boylston Street. We wandered around a little bit first and took in the sights and sounds of Beantown. It was a crisp, cold day, but the sun was shining, and I found myself getting premature spring fever. Even though we were in the heart of the city, it was beautiful, and I loved walking along the tree-lined streets while admiring the businesses and residences that coexisted quite naturally. The famous Newbury Street was out of my price range for nearly everything, but still, I liked to window shop and pretend that someday I would actually purchase something there without forfeiting food or rent for a month. Or a few months. Or a year. Whatever.

Once we settled in at the cafe, Doob ordered the left half of the menu, and I ordered a western omelet and chocolate milk.

It was time to get down to business. "Doob, thanks for taping your note to my face last night. I certainly wouldn't have found it otherwise. But more importantly, I am very curious about the scoop you found."

Doob smiled. "Well, from what I could tell, most, or all, of the names on Brenda's sheet are thugs of the Ramirez crew. Some of them have served some hard time in jail, and others have records of petty criminal stuff. They're almost all under thirty-five years old, but none of them really have an employment history. These guys have some hefty mortgages, car loans, boat loans, and credit card balances, but there's no record of employment, which is curious. I noticed no student loans—real shocker—so unless they paid cash for college, my guess is that Ramirez recruited these guys when they were pretty young. In my un-expert opinion, they're being paid handsomely for doing jobs that don't exactly end up on a credit bureau or a loan application."

"How can they get loans and credit cards if they can't prove their income?" I wondered.

"This is America, Meg. Buy on credit today what you probably won't be able to pay for tomorrow. Then try to get someone else to foot your bill."

Good grief. I didn't want Doob to get started on his vast plan for making this a great and wealthy nation once again. I'd heard the speech too many times, and I briefly envisioned a President Doobie, then shuddered.

I held up my hands, in the universal STOP gesture. "Doob, let's stay on track. That's great information, and I tend to agree with what you're thinking. I wonder if one of those guys would be willing to help us, but again, that involves phoning a complete stranger to see if he wants to snitch on his boss."

"A boss who's been overpaying those thugs for years and saving them from lifetimes of cleaning sewers."

"Is that a job?"

"I'm sure it is."

Our order arrived, so I asked if we could please change the subject of sewers while we ate. Doob didn't answer, rather he attacked his food with enthusiasm. I followed suit, and ten minutes later, we were both stuffed to maximum capacity. I'd had the foresight to wear some stylish sweat pants with elastic, and I was grateful for my earlier brilliance. There was no way the zipper on a pair of my jeans would have survived this breakfast.

"We have to take a cab home," Doob whined. "I don't think I can walk."

I laughed. "Before we leave, was there anything else you found during your cyber exploring last night?"

His mouth dropped open. "My God, I forgot to tell you about something I found! It might be the best part!" he said excitedly.

That got my attention. "Enlighten me, please."

"Remember that cop dude you told me you met when you were in Los Angeles?"

"Yeah, Officer Simonetta."

Doob snapped his fingers and pointed at me. "The very one. And how exactly did you meet him again, Meagan?"

I felt my face flush. "Ummm, when I got pulled over for speeding. He just gave me a warning, though."

Doob stared at me. "You *will* go to hell for lying, Meagan."

"Doob! Who cares? What about Officer Simonetta?"

Doob squinted. "At some point, I will find out how and why you really met him. But that's for another day. In the meantime, Officer Simonetta's name was on that list of Brenda's."

My eyebrows shot up. "Really? That's curious. I wonder if he's a bad cop."

"Did you seem like a bad cop when he pulled you over? For *speeding?*" Sarcasm was oozing out of him.

I shook my head. "Not at all. He seemed pretty solid, and I've talked with him about Bobby's case a couple of times since then. I just don't see it."

Doob twisted up his mouth. "Okay, let's grab a cab. I need to find a pillow quickly."

We spent the ride home in silence, finally giving in to our gluttony, and then we both picked a couch to collapse on back at the apartment. I woke up an hour later when Sampson licked my face, and then I saw him walk over to the other couch and lick Doob smack on the mouth as well. That would be the closest Doob and I would ever come to kissing.

We groggily sat up on our respective couches and then spent the next hour talking about all of the unanswered questions. Everything from the junkie who supposedly killed Bobby, to Carol, to Glenn, to Brenda, to Vince, to Officer Simonetta, to Ramirez and back again.

"Doob, have we missed anything on this spreadsheet?"

He shrugged. "You can look at it just as easily as I can, but there is one more thing. Brenda had some notes about people from the restaurant where Darrin worked."

"Sunny's?"

"Yep."

"How do you know they all worked at Sunny's?"

Doob rolled his eyes. "Well, it was super tough to figure out because on the spreadsheet there was a column heading titled EMPLOYMENT, and for a number of people, the name Sunny's was under the heading. I put two and two together. It was like a needle in a haystack, though."

I rolled my eyes. "Okay. So who was listed under that heading?"

"Well, there was Darrin and some general information about him. Then there was the manager. The info on him said he'd been the manager for about three years and was married with two young kids. There was a note indicating that the younger child might have been autistic. The wife was a schoolteacher, and his in-laws lived with them. Evidently the in-laws had lost their house, and there was some type of immigration scuttlebutt around them as well."

"Holy crap. What do we make of that?"

Doob shrugged. "Don't know. Like you said last night, she was obviously compiling all of this info for a reason."

"What else?"

"She also had some notes about a dishwasher who appeared to be getting paid under the table and who was covered in tattoos. He took the bus to work every day, and she thought he might be living in a halfway house."

I was impressed with Doob's powers of recall. I would definitely have to be looking at the computer if the roles were reversed.

"Is that it?"

He held up a finger. "Getting there. There were some notes about a waitress who Brenda thought might be selling drugs and/or sexual favors on the side. She'd also made a note to find out if the girl was a runaway. Her name was Josie or something like that, and Brenda thought she might be under eighteen years old.

"Anything else?"

"The last thing she'd listed was a blurb about that lady you met, Melanie."

"What did it say?"

"All it said was that she was an orphan and she'd spent some time as a stripper."

"A stripper?" That surprised me. Melanie didn't seem the type, but I didn't know any strippers, so who was I to say?

"That's what it says. Stripper and an orphan."

"Hunh. Melanie told me her parents died when she was a kid and that she then bounced around the southwest."

"That sucks," Doob said.

"It does," I agreed. "But why would Brenda have notes on all of these people from Sunny's? What do they all have to do with the Ramirez people? Does one of them work for both Sunny's and Ramirez? That doesn't seem likely."

"Meg, your head is going to spin off. I will go get my laptop and see if I can find a connection. In the meantime, why don't you organize the three-foot behemoth of paperwork you've piled up? We'll find something."

Doob brought his laptop over to the apartment and started clicking away as soon as we sat down. I stared at my pile of paperwork, and for the millionth time, I went through all of it and made sticky notes of the things that still didn't make sense. I passed the notes to Doob, and he'd stop clicking just long enough to read what I'd written, grunt, and then continue on.

We didn't speak for over two hours, and finally Doob stretched his hands over his head and cocked his neck from side to side. I raised my eyebrows as I watched him. He looked content.

"Did you find something?"

He shrugged. "I think so. You're going to prison."

CHAPTER 27

"Ummmm, Doob, you know I'd go to hell and back for you, but prison is out of the question. That's definitely not on my bucket list."

He smirked. "Where's your sense of adventure, Meg?"

"Cute, Doob. The big house is somewhere I have no intention of going. I do not look good in stripes, and I'm too little to fend off some of those beefy chicks who are mad at the world."

"Well, what about a men's prison?"

I raised my eyebrows at him further. "You want me to go to a *men's* prison? Oh, well why didn't you say so? That's so much better."

"Not forever, Meg. Just for a visit."

"And why in God's name would I go to a men's prison?"

"To visit Bobby's dad."

I narrowed my eyes as I tried to follow what in the world Doob was getting at. "Bobby's dad? What does he have to do with anything?"

"I'm not sure he has anything to do with anything, but I do think he was one of the last people to see Carol."

"Okay, lay it on me." I waggled the fingers on both of my hands towards myself.

Doob cracked his knuckles like a concert pianist before a big show and leaned back in his chair. When he is in his element, he doesn't mind being the center of attention.

"Here's the deal. Carol and Bobby were married for a few years, but she never updated her driver's license with her new last name. She was Carol McBride on their mortgage and other bills, but she left her license in the name of Smith."

"Hunh. I wonder why."

Doob rolled his eyes. "Have you ever been to a DMV Meg? My God, why would she do that to herself? She probably plans to update it when her renewal comes up, which is next year, by the way."

"Okay, so her license is still Carol Smith." I thought about that for a second. "So what?"

"Well, as we've talked about, it didn't seem like the authorities got too uptight about her as a missing person. They never came up with any leads, and since Bobby had flown the coop, evidently no one beyond Glenn was around to push them to find her."

That seemed awfully sad to me. "Didn't she have any family in the area?"

"Well, if she did, no one was barking loudly enough for her to stay in the public eye. There were only those initial two articles. I can do some more digging, but you can imagine the number of Smiths I'm going to come across."

I nodded. "Okay, but you still haven't told me why I should care about her keeping her license in her maiden name."

"Because there was a Carol Smith on a flight out of West Palm Beach to Boston on the night Carol supposedly disappeared."

"And the cops missed this?" I asked.

"Probably because they were looking for Carol McBride. That is, if they were looking at all."

I raised an eyebrow. "Doob, I'm thinking there are a lot of airlines that fly out of West Palm. You're good, but there's no way you hacked into every airline to check this out. No way."

Doob waved his white napkin in the air. "I surrender, Meg. But I do have a friend who lives in Port St. Lucie, which is about forty minutes north of West Palm, and she happens to work for Sky Blue Airlines."

"Love them! They have the little televisions in the backs of their seats, and they don't charge for luggage."

"Calm yourself. Anyway, I emailed her and asked if she could do an old friend a favor, and I had the answer within an hour."

"Couldn't that get her in trouble at the airline?"

He shrugged. "I doubt it. Carol didn't fly on Sky Blue. My friend got the answer from yet another friend at yet another airline."

"Why would she go to that trouble?"

"Meg, she survived a semester of advanced programming in high school because of me. She didn't mind doing the Doobmeister this one little favor."

I grinned. "The Doobmeister? Is that what she calls you?"

He instantly turned a million shades of purple. "It was just a silly high school nickname, Meg." He started fiddling with a hangnail that apparently had become quite interesting to him.

I laughed out loud. "Yes, you've clearly outgrown silly nicknames, haven't you *Doob?*"

"Anyway, my Sarcastic Sleuthette, Carol arrived in Boston just before that first article was written. It was back in September."

"But Bobby was in Santa Barbara by then. California. West." I used my arm to make a big arc. "Nowhere near Boston, my friend."

"Hear me out, please. Bobby was originally from Boston, but Carol was a Florida girl. So I tried to get into her head."

"This should be good."

"You'll apologize when I'm done," Doob continued. "Bobby had up and left her when he'd found out she was on the cheating side of town, and she'd had no luck finding him."

I butted in. "So she came to Boston to see if he'd returned to his old stomping grounds!" I was quite proud of myself.

Doob circled his head in kind of a figure-eight gesture. "Well, I thought about that, and she probably did try to track him down through his old friends. I'm sure she had some names and contact numbers in Boston that she called before she hopped a plane up here."

"Okay, so if we go with that theory, then she evidently didn't have any luck over the phone."

"Exactly. So if we try to think like Carol, maybe she'd rethought her relationship with Glenn-the-psycho. Maybe she was desperate to find Bobby because of the money, but she also wanted to get away from Glenn. She probably wanted to reconnect with her hubby, make amends, and damn well make sure she was still getting that million bucks."

I circled my hand to tell him to keep going.

"I think she came up here to see Bobby's father."

"You're gonna need to convince me, please."

"It makes sense. She wasn't having any luck with Bobby's friends, and she probably thought a plea to his dad might do the trick."

"But Bobby's dad is in prison. He's been in prison for . . . well, forever."

"I'm aware, Meg."

"So why wouldn't she have just called him to find out what she wanted to know? Why would she have hopped a plane for a possible dead end?"

"Because the dad was family and because she was desperate. Plus, she probably decided that an in-person visit was the only way to go."

"Why's that?"

"Think about it, Meg. Do you think a guy in prison is just going to spill his guts about his son to some girl who he's never met, even if it was Bobby's wife? Especially a cheating wife? Over the phone, he wouldn't have even been able to verify who she was. Further, did the dad know where Bobby was, and did he know that Bobby was sick? I can see why Carol would make a face-to-face visit for lots of reasons."

I mulled it over. "Okay, Doob, I'll buy into that for a second. But why in the world does that mean *I* have to go to prison?"

"You need to find out if Carol visited him. You need to go look this guy in the eye and find out what he knows."

I twisted up my mouth while I thought about it. "You know what's weird about this?"

"Besides everything?"

"What's weird is she seemed to come up here on her own. She took a flight, probably stayed in the Boston area for a day or two and also probably visited Vic. All of that takes planning. So why didn't Glenn know about it?"

Doob cocked his head. "What do you mean?"

"Well, according to the articles, Glenn wasn't a person of interest in Carol's disappearance, and he seemed to be looking for her as well. But the Zales account would imply they were close to being engaged or, at the very least, they were in a serious relationship. If that was the case, why wouldn't Glenn know of her plans? Why did she just take off without telling him?"

Doob mulled that over. "It's like I said a minute ago. Maybe Carol finally realized he was nuts and just took off."

"But what about the Zales card?"

Doob shrugged. "Maybe it was just some type of grand gesture. If they were on the outs, he was probably scrambling to keep his sugar mama close by. He'd get down on bended knee, hold the ring up, and ask her, and her million dollars, to marry him."

I thought about that for a little bit. "That's probably true. She'd obviously thought it out, and Glenn's recent behavior would indicate that he knew nothing of her plans. What I don't get is this—was Glenn really stupid enough to continue to chase after the money when there's been no sign of Carol for months? He had no claim to it whatsoever. And it still doesn't explain why he didn't ask about Carol when he threatened me."

Doob smiled. "Meg, you're thinking logically. This guy was probably cranked up on steroids twenty-four, seven. He was fired from being a cop because of drugs and a sixteen-year-old girl. He basically told Darrin in Los Angeles that he'd kill him, and then he drove across the country to threaten everyone in your family, including this guy right here." He reached down and ruffled Sampson's ears. "What we need to focus on is what happened to Carol."

I stared into his determined eyes and sighed. "I'm going to prison."

Doob beamed. "That's my girl!"

I spent the next hour or so learning a whole lot more about prison procedure than I would have liked to. It's not as easy as picking up the phone and asking for Prisoner #1234, unfortunately. It involves having to get on an approved list and a bunch of other bureaucratic necessities. In the end, I jumped through all of the hoops I needed to and then hoped Vic McBride would call me at his earliest convenience. I wanted to at least speak with him before I sauntered into the prison to discuss his murdered son.

In the meantime, I decided to concentrate on the information LaKeisha had sent me, and that meant a phone call to get some answers.

CHAPTER 28

He sounded out of breath when he picked up the phone.

"Hi Darrin, it's Meagan."

"Hey Meagan, I was just getting in. How's it going?"

"Okay, thanks. How are things with you?"

"Great, I got a bartending job at my buddy's place on Boylston Street that I told you about. I've been there a few days, and it's awesome. You'll have to come down tomorrow for St. Patty's Day. The first one's on me."

"I will do that, thanks. Hey, if you have a minute, I need to speak with you about a couple of things."

"Are they good things?" He sounded lighthearted.

"No." I didn't sound lighthearted.

There was a momentary silence on the other end. "Okay, what's up?"

I relayed the discussion I'd had with LaKeisha and heard him gasp when I told him Brenda had been murdered.

"Darrin, I'm sorry. Are you okay?"

"I just can't believe it." He sounded choked up.

"I know, it's awful. Since she was Bobby's broker, I was thinking you might have known her?"

"Yeah, he introduced us. We actually went out a couple of times, but nothing really ever came of it. I didn't exactly meet the income requirements she wanted in a guy. But still, she was a good kid. I can't believe she's dead."

"I'm so sorry. This must be quite a shock."

"Do they have any suspects?"

"From what the papers are saying, it doesn't sound like they're close to arresting anyone. I have an associate working on it, and we're trying to find out all we can."

I was met with more silence and felt incredibly guilty about delivering the bad news of Brenda's death.

"Darrin?"

"Yeah, I'm here. I'm just stunned." He sounded like the wind had been knocked out of him.

"I'm sure you are. It's weird that this situation is resurfacing, and I want to help."

"I wonder if it's that freak who was chasing me around in L.A., the same guy who confronted you the other day," Darrin suggested.

"So David filled you in on that?"

"Yeah, David called me from work and told me to be on the lookout. I didn't leave the apartment the entire day."

"Well, I thought it was that guy, too. The problem with that, though, is his body washed up in Boston Harbor on Friday morning, so no one will be talking to him now."

"What?" Darrin yelped.

I wished I could see his face. "Yep, it was in yesterday's paper, but we saw it online Friday afternoon."

"My God."

"And that's not all. To top it off, Carol is missing."

"Who?"

"Carol. Bobby's ex-wife. She's been missing for months, and no one seems to know where she's at. Meanwhile, the freak washes up right here in our backyard, so it's an understatement to say things are getting stranger by the minute. There are bodies piling up on both coasts, and it's a little scary."

"Holy shit." Darrin's voice was barely a whisper.

"You can say that again. Listen, Darrin, do you know anyone who might have wanted to kill Brenda?"

"Why would I?" He sounded defensive.

"Well, since you knew her, I just wondered if she ever said anything about being scared or followed or threatened by someone. Anything at all?"

"I think I'd remember that, Meagan. That never happened. How do you know it's related to Bobby or Roy anyway?"

"I don't. But Brenda arranged for LaKeisha and Roy to receive some information after her murder, and the contents of that package indicate that her death and the viatical policies might be related."

I was met with even more silence, so instead of my usual routine, I just kept talking. "There's another person that might be connected to all of this as well. Does the name Vince mean anything to you?"

There was a bubble of silence on the other end.

"Darrin?"

I could barely hear him. "Yeah, it does."

"Who is he?"

"He's kind of a ghost."

"Not a great answer, Darrin. That's not going to make this case easier to solve. Whoever he is, he might have had something to do with all of this."

"Why do you say that?" Darrin's voice was shaking.

"Because LaKeisha's package had a flash drive and some pictures in it, and Vince was the star attraction. She's mailing it all to me so I can give it to *you*." I didn't mention I'd already seen the contents. I wasn't in full disclosure mode at the moment.

"To me? What for?"

"That's kind of what I'd like to know. Is there anything you've maybe forgotten to share with me?"

"Forgotten?"

"Uh, yeah, forgotten."

"Like what?"

"Oh, I dunno. Think hard." *Like twenty thousand dollars.*

When Darrin spoke, his speech was very measured. "I'm not sure what you're getting at, Meagan, but I don't like your tone. I don't know what to think about this any more than you do, other than it's all pretty fucking scary."

"I couldn't agree more. So who's Vince?"

Darrin sighed loudly but didn't respond.

My voice went up an octave. "Darrin, who is Vince?!"

"Calm down, Meagan. Jesus, what a mess."

"I really don't want to ask you again, Darrin."

"I don't know! He's this guy who was kind of tied up in the whole thing, but I swear to God, I don't know how to find him. He contacted me."

"Contacted you for what *exactly*?"

"It's not what you think, Meagan."

"Really? Well, what I *think*—no check that—what I *know* is you're not telling me everything. What I also *know* is you came into twenty thousand dollars shortly before Bobby was murdered."

"How the hell do you—"

"It doesn't matter how I found out. The fact is you're knee deep in this, and I want some answers."

"Meagan, I'm going to hang up if you continue with this bullshit. I've told the cops everything I know, so who the hell do you think you are? You're some two-bit detective who found me in California and probably overcharged my brother for doing it. Big fucking whoop. At the end of the day, I didn't hurt anyone, and I certainly don't answer to you." His voice had grown increasingly louder, and he sounded absolutely furious.

"And I don't answer to you either, Darrin. I'm going to get to the bottom of this, and I don't give two shits if you end up being guilty as sin. I told your brother that on the day I met him, and I won't even overcharge him for getting you put away."

I heard him scoff. "Are you for real? I can't believe you think that I had something to do with Bobby's murder."

"Well, call me crazy. I'm just wondering why a dead girl would send LaKeisha a package and why the freak is now dead and why the ex-wife is missing and why this so-called ghost is suddenly involved and why you never bothered to mention him. Oh, and then there's this issue of another twenty thousand dollars, on top of the fifty you received after Bobby was *murdered*! I'm just trying to sort it all out. So forgive me for asking some questions, and forgive me for giving a shit. The poor kid was supposedly your friend, but maybe you're just a really good actor after all."

"Meagan, you're so far out of fucking line." I sensed that he was going to disconnect.

"Darrin, you can hang up on me, but we are going to finish this conversation. We can continue to exchange insults, or we can do this like adults. Your call. But rest assured, I will get to the bottom of this whole thing, with your help or without it."

There were crickets for about thirty seconds. I was surprised when I heard him sigh loudly and say, "I'll be working at the bar tomorrow night. You can come by if you want, and we can talk if I get a minute or two. You are pissing me off too much right now to continue this conversation."

"See you then," I said as the dial tone hit my ear. Meagan Maloney, Not-Very-Popular-Right-Now-Extraordinaire.

CHAPTER 29
MONDAY, MARCH 17TH

St. Patrick's Day had arrived in Boston, and that meant a lot of green clothes, green beer, but mostly just a general excuse to party it up. I'd invited Kayla to go along to the restaurant, thinking that having a third party might ease the tension between Darrin and me. I still wasn't sure if he was a good guy or a bad guy, so Kayla could double as my heavy. Additionally, she'd abruptly quit her job, and I wanted to hear about her plans for the future. Assuming she had any.

We met in front of the chic restaurant on Boylston Street around nine thirty that night. I wanted to get there a little after the dinner rush, hoping to get to chat with Darrin, but the bar area was still pretty packed. Gotta love Beantown on St. Pat's. We could see Darrin's head bobbing around as he worked the patrons at the long, mahogany bar. He had a pack of five female admirers along the far end, and he seemed to be having a good time despite the crazy pace of the place. There was also a pretty, blonde female bartender, and the two of them worked in tandem as if they'd been side-by-side for years.

Kayla and I scrunched our way through the crowd and hovered behind the people sitting at the bar, hoping that some of them would be getting tables for dinner fairly soon. We caught the pretty bartender's eye, and she whipped us up two margaritas while we waited for an open seat. To this point, Darrin hadn't seen us, or at least he was pretending he hadn't.

"He's hot!" Kayla yelped after getting a close-up of Darrin zipping down the bar with four beers in hand.

I was sipping my margarita with a straw and nodded in response.

"Does his brother look like that?" Kayla asked.

I finished my slurp and shook my head. "Not at all. They're stepbrothers, but they're both very good looking. David is tall, dark and handsome, and, well, you can see Darrin."

"Stout, blonde, and yummy! This night is shaping up to be all right." Kayla seemed happy for a recently unemployed person, and I was glad for that.

About midway through the margaritas, Darrin's five admirers were called to their table, and Kayla and I quickly maneuvered to grab two of the seats they'd left behind. One of the five lingered a bit longer than the others and scribbled something on a napkin. She handed it to Darrin and told him to call her anytime. Darrin smiled, folded it, and put it in his back pocket.

"Did you see that?" Kayla acted appalled. "What a slut!"

"Oh, good grief, Kayla. You just wish you'd done it first."

She smiled slyly. "You know me too well. But all I have to do is to figure out a way to get that number *out* of his pocket. That promises to be fun."

"If possible, why don't we let him finish his shift before you start removing his pants? I'd prefer to get kicked out *after* we eat. I'm starving."

"Well, he's pissed at you anyway. How is taking his pants off going to do any more harm?"

I'd filled Kayla in on most of the situation when I called to invite her out for the night. I turned my barstool to face her and did my best to be firm. "He definitely is pissed at me, Kayla, but I need him to *not* be pissed. Part of the reason you are here is to be charming and funny and to help get me back on his good side. He knows more about this whole mess than he's letting on, and I can't just ignore that."

From the corner of my eye, I saw Darrin approaching us. He gave a tight smile and a little nod. I lit up like a lighthouse and acted as if I was never happier to see anyone. Before I could get a word out, Kayla was on the move. She reached across the bar to shake his hand and managed to toss her soft blonde hair in the process.

"I'm Meagan's friend Kayla, and I love those pants," she cooed. Darrin's eyebrows knitted a bit, but he smiled slightly as he looked over at me.

"They are great pants," I nodded vigorously.

Darrin peered at us like we both had two heads. "Uh huh. Nice to meet you, Kayla. Are you ladies ready for another round?"

I thought we should get some food in our systems. "We'll actually take menus—"

"Yes, we'd love another round," Kayla cut me off with her shut-the-hell-up face. "We'll eat later."

I leaned across the bar towards him. "If we start asking for bus, train, or airplane schedules, please stop us."

Darrin grinned. "Two more margaritas and two menus coming up." We both watched him walk off, and Kayla whistled softly.

"Really nice pants."

"Would you please go hose yourself off?"

Kayla sucked on her lime. "Why should I? You're being a total buzz-kill, so please tell me what's up your ass."

I pulled a face. "Nothing is up my ass. I just need to get a little bit of work done tonight, so please help me."

Her eyes glanced at my near empty glass. "How nice that you can *work* while drinking tequila. I'm signing up to be a private dick just like you. How do I get a dick license?" Her voice carried to the next county, and a couple of guys just down the bar leaned over to look at us. Kayla made kissy faces at the leering men and then looked at me and stuck her tongue out.

Shortly thereafter, I convinced Kayla to order some food, and we had calamari and scallops to kick off the dinner. After that, we both went with the salmon and asparagus. There are few things in life as good as seafood in Boston.

Once we had some food in our bellies, I had to get to the task at hand. "Kayla, the whole evening is on me if you will help me out with Darrin."

"Meagan, I have enough money saved to get me by for a long time, so spare me the pity bullshit."

"It's not pity. It's showing my appreciation for you buttering him up."

"Baby, I'll slather butter all over him if that's what it takes."

"Kayla! I'm serious."

She bounced her finger off of my nose. "And that, my dear Meagan, is exactly your problem. Lighten up. We'll get your precious info, but we're also going to have a little fun with what's left of the night. I am so sick of ending up in my own bed. I think we should steal a Duck Boat later."

Good grief. Duck Boats are essentially double-decker-bus-type-vehicles for tourists. They drive all over the city and see the many cool historical sites in Boston, and then they proceed right into the water, scaring some of the passengers shitless. They float around and then hit the streets again. Attempting to steal a Duck Boat with Kayla would result in nothing but disaster.

"I think we should save that for a night when it's a little bit warmer, don't you agree?"

She scrunched her face. "Yeah, probably. I'm not exactly dressed for it anyway. My who-haa would get cold." She pointed at her crotch, emphasizing the miniskirt that wasn't covering much of her nether regions.

I had to change the subject. "The info I need is on this smoking hot biker guy named Vince. He might be single, I'm not sure." I embellished a little bit to get her interested.

Kayla perked up. "Sweet! Is he coming?"

"No, he isn't, sorry. Darrin knew him back in California, and I'm thinking he's not the nicest guy in the world. I need Darrin to give me some dirt on Vince to see if it's tied in with Darrin's roommate's murder."

Kayla craned her neck down the bar. "Speaking of, where did Mr. Hot Pants go? We need our drinks."

I was getting discouraged. Plying Kayla with alcohol and thinking she could be helpful had been one of my dumber moves as of late. "Take it easy, he's getting our round. Kayla, this is important, so try to be charming."

"Hey, I'm as fucking charming as they come." Then she belched.

Before I could respond, Darrin slid up and plopped two jumbo margaritas in front of us.

"So who the hell is Vince?" Kayla barked before taking a giant slurp of her drink.

Darrin cocked his head and looked at me accusingly. "Isn't there some type of client-investigator confidentiality with your cases, Meagan?"

I felt my cheeks flush, and Kayla continued to bellow. "You're not her client. Your hot brother is the client, who she is somewhat in love with, by the way."

I put my head directly down on the bar and pretended to be invisible. Some type of sticky something attached itself to my forehead and hair, and I couldn't have cared less. When I lifted my head about thirty seconds later, Darrin was long gone. I glared at Kayla.

"What's your problem?" she snapped. "You wanted to know about this Vince guy, so I cut to the chase."

I put my hands in my hair, and they stuck there. I was a mess. "Kayla, what happened to buttering him up?"

She smiled alluringly. "That happens later. I'll get him all lathered in butter and marmalade if it's the last thing I do."

I rolled my eyes.

Darrin understandably avoided us for a while, and when he finally came back our way, he wouldn't make eye contact with me. "You ladies need another one, or should I get your check?" He seemed to emphasize the getting-the-check part.

Kayla's mouth opened, and I put my hand over it. "You need to go to the ladies room *right now*," I instructed. She downed her margarita and pointed at her empty glass before she flounced off her stool and headed toward the restrooms.

I turned to Darrin. "Darrin, I realize you're pissed at me, and I'm sorry. It's just that I know you have some information that might help the case, and maybe if we put our heads together, we could figure it out. Could we please talk about it sometime soon?"

"We can talk about it now," he said. He looked around and leaned across the bar towards me. "I've thought about nothing else since you called me about Brenda, and I'm pretty sure that I set up her murder."

I nearly swallowed my lime.

CHAPTER 30

"**D**arrin, elaborate now, please."

"Well, of course I don't mean that literally. I didn't do anything intentionally, but now that I've had time to think about it, I think Vince was involved in her death. And I think I inadvertently helped. And that makes me fucking sick to my stomach." He appeared sincere, and more importantly, he was opening up to me.

I looked around, and it seemed like things had slowed down a little bit. "Is there any chance you could take a quick break? I need a smoke."

Darrin looked shocked. "I didn't know you smoked."

I winced. "I do about three times a year, always when I'm drinking. And generally when multiple homicides dominate the conversation. So I would love to sneak outside and take a puff or two with you."

"Actually, my shift is over in a few minutes. The other bartender is closing, so if you will wait a few, we can go outside and light up." He walked down the length of the bar and said something to the pretty girl he was working with. They put their heads together in conversation, and then he looked up and nodded at me.

Without warning, Kayla appeared out of nowhere and jerked me off of my stool.

"We have to leave!"

"Take it easy, we will in a minute." I'd about had it with her.

"We have to leave right NOW, Meagan!" She yanked at my arm like a child and tried pulling me towards the door.

I planted my feet and put my hands on my hips. "Exactly what is the big hurry?" I demanded.

"Muffy Bingston is here, and she knows I slept with her boyfriend before they broke up. Her friends literally had to hold her back just now when I walked by. They said they'd give me a one-minute head start. We have to get out of here, or we're going to get our asses kicked."

"*We?* What did I do?"

"Guilt by association. Pay Mr. Hot Pants, and let's go!"

"I'm so glad I invited you tonight. Good grief." I flipped over the tab Darrin had placed in a glass in front of us and begrudgingly left a hundred and fifty dollars on the bar. Like I had that kind of money. Kayla beyond sucked as a date.

Darrin saw me put the money on the bar and came over to pick it up. "I'll cash this out and then we can go have that smoke."

Kayla reached over the bar and grabbed him by the shirt. "Screw the smoke, you're walking us back to Meagan's apartment."

CHAPTER 31
TUESDAY, MARCH 18TH

The next morning, I was proud that I once again woke up in my own bed after a night out with Kayla. While my head was a little fuzzy and my wallet was a lot lighter, I was happy that Duck Boats hadn't become a part of last night's festivities. We'd clearly reached a level of sophistication and maturity I would never have dreamed possible.

I shuffled into the kitchen to grab some orange juice before brushing my teeth, only to find a lump of blankets on Moira's oversized couch. The lump moved, and I saw Kayla pop her head out from one end of the couch. I smiled and then saw Darrin's head pop out from the other end of the couch. Oh.My.God. I knew Kayla was doing a sleepover but didn't know that Darrin had stayed as well. I'd told him last night that I'd call him to discuss Brenda. There'd been no point in even trying to talk about it with a drunken Kayla in our midst. Yet here he still was on the couch. Maybe I should have mentioned to Kayla that I hadn't *completely* ruled Darrin out as a murderer. Somehow I didn't think now was the appropriate time to share that little tidbit of information. As I considered both of them, they simultaneously covered their heads and resumed lump status.

Before I could react to that whole scene, Doobie and Sampson strolled out of Moira's bedroom. Doobie was rubbing his eye with one hand and was being pulled by Sampson with his leashed other hand. Sampson turned his head around and clamped his mouth securely on the leash, in a futile attempt to pull Doobie along a little bit quicker. Doobie's gravity defying hair had reached a record level, even for him, and I wondered if he'd ever actually looked in a mirror.

"Whassup Meg?"

"Hey, Doob, no Moira again last night?"

"Nope. I think she's in love."

I wrinkled my nose at the thought of tight-ass Porter becoming a member of the family. "Gross."

Doobie shrugged as if it didn't matter to him one way or the other. "Are you making breakfast?"

I ignored the question. "Hey, when did you get here last night?"

"Probably around three or four this morning. Why?"

"Was that lump there when you arrived?"

Doob stared at me blankly, and I gestured to the couch. He glanced at the blankets and looked confused.

"Is someone under there?"

"Yes, Doob, two someones actually. Please tell me they weren't in Moira's room at any point."

"Nope. Do you know them, or do I need to take action?"

"Take action? Are you going to sic your hair on them?"

"Sticks and stones, Meg. Seriously, do you know who's under there?"

"Of course I know. It's Kayla and a, uh, friend of ours."

Doob raised his eyebrows up and down several times. "She's the hot one with the filthy mouth, correct?"

I didn't know Doobie ever noticed hot girls. It was reassuring for some reason. "That's her. She came home with me, and Darrin sort of escorted us."

"Escorted you? Were you at the prom or something?"

"Very amusing, Doob. Kayla almost got us into a bar fight last night, so Darrin got stuck with bringing us home. I was so tired that I went straight to bed, but I told him I needed to speak with him today." I looked at the couch. "I guess he just decided to stay."

"I'd stay with her too!" Doob said excitedly.

I shook my head and smiled. "She'd kill you in five seconds, Doob."

Doob looked back at the lump on the couch. "Hey, wait a minute. *Darrin* is the other lump? Is he the guy you drove cross-country with who might have—"

I cut him off abruptly. "Who works at the bar we went to last night, Doob. Yes, it's *that* Darrin." I bulged my eyeballs at him, giving him the shut-the-hell-up look that Kayla had given me the night before.

Doob bulged his eyes back at me. "Oh, well, I'll be glad to meet him. I've heard so many *nice things* about him."

"By the way, you really need to stop sleeping in Sampson's bed. Something's not quite right with that."

Doob continued to stare at the couch. "Are they clothed?"

"God, I hope so. Moira will flip if any bodily anything shows up on that couch."

A muffled sound came from said couch, and I'm pretty sure it was Kayla, but I couldn't understand her. I walked over and pulled the cover down just enough to reveal her face.

"We're clothed," Kayla growled. "Are you going to make some fucking food or not?"

Doob smiled gleefully. "It's definitely the hot one. It sounds like that dirty mouth needs some food ASAP."

Evidently the apartment had been transformed into a bed and breakfast without my knowledge. Maybe that's why Moira never came home anymore. I tromped to the kitchen area and opened the fridge. I was surprisingly pleased with the contents. Doob must have made a trip to the grocery store recently. There were some definite benefits about having a trust fund baby next door.

"Eggs, sausage, bacon, a mixture of fruit, some orange juice, and some milk." I opened a container to find some type of mystery meat which smelled disgusting, and I threw the entire thing into the trash. I then moved on to one of the cupboards and continued my breakfast pitch. "Okay. In this corner, we have some Frosted Flakes, Cheerios, and I can make some quickie blueberry muffins. I've got some instant coffee, which I won't touch, but I'll make it for you guys. Who's in?"

Doobie raised his hand like a third grader, and Kayla followed suit. She lightly kicked Darrin to see if he was coherent and was rewarded with a loud fart. Nice. Sampson whined and pulled Doob closer to the door.

"That's a yes," Kayla said.

I pointed towards Darrin's lump. "Please show him to a bathroom immediately, preferably the one as far from the kitchen as possible. Breakfast will be served in twenty."

As promised, the air was filled with bacon grease and blueberry muffin smell in no time, and we all chowed down like we hadn't eaten in months. Kayla helped herself to a second plate, something I'd never seen in my life.

She was incredibly thin and didn't let her weight fluctuate more than two ounces either way.

After we all stuffed ourselves, I cleared the table while the three of them stared into space. Who needed kids with this crew? Once everything was back in order, I asked Darrin if we could talk for a little bit.

"I suppose Doobie and I are going to get kicked out?" Kayla chirped.

"Well, you did eat that whole second plate. Maybe you could take Sampson for a quick walk. We probably won't be long."

"If there's a God," Darrin muttered. I narrowed my eyes at him.

Doob and Sampson had both started shaking their hind ends when they heard the word *walk*, even though they'd gone outside just before breakfast. Doob started belting out the words to 'Shake Your Groove Thing' by Peaches and Herb as he and Sampson gyrated across the room.

Kayla rolled her eyes but smiled in spite of herself. "All right, but it's only because I had that second muffin. Those things are fan-fucking-tastic."

Ummmmmm. "Thanks?"

Doob and Kayla grabbed their coats while Sampson spun in circles by the door. He looked like a hairy black and white tornado. There's something about a happy dog that is a joy to behold.

When the door closed behind them, Darrin looked like he was about to face a firing squad. He put his elbows on the table and ran both hands through his hair.

"Do you want anything else to drink?" I asked, and he nodded.

"I'll have a little more coffee, thanks. With some Bailey's if you have it." I raised an eyebrow at him. "Kidding," he said grudgingly.

I refilled his cup and placed it in front of him on the table. His face was weary, and he looked extremely tired. I felt sorry for him but then wondered if I was sitting at my table with a killer. That should have terrified me, but it didn't for some reason.

"Okay, Darrin, time to fill in the blanks." I stared at him. I was back to my tactic of not speaking, and for once it actually worked on him. He licked his lips and started his story.

CHAPTER 32

"Like I told you when we met, Meagan, I did not have anything to do with Bobby's death. He was my *friend*, for God's sake. I identified his body—"

"I'm aware! We're sitting here because of what you *haven't* told me. Start talking."

He took a deep breath. "One of the things I didn't tell you was that I'd been approached by this guy, Vince, who was pretending to be some type of vigilante."

"*Excuse* me?"

"Yep. He was on a mission to get revenge against this drug lord in L.A. It was the guy I told you about that first day—the dude who bought Bobby's policy."

"You're talking about Alberto Ramirez?"

Darrin looked surprised. "So you're way ahead of me. Then do you need to hear this, or do you already know everything I'm going to say?"

"Believe me, I have no idea where you're going with this. So what did Vince know about Ramirez, and what did you have to do with it?"

"Well, since learning of Brenda's death, I've come up with a theory that I'm convinced is the way it went down. But first, I'm going to lay out the story for you as it happened to me."

"I can't wait," I said dryly.

Darrin sighed. "It started one afternoon when I noticed this guy at the restaurant. He'd spent the whole day at the bar, but he didn't have more than two beers the entire time. He seemed a little *off*, kind of bizarre. It wasn't so much how he looked, although he was trying hard to look ultra-tough. He was decked out in this all-black, rugged getup. He had a beat up leather jacket with studs, scuffed up cowboy boots, long hair and some tats. But you see all kinds of shit in L.A., so that didn't faze me. It was more that I could tell he was there to start some shit. Every time I turned to look at him, he was glaring at me."

"So what'd you do?"

"It was getting near the end of my shift, and I was pretty fed up with his whole tough guy act. So I poured him a beer, put it in front of him and asked if there was a problem. I was hoping that if I went on the offensive he might back down a little, but he didn't miss a beat. He said that we definitely had a problem. Hell if I knew what, but at least we were making progress."

"So then what?"

"Well, there was an open booth towards the back of the bar, and I suggested that we take our conversation back there. When he got up, I told Melanie and the manager to keep an eye on us.

"So I joined him at the booth, and he got right to it. He said 'I know what you're up to, and I'm not going to let you kill your roommate.'"

"*What?!*"

"Yeah, exactly. I asked him what in the heck he was talking about, and he repeated his accusation. I told him he was out of his mind and slid out of the booth to leave. I figured he'd just escaped a loony bin or something."

"I take it you didn't leave, though?"

"No, when I stood up and started to walk off, he grabbed my wrist. He said he knew that they gave me the money to kill Bobby."

"Who is *they*? What money? The fifty thousand? Or the twenty thousand? Or was there more money?" Could there *be* more money? Good grief.

Darrin patted his hands down towards the table. "Slow down, I'm getting there. So this guy had a vice grip on my wrist, and I'll never forget the look in his eye or what he said next. He said 'Someone is going to be paid a lot of money to kill your roommate. If you're not in on it, then sit back down so that you can help me protect him.'"

"Did you believe him?"

"I didn't know what to believe. I shook his hold off my wrist and sat back down. Then we just glared at each other for a minute and cooled off."

"Then what?"

"Well, a few things. Number one, Vince told me this story about his brother, Pete. Number two, he showed me some pictures of myself and a

Ramirez goon chatting it up. And number three, he told me he knew that I'd just come into twenty thousand dollars."

I erupted. "You were with a Ramirez goon?!"

Darrin nodded. "Meagan, that was part of their plan. Yes, they had pictures of me with a Ramirez goon, but I can explain."

I threw my hands up. "This should be great. I think I will get that Bailey's." I got up and rummaged through the cupboard above the stove and came back with the liqueur, the coffee pot, and an empty cup.

He looked at me quizzically. "You said you won't drink instant coffee."

I shrugged. "Desperate times." I poured myself a little coffee, a lot of Bailey's, and then handed the bottle to Darrin.

Darrin added the dark liquid to his coffee, took a sip, and sighed. "Much better. Okay, I'm going to tell you things in the order that Vince laid them out to me. I'll get to the goon, I promise."

"Okay."

"So Vince told me this story about his brother who did one of those viatical policies and died of a supposed suicide. Ramirez was the investor behind Pete's policy, and Vince and Pete's widow were convinced that Ramirez was behind the so-called suicide."

"Why?"

"Because Pete's wife was expecting a baby, and Pete wanted more than anything to see his kid before he died. Vince said that there was no way that Pete would have abandoned his unborn child; he wouldn't have wanted the kid growing up thinking his dad had deserted him."

"Where was Ramirez when this alleged suicide occurred?"

"Basking in the sun in Miami, with about 100 witnesses."

"So he hired someone," I stated.

"Obviously. And since it was deemed a suicide, there was no real investigation. That didn't sit well with Vince, so he took it upon himself to make Ramirez pay for his brother's death. Vince had some rental properties in L.A. and didn't really have to work, so he dedicated himself to getting even with Ramirez."

"Why didn't he just go to the cops?"

"He said that he had, and they'd told him they were doing everything they legally could. The cops had been watching Ramirez for years on some other issues, and from the sounds of things, the feds were working a case against him as well. But to that point, no one had been able to bring a case against him that would stick."

I sighed. "Okay, so what about you and the goon?"

"On to the goon. As I've indicated, Vince was manic about making Ramirez pay dearly. Vince knew where he lived, where he dined, which cars he drove on which day, who serviced those cars, what tailor he used, what drycleaner he used, what day which particular maid or butler was off, the bodyguards' schedules, what supermarket his staff shopped at, the works. Vince could probably write a book on the inner workings of the Ramirez empire."

"And they never caught him lurking around?"

"Evidently not. It's not like he sat outside the iron gate at the compound. According to him, he was always nearby, in a café or on a street bench, and he latched on to one of the bodyguards early on."

"What do you mean?"

"Well, this one thug of a bodyguard looked really familiar to Vince, and he could never pinpoint exactly when they'd crossed paths, but he was convinced he must have seen the guy when Ramirez had set his sights on Pete."

"Vince thinks that particular guy might have killed Pete?"

"He didn't know for sure, but he was convinced the guy was following Pete around shortly before he died."

"Why would the guy have been following him?"

"Probably to monitor Pete's routine, figure out his habits, that type of shit. The Ramirez guy was basically trying to determine the best time and place to kill Pete."

"That's quite an assignment. So Vince followed this thug around when the thug wasn't playing bodyguard?"

"Exactly. Vince got to know the shifts and could predict them like clockwork. He figured out the guy's schedule, which didn't involve much more than going to the gym, pumping himself with steroids and bedding down several different women a few times a month. He seemed to have two or three regulars. When they weren't around, he'd get a high price hooker, an escort, whatever they're called these days."

"I still don't see where you come into this picture."

He suddenly looked a little sheepish. "Well, Vince happened to have some pictures of me talking with the Ramirez bodyguard he'd been following around."

I rolled my eyes. "Here we go."

"It's not what you think. The goon was just a customer at the restaurant. He'd come in for lunch about four or five days in a row, but I didn't know who he was. Since he'd gone to the restaurant on so many consecutive days, Vince got suspicious and took a few pictures of us talking. He knew the Ramirez lackey, but he didn't know who I was, so he conducted a background search on me, along with some of the other people who worked at the restaurant."

I thought of Brenda's spreadsheet with all of the names. "How did he do a background search?"

Darrin smirked. "Two-bit detectives aren't the only people who can do background searches, Meagan. Once Vince zoomed in on the restaurant, he had some help from a buddy. The guy is a computer programmer and evidently a bit of a hacker."

I smiled. "I know the type. Go on."

"So anyway, the computer dude did a little hacking and found out where I lived, who I lived with, where I worked, yada yada. He discovered that I'd come into some money—"

"*Some* money? Meaning the twenty thousand dollars?"

He nodded. "Yep."

I folded my arms across my chest. "Let's get to that right now. Where'd you get the money?"

He sighed deeply and looked down. "Unfortunately, L.A. isn't too far from Vegas, and it's an easy trip to make on a weekend. I'd made a few runs out there and got myself in a bit of a jam. I'd taken a bunch of cash advances out on my credit cards, and I had two that were completely maxed out."

"To the tune of twenty grand?"

He nodded but didn't say anything.

"Good grief," I exhaled.

"I know, I know. But I told Bobby I'd fucked up, and he gave me the money to pay off my credit cards. He made me promise I was done with the whole Vegas scene, and I told him I was, and I meant it. I never went back, and I'll never gamble again. I wouldn't do that to Bobby's memory." His chin wobbled a little, but I was determined to keep him focused.

"Okay, back to the computer dude and Vince, please."

He took a breath. "So after a little more digging, Vince found out that Bobby was involved in a viatical situation. He knew all about those because of Pete, so he put two and two together and approached me." Darrin spread out his hands as if that explained everything.

"Approached you about what?"

"He'd concluded I was going to kill Bobby."

"What? Why?"

"Try to stay with me, Meg. Vince's computer guy found out that I'd recently paid off quite a bit of debt, just like you uncovered." He cocked his head. "By the way, how did you find that? You don't strike me as a computer geek."

I didn't know if I should be flattered or insulted. I went for indignant. "Oh yeah? Why's that?"

Darrin smiled. "Oh, gee, I don't know. Maybe because the bill you sent to David was handwritten on what looked like a diner slip."

I felt my cheeks redden. "It's part of my charm as a two-bit detective."

"So how'd you get the dirt on me?"

I gave him a coy look. "I have my own computer geek. You just had breakfast with him." I gestured towards Doobie's empty chair.

Darrin nodded in understanding. "Those guys will get you every time. I should have been nicer to them in high school."

"We all should have. So let me see if I've got this straight. Vince was on a mission to get Ramirez, and he followed Ramirez's familiar-looking-goon to the restaurant. When it seemed that the goon might be up to something sketchy, Vince did some digging, found out about Bobby's situation, and further found out that you'd come into a good chunk of change. He assumed that the chunk of change meant that you accepted an upfront payment as a hit man. Does that sum it up?"

"Pretty much," Darrin said.

"So if Vince was that certain you were going to kill Bobby, then it was pretty ballsy of him to approach you at the restaurant."

"You don't know Vince. If you look up ballsy in Webster's, his picture is right beside it."

"So what did he want from you?"

"He said that if I really *wasn't* going to kill Bobby, then he wanted my help in bringing Ramirez down."

I barked out a laugh. "So the cops and the feds hadn't put Ramirez away, but Vince thought you two mighty crime fighters could manage?

That's cute. And what was Vince's master plan once you two super heroes caught Ramirez with the smoking gun?"

Darrin looked down. "I don't know."

I raised an eyebrow. "Bullshit."

His head stayed down, but his eyes moved up to look directly at me. His voice was stern. "Okay, so it's not too hard to figure out what he was planning. But he never specifically told me what he was going to do. And if those guys were out to get Bobby, then I wasn't going to stand in Vince's way." Darrin's chin jutted out as if to challenge me.

I rubbed my forehead and decided not to argue with him.

"Plus, there's something else," he said, his voice dropping a notch.

I sighed. "Of course there is."

"One of the women the goon was wining and dining was Brenda Alvarez."

Holy shit. "The same Brenda you dated? The same Brenda who was the broker for these policies? The same Brenda who's now dead?"

He blew out a huge breath. "That Brenda."

"My God."

"I know; it's all an intertwined mess. But anyway, Vince was convinced that Brenda was in on everything with all of the viatical policies."

"How so?

"She'd tell the goon what she knew about her clients. Things like their lifestyles, habits, whatever. Vince thought she helped Ramirez target certain people to kill."

"Holy cow. You went out with her. Did she seem that ruthless to you?"

"No, but we weren't all that close. At least not in the dating sense. We only grabbed dinner a few times, and it didn't turn into anything at all. She was totally hot, but she was very materialistic and high maintenance, and that's a complete turnoff to me. That being said, what Vince was saying about her was hard to believe."

"Well, her uncle works for Ramirez. He could have introduced her to the bodyguard and they got together. Or maybe they were just all insane lackeys who were part of the messed up inner workings of the Ramirez machine."

"Could be, I dunno."

"So what would make her tell the goon to recruit you as a potential hit man, assassin, whatever?" Was I really having this conversation?

Darrin leaned back in his chair and looked up at the ceiling. "Well,

Brenda knew that I never had any money. Vince thought that she'd already told the goon to check me out, and that's why he'd visited me at the restaurant. So Vince and I took it a step further and kind of came up with a plan."

"Kind of? What exactly does that mean?"

Darrin sighed loudly. "We set Brenda up."

I shook my head vigorously. "Please tell me I heard that incorrectly."

"Sorry, no. Vince thought that my relationship with Brenda seemed to be central to the whole thing."

"How so?"

"He said the Ramirez crew always found someone to do their dirty work for them, just like they did with Pete."

"Rule number one in the crime syndicate book, I believe."

"Yep, they'd find some loser who had a crack habit or who was cheating on his wife or who had gambling debts. They'd exploit the guy's weakness—show him pictures or threaten him or whatever. Once the guy agreed to take care of things, it was on."

"By 'take care of', you mean that the guy would do their killing for them?"

Darrin nodded. "Exactly. That way, they would make sure they were out in public when these things went down, and they'd all have alibis from here to Sunday."

I frowned. "Weren't they worried that the loser would talk if he ever got caught?"

"Not really. These guys operate in dark alleys and pay phones. They disguise themselves and then put hoods over people's heads and drive them to unknown locations. Even if someone they hired got caught, the person wouldn't know their names, their whereabouts or anything. They're pros, and the people they hire are desperate."

"So what did you do?"

His cheeks reddened. "I pretended to be one of those desperate people."

"How?"

"Um, well, we essentially decided to use me as bait."

"I am soooooooo not liking the sound of this."

"I was a little leery at first, too, but Vince made it sound so easy. He just wanted me to have a simple conversation with Brenda and work in the fact that I was in some dire straits financially. He said to also drop a hint or two that Bobby had been kind of a pain in the ass lately." Darrin pursed his lips and then rubbed the fingers of his left hand between his eyebrows. That caught my attention.

"Are you a southpaw? A lefty?"

Darrin rolled his eyes. "I know what a southpaw is, Meagan."

"So you've seen the *Rocky* movies?" I sprang out of my chair and started shadow boxing around the room. I hummed the music from *Rocky I* while doing my fancy moves and was thinking the whole thing was fairly impressive. Except for the fact that I was wheezing in a matter of seconds.

Darrin wasn't amused. "You're not going to have a stroke, are you?"

I scowled at him but realized it was possible. I sat back down to catch my breath.

"Okay, so to get back to it," I summed, "you were already a candidate for hit-man-of-the-month because the thug was checking you out. So what Vince proposed was that you should test Brenda to see if she would pass along some *new* information to officially get you the job, correct?"

"Exactly," Darrin said briskly. "I called Brenda and met her for the last dinner we had together. We met at Sunny's, as I said I couldn't afford anything else. I spent most of the dinner telling her how I owed a lot of money to some pretty shady guys in Vegas. I tried to act scared and preoccupied, which wasn't difficult, given the circumstances. I also worked in something to the effect that being around Bobby was pretty depressing." He paused for a minute. "I felt horrible saying that. He was anything but depressing, but I had to see what would happen."

"Did it work?"

He shrugged. "Well, that's what I don't know."

"What do you mean? What happened?"

"Well, the day after I had dinner with Brenda, the goon showed up at the restaurant. I was positive he was going to ask me to meet him somewhere later to discuss Bobby's situation."

I scowled. "Are you shitting me? I can't believe none of this has come up before now."

He didn't bother with a rebuttal. "But here's the deal—he didn't ask me for a thing. He ate his meal, had a couple of beers and went on his merry way. If it hadn't been for Vince telling me about him, he would have been like any other repeat customer, just a guy coming in for a burger."

"Did you ever see him again after that?"

"Nope. That was the last I ever saw of him."

"You're sure? Completely positive?"

He gave me an exasperated look. "Yes, Meagan, I'm sure. Believe me, I'd remember him."

"What did Vince have to say about the guy *not* soliciting you?"

"Well, that's where it gets weirder. It was odd enough that the goon came and went without asking me to do anything. But what was stranger was that Vince didn't even bother to find out what happened. He didn't stop by the restaurant, didn't call me, nothing. He just vanished. At first, I was scared something had happened to him."

"But?"

"Well, on the day I met Vince, he'd scribbled his name and phone number on a napkin from the restaurant. So I dug out the napkin and called the number, and it had been disconnected with no forwarding information."

"That seems a little peculiar."

"Yeah, I thought so, too. And another thing that was curious was he didn't put a last name on the napkin. Just the name *Vince* with the disconnected phone number. So I conveniently had no way of contacting him."

"Well, maybe the Ramirez guys caught onto him somehow and he got spooked. Maybe he dumped his phone and just disappeared for a while."

"I thought about that, too, but the lack of a last name really bothered me. So the first thing I did was to go into one of those websites where you can do the reverse phone number to see if I could get Vince's last name."

"So what did you find out?"

"Nothing."

I rolled my eyes. "That's helpful."

"I know. It was irritating. But then I remembered the manager at the restaurant had a sister who worked for the phone company."

"Ah ha, the old sister-at-the-phone-company routine. Works every time."

Darrin nodded. "So I spoke with her, and the number had been disconnected for over a month, and when it was an active number, it was a pawn shop."

I cocked my head. "So it was a bum number when Vince gave it to you?"

"Yep. And I just couldn't figure out why."

I mulled that over. "So the guy shows up out of nowhere, sells you a bill of goods about a brother who may or may not have existed, gets you to feed Brenda a bullshit story, and then disappears?"

"That about covers it."

I drummed my fingers on the table. "Why?"

"Well, I certainly wondered why at the time, but I couldn't piece it together. But now that Brenda is dead, I think I know what was going on. If she'd been working *with* Ramirez, then I probably would have been approached right away, correct?"

"Most likely."

"But I wasn't. I mean, the goon showed up and didn't say a word. And Vince was the one who convinced me to do the whole setup, and then he didn't even follow up."

"So what do you think now?"

"I think Brenda turned snitch on Ramirez. She might have been working with the feds or something, I don't know. But I think she was trying to set him up. And when she didn't take my bullshit story of financial problems back to the goon, they knew she'd turned on them."

"So why did the goon show up at the restaurant again?"

"I think he showed up and specifically *didn't* ask me to do something to Bobby, just so that I couldn't ever accuse him of anything. He knew what I was expecting of him, but he made a point of just being a regular guy, not a fucking thug. Brenda played with fire and got burnt."

I remembered thinking that Brenda might have been working for the good guys from the moment I saw her package. "Do you have any proof to back up your thoughts?"

"Not really. But that night at dinner, she kind of opened up about her situation and her family. She talked a lot about the viatical shit and said that Ramirez had invested in eight of those policies through her. Evidently he went to Mass every day and prayed for people to die. He was always calling her and asking her to check up on the terminal people, which really wasn't her job at all. She asked me if I'd ever heard the rumors about him."

"Had you?"

"Yeah, who hadn't? The guy had his hands involved in everything illegal in California and probably half of everything illegal in Mexico. The latest stories involved child prostitution in addition to the human trafficking and drugs he was well known for. I told her I'd heard some stuff about his enterprise, and she said she'd never work with him again. She talked a lot about leaving the area and starting over somewhere brand new. A fresh start and all that shit."

"Would she have left her family and career?"

"I certainly didn't think so. She definitely acted like she didn't approve of what Ramirez was all about. But the whole time she was talking, I kept thinking that she was bullshitting me. Remember, when we were at dinner, I was thinking that she was part of his crew, so I took everything she said with a grain of salt. I thought she was playing me."

"And now?"

He shook his head sadly. "I'm pretty sure I was wrong. I remember that towards the end of our dinner, I was just sitting there listening to her and wondering why she'd be working with such a scumbag. She had so much going for her, it just didn't make sense. I convinced myself that she'd gotten in over her head because she was so materialistic and money hungry. So I put my hand on hers and told her that if she ever found herself in trouble, or if she ever needed help, I'd be there for her."

"How did she react?"

"She got all teary-eyed and said that I was a good friend. Then she said that she had to go and left pretty quickly. I wasn't sure what to make of it. That's the last time I saw her." He paused for a moment and said softly, "What a waste."

A thought occurred to me. "Darrin, was this whole situation what prompted Bobby to go to Santa Barbara?"

"Yep," he said, his voice cracking. "We thought that we were being so smart. The whole thing backfired." He covered his mouth with his hand and looked away.

I leaned my head back and thought about everything Darrin had told me. If his theory proved correct, then Brenda had probably directed the package to him because of his kind words at the end of their dinner. And possibly her talk of a fresh start had something to do with the witness protection program. But if she was working against Ramirez, instead of with him, then why wouldn't she have sent the package to the authorities she was working with? Why send it to Darrin?

I then remembered Brenda's note requesting to not think poorly of her. Did she somehow feel guilty about the crimes that Ramirez had committed, even if she'd played no role? Did she feel that she'd inadvertently setup the people for whom she'd written viatical policies? Did she feel guilty for being a snitch and potentially hurting her uncle, thus hurting her own family? I wondered if Brenda's uncle had known what was going to happen to her. Here I thought that Uncle Larry was a handful, but he would go to hell and back for Moira or me.

My head was spinning, and then suddenly the room was, too. Kayla, Doob and Sampson bounded through the door all at once and landed in a pile of arms, legs, scarves, hats and dog hair.

Kayla screamed, "I won!"

Doob got up from the heap and rubbed the side of his temple. "You cheated."

"All's fair in love and war, Sucker. You have to help me tomorrow."

I raised my eyebrows at them. "Do I even want to know?"

Kayla pranced around as she filled me in. "Doob and I raced from the outside of the building, up the stairs. And I won!"

Doob kept rubbing his head and pointed at Sampson with his free hand. "He held me up."

I rolled my eyes and rubbed Sampson's head. He barked at me and headed towards the pantry for treats. "Yeah, the four legged one that weighs forty pounds was sure to slow *you* down, given the tip-top shape you're in. C'mon Doob, you're above blaming a dog, aren't you?"

Doob considered that. "Not really."

I jutted my chin towards Kayla. "So you have to help her with—?"

"Her resumé," he said grudgingly, but I saw a slight smile.

I looked at Kayla and put my hand on my hip. "And what, pray tell, were you going to do for Doobie if you'd lost the bet?"

Kayla briefly flashed her cat-that-ate-the-canary smile. "I didn't plan on losing."

"But if you had?"

"Doob would have gotten a glimpse of my tattoo," she said seductively.

That got Darrin's attention, and his eyes widened. "And where would that be?"

"Let's just say that even the tattoo artist was embarrassed," she replied. "I have to pee."

With that she flounced out of the room and left the three of us to wonder about how someone could get ink into certain parts of the body. She came back a minute later and pointed at Doobie, who'd plopped down on the couch.

"What time tomorrow CB?"

I looked quizzically at Doobie, and he blushed before quietly saying, "Computer Boy."

"Oh brother." Kayla would have him completely eating out of her hand by this time tomorrow.

Doob asked, "What time do you get up?"

Kayla shrugged. "Now that I'm unemployed, I pretty much get up whenever I want. It could be as early as seven thirty or as late as noon."

Doob pondered that for a second. "Sounds perfectly vague to me. I'll need some food, and we'll use this apartment."

I held my arms out wide. "Make yourself at home, people."

Kayla grabbed her coat and then skipped around the room, ruffling Doob, Darrin and Sampson's heads in the process. She then gave me a peck on the cheek and said, "See you tomorrow, Kid. Thanks for dinner." And then she was gone.

I sighed loudly and said to Darrin, "Let's get back on track. Do you mind if we fill Doob in? Three heads are better than two."

Darrin nodded. "That's fine, but if it's all the same to you, I'd like to get some fresh air. Do you guys want to go get some real coffee?"

Doob shot off the couch like a bullet and was back in his coat and out the door before Darrin or I could move.

I smiled. "I guess that's a yes. You're buying."

"Extra large, I presume?"

"Is there another size?"

CHAPTER 33

We arrived at the coffee shop about ten minutes later. En route, Doob had entertained us with some mundane trivia. Supposedly the Boston University Bridge is the only place in the world where a boat can sail under a train that is traveling under a car that is driving under an airplane. Doob is an encyclopedia of useless facts.

Once we arrived, we ordered our warm concoctions and got settled in at a table by the window. Darrin and I took turns bringing Doob up to speed on what we'd already discussed. Doob listened intently, and I could tell he was processing and storing information in his computer-like brain. Despite all of Doob's eccentricities, he's sharp as a tack, and I was glad he was there.

Once the story was recapped, I got back to business. "So Darrin, you just put this Brenda theory together after you spoke with me the other night, correct?"

"Yeah, why?"

"Did you call the cops in L.A.?"

His face reddened. "No."

I looked pointedly at him. "I *assume* you will call the cops as soon as we're finished here?"

"Done," Darrin said agreeably.

"Okay, good. Now, let's explore this theory about Brenda. If what you think is true, then Ramirez probably offed her."

Darrin nodded and Doob grinned. "I like it when you talk gangsta, Meg. Very chic."

"Glad you approve, Doob."

Darrin looked pained. "That's what I think. Vince had to have been involved with Ramirez. They were suspicious of her, and they got me to unknowingly set her up. Vince, the goon, and Ramirez fabricated the whole story, and I bought it."

I recapped. "And when Brenda *didn't* tell them about your supposed financial woes, they concluded that she'd turned on them, and that was the end of Brenda."

We sat in silence and sipped our coffees. If Brenda had been working for the good guys, then the fact that she put that package together before her murder was telling. She must have suspected they were on to her. What she hadn't known was that they'd sent her on a false trail, straight to Sunny's, with Vince leading the way. The notes in her spreadsheet about the Sunny's employees proved that she was doing her homework. She likely concluded that Ramirez was going to approach one of them who were down-and-out financially, with the obvious choice being Darrin. Yet for some reason, she still sent her package straight to him. She, for one, must have thought that Darrin was trustworthy. Had she been wrong about that as well?

My mind continued to jump all over the place, and then I had a thought. "Darrin, how many people knew Bobby was at that house in Santa Barbara?"

"Not many at all."

"Yet somehow, this Jethro dude who supposedly killed him knew exactly where to find him. What if the owner of that house wasn't really a friend of Bobby's at all? What if the supposed friend was in on it and hired this Jethro thug to kill Bobby?"

He shook his head adamantly. "No way, Meg. Absolutely no friggin' way. If the Ramirez people wanted him dead, they could have discovered where Bobby was staying easily enough. They would have just followed him from the hospital because he was still going for treatments several times a week. But I'm positive it wasn't the owner of the house."

"How do you know? Who was this friend? And how did they meet?"

"The house belongs to a guy named Dr. Marcus Wallingford, and he's a department head at the hospital Bobby went to for treatments. He's in his fifties, and he's been a fixture at that hospital for over twenty-five years. Bobby started seeing Dr. Wallingford when he got to L.A., and they hit it off from day one. The doc was like a father to Bobby. He'd call the apartment to check on his progress, and he took him to a couple of Lakers games over the winter. Believe me, the doc was doing everything he could to save Bobby's life."

"Don't you find it a little odd that a bigshot doctor took such a liking to a younger man? Was there any chance he had feelings for Bobby and Bobby might have rebuked his advances?"

Darrin laughed. "Meagan, you're not getting the picture. Doc has been married to the same woman for thirty years. She, by the way, is also a department head at the same hospital. They live in a mansion in Bel Air, and they have condos in Vail, Paris, and Turks and Caicos. They also have that house in Santa Barbara where Bobby was killed; it's up for sale now. They couldn't deal with the fact he was murdered there.

"They have three boys, and the youngest one just graduated from law school. His name is Rick, and he visited his dad at the hospital last year over his winter break. By chance he met Bobby that day, and the two of them became fast friends. Turns out that Rick is a whiz-kid as a student, but he's a complete numskull when it comes to mechanics. He was telling his dad and Bobby about the latest problem with his car, and Bobby told him he'd take a look at it. A day later, Rick's car was purring like a kitten, and Bobby's relationship with Rick and Dr. Wallingford was solidified. It was great for Bobby. Rick invited us both over for a party at their place on New Year's Eve, and it was like nothing I've ever seen before. Twenty-five thousand square feet, six fireplaces, ocean views, granite everywhere, except for the floors. Those were all Italian marble.

"The Wallingford family is the American dream, Meagan. They were devastated when Bobby was killed. They started a foundation in his name and donated half a million dollars to cancer research."

I still wouldn't let it go. "Maybe the good doctor only did that to take the suspicion off of him."

Darrin rolled his eyes. "Come off it, Meagan. No way."

"Okay, so maybe it was the kid? This Rick guy. Maybe he was jealous of his dad spending so much time with Bobby. Or maybe he needed some cash and he thought Bobby was going to leave something to him."

"Meg, the kid is from a family with millions, and he's on his way to a private law firm where he'll make partner in no time. And he treated Bobby like one of his brothers. I know that you want an easy answer, but you are way off base. Could you just *consider* the fact it wasn't the doc's family and focus on someone else?"

I raised my eyebrows. "Fine, I'll focus on someone else. Didn't the cops suspect *you* of being involved after Bobby was killed? *You* knew where he was staying."

Doob piped up with a mouthful of powdered sugar donut. "And *you* got a shitload of money when he died."

Darrin looked back and forth to both of us. "Thanks so much for those reminders, Ms. Holmes and my dear Watson. And, yes, they wondered about me initially.

"Like I told you before, I had an alibi for that night. Melanie and I both worked that day and were done around eight. I went to her place after work to catch a movie, and I was tired so I stayed on her couch."

"So she vouched for you?"

"Yep. She woke up around one o'clock to go to the bathroom and told the cops that I was sound asleep on the couch, snoring like a bear. They'd calculated Bobby's time of death around one that morning, and the place where he died was nearly two hours from Melanie's apartment. There was no way that I could have traveled to the spot he was killed and been back on her couch by one if I was supposedly killing Bobby at that exact time. Thank God she had to pee when she did."

Something struck me. "So how in the heck did the police find Bobby so quickly?"

He looked at me quizzically. "Hunh?"

"Well, supposedly hardly anyone knew he was up in Santa Barbara. How was his body found so quickly?"

"Oh, that. The mail comes early in that area. The mailman saw Jethro slumped in the car and called the cops. They arrived and found Bobby shortly thereafter."

"And how did they know to find you at Melanie's house when they came to talk to you?"

He shrugged. "I'm not sure. Cops are pretty resourceful."

I nodded. "Did you tell them about Vince when you found out that Bobby had been murdered?"

Darrin looked confused. "No, I didn't tell them *specifically* about Vince. What would I have said? That a dude introduced himself to me one day and assured me that he wanted to *protect* Bobby? Oh, and by the way, that dude has subsequently disappeared? I would have looked like a nutbag to the cops. Plus, they had their guy. Vince was long gone as far as I was concerned. But they did know about Ramirez and the viatical policy. I told you that on the day we met, Meagan."

I thought about that while Doob said he was going to grab another round of coffee. Darrin and I sat quietly for a while, and he eventually said, "I keep thinking about Vince and what happened to Brenda. I feel awful."

I wasn't sure what to say, so I said nothing. Shortly thereafter, Doob made his way back to the table, toting three large coffees in a to-go tray.

"We're taking these home?" I inquired.

Doob nodded. "Your sleuthing powers constantly amaze me, Meg. I've got five movies from Netflix, and I propose an afternoon of cinematic entertainment and junk food. We need a break from this murder talk." He lifted Darrin's coffee from the tray and held it out to him. *Here's your hat, what's your hurry?*

There was a moment of awkward silence before Darrin said, "Well, you guys have a good time. I guess I'll see you later." He grabbed his coat and left without taking his coffee.

I was astonished. "Doob, that was the least subtle moment you've ever had in your life!"

Doob shrugged. "Sorry, Meg. But I'd had enough. We can talk about all of this Vince crap tomorrow. It was making my hair hurt."

As we walked back to the apartment, I felt guilty that we'd excused Darrin so abruptly, but Doob was right. We needed a break. While I was ninety-nine percent certain that Darrin was incapable of killing anyone, there was still that nagging one percent.

CHAPTER 34
WEDNESDAY, MARCH 19TH

After the day of junk food and general laziness, it was time to find out about Vince. I was hoping that Doob's busy schedule would allow for some snooping.

I was still in bed and called him from my cordless phone. He seemed up for the job, and by the time I brushed my teeth and dressed, Doob was sitting at the table, laptop at the ready. He cracked his knuckles and raised his eyebrows twice.

"What's for eats?"

"Good God, Doob. How do you stay so skinny when all you do is eat crap?"

He shrugged. "I don't know. But I only eat when I'm hungry. It just seems I'm always hungry."

Suddenly a smell in the room got my attention, and I started sniffing the air. Doob looked sheepish and his eyes started darting around. I walked right up to him and sniffed his neck a couple of times.

"Doob!"

He turned purple. "What?"

"You showered!"

Doob started to get up from the table, but I grabbed his arm and studied his head. Then I pried his lips open with my thumb and forefinger before he pushed my hand away.

I sat down across from him, leaning my head forward and speaking in mock astonishment. "You've also brushed your hair and teeth, and I believe," I held up a finger and sniffed the air a couple more times, just for effect, "that I detect an odor of cologne. Can it be? Who are you and what have you done with my neighbor?"

By now, Doob was nearly crimson. "A guy can clean up occasionally, can't he? What's for breakfast?"

I smiled wide and decided to not bruise his ego by telling him that Kayla would crush him if she didn't like his new odor. I rummaged around in the kitchen and spoke to him through the pass-through. "We have most of the breakfast stuff we had yesterday."

Doob shook his head. "Old news. What else?"

I rolled my eyes. "Beyond that, we have a half box of hot tamales, four miscellaneous donuts, an almost-full bag of Doritos, a bowl of stale popcorn, three Diet cokes, two beers and one Red Bull."

Doob held out his hand. "Two of the donuts and the Red Bull, please."

I delivered them promptly and took the remaining two donuts and a Diet Coke for myself. We ate in companionable silence, and I felt my jeans getting tighter with each bite. I had to get to the grocery store and buy some fruit or some other such nonsense, but the store was just such a pain. Instead of dealing with my waistline getting bigger, I went into my room and changed into sweats. Then I returned to the table to watch Doob finish his junk food.

His tummy satisfied, Doob took his plate into the kitchen. He then rinsed out his Red Bull can and put it in the recycle bin. I was impressed. Maybe Doob could be trained after all. When he came back to the table, he sat down and again cracked his knuckles.

"All right, Meg, what's the mission today?"

"Kind of a hodge podge of stuff. I need my sticky notes." I grabbed my purse from under the table and started digging.

Doob crossed his arms. "Well, this looks promising. Should I come back in an hour or two when you get through with the excavation?"

I popped my head out of my purse like a groundhog on February 2nd. "You want to compare slovenly habits?"

"Touché. But unless I'm mistaken, you've been bribing me with food for the past couple of days for a reason. Or several reasons. I'm just wondering what I'm in for."

I went back to digging and came up with three yellow sticky notes, globbed together by something dark and gooey. I very much hoped it was chocolate. I held them out to Doob.

He wrinkled his nose, which was saying something. "Nice, Meg."

"Oh, I'm so sorry, Computer Boy. Have you suddenly gone all clean-freak on me? You and your fancy cologne are now above gunk?"

Doob flushed three shades of red. "That's not my name, jackal."

"Well, you certainly didn't mind when Kayla was calling you that yesterday," I teased.

"That's different Meg. She's a totally hot chick with a flair for the outrageous. You're—"

"Don't even think about finishing that sentence, Doob."

He nodded agreeably. "Good advice."

I was hoping to get some production out of Doob before Kayla sauntered in. After her arrival, he'd be useless. "You don't know what time she's coming over, do you?"

Doob raised his eyebrows like Groucho Marx. "The sooner, the better. Yum."

I laughed out loud. "Doob, she would absolutely kill you. Ransack your liquor cabinet, spend your money, wreck your car, and then leave you in the gutter to rot."

Doob smiled. "I know," he said wistfully.

I shook my head. *Men!* "Well, before she gets here, I was hoping you could help me with some stuff."

"The hodge podge?"

"Yes, it's a few different things. But *I think* they all matter." I had no idea.

"So enlighten me, Maloney-Wan-Kenobi."

I raised an eyebrow and thought of our Netflix movies from the previous day. "The *Star Wars* trilogy is going to be with us for a while, isn't it?"

"Yep," Doob said and reached across to put his hand on my shoulder. "Meg, I am your father."

"Good God, Doob. Get a grip. My real father would never smell like that. So here's the deal. I still haven't completely ruled Darrin out. I think there's a one percent chance he might have done something bad, but that's a very small percentage."

"Are you *shitting* me?" Indignant-Doob. "So that's why you had him over here all friggin' night on Monday? On the couch with Kayla, no less? I can imagine how you'd treat someone you *don't* suspect of murder."

"I'm sorry. But I didn't know that he'd stayed overnight. Plus, with you and Kayla around, he wouldn't have chopped us all up. And he does seem like a good guy, but all of these things keep creeping up that make me second guess him. So I need you to find Vince for me."

Doob rolled his eyes. "With no last name or phone number. Yet again."

"Well, if Brenda was convinced he was part of the Ramirez crew, then I'll give her the benefit of the doubt."

"I'll do my best."

"I just wish she'd written more in her note. I've been thinking about that, and the only thing I can think of was that she wrote it in a hurry. Like she knew someone was after her."

Doob looked sad. "Poor lady."

"It's terrible. One other thing, Doob. Please check and see if you can verify anything about some dude named Pete committing suicide."

"Is that the story about Vince's brother? Pete, who also has no last name?"

"His *supposed* brother, yes. I'm thinking he made up that story to win Darrin's sympathy. If you don't find anything, then I'm guessing there never was a dear-departed brother Pete."

"Will do. Please tell me that's it."

I winced. "Ummm, not quite. If you can find a connection between Brenda and Officer Simonetta, that would be great. But that's the last priority. I will call him directly if I have to."

"Okay. So, number one—try to find Vince. Number two—try to find out if his brother ever existed. Number three—try to figure out a commonality between Brenda and Officer Simonetta. And what exactly will you be doing while I'm slaving away?"

"Well, I have that other case I'm working on—"

"Jim's?"

"Yep. I'm going out for a few hours to wrap it up, so please call me if you find anything. And, you and Kayla? Don't do anything I wouldn't do." I smiled mischievously, and Doob turned scarlet.

I plopped a quick kiss on Doobie's forehead and ruffled Sampson's ears on my way out. As I locked the door behind me, I saw Kayla walking down the hall.

She had her perky little nose up in the air and said, "Someone's cologne smells like ass."

I laughed and kept walking. Poor Doob.

Four hours later, I'd almost completed my final hours on Jim's case and had absolutely no proof, nor any reason to think, that his ex-wife was cheating on her current man. I was secretly glad. Jim was an asshole.

Doob had called while I was on my sucky stakeout to give me an update. He'd made no headway finding Vince, and he'd also had no luck finding any articles or any information whatsoever on a dead Pete. We concluded that Vince was indeed a Ramirez lackey, and we also decided that his story about his brother was completely fabricated. Doob said he hadn't been able to look for a connection between Brenda and Officer Simonetta because he'd been working on Kayla's resumé for most of the afternoon.

I was satisfied that we'd come to some resolution on the Vince situation and his entire bullshit setup, but the Officer Simonetta thing was still nagging at me. I decided I would make a phone call to him directly and give Doob a break.

After I thanked him for all of his help, Doob asked if I wanted to meet Kayla and him for a matinee. It sounded fun, but I wanted to finish logging the hours I owed Jim. Kayla was yapping away in the background, and I was pretty certain I'd heard a bottle of wine being opened. God help Doob. I told him to have fun and that the apartment better be in one piece when I got home. While laughing, Doob said he'd do his best.

After we rang off, I fished out his card and dialed Officer Simonetta's number. After exchanging pleasantries, we began talking about Brenda Alvarez.

"Officer, I have reason to believe you knew Brenda, and I just wonder if you have any leads in her murder."

"And why would you have reason to believe that, Meagan?"

Uh oh. I reminded myself that LaKeisha had been routed to Officer Simonetta when she'd initially called the police. I also remembered she'd sent him the same flash drive she'd sent to me. I didn't want to get her in trouble.

"I can't reveal my sources?" I said this more as a question than a statement.

"Meagan, all I will tell you is that I did know Brenda Alvarez, and I'm working closely on her murder investigation."

"Would you mind telling me how you knew her?"

"Meagan, do you have any information that might help with her case?"

I decided to show my cards. Kind of. "I think she was somehow working with the authorities against Alberto Ramirez and that it very likely had something to do with her death. I think Ramirez became suspicious of her and gave her a little test, and when she failed that test, he had her killed."

My statement was met with silence.

"Officer?"

"I'm here." His voice was quiet.

"Is that of any help to you?"

"Would you mind telling me about this test, Meagan?"

I proceeded to tell him about Vince, Vince's supposed brother, the thug who'd visited Sunny's and spoken with Darrin, the pictures of the thug and Darrin in Vince's possession, Darrin's subsequent phony story to Brenda, and finally the fact that Darrin hadn't heard a peep from Vince since then. I felt like I'd run a marathon when I finished, and again, I was met with silence.

"Officer, you better still be there, because I don't think I can repeat all that."

I heard a soft chuckle. "I appreciate the information, Meagan, and I will certainly look into it. It could definitely be helpful."

"So how about a little quid pro quo? Would you mind telling me how you knew Brenda? And if I'm on the right track?" *Because I really want to think you're a good cop and not yet another creep on the Ramirez payroll.*

I heard a loud sigh, and I thought he was going to tell me to pound sand. But he surprised me.

"The short story is that I met Brenda outside of a restaurant a few miles up the road from where I met you, Meagan. The guy she was with was all drugged up and making a scene in the restaurant. It's a half-ritzy place, and they called us before throwing him out. I arrived on the scene to find him smacking her around in the parking lot, and we hauled him off to jail. I gave her my card and told her to call me if she wanted to press charges." He scoffed. "So many of those women never do. It makes me crazy."

"Did she call you?"

"She did," he replied.

"And?"

"Turns out that it didn't have anything to do with the guy who'd smacked her around."

"Then why did she call?"

He was silent for a few seconds. "She called to see if I had any contacts at the FBI."

Gulp. "And did you?"

"I did."

"Oh." That certainly seemed to confirm that Brenda had been working with the feds. "May I ask you one more thing?"

"Sure."

"Hypothetically, if Brenda was working with the feds and had some information for them, wouldn't it make sense for her to send a hypothetical package directly to them?"

He was silent again, and I crossed my fingers. He sounded sad when he finally responded. "Hypothetically, yes, that would make sense, Meagan. But hypothetically, even feds can go bad."

My stomach lurched. "Oh my God." Ramirez had everyone on his payroll. Brenda had known she was in a shit-storm but couldn't get out. Then something struck me.

"Hypothetically, if Ramirez had a mole within the feds, then why did he go to the bother of giving Brenda that one last test? Why didn't he just kill her?"

"Good questions. Hypothetically, my guess is that he was testing the mole's information. Ramirez knew that either the mole or Brenda had to be lying, and he needed to flush that person out. It was one of two things. One—the mole was lying about Brenda working with the feds, or two—Brenda had turned on him. Given the family relationship with Ramirez, he probably hoped she hadn't turned snitch.

"That's all that I can tell you, Meagan. But I really appreciate your call. We'll get the bastard who did this to her. And we'll nail anyone who sold her out, too. You have my word on that."

I could hear the determination and guilt in his voice. I finished my stakeout and thus my obligation to Jim soon after hanging up with Officer Simonetta. The apartment was quiet when I arrived home, and as promised, nothing was out of place. I only hoped that Doob wasn't on his way to Buffalo.

CHAPTER 35
THURSDAY, MARCH 20TH

After a short night of tossing and turning, I got up very early the next morning and decided to do some cleaning around the apartment. I usually feel a sense of accomplishment after doing a bit of serious scrubbing.

While I was giving the stainless steel fridge a rub down, Doob sauntered in with a box of cupcakes and his laptop. I couldn't believe he was up before six. Then I realized he probably hadn't been to bed.

"How was Buffalo?" I asked.

He cocked his head and looked confused. "Hunh?"

I smiled. "Never mind. How did it go with the resumé and the movie?"

"It was fun. Kayla is super cool." He turned a near-fuschia color, and I decided to not pick on him for once.

"She definitely is," I agreed.

"Want one?" He lifted up the box of cupcakes, and I opened my mouth to chastise him for such shitty eating habits.

"Yeah, why not," I heard myself say. "I can't believe how quickly food disappears. Once I'm done going through this refrigerator, we will officially have more dog food in this apartment than people food."

Doob got his deer-in-the-headlights look. "So?"

"So, we need to go to the grocery store, which I hate. The stupid food is supposed to be all lined up to make sense, but it makes no sense to me, and the cold stuff gets warm by the time I'm done looking for friggin' everything."

"I see you're in a fine mood today, Miss. P.I. What's up your ass?"

I sighed. "I don't know. I'm never up this early. I slept like crap because

I had all these weird dreams about Darrin. I keep going back and forth on my suspicions of him. Maybe it's my guilt manifesting itself in my dreams. I guess I feel bad for accusing him of being a murderer."

"I would think so," Doob said, with a touch of snootiness that I wasn't in the mood to hear.

"You can get your nose right out of the air, Cupcake Boy. You thought that additional twenty grand was pretty fishy as well. Not to mention that you basically escorted him right out of the coffee shop the other day."

"Guilty," Doob quipped. "So what do we do?"

"I need to know with one hundred percent certainty that Darrin didn't have anything to do with Bobby's murder. I've got to get off of this merry-go-round of thinking he's a good guy and then that he isn't. Based on the story he told us, he supposedly told Melanie all about Vince. I might call her to see if she can verify everything."

He thought about that for a second and nodded. "I guess it couldn't hurt."

"I have to wait until it's a more sane hour in California, though. I'll give her a call later. Or tomorrow." I shrugged and went into my room to change.

I scrutinized my closet and selected some light brown pants that were suitable for church. As I pulled them on, I felt myself having to extra-suck in my gut to get them buttoned. How the hell had all my clothes gotten smaller over the winter? I had to get on the treadmill very, very soon. After figuring out how to breathe despite the pants, I headed back into the living room and grabbed my coat.

Doob watched with curiosity. "Where are you going?"

"It's my dad's birthday today, so I'm going to head to church with the folks. They attend eight o'clock Mass every weekday, rain or shine, and a prayer or two on my part probably couldn't hurt matters."

"Didn't your mom just have a birthday?"

I cocked my head at him. "Why yes, Doob, she did."

"Wild."

I rolled my eyes and didn't even ask what that was supposed to mean. "Doob, I'll probably spend the day over there. It's always good to earn a few brownie points, plus I know that Ma will make something wonderful to eat. Do you want to come along?"

Doob looked panicked. My pop and he aren't exactly cut from the same mold. Truth be told, I think Doob is terrified of my father. "Uh, no thanks. I'll work on this, uh, stuff that I'm, uh, working on. Tell them hi, though."

A half hour later, I was pulling up to my parents' house just as they were coming out the front door, and I saw Ma's face light up like a Christmas tree. I started to smile back, but then I saw Moira and Porter following behind her, with Pop bringing up the rear.

I got out of the car and hugged Ma when we met on the sidewalk. "Meagan, I'm so glad that you made it after all! Moira said you weren't feeling well."

I swung my head towards Moira, and her blue eyes were begging me not to tattle that she'd been shacking up for days on end. Pop would probably drop dead on the front lawn.

"Well, I decided that church might help me feel better." Then, just to stir the pot, I continued. "I planned on stopping by this afternoon, but since Pop is going to be gone, I wanted to be sure to see him." They all looked confused for a moment, and then Pop jumped in.

"What do you mean I'm going to be gone?"

I covered my mouth as if I'd told a big secret. Then I looked at Moira and Porter. "I'm so sorry. Did I let the cat out of the bag for Pop's birthday?"

Porter took a step backwards, and Moira narrowed her eyes at me. "Yes, Meg, I'm sure you did."

"What the hell are you talking about?" Pop asked.

"Language, please." Ma never missed a beat.

I smiled sweetly. "I'm so sorry, Porter, I didn't mean to spoil your surprise." Porter looked like he'd just sucked on a lemon.

Ma was intrigued. "What surprise, Porter?"

I knew the tight-ass couldn't think on his feet, so I jumped in on his behalf. "Well, since it's going to be such a beautiful day, and since it's Pop's birthday, Porter was going to see if he could get you two a tee time for this afternoon. The course has the temporary greens ready, and it would be a great day to go golfing, wouldn't it Pop?"

Pop looked like he might start doing a jig. "Really?" All eyes were on Porter.

He cleared his throat and shuffled his feet a little bit. "Well the reason I didn't bring it up, Mr. Maloney, is because I did call the club, but they aren't open just yet because of all of the rain we've had lately. They will probably be open in the next week or so. I'm sorry that *Meagan* got your hopes up."

Leave it to that prick to make me look like an asshole. I guess I deserved it, though. Moira was glaring at me, and Pop looked crestfallen. Ma herded us all into their massive Buick, and we survived church without further incident.

Moira treated everyone to breakfast after Mass, and then we all went back to the south side so that she and Porter could grab her car and head in to work. They'd both taken a few hours of vacation time to hang out with Pop on his birthday, and that endeared Porter to my parents even further. Gross.

I spent a very lazy day on the couch hanging out with my folks, and it was nice. I ate way too many sweets, and Pop and I channel flipped all day while Ma read one tabloid magazine after another. It amazed me that my prim and proper mother liked to keep up with the latest celebrity gossip.

After a large late-afternoon snack, I was certain my pants were not going to survive the rest of the day. I had to get up and get moving, or I would fuse into the couch cushion, stuck there until the end of my days.

I bid my parents farewell and decided to stop by Faneuil Hall to do a little shopping. One of my cousins was having her third baby in early April, and Kayla's birthday was also coming up, so I had a couple of good excuses to go spend some money.

Faneuil Hall Marketplace is in the heart of downtown Boston, and it's a wonderful compilation of food, entertainment, and shopping. I think of it as a modern, outdoor mall that collided with the 1700s. When it was built in 1742, the marketplace was home to fishermen, merchants, and meat and produce sellers. It also provided a forum for some of the country's most famous orators and was where the colonists first protested the Sugar Act in 1764. In my mind, the Boston "attitude" came about when those opinionated folks way-back-when established the doctrine of "no taxation without representation".

Today, retailers, restaurants, and bars outline the perimeter, and there are beautiful trees in the middle section of the cobblestoned walking area. During the day there are jugglers, magicians, musicians, mime artists, and other performers who entertain the crowds, and at night the trees have twinkling lights in them that radiate a wonderful, New England feel. The Marketplace is bordered by the waterfront, the financial district, Government Center, the North End, and Haymarket Rail. I've made a habit of bringing out-of-town friends to Faneuil Hall on their first visit to Boston, and we inevitably end up on a Freedom Trail tour or walking to the nearby New England Aquarium. It's simply a marvelous place and contributes to my love for my city, despite the occasional twisted ankle amongst the cobblestones.

In spite of the mid-March date, the warm weather had people out in droves. Spring fever was definitely in the air. It was infectious, and I found my mood picking up just a little bit as I weaved in and out of the little displays. I found the gifts I was looking for fairly quickly and also splurged on a new Red Sox hat for myself. I promptly plopped it on my head and realized that it didn't match the shirt and miserably tight pants I'd worn to church and lounged around in all day, but I didn't really care. My black and red pocketbook didn't match anything either, which Moira had pointed out as soon as she'd gotten the chance.

One of the little food stands I came upon actually had cotton candy, and I decided *what the hell, my pants don't fit as it is.* I waited in line behind a young couple with three children and then paid far too much money for a beehive looking swirl of sugar.

So there I was eating cotton candy like a three-year-old with my mismatched ensemble. I could feel the residue of the sticky mess all over my face when David Fontana and Gina Giovanni strolled into my space. I was so surprised that I dropped the remaining swirl to the ground. Ever the gentleman, David picked it up for me and then surveyed the damage.

"Five second rule?" I asked in an attempt to diffuse my embarrassment. Gina wrinkled her nose like she'd never heard anything more disgusting.

David smiled and shook his head. "Sorry Meagan, but I don't think you'll be able to finish this." I was trying to think of a witty retort when Gina hooked her arm through David's. She looked back and forth between David and me and scrunched up her perfect face even further.

"*You* know *Meagan*? How in the *world* do you two know each other? I can't imagine that Meagan's tax returns are very involved." She giggled like a school girl and looked at David expectantly, waiting for an answer.

I jumped in. "We've known each other for a while, Gina. It has to do with my line of work, but it's confidential."

I was hoping the uncertainty of my relationship with David might bother her, but it didn't seem to.

She rolled her eyes and said, "Yes, I'm sure it's very top secret." Then she cupped a hand to her mouth. "Alert Homeland Security. Meagan has some information."

David was still holding my ruined cotton candy and was looking terribly uncomfortable. "I've been meaning to call you Meagan, so I'm glad we ran into you. Is everything okay with the situation we discussed the other day?"

"It's fine," I said tightly. *What in the hell was he doing with the priss-bitch-of-the-decade?* "But there was a development you might be interested in. Why don't you give me a call when you don't have big fat ears and an even fatter mouth around?"

Gina smiled a humorless smile. "Speaking of fat, Meagan, how are those pants working for you?" She looked me up and down and whistled lightly.

David saw my fists clench, and his face registered instant panic. He tried to politely steer Gina away from me with his free hand. His other hand still had what was left of my cotton candy in it. Gina stood firmly in place and glared, and I swear she was daring me to make a move.

Caught between two hostile females, David started stammering in a quick tempo. "Well, uh, it was great to see you Meagan. And ummm, I will definitely call you soon. Very soon. As soon as I can. So that'll be good. So that's that. And we're just on our way to grab a bite to eat, so we'll just be on our way." He quit sputtering and tried to usher Gina along, but she wasn't having it. She just couldn't leave well enough alone.

"We should probably invite you along Meagan, but three would *definitely* be a crowd. Plus, given those pants, you could afford to skip a few meals. However, if you get really hungry, you can just finish eating what's all over your face. You really should see yourself!" She scoffed at me, and David was looking more miserable by the second. I simply couldn't let her one-up me, so I went for broke.

"Gina, I heard you're separated from the Golden Boy and his wallet. Did you two get sick of fighting over all of the mirrors in the house?"

David's head turned sharply to look at Gina, and I knew I'd scored a point. Small victory, since I was still standing there with my huge ass, along with sugar smeared all over my face.

Her eyes blazed and her sizable fake chest swelled in anger. "Well, how absolutely *tacky* of you to bring that up, Meagan. I am going through a divorce, yes, and it's an extremely painful time in my life. I guess you wouldn't understand much about relationships, though, as I hear the only one you have is with that freak neighbor of yours. I heard his parents abandoned him and that he can't even hold down a job. Nice catch, Meagan, really." She looked around as if searching for someone. "Where is he anyway? Trolling for some ketchup packets or digging through a dumpster somewhere?"

I saw red. That bitch could say what she wanted about me, but I'd be damned if she was going to say anything bad about Doobie. I dropped my packages to the ground, swiped the ruined remnants of my cotton candy from David and shoved it into Gina's perfectly made up face and glossy hair. She started screaming and swinging her Louis Vuitton pocketbook at me. She was the poster child for fighting like a girl. While swinging the massive purse, she lost her footing on the cobblestones, and I happily watched her fall on her tiny ass. Then I pounced. She was trying to get up, but the momentum of my pounce combined with her upward movement caused us to roll around a couple of times. We had to have looked like a huge designer-meets-grunge tumbleweed. I felt my hat fly off but couldn't worry about it at that particular moment. I ended up on top and got a couple of good slaps in before David pulled me off of her. She landed a good kick to my shin before I was out of range. I yelped like a stuffed pig and tried to lunge at her again, but David was much stronger than me, and I couldn't get back to her. I swear he was trying not to laugh, and I could have hugged him for it. A small crowd was gathering, and it was probably a matter of seconds before the horse mounted police would show up and haul my enormous ass off to jail.

As David steered me away from Gina, he shoved my hat in my hands and spoke quietly into my ear. "She had it coming, Meagan. Now get the hell out of here. Put your hat on and blend into the crowd." He gently pushed me away from him and then turned and walked back to Gina, who was giving an Academy Award winning performance for the onlookers.

I made it to my car and got the hell out of Dodge with no one the wiser. That's when I realized I'd left my gifts on the sidewalk at the scene of the, well, scene. Good grief, I'd lost my mind. But what the heck was David doing with Gina Giovanni anyway?

When I got back to the apartment, Doobie was sitting at the table with junk food wrappers all over the place. He was clicking away at his laptop and probably hadn't moved since I'd left him there that morning.

He looked up at me for a moment, studied what he saw, and then went back to clicking, his eyes glued to the computer.

"You have what appears to be cotton candy completely covering your face and throughout what I can see of your hair, Meg. You also seem to have a number of cuts and abrasions on your arms, and your pants are filthy."

At least he hadn't pointed out how tight they were. "Good to see you, too," I responded and went into my bedroom to change.

After literally busting out of my god-awful pants, I dug through my bureau and found the biggest pair of sweats on earth. My stomach actually had indentations from the zipper and seams of those miserable pants. It was totally disgusting. I vowed that I would lose ten pounds. I would start dieting immediately. Tomorrow. Before the end of the month. April 1st would be a good day to start a diet.

Before going back to see Doob, I caught a glimpse of myself in the mirror, and I was actually startled. I cocked my head and studied myself and wondered if this was what it was coming to. Even so, I didn't bother addressing the cotton candy in my hair. It actually smelled kind of good. And I liked the Red Sox hat. I went back into the kitchen and started rummaging around for food I knew wasn't there.

"How are your folks doing?" Doob chirped. It was nice of him to ask, but I got the sense he didn't give a rat's ass. He gets completely absorbed when he's hacking.

"They both got naked lady tattoos after church, pierced their nipples, dyed their hair purple, and then chartered a rocket to Mars."

"That's cool," Doob said. He was oblivious.

"They taught the Martians how to do the limbo, and then they all doused themselves in kerosene and lit themselves on fire. The whole planet is burning as we speak. It's on CNN this very minute."

Doob nodded indifferently. "Don't forget that you need to call your friend Melanie."

"Who?"

"The chick from Los Angeles who Darrin lived with right after Bobby died? You know, the girl who was his alibi? Helllllllllllllooooooooooo? Earth to Meg? Weren't you the one who said you needed to call her?"

I smacked myself on my Red Sox hat. "Sorry, sorry. Yes, my brain is elsewhere, Doob. I *definitely* need to call her. There are still way too many loose ends for my liking."

Doob looked at his wrist for a watch that wasn't there and then scanned the room to find the clock. "It's late afternoon there."

I shrugged. "No time like the present."

Doob pointed at me. "Giddy-up Meg."

CHAPTER 36

Melanie answered her cell phone on the third ring, and after an unsuccessful attempt at small talk, I cut to the chase.

"Melanie, I'm sure you're busy, so I'll get to the point. Darrin and I are still kind of tying up some loose ends with Bobby's case, and I just wondered if you could give me your take on Vince."

There were several seconds of silence, and I wondered, and sort of hoped, that I'd caught her off guard. If she was lying for Darrin, then maybe she was scrambling right now to figure out who Vince was.

"Are you talking about the tough guy who approached Darrin at Sunny's?" Her voice was nonchalant. Okay, so maybe Darrin was on the up-and-up.

"Yeah, that's the guy. I'm just wondering what your take was on him?"

"My take?"

"Your thoughts, impressions, whatever."

I heard a huge sigh and nearly made a sarcastic quip, but I bit my tongue and waited. "I don't know what exactly to tell you, Meagan. Basically Vince came to the restaurant one day and spent the whole day leering at Darrin. I guess Darrin told you about that."

"He did. He said it was pretty weird."

"Yeah, it was." I heard her take a breath, and it sounded like she was going to say something else, but she didn't.

"But?"

"But what?"

I rolled my eyes. "It sounded like you were going to say something else."

She conceded. "It was definitely weird, but it was also kind of sexy."

Ummmmm. "Okay? How so?"

"Vince had the whole bad boy thing going for him. Black leather jacket with studs on it, worn out blue jeans, and his hair was a little longer than the normal guys. Kind of Billy Ray Cyrus from back in the day."

Good grief. "He had a mullet?"

"No, just some shaggy hair. Anyway, Darrin finally asked Vince if there was a problem, and Vince basically said there was. It was pretty evident that the shit was going to hit the fan."

"So what happened?"

"Darrin said they were going to sit in the back corner in case things got heated. He didn't want to upset any customers. He asked the manager and me to keep an eye on things."

"And you did?"

"Yep. I was checking on their table the whole time they were talking, and I saw some pictures that Vince had shown Darrin."

"Did you get a good look at them?"

"Yes."

"And?"

"And they were pictures of Darrin talking to some hulking guy at the restaurant."

That must have been the Ramirez goon. "Did you see that particular guy at the restaurant when he was talking with Darrin?"

Another huge sigh erupted. "Meagan, I see all kinds of people at work every day. I have no idea if I saw this guy or not. I don't pay that much attention. And now that I think about it, why are you asking me about all of this if Darrin has already explained it?"

"I'm just verifying his story, Melanie. I'm trying to see if anything new comes out of your version. Seems this Vince guy is a ghost, and maybe you'll remember something that Darrin didn't."

"Well, I highly doubt it. Besides, they got the guy who did it, Meagan."

"I'm not so sure. They got a guy, but maybe not the *right* guy."

I heard Melanie scoff. "Are you kidding me?"

"Not at all."

"Fine. Even if they didn't get the *right* guy, you've had to have spent enough time with Darrin to know that he didn't do it."

"One day I feel that way, and the next day, I don't. I just need to know once and for all."

"Meagan, why are you doing all of this?"

"Doing all of what?"

"I mean, why do you keep pushing this? The case is *closed*."

I shrugged, even though it was a gesture she couldn't see. "I dunno. Something just doesn't feel right."

She sighed again. She was going to be out of air soon. "Well, if I were you, I think I'd let it go."

Easy for you to say. "Yeah, well, be glad you're not me."

"If there's nothing else—"

Evidently Melanie wanted to get off of the phone. "No, there really isn't. Thanks for your time, Melanie. Please call me if you think of anything else that might help me. No detail is too small."

She chuckled. "I will definitely call if I think of anything, Meagan. But I really don't feel there's anything more to look into. You need to let it go." She obviously wanted to hang up, and I couldn't come up with any good reason to not let her. But then it hit me.

"Melanie, just one last thing, real quick," I said with some urgency in my voice.

"Yeah?"

"You were Darrin's alibi the night Bobby was killed, correct?"

Her voice came over as extremely impatient. "For the umpteenth time, that's right. I've been over that with you, the cops, and anyone else who cares to talk about it."

I ignored her tone and developed a bit of one myself. "Well, I gotta ask. Was he *really* at your house, or were you just being a good friend by giving him a cover?"

Crickets.

"Melanie?"

"I'm just surprised by the question, Meagan. You're sounding like you don't trust Darrin. Or me, for that matter."

I shrugged again, to no one but myself. "I'm sorry you feel that way, but I had to ask." She remained silent, so I tried to bait her. "I haven't heard an answer yet, either."

"Even if I did lie to the cops, Meagan, and I'm not saying that I did, what makes you think I'd now change my story and confess to *you*? And open up a whole can of worms that you're hell-bent on opening? I don't think so. I said he was at my place all night that night, and that's that.

So back off. Now, if you don't have any more straws to grasp at, I really need to go."

"I guess there's nothing else for now Melanie, but please call me if you want to come clean on anything. You might just feel better."

"I feel just fine. Bye Meagan."

CHAPTER 37
FRIDAY, MARCH 21ST

The next morning I got up early again and spent the first few hours doing some online bills, responding to a plethora of personal emails that had piled up over the last couple of weeks, and then I actually went into the third bedroom where the dreaded treadmill lived. I managed a brisk walk for about forty minutes and thought I might need the paramedics once I'd finished. The things that had kept me motivated were envisioning Gina's sneering face, my curiosity over Melanie's vague answer about being Darrin's alibi, and the fact that Vince-the-ghost was nowhere to be found.

While showering, I decided that only another chat with Darrin would give me some answers. Of course he'd be thrilled, but I didn't see another way. I threw on some sweat pants and a Red Sox sweatshirt and approached the phone in the kitchen like it was a guillotine. It was almost eleven, so I couldn't use the it's-too-early-to-call excuse.

I blew out a huge puff of air as I punched the buttons for Darrin's number very slowly. Usually I try to halfway rehearse my blather, but I didn't even bother. My rehearsals never come to fruition, so I decided to just wing it. Maybe he wouldn't even be home.

"Hello?"

Maybe I should have rehearsed. "Hey Darrin, it's Meagan." *I'm calling because I now think your alibi is bullshit, and I'm back on the side of thinking you're a murderer. Care to defend yourself? Again?*

His voice dropped a notch. "Oh, hey Meg." He sounded like I was the one who told him about Santa or the Easter Bunny.

I *definitely* should have rehearsed. I had nothing. "So, anything new with you?" Good grief.

"Actually, yeah. You remember Melanie?"

Oh shit! Had she called him? Did he know I'd been checking up on him? *Shit shit shit!* Since I wasn't sure what he knew, I decided to play dumb, which is so very easy sometimes. "Um, your friend Melanie from Los Angeles?"

"That's the one. I'm picking her up at Logan in a couple of days."

That got my attention. "She's coming *here*?"

"Yep. You sound surprised."

Weird. I'd just talked to her the night before. She hadn't mentioned coming to visit. Something was up. "I thought you two were just buddies," I said, sounding confused, which I was.

"We are, I told you that before. She has to come to a funeral out here, and she wanted to know if she could crash at the apartment."

"Oh jeez, that's too bad. When I met her, she said something about having relatives out here, but it didn't sound like they were close."

"Yeah, she said it was some relative of her dad's who she's never even met."

I scrunched up my nose. "That's kind of awkward."

"Yeah, I thought so, too. But whoever called led her to believe that there might be some money in it for her. I guess it was some spinster great-aunt or something, and she put Melanie in the will when she was just a baby."

"I guess that's nice, but it seems odd that someone would leave money to a relative who's a stranger."

"Ever the suspicious one, Meagan. Maybe you could stand outside the funeral home and accuse the people paying their respects of grand theft auto or embezzlement while you're there."

I ignored the barb. "So when did you find out she was coming?"

"About two hours ago."

"Oh. Well, that explains it." I'd spoken with her yesterday afternoon, California time, so she must have received the news sometime after talking to me.

"That explains what?"

Uh oh. If I told Darrin I'd talked to Melanie yesterday, he would want to know why. And if I was honest, which I try to be, mainly because I don't have a good enough memory to lie, then I would have to tell him that I was checking up on his Vince story. As well as his alibi, although that had been spur of the moment.

"Meagan? Are you there?"

I abandoned my whole reason for calling and opted for the mature way out. "Darrin, I'm so sorry, but I've got to run. Please give my best to Melanie when you see her. We'll have to get together for, uh, something, when she's in town. Bye."

I hung up as fast as I could and then pictured Darrin staring at his phone. I simply couldn't tell him I'd been checking up on him. I'd changed my mind about Darrin's involvement with Bobby's death a hundred times, but he didn't need to know that. The curious thing was that Melanie hadn't told Darrin about our chat either. But maybe she was caught up with getting a flight and getting out here. For the funeral of someone she hoped to profit from. There seemed to be a little too much of *that* going around.

As I was staring at my cell phone, it rang, which startled me.

"Meagan Maloney," I answered.

There was a moment of silence, and then I heard his voice. "Meagan, this is Vic McBride."

CHAPTER 38

After speaking to Vic McBride for about twenty minutes, he agreed to let me visit him at the prison the day after next. And even though I'd just spoken with him, I called Darrin back and asked if I could borrow the photo albums Bobby had left behind. Back during our cross-country drive, Darrin had mentioned he had a few boxes of Bobby's things, and I wanted to show Vic a picture of Carol to see if she had visited him on her Boston trip many months prior.

Darrin surprised me when he asked if he could go along to visit Vic at the prison.

"Ummmm, I guess so," I said uncertainly. "We'll need to get you on the approved list, but that shouldn't be a big deal." He answered my unasked question before I could bumble into asking it.

"I'd just like to tell him that he had a great kid and share some stories. He might not care, but I feel like I owe it to Bobby." Darrin sounded determined.

And just like that, any on-again-off-again lingering suspicions that I had about Darrin vanished for good. I couldn't fathom that he might have had something to do with Bobby's murder, yet wanted to go visit his father to tell him about his great son. Unless it came from guilt? I just couldn't see it.

After I gave Darrin the instructions as to how to get on the visitor list at the prison, we agreed on a time for the day after next, and I told him I'd swing by to pick him up. Hopefully I wouldn't run into Gina at their apartment. Sigh.

CHAPTER 39
SATURDAY, MARCH 22ND

I slept in a little bit the following morning and was glad the previous couple of days were in the history books. Whatever David had been doing with Gina was clearly none of my business, and if that was his type of girl, then it was best I'd never gotten around to asking him out to dinner. I'd keep telling myself that until I managed to believe it.

After brushing my teeth and making the bed, I shuffled into the kitchen. I fully expected Doob to be drinking out of Sampson's bowl, but all was quiet. Moira's bedroom door was shut, which was almost a sure sign that she was home. That was very odd for a Saturday morning when she usually goes into work for a few quiet hours while the office is unoccupied. Doobie's laptop was on the kitchen table, but he wasn't sprawled out anywhere, so he must have actually been at his own apartment.

I grabbed a couple of frosted mini chocolate doughnuts and turned on Doob's laptop. I could have used my own, but his runs so much faster, probably because of the nine billion emails I haven't purged from my system. Or possibly because I don't have an anti-virus what-chacallit, that can't help either.

I used Doob's password info and logged on to the laptop in no time. I checked my email and found a few jokes, some coupons for various retail outlets, and a notice that my credit card statement was ready for viewing. Yeah right. View this.

I sent Doob an email, asking if he was up. If he was on one of his other laptops, the response would be quick. God forbid we use a telephone.

As expected, Doob responded immediately that he was up and at 'em. I wrote back that I'd buy if he'd go to the coffee shop, and shortly thereafter

I heard keys in the lock, and Doob walked in with his hand out. He had an orange and yellow knitted cap on that looked like it had been made sometime at the turn of the 19th century, but at least it covered his hair. For clothing, he'd managed a faded jean jacket over a purple tee shirt, the latter which appeared to be full of holes. His getup was topped off with black sweatpants and bright blue flip-flops that revealed some very white feet, with a few hairs sprouting from the toes. I had a flash of what I'd probably looked like at Faneuil Hall two days ago.

"That was fast," I said with a smile and grabbed my purse. Rummaging for my billfold, I unearthed twelve dollars and held it out. "Will this do?"

Doob shrugged. "I can probably make that work. I'll just make your coffee smaller if it isn't enough."

I raised an eyebrow and gave him the money. He asked, "Should I take Sampson out before I go?"

I gestured my head towards Moira's room and said, "Moira must have taken a day off, and I think they're in there sleeping. If you're brave enough to go in and get him, go right ahead. Personally, I wouldn't attempt it for any amount of money. If she's missing work, then there's definitely a good reason."

Doob looked crestfallen. He was simply cuckoo about that dog.

"Tell you what, Doob. I'll probably make enough noise that they'll be up by the time you get back. You can take Sampson out then." I had no intentions of waking them up, but I hated to see his pout under that pathetic little hat.

His face lit up. "Cool. See you in a little bit. Do you think Moira will want anything?"

"God, no. She'll have her bottled water and strict regimen of vitamins and yogurt when she gets up."

He considered that for a moment. "It's weird that you two are related."

I was being very quiet so as not to disturb the sleeping beauties, but Moira's door opened about fifteen minutes later, and Sampson bounded out and presented himself in front of me, looking for some petting and cooing. His tail was wagging and he was full of doggy optimism, ready to face another day of eating, sleeping, walking and passing gas. I don't think I believe in reincarnation, but if it does exist, then I want to come back as a pampered dog.

Moira strolled out in a white robe, with her hair loosely twisted around a clip on top of her head. Even without makeup, she looked like a flower in bloom. I fully expected birds to start flying around her, chirping a lovely little tune, straight out of *Cinderella*. I couldn't help but wonder at the injustice of the whole thing.

"Hey Meg." She had her scratchy morning voice.

I smiled. "Hey yourself stranger. It's good to see you. You taking the morning off?"

She raised a shoulder lightly. "Yeah, I have a lot of vacation time built up and decided to use some of it. I'm taking all of next week off."

There was something in her voice that gave me a funny tummy. Upon closer inspection, her eyes looked a little puffy. For most people, that is normal in the morning. But Moira is not normal. She's never puffed. She's always perfect. I cocked my head at her. "A whole week? That's not like you."

Another raised shoulder. "Yeah, well. I've been missing you and Sampson, and it's nice to be at my own apartment now and then."

Hearing his name, Sampson zipped over to her, and she ruffled his ears. He leaned in towards her, indicating that he would only put up with that type of behavior for a few more hours.

"Is Porter here?" I dreaded the possibility.

"No." Her answer was clipped, and she wasn't making eye contact.

"Is everything okay?" My older sister radar was blaring like a fire alarm.

"Not really, but it's kind of hard to talk to you about it. I know that you hate him. You'll be glad to know we're finished, so you won't have to deal with him anymore."

"I'm sorry you're hurting," I said lamely.

"Whatever, Meg," she responded.

And that's all it took. "Listen, Moira, the guy is a totally self-absorbed-douche-bag-egomaniac. A stuffed shirt and a smug, pompous asshole. There's not one single redeeming quality about him. He sucks. He *worse* than sucks. He's not good looking, and he gets even less good looking when he opens his fat, I'm-better-than-everyone mouth. There is clearly something shoved up his ass at all times. I'm truly sorry you're bummed out, but you can do so much better than that little prick. There are a ton of guys who would love to go out with you, but you don't even see them because you've wasted so much time on that jerkoff. You're ten million times better off without that little yuppie yard gnome."

I braced myself for the verbal onslaught that was sure to come my way, but Moira just gaped at me. Then she twisted up her mouth, which meant she was thinking. "When did you realize that you disliked him so much?"

"The truth?"

She narrowed her eyes and folded her arms.

"The second I met him."

Her face fell. "Was he that bad?" She seemed sincere.

"Yes."

She nodded to herself and then went into the kitchen and started rummaging around. Sampson was running back and forth between us, looking to see who was going to take him out to do his business.

I heard a knock on the door but didn't feel like getting up. "Who is it?" I bellowed.

I heard Doob's muffled voice through the door. "It's me!"

"Use your keys, Doob! That's why you've got them!"

"I can't!"

Oh, for goodness sake. I got up and stomped to the door. I whipped it open with my what-the-hell face and stared right at Doob and David Fontana. God above, and here I thought I'd looked a fright at Faneuil Hall. My yellow terry cloth robe and tattered pink bunny slippers undoubtedly couldn't compete with Gina's sexy sleepwear.

Doob was looking extremely uncomfortable. "Sorry Meg, but I saw this guy at the coffee shop. Then I noticed him coming into the building, and then he followed me to your apartment. He said he knows you, but with everything that's happened, I just wanted to make sure."

Good grief, and here I was stomping around because Doob didn't use his key. I should have known better. Doob is always so well intentioned that it makes me feel guilty at times.

"Thanks, Doob. Yes, this is David Fontana, the client of mine who we've talked about." I gestured to have them come in and gave David a tight smile. He had two coffees and the packages I'd dumped at Faneuil Hall the other day. I didn't deserve either of these nice men coming into my home.

I took everything from David while he and Doobie shook hands. I placed the coffees on the table and the packages on the floor, then turned around to face the music.

"Well, David, thank you very much for stopping by. I'm surprised to see you."

"Well, not half as surprised as I was to see you on Thursday."

244

I felt myself flush. "Uh, yeah, about that. I'm sorry, if, uh—"

"It's okay, Meagan. I haven't seen a good catfight in a long time. It was actually pretty entertaining." Speaking of cats, he was smiling like a Cheshire and looking pretty darn proud of himself.

Doob's eyes grew to the size of pie pans. "What catfight? Meeeoooooowwwww!"

They both looked at me expectantly, and I looked to the heavens for some help. None came.

"Doob, it was nothing, really. I ran into Gina and David at Faneuil Hall a couple days ago, and Gina and I exchanged some unpleasantries."

Doob smiled knowingly. "And you punched her? Meeeoooooowwwww!" Doob shadow boxed around the room like an uncoordinated puppet.

"No, I didn't punch her!"

David cocked his head, and I knew he would spill the beans if I didn't give Doob some details. They were enjoying themselves just a little too much, and I hated being the subject of a catfight. Men always seem to find them so titillating.

I threw my arms in the air. "Okay, fine. Gina was being Gina, and I kind of smashed some cotton candy into her face and knocked her over. David was smart enough to break us up, and I accidentally left my packages behind."

Moira came out of the kitchen as I was finishing my story, and she noticed David in the room. "Well, hello there." She looked at me questioningly.

I spun around, thankful for the diversion. "Moira, this is David Fontana, the client we've briefly discussed." I turned to David.

"David, Moira and Doobie are on my payroll for a whopping dollar a year. That way, they can help me with various aspects of my cases, but it's all held in the strictest of confidence." I flashed back to Ma's birthday when Moira had blabbed David's name, and I felt my face redden again. I would have internal sunburn by the end of the day.

David smiled even wider. "Nice to meet you, Moira. Should we have some coffee?"

That was the best idea I'd heard so far today. Between the two coffees David had picked up and the two from Doob, we had a total of four, and they smelled great.

"Moira, we've got an extra coffee, so we'd love if you'd have one of them with us." I didn't think she'd join in, but she surprised me by gesturing to the table.

"Why not? Guys, have a seat while Meg and I get out of our pajamas. Doob, you know where everything is, so make yourself at home."

Moira and I departed to our respective rooms, and I heard her get back to our guests before I did. She was unbelievable. I joined them two minutes later, and David had evidently given Moira and Doob some additional details about the altercation with Gina. They were all laughing, and Moira shook her head at me when I returned.

"Meg, just let me know when to clear my calendar to defend you for assaulting Miss Silver Spoon."

"Hey, I've got a big bruise on my shin from her pointy overpriced shoes, so I could sue her bony ass as well. Anyway, I'd gladly do it again." I paused. "Except this time, I'd remember to grab the packages. I'm really sorry you had to get those for me, David. You should have just left them there."

"Well, if it had been up to Gina, we'd have thrown them in the nearest dumpster."

"Sorry. I hope I didn't mess anything up for you two." I waited for my nose to grow, but it stayed in place.

Thankfully, Moira changed the subject. "So David, how is your brother doing?"

David's light mood changed quickly. "I dunno. He's got his bartending gig, but he's working really late and rolling in around three or four o'clock in the morning most days. I'm wondering about some of the types that he's meeting and hanging out with. Hopefully he's not blowing all of his money. I guess that I just wish he'd get more of a nine-to-five job, but he's a big boy, so I'll keep my mouth shut."

Moira looked pointedly at me and raised that friggin' eyebrow. "A shut mouth? How unusual for an older sibling." I rolled my eyes.

David laughed. "Yeah, well, I try to avoid confrontation unless it involves two women at Faneuil Hall." I winced while Moira and Doob smiled, and David continued.

"I'd say something to Darrin if I thought it would help, but he's a free spirit. I'd offer him a stable job, but he's not an office type." David then turned towards Doobie. "What do you do, Doob?"

Doob was slurping on his coffee and looked stunned that he'd been asked a question about his employment status.

"I, uh, do this," he said and kind of looked around the room. He then sunk down in his chair. "I guess I don't have a real job, sorry."

I could tell that Doob felt inadequate, and I immediately jumped to his defense. "Doob is being modest. He is unbelievable with computers, and he does a lot of freelance projects. He was actually a tremendous help to me on your case."

David looked impressed. "Really? Well, thank you very much. You and Meagan did a great job."

Doob turned three shades of red, which made my reds look pale. He doesn't do well being the center of unwanted attention. "No problem. Does Sampson need to go out?" His look was pleading.

Moira said, "He's been waiting for you, Doob. Do you mind?"

"Not at all. Come here, boy!" Sampson galloped over to Doobie, and they raced out the door.

David had sensed Doob's discomfort and said, "Sorry, I didn't mean to make him feel bad."

I explained. "Moira and I love him like a brother. He's not really unemployed; he's a bit of a trust fund baby and really is brilliant with computers. Companies have actually paid him to hack into their websites to show them where their weaknesses are, but he just doesn't need regular work."

David smiled. "Well, that sounds like a pretty great gig. Good for him."

I nodded. "That's why I lost it with Gina. Do you remember when she referred to my loser neighbor?"

"I do. That's when you smashed her face with the cotton candy."

Moira shook her head and laughed. "Nice, Meg."

"No, it wasn't nice, but I'll say again that I'd gladly do it all over. When she said that, she was referring to Doobie, and he's far from a loser. He was born with money just like her, but he's got the best heart of anyone I know. I doubt that witch even has a heart, and I just wasn't going to have her badmouthing him." Meagan Maloney, Best-Neighbor-Ever-Extraordinaire.

David nodded like he understood things a little more clearly, and Moira looked at me with something resembling admiration. "I wish I could have seen it," she said with a smile.

"Joe Fraser has nothing on this one, let me tell you," David said. He reached over and tousled my already unruly hair, and I thought I would faint from giddiness.

Moira turned to him. "So David, are you dating Gina regularly, or was that just a one-time silly thing?"

My eyes bulged. "Moira! That's really none of our business."

David chuckled and held up his hands. "It's okay, really. I recently got out of a long-term relationship—"

"Jocelyn," I quipped. *Whoops.*

David looked at me questioningly. He must have forgotten her name had come up when Darrin was moving in. I certainly hadn't forgotten.

"Um, yes, Jocelyn. We lived together for a couple of years before it fell apart. I won't bore you with the gory details. A few of my friends have been encouraging me to get back into the whole dating scene, and a friend of a friend set up Gina and me. Thursday was the first time we'd met," he said. "You made it a very memorable first date, Meagan." Hearing him say *Gina* and *dating* in the same sentence made my stomach flop.

"Well, you seem like much too nice of a guy to be hanging out with snobs like her," Moira chimed in. "Will you be seeing her again?"

Oh.My.God. Moira simply couldn't *not* be a lawyer, and this cross-examination was so transparent that I might as well have announced my huge crush for him right then and there.

David's face reddened a little bit, and he shifted in his chair. "Um, I don't know for sure. The date kind of ended abruptly after we saw Meagan. She thought she was getting a migraine because of where Meagan pulled her hair—"

"Sissy," I said under my breath.

David smirked. "I told her I'd call her in a day or so, to see how she's feeling, so I'll probably touch base with her later today. I think she might have played up her injuries just a little bit. There were only seventeen stitches."

"What?!" Moira's head snapped over to look at me, and I briefly wondered if she could give herself whiplash.

I grinned. "I bet it was only eight or nine stitches at the most."

We continued talking until the apartment door burst open, and Sampson bounded into the room, headed straight for the pantry. Moira jumped out of her chair and tended to his majesty. Doobie then sauntered through the door, wearing a headband that had been fashioned into a pair of sequined, black cat ears. He'd used them when handing out candy the previous Halloween, and the kids had loved it.

"Meeeeowwwwwww!" he screeched and looked incredibly pleased with himself.

"Hilarious, Doob. I'm so glad you're getting such a kick out of this."

"I really am," he said, beaming. "I think these would be much more appropriate on you, though." He plopped the cat ears on my head.

Moira came back into the room and raised an eyebrow when she saw me. "So David, have you received any information about who broke into your office?"

He shook his head and took a sip of coffee. "No, but Meagan and I are pretty sure that we know who did it. It's got to be that guy who grabbed her on the street. But the police didn't find any fingerprints or other evidence, so it's going to be tough to prove."

Moira said, "Well, it'll be even tougher now."

David's face registered confusion, and he looked at me. "What does that mean? I thought I'd asked you about that the other day, Meagan."

I winced. "I'm sorry, but I thought Darrin would have told you. Plus, it wouldn't have been appropriate to discuss in front of Gina."

Moira laughed. "*You're* talking about being appropriate? Was this before or after you knocked her to the ground?"

I ignored her and turned back to David. "Anyway, the guy who grabbed me on the street ended up dead in the harbor."

David's eyes grew wide. "Are you kidding me? What happened?"

I gave him the abbreviated version of what we knew, and, of course, David asked the logical question. "Did you call the police?"

Oh no. "Um, no, I didn't."

"Well, shouldn't we? Let's call them right now." He looked from me to Moira to Doobie and back to me. Doob was staring down at the table, while I gazed into the hole in my Styrofoam coffee cup lid, and Moira became very interested in rubbing Sampson's ears. David tried to wait us all out and then leaned forward, both arms on the table.

"All right guys, what's up?" David's voice sounded stern, and I saw Doob physically shrink inward.

No one responded, and David took his cell phone out of his pocket. "Meagan, I am dialing the police in five seconds if you don't start explaining."

"Okay," I said and put my hands up. "The thing is, I might, uh, I might know—"

David's face went white. "You didn't have anything to do with this, did you?"

Moira slammed her hand on the table, and Doobie jumped so high out of his chair that he was definitely going to need a change of underwear. "Of *course* she didn't! Who the hell do you think you are? You've got a lot of nerve waltzing in here and saying that when she was the one who was attacked!"

David leaned back in his chair and rubbed his forehead. "I'm sorry. It's just that she hasn't called the police, and I saw her go after someone—"

I interrupted him. "David, first of all, I'm sitting right here, so don't talk about me like I'm not in the room. Second, I am more than a little pissed that you think I could do something like that, but in lieu of the events with Gina, I'll cut you some slack. But knocking her down and dumping someone into the harbor are very different things, don't you think?"

"Yes, I do. So why won't you call the police?"

"I'll tell you two things, and then you've got to trust me on the rest. The first is that I had *nothing* to do with what happened to that guy. The second is that I might know who did, but I'm not sure what to do about it."

He sighed. Then he leaned across the table again and spoke very softly. "Meagan, do you remember the day we met?"

How could I forget? "Of course."

"Well, a couple of things struck me about you right away. The first is that you were very direct, and second, you seemed honest."

"Those things are both true," Moira said, her voice filled with irritation. "What's your point?"

He didn't glance her way but kept his eyes locked on mine. He pointed a finger across the table at me, and I was surprised Moira didn't slap his hand away.

"My point is that you told me from day one that you'd go to the authorities if you'd found anything illegal going on with my brother. I believe you used the word *hinky*, and you made it very clear that you weren't going to be a party to anything that was out of bounds. Also, you were a little upset with me when I told you that I'd misled you about opening the briefcase. You're a straight shooter, Meagan. So why is this situation different?"

I momentarily hated him for throwing my words back in my face. After all, we were talking about Uncle Lare.

"It just is," I said weakly, knowing it sounded lame.

David stood up. "Well, maybe I misjudged you, Meagan. Take care of yourself." He left his coffee on the table and walked out of the apartment.

CHAPTER 40
SUNDAY, MARCH 23RD

Around eleven thirty the next morning, I pulled up in front of David and Darrin's building. Thankfully Darrin was outside waiting for me at the top of the stairs. I absolutely didn't want to have to go up to their apartment and possibly see David. I flipped on my hazard lights and watched Darrin meander down the steps. I noticed that he had what looked to be a bright blue book in his hand.

When he got to the car, I noticed the words *Photo Album* in gold lettering on the front cover. He opened the car door and popped his head inside. "I'm sorry, Meagan, but I just found out that a guy I work with got in a car wreck last night, and I've got to take his shift this afternoon. But it wasn't a wasted trip for you, because I know you wanted these." He handed me the photo album, and I flipped it open to see a lot of pictures of Bobby and his friends.

I looked back up at Darrin. "No worries, I hope your coworker will be okay. And I really appreciate the pictures. I don't know how receptive Vic is going to be to any of this, but hopefully he'll want to see some photos of his son."

"Yeah, I went to CVS yesterday and made copies of every single picture that Bobby had."

"That must have cost a bundle."

He shrugged. "It wasn't cheap, but I had an ulterior motive. I want Vic to have some pictures of Bobby, but I want some memories, too, so this seemed like the most logical choice."

A horn beeped behind me, and I gave the one finger salute. "Do you mind hopping in and I'll drive around the block so we can talk for a second?"

253

"Not at all."

I smiled over at him as I pulled into traffic. "That was really nice of you, with the pictures. I don't know if the guards will let him keep the whole book, but I'll do my best."

"Well, with him getting out soon, I don't think they're going to be too worried about a fifty-year-old guy with a photo album. It's not like he's going to use it to bust out."

That totally caught me off guard, and I almost side-swiped a taxi. "Darrin, what are you talking about? Vic is getting *out*? When?"

"Yeah, it turns out the person I spoke with about visiting privileges was a girl from my high school days."

"Small world."

He nodded. "Yeah. Anyway, we got talking a little bit, and she said it was odd that Vic is finally getting some visitors when he's so close to getting out. I asked what she meant, and she said that he's being released in less than a week. I can't remember the exact date."

"Holy cow," I murmured. "I wonder what he'll do."

"I dunno," Darrin said quietly. "It kinda sucks."

I immediately flashed to one of my favorite movies of all time, *Shawshank Redemption*. There's a scene in which one of the old men, Brooks, gets out of prison after years and years. He can't adjust to the modern world that he's reentered, so he hangs himself in a dismal little room in the boarding house he'd been living in. It was terrible. I thought of Vic McBride having no family and trying to start his life over at fifty years of age. I got a lump in my throat.

Darrin was studying me. "*Shawshank Redemption?*"

That surprised me. "How'd you know?"

"It just seems fitting. I hope you find out that he's a decent guy. That probably sounds odd, considering where he's been for twenty-five years, but I'm finding myself rooting for him."

I nodded. "I know what you mean."

"Do you know what he was locked up for?" Darrin asked.

I considered that. "I don't think so," I admitted. "What'd he do?"

"You probably remember back when we were kids that Boston was pretty well known for armed robberies?"

"Yeah, sure," I replied. "They were on the news all the time. I remember my Uncle Larry telling us that he carried a gun every time he went to the bank. He tried to get my pop to do it as well, but Ma wouldn't hear of it."

"Okay, so you know the deal. Anyway, there was a botched robbery that went down about twenty-five years ago, and Bobby's dad was the driver of the getaway car."

I shook my head. "Ah, jeez."

"I know. Supposedly that was the first time he'd been in on it. The guys with him had already done a couple of small-time convenience store robberies. They had a guy on the inside at the bank and told Vic that all he'd have to do is drive them there, wait outside, and drive them away afterwards."

"Yeah, it always sounds easy, doesn't it? Obviously something went wrong."

"Understatement. They went in the middle of the night, and the guys got into the bank well enough. It was in some type of a strip mall, and Bobby's dad was waiting outside and not seeing any activity. However, just as the guys came out of the bank, all these cop cars appeared out of nowhere. Lights flashing, sirens blaring, and the guys jumped in the car and started screaming at Vic to get the fuck outta there, so he peeled out."

"Holy shit."

"You can say that again. Anyway, for whatever reason, this rookie cop got out of his vehicle and basically jumped in front of the car Vic was driving. As the story goes, he was in a shooter's stance and was screaming at Vic to stop."

"Why would he do that?"

"Take on a moving vehicle? Who the hell knows? The awful thing is that Vic stomped on the brakes when he saw the cop, but it was winter, and the fucking car just started sliding. That part of the parking lot must have had some black ice. Anyway, when the cop finally realized that the car wasn't stopping, he tried to jump out of the way, but he was on slippery ground as well, and the car hit him."

I felt nauseous. "Did it kill him?"

"Not right away, but it launched him into the air, and he died of internal injuries a couple of hours later."

"I can't believe they didn't kill Vic," I said softly.

"The other cops?"

I nodded.

"I agree with you there, Meagan. There's no working bond greater than the boys in blue. And those guys hardly take it well when someone kills one of their own. But apparently at the trial, one of the testifying captains said that Vic was a mess at the scene, sobbing and saying that he was so sorry. He'd begged to see if the cop was okay, but the other police wouldn't let Vic near him. They dragged Vic to the back of the police cruiser because he couldn't even walk. I don't think the typical term of cop-killer applies to him, but at the end of the day, he killed an officer, and he's served his time for it."

I shook my head and wondered about a then twenty-five-year-old Vic. What made him so desperate to make a few bucks that he would do that? And did the rookie cop have a family? And how had their entire lives been affected because of his death?

I finished my trek around the weird city block and told Darrin I'd let him know how my visit went. He got out of the car and shut the door but then immediately knocked on the window. I let it down, and he leaned in the doorframe.

"Do me a favor, Meg."

"What's that?"

"Please give Vic my number, and tell him that I plan on visiting him soon, even if it has to wait until he gets out and gets settled."

I smiled. "I will definitely do that. I've gotta think he could use a friend once he gets out of there."

"Thanks, Meagan. Talk to you later."

With that, I pulled back into traffic and headed towards the Souza-Baranowski Correctional Center in Shirley, Massachusetts.

CHAPTER 41

The next few hours were ones that I'd probably never want to repeat, but nonetheless, I was glad I had made the decision to go see Vic. I reviewed the whole scene in my mind as I drove away from the prison late that afternoon. Nothing like a little quiet, highway time to let the mind wander and reflect.

After arriving at the prison, I was made to remove nearly half my clothing, fill out a visitor form, give up my pocketbook, and essentially get cavity searched. I then handed over the photo album for a guard to rifle through.

The guard was a mountain of a man, with tons of red hair and freckles, as well as about thirty extra pounds around his midsection. I considered asking him if we might be related, but he didn't seem in the mood for chitchat. As suspected, I wasn't able to give Vic the entire album, but the guard said I could give him five of the individual pictures. I wondered how in the hell that made sense but didn't ask.

After going through a metal detector, I waited in an area called the Pedestrian Trap for my one o'clock scheduled visit. It was unnerving and the closest, I hoped, to ever being incarcerated.

Once I got in to see Vic, it was pretty awkward. He was a small, wiry man with closely cropped gray hair and pale blue eyes. The rules stated that we had to sit on the same side of a long table that reminded me of the cafeteria tables from high school. Our close proximity added to the uncomfortable atmosphere.

The walls in the visiting area were a puke-colored green, and it must have been the cheapest, ugliest paint ever made available to the state. There were other prisoners and visitors in the room, and everything smelled overpoweringly of disinfectant, which wasn't doing a very good job of covering the body odor that permeated the air.

Initially, Vic was very guarded with me, and I couldn't blame him. I hated having to discuss his murdered son, especially given the fact that we'd just met. After I'd told him who I was and why I was there, he warmed up a little and seemed like he wanted to help.

I started off by giving Vic four of the pictures, and a lump formed in my throat as I watched him flip through the photos again and again. I didn't know when he'd last seen Bobby, but Vic must have recognized his face because he didn't ask me to point him out. I felt like an imposter since I'd never met Bobby, never been his friend, but Vic didn't seem to mind. I apologized for not knowing everyone in the photos but told him about Darrin and his eagerness to meet. Before entering the visiting area, I'd scribbled Darrin's cell number on the back of one of the pictures for Vic. When he learned that Darrin helped Bobby with the viatical policy there was a curl of a smile on the side of his mouth.

I purposely saved the picture of Bobby and Carol's wedding for last and found it extremely sad that Vic had never seen a photo of his son and daughter-in-law on their wedding day. When I gave it to him, the recognition registered instantly on his face, and he nodded several times. "That is definitely the girl who came to see me last year. She seemed pretty desperate to find Bobby."

"And you knew where he was at the time?"

"Yeah. He'd contacted me after moving to Los Angeles. He was sick, and I guess he wanted to reach out to his old man."

"Vic, this is important. Did you tell Carol where Bobby was living?"

He had looked down before answering and then glanced over at me. "Yeah, I did. I may have been wrong to do it, but she seemed sincere about wanting to find him. After twenty-five years in this place, I didn't want my boy dying alone." His eyes filled with tears, and it was all I could do to not break down myself.

After he regained his composure, Vic and I went on to discuss politics, movies, current events, and how different the world was now compared to twenty-five years ago when he was last free. It was like talking to a friend.

When the guards signaled the five minute warning, I was shocked that two and a half hours had flown by. When I stood up to leave, Vic also rose and reached out his hand, his eyes again full of tears.

"I hope you'll let me take you and Darrin to lunch when I get out of here, Meagan. It's hard to believe that I'll be free in a matter of days."

I smiled cautiously at him, not knowing if he was happy, scared, or both. He continued.

"I appreciate all you're trying to do in Bobby's memory, and I hope that you find Carol." He hesitated, and I felt like there was something more he wanted to say.

"Is there anything else you want to tell me?" I asked.

He looked at me curiously. "You didn't ask me why I did it."

I was startled. "I figured it was none of my business." We looked at each other for an awkward moment, and I cocked my head. "Do you want to tell me?"

He smiled sadly. "Did you know that Victoria was pregnant when I committed that crime?"

Yet another surprise. "Ummm, no, I didn't. So you have another child?"

He nodded. "Somewhere out there, yeah. That's why I did it. We didn't have any money, and I thought it'd be an easy score. I didn't mean to hurt that cop, not for a second."

To think he committed that crime for his family and now had no family didn't seem right. The wonderful world of irony. My heart ached for him. "I believe you."

He kept talking, almost to himself. "Victoria had to give her up. She couldn't afford Bobby, much less a newborn."

"You said her. *The baby was a girl?"*

He nodded and looked down. After his chin stopped quivering, he finally spoke, his voice very soft. "Every September 18th, I say a silent happy birthday to my baby girl."

Somehow I managed to keep it together, despite the emotions churning through my system. "I'm really sorry, Vic. I know you've got things to take care of once you get out of here, but maybe we could work on finding your daughter once you're all settled."

He looked at me with such hope in his eyes that it actually scared me a little.

"I'd like nothing more, Meagan. And before you leave, I just need to say that I'm sure your parents are incredibly proud of you." I blinked back tears and said that I'd be looking forward to that lunch.

As I was driving along and revisiting the afternoon, my cell phone rang. I checked the caller ID, and it was my apartment number.

"Hi Doob," I said, my voice sounding tired.

"How'd it go?"

"It was nothing I'd like to do again in this lifetime, but Vic seemed like a solid guy. And you were right—Carol visited him last fall."

"Well, that's progress. Now we just need to figure out where she is."

I groaned loudly.

"Are you on your way home, Meg?"

"Yep. Why? Do you want some food?"

"No. I'll order a pizza. Moira is home, and I brought her up to date on everything." He paused.

"And?"

"And she's got a theory."

I rolled my eyes. "Is this going to throw another wrench into everything?"

"Yep. Just drive safe and get home soon, Meg."

I heard a click, and Doob was gone.

When I entered the apartment, my nose perked to the smells of pepperoni, garlic, and possibly something chocolate?

I put my coat in the closet and yelled towards the kitchen. "Do I smell cupcakes?"

Doob came out of the kitchen wearing what appeared to be only a blue and white checked apron. He had a kitchen mitt on each hand and was holding a big white bowl with one mitt and a mixing spoon with the other. There was chocolate all over his face.

"Doob, tell me you have clothes on under the apron, or I swear to God, I will light you on fire."

Doob looked down and then turned purple. He twirled around, and from his backside I saw that he had on cutoff jean shorts and a ribbed tank top that used to be white but was now more yellowish in color. He looked like some type of 80s kitchen porn star.

"Thank God," I said and plopped on the couch. "Tell me that Moira knows what you're up to," I said in a stage whisper.

"Take it easy. She actually gave me the apron." He looked down at himself again. "Like I care if something gets on my clothes, but evidently she does."

"She's probably more worried about something jumping off your clothes and getting into the batter. What are you making anyway? Judging by your face, it's gotta be chocolate."

"Correctomundo, Sherlocka Holmes. Chocolate cupcakes, chocolate frosting. We'll only have about half of what the box says, as I've already eaten the rest."

"Yum. Where's Moira?"

"She jumped in the shower. The pizza just got here, so let me finish this, and we'll eat in five."

Assertive-Doob was cute. I lumbered into my bedroom and tidied up a few things until I heard voices in the kitchen. I went out to join the meal and smiled when I saw Moira.

"Hey Sis. I hear you have some thoughts on my case."

Moira was putting plates and pizza boxes on the table, and I grabbed some napkins and three diet Cokes. Acknowledging my addiction, I then grabbed a fourth.

"I do." Moira sounded decisive.

"So, let's hear it, Counselor."

"Well, to me, Carol is the obvious choice for the murders of Bobby and Glenn."

I cocked my head. "I'm listening. Carol is missing, by the way."

"How convenient," Moira replied.

I sighed. "Maybe."

"From what Doob told me a little bit ago, your visit with Vic today confirmed that Carol had tracked Bobby down. Very simply, she murdered him because she thought she had a million dollars coming.

"Then we move on to Glenn, who also thought that Carol had a million dollars coming. He up and died in Boston Harbor under less-than-normal circumstances."

I lulled my head back and forth. "Elaborate, please."

"Well, Bobby is obvious. She didn't know about the viatical policy, so that's a follow-the-money scenario. She thought the million was hers the minute that Bobby died, case closed.

"Glenn isn't as obvious, but I've got a theory. At some point after Carol had Bobby killed, she discovered that she'd been cut out of the money, so she disappeared, this time for good. My guess is that Glenn wasn't so quick to give up on the million bucks, and that's when he started running around terrorizing people, trying to find out what happened to the money. We all agree that Glenn wasn't the brightest bulb. Carol obviously knew that he was a loose cannon and that he'd go ballistic when he found out that the money wasn't hers. Glenn likely knew what she'd done to Bobby, so she decided to get rid of him as well. Carol is only missing because she *wants* to be missing. It's all speculation, but that's my two cents."

The three of us pondered Moira's assumptions while we chowed on the pizza. Doob then chimed in with a mouthful of food. "So if we go with

Moira's thinking, is it possible that Carol killed Brenda, too, or do we still think Ramirez was behind that?" Half a piece of pepperoni flew from his mouth and landed on one of the daffodils in Moira's centerpiece.

I rubbed my forehead. "Seriously, Doob. We'll still be here if you want to actually swallow before asking your next question. That's disgusting."

Doob delicately picked the piece of pepperoni out of the flowers.

Moira glared. "If you even think about eating that, you are out of here."

Doob's eyes lit up. "Sampson?"

"No!" Moira and I said simultaneously. Sampson had been relegated to Moira's bedroom while we were eating, so as not to torture the poor dog. Doob got up and went in the kitchen to throw out his half-chewed piece of food.

"My money is still on Ramirez for killing Brenda," I yelled after him in response to his question.

Doob came back and cleared his throat in that uncertain way of his. Moira and I both looked at him expectantly. "Does the peanut gallery have something to add?" I asked.

Doob scratched his unruly head of hair. "Can chicks really be serial killers?" he asked sincerely. He sat down and grabbed another piece of pizza.

"Of course, Doob!" I exclaimed. "For as smart as you are, you ask the silliest questions sometimes. Plus, we don't know if Carol is a serial killer or just a regular killer."

Doob scrunched his lips to one side of his mouth. "Regular killer?"

Moira jumped to Doob's defense. "Okay Meg, be nice. Regarding serial killers, that's actually a decent question because over ninety percent of serial killers are men. Women don't tend to play in that club."

"Exactly why do you know this?" I asked.

"True Crime Television," she responded simply.

I snickered before I could help myself. "Is that what you and Porter watch?"

"*Used* to watch," she corrected, and I felt bad for reminding her of the breakup, but she continued. "And we watched it because I really enjoy it, not because of him. Anyway, there was a show on just the other night about this exact topic. It talked about the small number of serial killers who are women, and it discussed the common traits."

"Which are?" I asked.

"Well, I don't know if I can remember all of them, but I'll give it a shot." She started clicking her fingers. "They tend to be intelligent, with IQs well above normal. Despite that fact, they almost always do poorly in school, have trouble holding down jobs, and often work as unskilled laborers.

"Let's see, they also tend to come from very unstable families. There's generally a history of alcohol, criminal, and psychiatric problems, and there is almost always some type of abuse involved, be it psychological, physical or sexual. Most of the time the abuse is perpetrated by a family member, and suffice it to say, the serial killer ends up hating his or her parents as a result."

I smiled. "Not bad for just watching a television show." Doob nodded.

Moira held up her finger. "They're often fascinated with starting fires as well. That's all I've got."

I snapped my fingers as a memory struck me. "You know what? Darrin told me that Bobby's mother died in a house fire!"

"When was that?" Moira's face lit up with curiosity.

I shut my eyes and thought hard. "If I remember correctly, in the span of several days three major things happened in Bobby's life. He found out about his illness, he discovered that Carol was cheating on him, and his mom died in that fire."

Moira leaned across the table and looked at me intently. "In what order did those things occur?"

I thought about it and then shrugged. "I'm not sure, but I'm also not sure that it matters. If Bobby found out about Carol's infidelity first, would that entice her to burn down his mother's house? That doesn't make any sense. How would she benefit from that?"

Moira leaned back in her chair and pondered the question. "Maybe she thought Bobby would be so distraught over his mother that he would lean on her for support and eventually forgive her. Assuming that he didn't figure out that she burned the house down."

I moved my head from side to side, mulling it over. "I suppose that's possible. I guess I need to know a little more about Carol's background."

Moira and I both looked at Doob, and we didn't need to say anything. Doob saluted. "I'm on it. I'm gonna need some quiet, though."

I looked at Moira. "Wanna go see Ma and Pop?"

She nodded. "That's a good idea. I haven't seen them enough lately, and maybe Ma will make something sweet while we're there." She caught Doob's crestfallen look and quickly recovered. "Although we'll obviously both save our appetites for your cupcakes when we get back, Doobie." Doob beamed. He was so easy to please.

Moira looked over at the pooch. "Sampson, do you want to go for a ride?"

I saw a black and white furry tornado headed towards the door before the words were even out of Moira's mouth. Sampson was spinning and howling and yipping like there was no tomorrow. It was happy-speak in dog language, and from what I could surmise, Sampson was telling Moira that he absolutely, completely, definitely wanted to go for a ride.

As we weaved through the traffic en route to the South Side of Boston, a thought struck me.

"Moira?"

"Yeah?"

"Earlier you said that ninety percent of the serial killers are men, correct?"

Moira looked over at me. "Yes. Why?"

I looked out the window and mused. "I just think that ninety percent of the serial killers who have been *caught* are men."

"Meaning what?"

"I think women make up a larger percentage than we know. It's just that they don't get caught as often."

Moira smiled and snuck a quick glance at me. "Because women are smarter than men?"

"I don't know about smarter, but they're probably more conniving and definitely more vindictive."

Moira considered this. "Smarter."

"Smarter," I agreed and laughed.

I leaned my head back and shut my eyes as Moira wound us through the streets of Boston. I was feeling relaxed.

"Moira?"

"Yeah?"

"It's supposed to rain like crazy tomorrow. I propose that we do a spa day."

"Oh, I like it!" Moira gushed. "Let's do the works! And I know just where to go. One of the partners at the firm has a kid sister who works at that new place on Newbury Street. Her sister can get us a deal if we book a package. Let's email her right now." She handed me her Blackberry, and I pulled up the partner's email and started clicking away.

We got to the folks' house and did the requisite hugs, eating, and general kibitzing. Ma clucked over Sampson as if he was a newborn, and I wondered if he'd even bother coming home with us. Moira heard back from the partner at her firm, and we were booked for facials, manicures, pedicures, and full-body massages the following day at noon. Three hours of heaven.

Moira, Sampson, and I stayed at Ma and Pop's well into the evening, and it turned out to be a very nice visit. Tomorrow looked promising as well. If I'd only known what was coming in twenty-four hours, I wouldn't have left their house.

CHAPTER 42
MONDAY, MARCH 24ᵀᴴ

I woke up the following morning around eight thirty and tried to talk myself into sleeping for another hour, but my brain was having none of it. Doob hadn't been at the apartment when Moira and I'd gotten home the previous night, which had been unusual, so I gave him a call.

He answered in an extra-sleepy voice. "H'lo?"

"Doob, it's me. Are you up?" Duh. From the sound of him, he'd been in deep slumber.

"No." Then I heard a click and stared at the phone. I immediately hit redial. This time he picked up and didn't say a word.

"Doob! Just listen to me for five seconds. I'll go get some food if you come over and tell us what you found out about Carol."

"Meg, I went to bed about twenty minutes ago. I looked for stuff on Carol all night, and there hasn't been a sign of her since last fall. No credit card usage, phone usage, nothing. I'm sorry." Doob sounded exasperated, and he was probably the most patient person I'd ever met, so I knew he was exhausted.

"I'm sorry, Doob. Go back to sleep. Moira and I are going to the spa today from noon until three. Why don't you come over afterwards, and we'll grab some chow?"

"Later Meg," Doob said, and I heard another click.

Moira and I arrived at the spa about fifteen minutes early, and I was very happy that we'd decided to take a cab, because several spa ladies shoved champagne in our hands the minute we walked in. They reviewed our various appointments and smoothly upgraded us to the deeper massages and the fancier facial creams. With an almost scolding air about her, one matronly woman behind the desk reminded us that we were here to *relax*, not to yap, and with that, she commandeered our cell phones. I handed mine over easily. Moira was a little less enthused, but she did as she was told.

After confirming the time slots for our various procedures, Moira and I changed into ridiculously white, fluffy robes. I felt wrapped in a cloud. We then went to separate facial rooms where our faces were slathered with some type of heavenly smelling green concoction. A half hour later, Moira and I reconnected to get side-by-side pedicures. The spa ladies filled up the basins at our feet with warm, soapy water and bubbles, and then they plopped a couple of cucumber slices on our eyelids so we could relax during the process. Ahhhhhhhhhhhh.

The three hours flew by, and Moira and I were all smushy, gushy, and half tipsy when the cab pulled up to take us home. We heard a shrieking sound when we opened the door to leave.

"Ladies, ladies!" The lecturing matronly woman from earlier was rushing towards us with our phones. She smiled broadly as she handed them over. "We know we've done a good job when people nearly forget these wretched things. Please come back again soon."

We thanked her and headed out to the cab. I couldn't believe how the weather had turned in just the span of three hours. The temperature had dropped at least fifteen degrees, and the sky was an ominous dark gray. It looked more like a snow sky than a rain sky, but I'm no meteorologist. I'm not even sure if the term *snow sky* exists.

We hopped into the back of the cab, and Moira immediately checked her phone for messages. She looked bummed when there weren't any, and I assumed she was hoping for a message from that tight-ass, Porter. I was secretly glad she hadn't heard from him but then felt guilty for feeling that way.

I purposely didn't check my messages, or even look at my phone, because I didn't want to have a dinner invitation from some Greek god, which would have made Moira feel even worse. I decided to just enjoy some post-spa peace and quiet, sans cell phone.

Moira and I arrived back at the apartment around three thirty and found Doob and Sampson watching television in the living room. They were both cuddled on the floor, as Moira has a no-Sampson policy on the furniture. Doob claims that he doesn't want Sampson getting an inferiority complex, but my thinking is that Doob would be on the floor despite the policy.

"Ladies, you're both looking lovely," Doob said with a smile. "What's for eats?"

I laughed. "Well, at least you're smart enough to compliment us before asking for food. What are you in the mood for?"

"Chinese!" Doob yelled like a child. I shuffled over to the kitchen pantry and dug out the menu for the local delivery place. By four fifteen, we were covered in remnants of steamed rice, pan-fried noodles, Mongolian beef, kung pao chicken, pork lo mein, and several vegetable spring rolls. I then moved on to my favorite part of the meal, which was the fortune cookie. I didn't care one way or the other about the taste of the cookie, but I liked to read the fortune and then tie it into the current state of my life.

I tore it open and read the following: *Procrastination will cost you dearly.*

Hunh. Well, that fortune sucked, but I couldn't really think of anything I'd been putting off. Then I remembered my cell phone and decided to check for messages. I went into my bedroom and grabbed my pocketbook off the bureau. After digging around a little, I came up with the phone and heard a little chirping noise. The battery was nearly dead. It must have been turned on when I gave it to the lady at the spa.

As it turned out, I'd missed two calls, one from a number that seemed familiar, but I couldn't place it. The second was from Darrin. My phone also indicated two voicemail messages, so I dialed my code and waited to hear the voice from the number that I couldn't quite figure out.

"Hi, uh, Meagan. It's Vic McBride. I'm sorry to bother you, but something kind of weird happened today. I'll try to be brief, but the gist of it is that a lady came to the prison to visit me today, saying that she's a reporter for one of the Boston television stations. She said she'd like to do a story on me, with the angle being about what people do when they're released from prison, how they adapt, all that stuff. She looked really familiar to me, and I figured I must have seen her on the news at one time or another. But after she left, I got looking at the pictures that you gave me, and I realized she looked familiar because she's *in* one of them. I'm positive that it's the same lady. I'm going to call Darrin to talk about this, too, because it just seems odd. If she knew Bobby, why wouldn't she have told me? Anyway, I'll call you back the next time I'm allowed to use the phone, but in the meantime, please talk to Darrin and see what you can figure out. Thank you, Meagan. I hope this is no big deal, but something seems wrong."

Indeed.

CHAPTER 43

My heart rate accelerated as I retrieved the second message.

"Meagan, it's Darrin. Something is majorly fucked up, and I need to talk with you as soon as possible. I spoke with Vic, and he said he left you a message, so I think you kind of know what's going on. The deal is that some lady who said she's a reporter came to visit Vic out of the blue today. He met with her to discuss some story she supposedly wants to write, and then she was on her way. But then Vic recognized the same lady later in one of the pictures you gave him, and those are all pictures from L.A. I have the copies, so Vic had me get out the one in question while we were on the phone. I also scanned the picture and emailed it to you so you can look at it when you speak with him. But Meagan, the girl in the picture is *Melanie*. What the fuck?! Why in the hell would she be visiting Vic, and why would she be impersonating a reporter? She borrowed my truck today to *supposedly* attend the funeral of her long-lost relative, but I think that's utter bullshit. My head is spinning. I hope you get this before she gets back so we can confront her together. Anyway, the phone is beeping, so I'm almost out of time. I'm sorry for the long message, but this has got me totally freaked out. Call me, thanks."

I immediately dialed Darrin's cell phone, but it went right to voicemail. I told him to call me back the second he got the message. I then stumbled out of the bedroom in a state of confusion.

"People, we need to brainstorm," I said with some urgency. Moira and Doob were still in their food stupors at the table. But they both perked up at the sound of my voice.

"What's up?" Moira asked.

I grabbed three Diet Cokes and divvied them out as I brought Moira and Doob up-to-date on the messages.

271

Moira recounted everything once I finished relaying the information. "So Darrin thinks Melanie is here under false pretenses and that she went to visit Vic today in prison? Why would she do that? Further, how certain is Vic that the two ladies are the same person? He's been locked up a long time. Does he wear glasses? Is he absolutely certain?"

"He said on the message that he's *positive*. But unfortunately, I can't talk to him until tomorrow when he's allowed another phone call. And Darrin isn't answering his cell, so I can't pick his brain right now, either."

We sat in silence for a minute, and then I remembered that Darrin had sent me the picture. I ran to my room, pulled up the email and printed it. I brought it into the living room and showed it to Moira and Doob, pointing out Melanie, Darrin, and Bobby in the group of eight people.

Moira studied it. "She'd be more attractive if she was smiling."

Doob also took a close look. "It looks like an Abercrombie and Fitch advertisement. Very attractive people. But Moira is right. That girl should mix in a smile."

Then something that had been niggling at my brain since I'd heard Vic's message clicked into place.

"I've got a thought, guys. Doob, remember when I wanted to call the police after we learned about Glenn, but you were worried that they'd suspect me?"

He nodded vigorously. "I was mainly concerned that I wouldn't make a good alibi for you, as I sleep like the dead. And since I wasn't on the couch, they might have accused you of sneaking out without my hearing you."

Moira narrowed her eyes at Doob. "If you weren't on the couch, where exactly were you?"

Uh oh. Doob turned scarlet and his words churned out as fast as his mouth would allow. "I was kind of in your room, Moira, but I stayed on Sampson's bed. I didn't mess up any of your stuff. Swear to God." Doob was panting as if he'd just finished a hundred yard sprint.

Moira narrowed her eyes further but let the moment pass. "So you were in my room, and Meg was in her room. Neither of you can say with complete certainty that the other person was home all night long. The police might have suspected *you*, Doobie, as far as that goes."

Doob looked like he'd been slapped, but Moira was absolutely correct.

I shook my head, disgusted with myself. "And *that* is exactly the point. I totally fucking missed it. Everyone did."

"What are you talking about?" Moira asked, confused.

I was off my feet and pacing back and forth. "Doob said the police might have suspected me of Glenn's murder because I could have snuck out in the middle of the night. Moira, you just made the point that Doob could have snuck out, too."

I thought I might start hyperventilating. *"Melanie* was Darrin's alibi the night Bobby was killed. I've read the police report about ten times, and I've also talked to Officer Simonetta about it. Both Melanie and Darrin went to bed around ten thirty that night, Darrin to the couch and Melanie to her bedroom. Melanie claimed she got up to use the bathroom just before one in the morning and saw Darrin on the couch. Bobby's death was deemed to have been between one and two o'clock, so Darrin was cleared because the timelines didn't match up. Since he went to bed around ten thirty, it would have been impossible for him to drive to Santa Barbara in a rainstorm, kill Bobby, and return back to the couch in order for Melanie to see him."

"You're absolutely certain?" Moira's face was intense.

I nodded and continued. "The home where Bobby was staying is just under two hours from Melanie's sublet, so a round-trip would take a little less than four hours. Even if Darrin had left at ten forty-five, the *absolute earliest* he could have been back at Melanie's place was two thirty. Plus, the weather was bad, so it probably would have taken a little longer than a typical trip. Finally, killing both Bobby and Jethro would have eaten up some time as well. The timeline doesn't work for Darrin being the murderer, but that all hinges on what *Melanie* told the police."

Moira held her hands up, trying to slow me down. "Okay, Meg, I'm with you. So what are you flipping out about?"

"I'm flipping out because I hadn't fucking thought of this before— what if *Melanie* was the one who snuck out? What if her whole alibi for Darrin was bullshit because she was covering for *herself?"*

Moira and Doob thought about that for a second, and then Moira scowled. "Oh, I don't know, Meagan. There's this little thing called motive. Did she get any money from Bobby?"

"Not that I know of," I admitted. "But this phone call from Vic has me thinking, and Darrin is suspicious as well. Something is definitely off with that girl."

"So we'll go with the 'something is off with that girl' plea," Moira said in a singsong voice. "The jury will undoubtedly go for that one."

I ignored her and kept talking rapid fire. "Something else I just thought of is when Darrin and I were driving cross-country, Darrin said Melanie could barely wake him the morning they were notified of Bobby's murder. The police were at the door, and evidently he didn't hear the doorbell and said that Melanie had to shake the shit out of him to wake him up. He said his head was foggy and he felt completely hungover, despite the fact he'd had only two beers the previous night. By the time the cops arrived, he'd been asleep for over ten hours."

"Your point?" Moira asked skeptically.

"My point is that Melanie could have drugged him, snuck out, and pretended to be *his* alibi. All the while, *she* was the one who drove to Santa Barbara, *she* was the one who killed Bobby and Jethro, and *she* was the one who needed an alibi."

Moira put her hand on her forehead. "Motive, Meg. We need motive."

"I have no fucking idea, Moira."

It was barely audible, but I heard Doob say, "Oh boy," as his chin slumped down into his chest.

I narrowed my eyes at him. "What Doob?"

He exhaled loudly and looked like he was going to be sick.

I ran over to him and got in his face. "Doob! Oh boy what?!"

He started trembling. "Remember the night that you were in Los Angeles sleeping in the rental car?"

"*What?*" Moira's voice had gone up two decibels.

I held up my hand. "Not now, Moira. Yes, Doob, of course I do. Why?" I was doing my best to not shake the shit out of him.

"Well, when we finally talked once you got back to your hotel, I told you I hadn't found Melanie's California address. I'd found a little other background information, but you were too tired to take it down."

"Doob!"

He started sputtering. "And then Darrin contacted you, and you guys met, so we didn't ever go back to talking about Melanie. I never thought about her again because you'd found Darrin. End of story."

"But I'm guessing you found something that you think might matter now?"

He nodded. "When I went digging, Melanie's most recent address had been in Nevada, Vegas specifically. So I dug around a little more in her life, and her bank was also still in the Vegas address."

"Okay?"

"Okay, well, that Jethro dude who they blamed for Bobby's death was some drifter, right?"

I nodded vigorously. "Yeah, Jethro Hackett. He overdosed in the front seat of his car afterwards. They never pinpointed the motive, but I don't know that they tried too hard, either."

Doob rubbed his chin, and I anticipated something profound. "What if Melanie knew him? Like we've already talked about, when I poked around in his past, there wasn't anything there except for a lot of addresses. Something like thirteen of them in the past ten years, if I remember correctly."

Doob sprang to his laptop and did some major league typing.

He looked up at me. "One of those addresses was Boulder City."

"Where is that?" I demanded.

Doob's fingers kept flying. "Twenty miles from Vegas. I didn't make the connection because I never really thought about Melanie living in Vegas beyond the first night when you were in Los Angeles. And then the case looked to be solved, so I didn't think about her anymore. If we're looking at her as a suspect now, then that changes everything."

My heart started pumping wildly. "Okay, so let's think about this. They met in Vegas at some point and stayed in touch. And then maybe she hired him to kill Bobby, or maybe she met up with him that night, and they did it together? Then he either killed himself out of guilt, or maybe she killed him?"

Moira threw her hands in the air. "Maybe the guys from the grassy knoll were in on it, too! What is the *motive*?"

I was exasperated and lashed out at her. "Moira, you're the hot shot! The big brain in the family! Open your compartmentalized mind for one second please and pretend that you have to prove to a jury that Melanie is the one who killed Bobby. How would you argue? What would you need to know?"

She yelled back. "I would need to know the *motive!*"

We glared at each other, and I thought I saw Doob physically start shrinking. If we didn't tone things down, he would actually disappear in front of our eyes.

"Doob, are you shrinking?"

"Yes," he squeaked. "Please don't fight. I usually love chick fights, but this one sucks. You guys aren't together enough to fight."

Moira's demeanor softened instantly, and I took a big breath and nodded.

I spoke quietly. "Moira, I'm serious. I'm definitely grasping at straws, but it at least seems plausible, doesn't it?"

She nodded a quick, curt nod. "As a lawyer, yes. You have to look at every possibility and rule nothing out until you're convinced that it's absolutely not a possibility anymore."

Baby steps. "Okay, good. So now what?"

"We brainstorm," Moira said. "No idea is too insignificant or stupid at this point. You're the only one who's met her Meg, so this is your show. What's she like?" Moira and Doob looked at me expectantly.

I blew out another huge breath. "When I met her, she was very stand-offish, but I thought that was because she was protecting Darrin's whereabouts."

"Or protecting herself," Doob interjected. Moira nodded, and I kept going.

"I spent a little time in the car with her one night, and she said she'd moved to L.A. to get away from a guy."

"Who?" Moira demanded.

"I have no idea."

"Could it be this Jethro guy?"

I shrugged. "I suppose so. She said he was a not-so-nice guy and they'd had a disagreement about her owing him some money."

Moira was getting into it now. "Okay, what else? No detail is too small."

"She said he'd tracked her down but that she'd sent him packing. At least I think that's what she said."

"What does that mean?" Doob said.

"No idea," I replied.

"Keep going," Moira encouraged. "What about her personality?"

I thought of her snotty Iowa comment. "She wasn't exactly what I'd call a cheery person. She seemed quiet and introverted but also a little bit snippy."

"Could you picture her murdering someone?"

I threw my hands up. "I don't know. I can't really picture anyone murdering anyone. And even if she would and could and did do it, it goes back to your question. Why would she pick Bobby who was going to die anyway? Is she just some kind of nutcase?"

We sat in silence for a moment, lost in our thoughts. Then Doob spoke up. "Moira, what are typical motives for murder?"

Moira clicked off her fingers. "Greed, jealousy, revenge—"

I held up both of my hands. "Okay, okay, let's do them one at a time."

Doob chimed in. "Okay, greed."

Moira took it from there. "It's accurate to say that we don't think Melanie received any money from Bobby's death, correct?"

"That's right. I saw her house, which was a one-bedroom sublet, and I got a general sense of her lifestyle. It certainly didn't seem like she was living the high life. She was waitressing at a decent enough place, but it wasn't a hangout for rock stars. I didn't get the feeling she was rolling in money, nor did it seem like she was expecting a windfall."

Doob and I stared at Moira as if waiting for a verdict. "Okay," Moira said. "Take your own advice and make the argument for the other side."

"Hunh? I just gave you my argument."

She shook her head quickly. "I know, that's the whole point."

I cocked my head at her. "Sorry? Not following."

"Let me explain. When I was in college, I took this great debate class. I friggin' loved it."

"Shocker," I mumbled, and Doob tipped his head in agreement.

Moira ignored us. "Anyway, I will never forget this huge group assignment that we had towards the end of the year. We wrote up a fifty-page argument on the side of a topic that had been picked by our professor."

"What was the topic?" Doob asked.

"Gun control," Moira said.

"Which side did you have to argue for?" I inquired.

Moira lit up. "Well, that's the thing. We spent weeks preparing our argument, we got to class, and the professor had lined up the desks so that we were facing the other team. He went over the rules of the debate, and both sides were raring to go, but just before we started, he said, 'By the way, scrap your research. Today you will be arguing for the opposite side you were assigned.'"

I smiled, and Doob said, "What the hell?"

Moira laughed. "The point was that the professor made us think on our feet. We were so cemented into our side of things that we hadn't given so much as a thought to the other side. Then he pulled the rug out from under us, and we had to scramble to argue against all the work we'd done."

"How did the debate go?" Doob asked.

"It was great! It was the most fun I ever had in college, at least from a scholastic standpoint. That day confirmed my choice to be an attorney. I wanted to make arguments and anticipate the reasoning that would be flying back at me. It was exhilarating."

I smiled. "Moira, you look radiant. Do you need a cigarette or something? My God. I wish I had that kind of passion for anything."

She tilted her head. "You do, Meg. You've just hit a few speed bumps along the way."

I felt that weird lump forming in my throat and tried to get Tom out of my head. Thankfully, Moira got me back on track.

"Okay Meg, so this little sidebar has brought us full circle. I want *you* to make the argument as to how Melanie might have received some money and profited from Bobby's death. I want you to go against everything you said a few minutes ago and tell us how it's possible."

I took a deep breath and decided this little game of Moira's might be fun. "Okay, well it's *possible*, I suppose, that he willed something to her, but in his note to Darrin, he mentioned animal shelters and single moms and a couple of other things. He definitely didn't mention Melanie."

Doob piped up. "Could he have given it to her before he died?"

I shrugged. "I guess so, but that would eliminate the motive to kill him. She would have already had the money. Why kill him then?"

"Maybe she thought there was more for her," Moira said.

"Maybe," I conceded. "That doesn't feel right, but maybe." Then something hit me. "Although—"

Moira nodded encouragingly. "Although what? Keep brainstorming."

"Well, this might be a stretch, but this whole mess started when David got a wad of cash from Darrin, fifty thousand dollars to be precise."

"Right," Moira said. "And that means what exactly?"

"Well, Darrin said the money was in a laptop case under the bed. He remembered Bobby telling him to look in it after he died, and Darrin was shocked to see that much money hidden not-so-well in their apartment. He said anyone could have found it."

"But obviously no one did," Doob countered. "Or, if they did, they didn't take it."

I rocked my head from shoulder to shoulder. "Well, we don't know that for sure. Maybe that case initially had a hundred thousand in it. It's not like there was a receipt in there, and Bobby's note didn't specify the amount. What if it had originally had a much higher amount—"

"—and Melanie killed Bobby to make sure he never found out that she took some?" Moira finished my sentence and looked like a kid at Christmas. "You did it Meg! You made the argument for greed."

Her excitement was contagious, but then I deflated a little. "Moira, that's great, I guess, but what did we just accomplish?"

"You paved the path for motive. If she's the one you're honing in on, you've got to see both sides of it and then figure out if you're insane or if she is."

"Even odds," Doob piped up and grinned.

I rolled my eyes. "You're a comedian, Doob."

Doob responded, "So greed stays as a motive, correct?"

"Yes," Moira and I said at the exact same time.

"We're on to jealousy," Doob stated. Then they both looked at me.

I shook my head slowly. "I don't know, but Darrin certainly didn't mention Bobby and Melanie being an item, and I think it would have come up. If they had been dating, the cops probably would have questioned her about his death, and nothing I've heard or read leads me to believe that."

"Okay," Moira said. "But the cops thought they had their man, so they might not have looked into it much beyond him."

"Well, they looked at Darrin," I countered.

"Did they really suspect him, or did they just ask him some questions? After all, he was Bobby's roommate."

"I don't really know. All I know is Melanie provided his alibi. Whether he truly needed one is probably up for debate."

Moira considered that for a second. "Okay, make the other side of the argument."

"Ummmm, maybe they had some one-night gig that meant more to Melanie than it did to Bobby. And maybe when he started dating other people, she couldn't take it. The classic case of if-I-can't-have-him-no-one-can-have-him-cuckoo."

"That one is weak. We'll leave it low on the list for now."

"Moving on to revenge," Doob said.

"Revenge," I repeated. "For what?"

Doob shrugged. "I'm the one asking the questions. The sisters Maloney need to figure out the answers."

Moira took it from there. "But it's the right question, Meg. For what?

Did Bobby somehow burn her? Did he do something so terrible that it would make her want to kill him?"

"Sounds a little far-fetched," I said. "Bobby sounded like a pretty stand-up guy. I don't know what a kid dying of a brain tumor would do to generate that type of hatred."

"Maybe a kid dying of a brain tumor was living for the moment and didn't really give a crap about how he treated people anymore. Maybe he was mad at the world for the hand he'd been dealt." Moira said.

"Far-fetched," I repeated. "If someone knows they're dying, they're probably trying to live their final days as a model citizen. You know, before meeting the Big Guy." I cast my eyes heavenward.

"People react differently to news like that, you never know."

"Moira, I'm telling you! They didn't know each other very long. What could he have done in that timeframe to make her want to kill him?"

Moira glowered. "I'm just trying to look at all the angles. And how do you know that they didn't know each other for very long? And what does that matter anyway? You're acting like there is a minimum timeframe two people have to know each other before the desire for one of them to murder the other is reasonable."

I thought about that for a second. "Well, they met through Darrin, I guess. I think." I cocked my head. "Right? Darrin and Melanie worked together, and Darrin and Bobby were roommates. Darrin is the common denominator."

Moira cocked her head back at me. "That's what you *think*. What if they somehow met in another time and another place?"

I threw my hands in the air. "Then they probably both would have acknowledged that when they reunited. They would have said something like 'Oh hey, I remember meeting you at such-and-such' or anything like that. They wouldn't have pretended to not know each other. Why would they do that?"

"What if Melanie somehow remembered Bobby but he didn't remember her?"

"Yet he did something so awful that she killed him for it? I've got to think that would be fairly unforgettable for him, Moira."

She shrugged. "Maybe she's unstable and he wronged her in her own warped little mind. Maybe it happened so long ago that he didn't remember."

And suddenly it all clicked into place.

CHAPTER 44

I heard myself screaming. "Doob, start typing, start typing! Oh my God!"

Doob and Moira both looked at me like I was crazed.

Doob spoke first. "Calm down, Meg. Tell me what I'm looking for."

"You just talked about doing some digging on Melanie the night I was in Los Angeles."

Doob nodded vigorously. "I did."

"Okay, get digging again, as fast as you can. I *have* to know Melanie's birthday. Whatever it takes, Doob. I have to have that date. Now!"

Doob didn't say a word and started typing like a superhuman. While he did that, I tried Darrin's cell again, but it went straight to voicemail. I left an urgent message for him to call me back and resumed pacing. Moira watched me like a tennis match.

"Why do you need her birthday, Meg?" Moira asked quietly.

I slumped back down beside her at the kitchen table. "Vic told me that his wife, Victoria, had a baby a few months after he went into prison. Victoria had to give up the baby because she couldn't support it. It was a baby girl, and we even talked about trying to find her once Vic gets out of jail. She was born in mid-September."

"What date?" Moira's voice was barely audible.

I couldn't say it out loud. I grabbed a sheet of paper and wrote down the number eighteen and retraced the curves in the number eight again and again and again.

We listened to Doob's maniacal clicking, and then it suddenly stopped. I thought that my heart would stop as well.

"Tell me," I said evenly.

"September 18th."

I lifted up the sheet of paper and showed it to them.

Doob's mouth dropped open, and Moira gaped at me. Doob then picked up the picture and studied it. Melanie was on one end, Bobby on the other. Doob folded the picture in on itself vertically so the only two people we could see were Bobby and Melanie.

"If we'd known what we were looking for, that would have been a dead giveaway," Doob said softly. "They almost look like twins."

Moira looked ill. "My God, Meg. It seems you won't have to look very far to find Vic's missing daughter."

My head was roaring. "The mother died in a fire, Bobby was murdered. She's in town to kill Vic."

CHAPTER 45

I was out of my chair in the blink of an eye. "I'm going over there."

"We're going with you," Moira insisted.

"No fucking way," I said adamantly. "I don't need anything happening to either of you. Plus, I need someone here to hold down the fort in case I need help. You two will do me more good here."

"Yeah, right," Doob said sarcastically.

"This is not up for debate, guys." The adrenaline was kicking in, and my heart was racing. I ran into my bedroom and retrieved the gun from the nightstand. I shoved it in the back of my pants, hoping that Moira and Doobie wouldn't notice. When I went back into the living room, there was a mixture of worry and fear on their faces.

Moira put up her hands and did her best to slow me down. "Meagan, just take a breath and think about this for a second. If Melanie is in town to hurt, or ummm, to kill, Vic, then why would she involve Darrin? Why contact him? Why borrow his truck? She could have just come to Boston, waited for Vic to get out, and then gone back to Los Angeles, all nice and tidy. Involving Darrin would only complicate things, and she doesn't need that."

I erupted. "Moira, she's using him again! She used him to cover up Bobby's murder, and she's going to somehow use him when she kills Vic. Right now, we're the only people who have made the family connection, but Melanie doesn't know that. In her mind, the police probably won't connect her and Vic after she kills him—further, they might not even *care* if a cop-killer ends up dead in a shabby apartment somewhere. But if, by some way, something tips them off, she's setting up her alibi ahead of time."

"How?" Moira demanded.

"I don't know, but I'm going to stop her," I replied and pointed at Doob's laptop on the coffee table.

"Doob, please keep digging while I'm gone, and let me know if you come up with anything else. If you don't hear from me within an hour, please call the police and give them David's address. It's on his invoice on top of my bureau."

"And what in the world should we tell them?" Moira pleaded.

"You'll need to tell them it's an emergency." With that, I ran out the door.

When I pulled out of the parking garage, it was chaos. The drop in temperature had changed the predicted buckets of rain into a full-on blizzard. I began driving, rather sliding, through the snowy streets of Boston while simultaneously fumbling with my cell phone. I jammed the earpiece so hard into my ear that I yelped. I dialed David and Darrin's apartment and prayed that someone would pick up.

"C'mon c'mon, c'mon!" I shouted into the phone. I waited impatiently to hear a voice on the other end, but instead I heard more little chirping noises, announcing that the cell battery was almost dead. I'd never gotten around to buying a charger for my car, so it was only a matter of seconds before it would be useless.

The answering machine picked up after about eight rings, and I screamed in frustration. I then dialed David's cell phone but was greeted with his outgoing message. After he'd stomped out of the apartment the other day, he probably didn't want to talk with me.

In desperation, I dialed Darrin's cell phone one last time. I nearly drove off the road when it was answered.

"Hello?" Darrin's voice sounded weird—kind of muffled—but I didn't have time to digest that just then.

I spoke as quickly as I ever have in my life. "Darrin, thank God! I got your message, and we have to get together. Now! Melanie has been behind all of this, and she's fucking crazy. If she's there, get the hell away from her, and tell me where we can meet."

Silence.

"Darrin? Darrin?!"

"Hi Meagan." Melanie's voice made my skin crawl.

"Put Darrin back on the phone right now." I tried to keep my voice level, but I could hear it shaking.

"Darrin was never on the phone, Meagan. That was me. Shouldn't a hot shit detective like you be a little more careful about who you're speaking with?"

Shit, fuck, damn! Darrin's voice had sounded weird because it wasn't Darrin at all. "Where is he?!" I demanded.

"Meagan, my feelings are very hurt. You and Darrin should have left well enough alone. But you've both gone and upset me."

I exploded. "You crazy bitch! Where is Darrin? I'm calling the police right now!"

"If you do, I'll disappear, and you'll never see Darrin again. I promise you that." The calm in her voice gave me goose bumps. Then she was gone.

I looked down at my lifeless phone and screamed some more while banging my hands on the steering wheel. Then I had a sickening thought and hoped that the dead battery was the only reason that Melanie and I had been cutoff. God only knew what she was doing right now.

CHAPTER 46

I double parked in front of David and Darrin's building and sprinted as best I could up the slippery, snowy steps. Rather than wait for the elevator, I took the stairs the four levels up to the apartment. I was totally out of breath by the time I arrived at their door.

I didn't bother knocking but went right for the doorknob. To my surprise, it opened. I pulled the gun out from the back of my pants and lightly kicked the door open, pointing the gun into the apartment with both hands. I stayed in the building hallway and poked my head inside the front room, hoping I wouldn't be trigger-happy if David or Darrin walked out. However, it was quiet and seemed uninhabited, and I breathed a little easier, thinking that Melanie might be gone. Maybe she'd assumed I'd called the cops.

Out of nowhere I felt something cold and hard at the back of my neck and instantly froze. Without having to see it, I knew that it was a gun. Then someone had a fistful of my hair and guided me firmly into the apartment. The pressure on my head hurt like hell, but I remained quiet. I didn't want to scream and be rewarded with a bullet to my spine. The door slamming behind me sounded louder than it should have, as all of my senses were on full alert. It was understandable why cops work with partners. Unfortunately, no one was with me, and there were definitely no eyes in the back of my head.

"Drop the gun, Meagan."

I debated it for a moment. The gun was my lifeline, but she had the upper hand. I dropped the gun to the floor and watched Melanie move from behind me to kick it under the sofa. Then she leveled her own gun at me.

"It's nice to see you, Meagan, although you're looking a little pale. Would you like something to drink?" Melanie smirked as I glared at her.

"Where's Darrin?" My stomach was doing flip flops, but thankfully my voice sounded strong.

"He's unavailable."

"Where is he?"

"All in good time, Meagan. You'll be together soon."

"Where is he?!"

She held out her free hand. "Give me your phone."

I noticed something about her. "Where's your cast?"

"I'm all healed, thanks for your concern. Give me your phone. Now!"

"I don't have it," I replied. There was no reason to lie, since the battery was dead, but I didn't want to give it up.

She took a step closer and pointed the gun directly at my face. "It's in your front right pocket, Meagan. Give me the fucking phone. Slowly."

I did as told and handed it over. I was devastated to see it go, despite the fact that it was useless. She walked a few steps over to David's gas fireplace. Then she flipped the light switch on the side of the mantle, and a tidy fire popped up. I watched in what seemed to be slow motion as Melanie tossed my phone into the fireplace. It sparked a little and then started to melt. A disgusting smell instantly filled the air.

"You bitch!" I shouted reflexively.

"We're going for a little ride, Meagan, so let's head down to the garage. If you make one peep or make a run for it or have any other foolish ideas, Darrin is as good as dead. I promise you that. Now move."

"Are you out of your fucking mind?" I gaped at her.

She looked up at the ceiling and pursed her lips. She seemed to be seriously pondering my question. "Yep," she said airily. "Let's go."

CHAPTER 47

Melanie and I took the elevator down to the parking garage and didn't see a single person. Not that it mattered. I didn't know if I'd have the courage to scream for help even if we did run into someone. I was too worried about Darrin's fate to call Melanie's bluff, and sadly, I didn't see any security cameras.

I heard a car chirp and saw that Melanie had the keys to Darrin's truck in her hand. He'd only had it for a week, and David had graciously given up his one parking spot for Darrin's new Chevrolet. I also noticed that there were puddles around it. Someone had driven it recently.

"Why do you have Darrin's keys? Where is he? How in the hell do you think you're going to get away with this?" My mouth was running as fast as my brain was coming up with the questions.

"And what exactly do you think I'm trying to get away with, Meagan?"

Good question. "Where are we going?"

She handed me the keys and made me get in on the passenger's side so she could keep the gun on me. "Just move over and drive, Meagan, and keep your fucking mouth shut. You're giving me a headache, and I can be *extremely* cranky when I have a headache."

I thought about smashing her face into the dashboard. But two things kept me from doing that. Number one was the weapon leveled at me, and I noticed that Melanie's gun-hand wasn't shaking in the slightest. The gun seemed to be a natural appendage. Her other hand was bouncing up and down on her leg, and her nails were chewed to the nub.

The second thing that kept me from trying to beat Melanie senseless was because it was going to get me nowhere closer to finding Darrin. Assuming he was amongst the living. I had to play by her rules for the time being, but I didn't have to like it.

"So would you like me to just drive around aimlessly in the blizzard, or do we have a destination?" I wondered what I could run into that might disable the truck, but again, that wouldn't do Darrin any good.

Melanie sighed loudly, as if I was trying her patience. She played with the GPS for a second and told me to drive. Since the address was already programmed, I surmised that's where she'd taken Darrin. And then she must have driven his truck back to the apartment. Why? To wait for me? And where was David?

I looked at the navigation system as we pulled out of the underground parking garage. "This just tells me the next street to turn on. I'd like to know where exactly we're going," I persisted. Because I hoped to somehow get help to the same locale, but God knew how.

She rolled her eyes to glance over at me. "I'm sure you would, Meagan. Shut the fuck up and drive."

Okey dokey bitch. I noticed the navigation system showed us arriving at the mystery destination in about thirty minutes. Given the snowstorm, that would translate into approximately two hundred hours.

I inched my way into traffic and started to move at a snail's pace through the snowy streets. Evidently the whole city of Boston had decided to leave work early because the criss-crossed streets were jammed with cars. Horns were honking and gloved middle fingers were in abundance. Normally I would be of the same ilk, but these circumstances were different. How in the hell could I contact the police or Doob or Moira? Or Norman? Fine time to take a vacation, Boss.

My car was still double parked in front of David's apartment building, and it would undoubtedly be towed, but that didn't help. It's not like the tow truck driver would diligently try to find me. Plus, with the weather, it would be forever before they got to my car anyway.

Doob and Moira wouldn't have called the police yet, and even when they did, they'd direct the cops to David's apartment. Hopefully someone had noticed Darrin's truck leaving the building with two women in it. But this was Boston. People tended to mind their own business, especially when a nor'easter was in progress.

I noticed that Darrin's truck was equipped with OnStar. If I could just push the blue button above the rearview mirror, an OnStar operator's voice would fill the vehicle and ask how they could help. What would I say? And again, for the umpteenth time, if Melanie shot me and made a break for it, how would that help Darrin?

I decided to try to engage Melanie and see if I could get anything out of her. "Melanie, why are you doing all of this?"

"Did you *not hear me* when I told you to shut your mouth? Fuck!" She was pissed, and I wasn't sure if I was glad or worried. I didn't really feel scared, but that probably had a lot to do with the fact that we were out-and-about. When the environment changed, my attitude would probably change right along with it. Therefore, I decided to go for broke.

"I'm aware that you don't want to listen to me, Melanie, but I just have to know. Why are you hell-bent on killing your biological family?"

I shot a quick glance her way and saw her whole body shudder. She stared straight ahead, and I could see her jaw and neck muscles clench.

She spoke menacingly. "You think you're pretty fucking smart, don't you Meagan?"

I ignored the question. "When we met in California, you told me you had a brother who had died. That was Bobby?"

"Yep," she said simply.

Wow. Okay. There it was.

Melanie starting shaking her head violently, in a way that made me feel like she was hearing voices, and then she abruptly stopped. "To people like you, Meagan, I'm sure that Bobby and mommy dearest seemed to be just the typical white trash single-mother, loser-son combination. But families aren't always what they appear."

She paused, and I didn't fill the silence.

"Did you know that their names were Vic and Victoria? Cute, eh?"

"I knew that, yes."

"Did you know that dear old Vic went to prison when Bobby was a kid?"

"Yes. Melanie, your mom was faced with a terrible situation. She tried to do the right thing," I said softly.

Her face turned purple, and she started screaming at the top of her lungs. "The right fucking thing?! Vic went to prison, and Victoria found out she was preggers with me and gave me to the fucking wolves! She didn't want another mouth to feed, so I was cast off, given away, and Prince Bobby got to stay. Is that your definition of doing the right thing, Meagan?" She'd been screaming so loud that she started coughing. I thought about lunging for the gun, but I chickened out.

I waited for her coughing fit to subside. "Melanie, what did you mean by *she gave you away*?"

Melanie waved her free hand around. "Adoption, if that's what you want to call it. But Mommy didn't go through the most reputable place. It wasn't even an agency. Things were a lot looser back then. She got a thousand dollars for me. How's that grab you, Meagan?"

"So who took you? Where'd you go?"

"I ended up in bumfuck Arkansas. I was there for those precious formative years until my adopted parents died."

"How?"

"Murder, suicide." She said it as flippantly as if she was discussing the snowstorm.

"What happened?"

"My adopted mother was fucking nuts. She shot my adopted father in the head and then put the gun in her mouth and pulled the trigger. I watched it all from under the kitchen table. Six years old."

The empathetic side of me wanted to say I was sorry to hear it, but the words wouldn't come out. I could tell that she noticed my internal struggle because she smirked. Then she leaned in towards me and spoke softly.

"It's too bad that Victoria gave me away. Did you know she died in an *accidental* house fire in Florida?" Then she smiled broadly, looking like a proud cat who'd just brought a mouse home.

My stomach lurched as she confirmed what I'd already suspected. "You wouldn't know anything about that, would you?"

She shrugged a shoulder and her smile widened. "I might know a thing or two," she replied coyly. "I know she had ten one-hundred dollar bills rolled up and shoved in her mouth before she died. The doc checking the dental records probably didn't catch that. Money well spent, in my opinion."

"One thousand dollars," I said softly. "Bobby had the same amount in his mouth."

She stared at me, and since we were still sitting in traffic, I stared back. I could feel the heat in my face and knew my Irish skin was giving me away. Was she really this screwed up? Did she set her mother's house on fire? And then found Bobby and killed him as well? Her whole miserable, waste-of-a-life had been focused on killing her biological family?

"Melanie, what happened to you after your parents died?"

"After my *adopted* parents died, you mean?"

Choosing not to argue semantics, I nodded my head.

"Well, several things happened. First, I was sent to live with my dear auntie on my adopted mother's side. They'd have been better off willing me to a whore house. She was a total slut and a loser. She couldn't hold down a job for more than a few months at a time. Her way of dealing with me was to ignore me, and God knows what she did with the little money she'd received from my *adopted* parents' deaths. That's probably the only reason she'd agreed to be my guardian if anything ever happened to them. People who do that never really think they'll actually have to take on a kid, you know?"

"That's probably true," I said softly.

"Anyway, I did the best I could for being six years old. I got myself up every day and made breakfast, got myself to and from school. I wore the same pair of pants all the time, and the kids at school made fun of me nonstop." She paused and studied her horrible nails on her left hand. Her lower lip curled up, and I wondered what demons were running through her head. And then she continued matter-of-factly.

"The bitch wasn't home most nights, and that was almost a relief. That is, until bedtime. That's when I'd get scared. There was always loud music and fights at the other trailers. Everyone was constantly drunk, and there were drug deals going on all the time. At about nine every night, I'd hide under my bed, hoping that no one would break in and hurt me. It was probably a lot like your childhood, right Meagan?"

She paused and was evidently waiting for a reaction. I didn't give her one, although I was working hard to fight the image of a scared little girl under her bed. I made a mental note to bear-hug my parents if I ever saw them again.

"How long did you live with your aunt?"

"Until I was thirteen."

"What happened then?"

She scoffed. "I hit puberty."

I narrowed my eyes. "Sorry?"

"God Meagan, you are so naïve. Let's just say it got to a point where my aunt's boyfriends—if that's what you'd call them—preferred to come into my bedroom over hers."

"Did she know about it?"

She rolled her eyes. "I don't know how she wouldn't. But since she was high most of the time, maybe she was passed out when they came to visit me. It's hard for me to believe that she didn't know."

"But you never told her?"

"Nope."

"What did you do?"

"I stabbed one of the guys."

As much as I was trying to not react, I felt my eyes widen.

"Did you kill him?"

"Unfortunately, no."

"So what happened?"

"Well, it was my word against his. He said he heard me crying and thought I was having a bad dream. So he supposedly came into my room to check on me. According to him, I was waiting with a knife and attacked him. He said I was crazy and jealous of his relationship with my aunt."

"What did she do?"

She spit the words out. "Not a *fucking* thing." Then she looked off into the distance, shaking her head slowly.

"So that's when you left?"

"I didn't exactly leave. I was basically carted off. Somehow I ended up being the problem and was sent to this big white fortress in the country for—what do they call it? Oh, that's right. I went to a place for *troubled girls*, where they supposedly fix you all up and get you ready for society." She sneered. "That place made my aunt's trailer look like Disneyland. Overcrowded, all different ages of crazy girls, and perverted guards."

"Sounds like you couldn't catch a break," I said lamely.

"Yeah, I really landed the fucking trifecta, what with my adopted parents, my adopted aunt, and then that nuthouse. And I owe it all to the family who abandoned me."

I could see she truly believed that. "When did you get out of there?"

"Just after my eighteenth birthday."

"And then what?"

"Well, before getting out, I had a whole lot of time to think. That tends to happen when you're locked away in the middle of fucking nowhere.

"Anyway, they did let us read some books, and I read a book called *The Count of Monte Cristo*."

"Alexandre Dumas," I said idly.

"It changed my life," she replied, almost wistfully.

"How so?"

"It gave me purpose. I loved the fact that he got revenge on all of the people who wronged him, and I decided to do the same thing."

"Meaning what?"

"Well, I came up with the idea that I would hunt down my real family and kill them."

I felt the bile rise in my throat, and again, I reminded myself to not react. "Suffice it to say the therapy at the facility didn't help much?"

Melanie's eyes lit up, and she threw back her head and laughed what appeared to be a genuine laugh. "That's rich, Meagan. The only thing that place did for me was solidify my resolve to pay my real family back for the shit that happened to me."

I shook my head at her. "Surely you can see that no one could have predicted what your life was going to be like. Your mom probably believed she was giving you a better chance than you would have had with her."

"You and the doctors can rationalize all you want, and you can make excuses for the lowlife bitch, but she was fucking wrong."

"I got that."

"And she paid for it."

I stared into eyes that had quickly changed from laughter to menace. "I got that, too."

"And you and Darrin are going to pay as well, because I'm not ever going to be locked up again." She shrugged one shoulder simply.

I ignored my galloping heartbeat and tried to keep her talking. Looking over at her, I lifted my chin at the gun. "How'd you get that thing on the airplane anyway?"

She tilted the gun a little bit, as if she needed to clarify what I was talking about. "This?"

Duh. "Yeah, that," I said flatly.

"I didn't. I drove."

I narrowed my eyes. "Hunh?"

"I drove from L.A. I traveled with too many things that the TSA folks at the airport might not have liked."

I cocked my head. "But Darrin picked you up at the airport."

Melanie rolled her eyes. "He sure did Meagan. Right after I parked my rental car in Central Parking and walked to the terminal. I came out to meet Darrin as if I'd just gotten off a plane."

I nodded. "So what besides the gun did you need to hide?"

"Darrin has a pretty good idea of my travel items."

"Is he even alive? Or are you just acting like he's alive to keep me on a leash?"

"You'll find out soon enough, Meagan, and then you'll regret wanting to know."

CHAPTER 48

I've heard the word *surreal* used when people describe certain situations they've faced, and it definitely applied to the mess I was in. I was behind the wheel of someone else's vehicle, in a blizzard, with a crazy woman holding a gun on me. Despite the fact that there were cars all around me, I had no mode of communication, and even if I did, I wouldn't use it because I'd get myself killed and would never find Darrin. That is, if he was even alive.

Because I had nothing better to do, I kept talking. "So, how do Darrin and I fit into all of this? We certainly didn't do anything wrong by you."

"But you both know what I did," she said simply.

"What exactly does Darrin know?"

"Don't be coy, Meagan, it doesn't suit you. I know he left you a message, and he jumped my shit the minute I walked through the door. He hadn't put the family ties together, but he'd figured out the rest. He knew that I wasn't in town for a funeral and said that the jig was up. He wanted to know why I'd visited Vic at the prison and why I'd posed as a reporter. And then he made the mistake of telling me that he was going to call the cops if I didn't start talking." She smirked.

"Why *did* you visit Vic?"

"Well, I wanted to see Daddy-o and find out exactly when he's getting out of the joint. Darrin was wrong when he said I wasn't in Boston for a funeral. Vic's funeral is going to be sooner rather than later. I just needed to find out his release date so I could make my plans accordingly."

I was appalled. "So we're all just expendable?" My voice came out shakier than I wanted it to, and it pissed me off.

She ignored my question and looked reflective for a moment. "You know what's weird? None of them knew me. *My own mother*? Can you imagine? Hell, I hung around Bobby a few times, and I actually sat down with Vic and had a face-to-face conversation. They all treated me like I was a stranger."

"You *were* a stranger, Melanie."

"Their own flesh and blood, their own eyes looking into theirs, and they didn't fucking know. Shame on them."

"Melanie, something tells me that you would have killed them anyway, even if they'd somehow recognized you."

"Yep," she said quickly.

"And do you honestly think that killing all of them will make up for whatever hell you went through as a kid?"

She shrugged. "Can't hurt. None of them deserved to be living the good life while I was being tortured like an animal."

I scoffed. "The good life? Your mom lost her husband to prison, had to give up a baby, and moved away from the city she grew up in. Vic has spent the last twenty-five years locked up and will never forgive himself for his crime and for breaking up his family. Bobby was diagnosed with a disease at the ripe old age of twenty-seven, saw one parent die in a fire while the other rotted in prison, and married a sweetheart of a girl who cheated on him. If that's your version of the good life, then you're even more fucking crazy than I thought."

With surprising speed, Melanie struck me in the mouth with the gun. I saw stars and tasted blood, but to my credit, I didn't make a sound. Rather, I just put my right hand to my lips in an attempt to stop the blood flow. I hoped that I wouldn't come up with a fistful of teeth when I finally removed my hand.

"Crazy is going to get the better of you, Meagan."

I glared at her and mumbled through my hand. "It's certainly easy to say that when you're the one holding the gun. It would be an interesting fight if the stakes were even."

She smirked. "You're probably right. If you'd survived today, you'd probably have a good chance of pinning Bobby's murder on me, but I doubt you'd have any luck with poor Victoria's demise."

I moved my hand away from my bloody mouth. No teeth fell out. "Why don't you give me a shot? I'm pretty sure I could place you in Florida about the time Victoria was killed." I flashed back to Moira saying that serial killers have a fascination with starting fires. That discussion seemed like weeks ago.

"Victoria was a chain smoker and half a drunk, so they concluded that she fell asleep in bed with a lit cigarette. She was charbroiled, too. They found her burnt body in the bed as if she'd never moved. She was too out of it to even try and save herself."

Between that visual and the taste of blood in my mouth, I thought I might vomit. "I hope to God she didn't feel anything," I said softly.

She ignored me. "So, the last I checked, no one suspected homicide in Victoria's death."

"You seem pretty sure of yourself, Melanie. What if you're somehow wrong about all this?"

"About all of what?"

"The fact that these people were your biological family."

"I'm not."

"You're positive?"

"Totally positive, Meagan. I was very resourceful when I got out of the funny farm. It didn't take me long to make some real money and get the help I needed to track down the people who had abandoned me."

"Make some real money? Hunh. Did you ever finish high school?"

"Not exactly."

"GED?"

"Yeah, I had to do that before they let me out of the loony bin."

I rested my elbow on the driver's door and touched my mouth with my middle finger, lightly dabbing at the blood. I recalled Brenda's spreadsheet. "So we've got a pretty girl with a GED for an education. Let me think. What career path would an eighteen-year-old girl take in order to make some real money?"

Melanie framed her face with her hands. "Vegas likes girls who look like me."

"So you went with stripping, hooking, or selling drugs?" I braced myself for another smack to the mouth, but it didn't come.

She smiled condescendingly. "You're so self-righteous, aren't you?"

"Yeah, I'm the asshole here, right? If you won't answer, I'll just assume you went with stripping."

"Wrong, Meagan. But it was actually kind of a combination of two of the three things you mentioned. I worked as a waitress at a strip joint, and sold some drugs on the side. The money was pretty steady."

"Good for you," I said dryly. "So what'd you do with it? Besides burn some of it, that is."

"I got a private dick, just like you, except he was smart. He did some snooping, and in less than a month, I knew all about my humble beginnings right here in Boston."

"And you couldn't just leave well enough alone?"

"Of course not," she snapped. She looked at me like I was the one who was crazy. "The people who did this to me needed to pay."

"So you killed them."

"Two out of three." Then she corrected herself. "Well, that's the count for family members. You and Darrin are just collateral damage. And then there was—" She shrugged. She was so matter of fact about it that it was unnerving.

I watched the snow falling down on the cars around us. Windshield wipers were doing their best but losing the battle of the elements. Every now and then, a person would jump out of his or her car to clean the excess snow off their blades. Exhaust from the vehicles made mini smoke swirls all over the road and rose up, eventually disappearing into the atmosphere. I wished I could follow them up, up and away.

A honking horn snapped me out of my reverie, and I couldn't help but smile. We'd been sitting in the same spot for twenty minutes, as had every other car around us, but someone evidently felt that honking the horn would get everyone moving. I loved this city. I wondered if I'd ever see it again.

My eyes got misty as Tom's smiling face popped into my mind, and I was saddened because his image wasn't as clear as it used to be. I wanted to see him and touch him and hold him and be wherever he was, and for a second I actually thought that killing me maybe wouldn't be the worst thing Melanie could do to me.

Despite that feeling, the urge to flee was almost overwhelming. I could have jumped out of the car and easily lost her in the traffic and snow. I didn't know if she'd chase me, but it was irrelevant. I needed to know if Darrin was okay. I needed to know if he was alive. I needed her to keep talking, and I needed to keep my head.

"Melanie, I know you're telling me all of this because you plan on killing me and skipping town. But I have plenty of people who share my suspicions of you, and they won't let this rest. Are you aware that the police have reopened Bobby's case out in Los Angeles?"

I saw the tiniest flash of worry cross her face, and then it was gone. "Yeah, I knew that."

"You're lying." I only knew that she was lying because I was lying first.

"Whatever. Who cares?"

"It won't be long before they tie you to it, Melanie."

"We'll see."

"Why don't you tell me about Jethro Hackett?"

Her left eye twitched. "Who?"

"Melanie, please. As much as you insult me, I'm not an idiot. Was Jethro the not-so-nice guy you told me about when we met? Did you two meet in Vegas and have a little spat? Did you owe him some money and somehow set him up for Bobby's murder? Two birds with one stone, and all that. You can tell me. You're going to kill me anyway."

"None of it matters, Meagan. What do you care?"

"I probably shouldn't, but I'm curious by nature. One of the things that bugs me about Bobby's murder is that the cops could never connect the dots between him and his supposed killer. And I certainly don't blame the cops for not looking into it any further. They had a dead druggie with the murder weapon in his car, case closed. But it just didn't add up."

"Seems pretty cut and dry to me."

I ignored her. "So I started doing some digging, trying to learn about this drifter named Jethro Hackett. The long and the short of it is that I know you and Jethro crossed paths at the strip joint you worked at in Vegas." I hoped Doob's speculation had been right.

She considered this for a moment and then nodded in concession. "I was running from one guy and chasing another."

"You were running from Jethro and chasing Bobby?"

"Yep. What a friggin' hick that Jethro was. He thought he was a real cowboy, but he was actually a real douche bag. Anyway, he thought I owed him some money, and I don't know how he found me, but he did, and he was pissed. He was threatening to kill me if I didn't pay up. Said I ruined his life, as if he'd had one to begin with. Fucking idiot."

"How much are we talking?"

"Ten grand."

"What happened?"

"It's a long story."

I raised my eyebrows and looked around at the snowy traffic jam. "I've got some time."

She gazed out the windshield and sighed. "Not as much as you think,

Meagan. And anyway, why do you want to know all this shit? It isn't going to change a thing, and it's not going to save you."

I shrugged and tried for some false praise. "I'm a snoop. It seems like you've been at least one step ahead of a lot of people for a long time, which takes smarts. I'm curious as to how you pulled it all off."

"Seriously?" She seemed flattered.

"Absolutely. Like you said, what can I do with the information anyway?"

I think she actually blushed. "Well, I guess it wouldn't hurt to tell you." Her personality changed before my eyes as she turned in her seat to face me. She smiled slyly and seemed almost giddy, like we were two friends at a sleepover ready to tell our biggest secrets.

"Okay. Well, as you know, I was working at a strip joint in Vegas, as a *waitress*. The clothing was skimpy, fucking degrading. And Vito, the boss, was into all kinds of shit. Strippers, prostitutes, loan sharking, drugs, you name it, Vito was into it. Vito and Vegas were made for each other.

"Anyway, I was the only one who was allowed to serve Vito, and his slimy guests, drinks in his back office. He liked me because I kept my mouth shut, head down, and didn't do any drugs. Most of the time he and his buddies were all coked up out of their minds, and his fat fuck friends would always play a little grab-ass with me. I put up with it, because what the fuck else was I gonna do, and Vito appreciated that I didn't get all put-out when his scumbag friends were feeling me up. He even threw me a couple of extra bucks now and then for tolerating their bullshit. All in all, Vito wasn't too bad a guy."

"Except for the hookers, the drugs, and the loan sharking?"

She gave me a withering look. "It's easy for you to judge, you little princess. But you wouldn't last two seconds in that environment."

"I wouldn't have to."

She glowered but continued. "So anyway, I was always the one who brought Vito a drink at the end of the shift, which was usually around four in the morning. There were a few times when he'd be putting shitloads of cash into a wall-safe behind this big picture, just like outta the movies."

"What do you mean?"

"It was a narrow walk-in safe with three shelves on both sides. He had boxes of cigars in there and tons of jewelry. It also looked like a warehouse for cell phones because I swear he had twenty different kinds in there. Different passports, too, and a whole bunch of guns."

"That's a lot of stuff."

She nodded and was getting more animated by the moment. "The safe was pretty big, and the picture covering it was even bigger. The picture was of this huge fucking pear, and it was totally ridiculous.

"Anyway, one night I found out Vito went to South Beach for a long weekend. Cowboy Jethro had been at the club off-and-on for a couple months and was a total junkie. He'd hit on me every time, but I'd always told him to screw. But after hearing that Vito was out of town, I decided to be nice to Jethro that night. I'd heard he was kind of a handyman, and I'd been biding my time and wanting to get the fuck out of Vegas for a while, so I made him a deal."

"Which was what?"

"I told him I needed to get into Vito's office."

"What for?"

"Well, this one night last year, I'd taken Vito his drink, and he was by himself. He had several stacks of money on his desk, and his suit and hair were all rumpled and shit. His unlit cigar was down to a nub and was barely hanging out of his mouth. He stunk, and it looked like he'd slept in his clothes for about a week. He was totally fucking fried, and I think he'd done enough cocaine to kill an elephant.

"He told me to put his drink on the end table by the sofa and then told me to grab half the cash. I hesitated, because I didn't know what he was getting at. He laughed a little and said he wasn't worried about me skimming because I didn't have anywhere to put it. Standing there in what amounted to a bra and boy shorts, I had to agree with him, so I grabbed a bunch of the money. The stacks had rubber bands around them, and it was amazing. All I could see was hundred dollar bills. I couldn't even compute how much money I had in my arms, but my heart was pounding.

"So Vito grabbed the rest of the money and motioned me over to the fucking pear with his head. We got to the picture, and he unlatched it and was working on the combination to the safe. I made a big show of turning away from what he was doing. I didn't want to see the combination, because I didn't want to be accused of anything down the road.

"So I'm waiting for Vito to open the safe, and he's grunting and cursing, and I can hear the dial clicking around, but it wasn't opening. I assumed he was either too high or too tired to get it open, and he made some comment about his memory going to shit, so I figured he'd forgotten the combination to his own safe. Fucking moron. He suddenly put his pile of money in my arms, so I was standing there holding these stacks of hundreds like you'd hold a newborn baby. Unbelievable." Her eyes were sparkling.

"So then what?"

"Well, I was positioned at this awkward angle, because I was trying to balance all of the money, and Vito walked back over to his desk. Evidently, that was where he kept the combination to the safe. So again, I turned away so I wouldn't see where he kept the combination, but I looked right into a mirror that was directly across from the desk."

"You saw his hiding spot?"

"I sure did. He had this disgusting, filthy ashtray that he kept on his desk. I saw him lift it up and unscrew the bottom of it. It was like a little secret compartment. He took out this tiny piece of paper and stared at it for a few seconds and then went back to the safe.

"He got it open this time, took the money and thanked me. I went on my merry little way. I was probably in his office fifty times after that and never let on that I knew about his hiding spot. I just continued on like business as usual."

"But you were biding your time."

"Fucking A. That money was my ticket out. I'd been working for over five years, but it was tough to save the type of coin I needed in order to travel around and not work for a while."

The fact that she'd planned out approximately how much money she would need to track down and kill her family made me shudder. "How much are we talking?"

"I didn't need it all. I wasn't that stupid. I just wanted enough to get out of Vegas and track down Victoria and Bobby. I figured Vito wouldn't notice if I took a hundred grand, maybe a little more."

"So when you heard he was gone for a few days, you decided to act quickly?"

"Yep, I would have rather handled things myself, but I didn't know how to pick a lock, and I thought Jethro would probably split if I promised him some money."

"So what happened when you approached him?"

"I told him I'd give him ten thousand just for getting me inside, and he agreed to do it."

"So then what?"

"Towards the end of the night, I snuck Jethro back to Vito's office. I stood watch, and it took him less than a minute to get the door open. I told him to go back out and watch the girls just like any other night. I was going to slip him a note when I delivered his next drink as to where we'd do the handoff."

What she'd previously said about her bra and boy shorts made me wonder. "How were you going to get the money out of there?"

"I'd thought of that. A few months prior, I'd started bringing a gym bag to work and pretending that I'd been to the gym before starting my shift. Sometimes I actually went. But that night, I'd brought an empty bag, and that's where I was going to put the money."

"Sounds like you'd been thinking ahead."

She narrowed her eyes. "No shit."

"But it didn't go according to plan?"

"Fucking understatement of the year. After Jethro got the door open, I sent him back to the entertainment area and locked the office door behind me. There was a nightlight in the office, so I didn't even need my flashlight at first. I ran to the ashtray, read the combination to the safe, unlatched the fucking pear picture and managed to get the safe open. It was the second time I'd stood there with my heart nearly pounding out of my chest.

"I then used my little flashlight and was trying to figure out how to take some of the money without it being obvious. I grabbed a stack and fingered through it, and it was all hundred dollar bills. I figured they were bundled in piles of about fifty thousand dollars."

"How many bundles?"

"At least forty. So if my guess was right, it was about two million dollars."

"Were you just going to grab a couple stacks or what?"

"Yep, I'd decided I was going to take two bundles towards the back of the safe. It wasn't wide at all; it was narrow and long, so my hope was that Vito wouldn't notice the missing stacks at the back until sometime well after I'd flown the coop."

"You hoped he *wouldn't notice* that he was missing one-hundred thousand dollars?" I was incredulous.

She rolled her eyes. "He was a friggin' cokehead, and he was out of town. Those two things were in my favor.

"So I was literally standing in the back of the safe when I heard muffled voices and a giggle outside the door. I almost shit myself. I jumped out, shut the safe, and I tried to put the fucking pear picture back in place, but it didn't latch. I then heard what sounded like keys jingling outside the office door. I ran and hid behind this six-foot decorative screen just as the door was unlocked. I assumed that the pear picture would fly open and that I would be discovered."

She took a deep breath and looked a little reflective. I prompted her to keep talking. "But obviously that didn't happen."

"No. As it turned out, one of the bouncers was treating Vito's office like a little love shack while the boss was gone. One of the strippers and him were all over each other, but thankfully they hadn't turned on the lights. I stayed low and had to endure the sounds of their frivolity from my hiding place. I even took a peek or two from the crack in the screen, but it was nothing worth watching. And the pear picture hadn't betrayed me, which was amazing with everything that was flying around.

"Anyway, I figured I could just wait them out, but this guy was quite a performer, and it was about forty-five minutes before things came to a climax, so to speak."

"Probably the steroids."

"What?"

"Never mind. Then what?"

"In the meantime, I had calmed down to some degree but was worried that Jethro would be getting antsy. As it turned out, I was right.

"After the whole production, the butt-naked Romeo was picking up his clothes off the floor, and in walked fucking Jethro like he owned the place. Romeo and Jethro made eye contact, and Jethro hauled ass, with a naked Romeo right on his tail. The stripper picked up her band-aid-sized clothing and went screaming after them.

"I was absolutely frozen and could hear the mayhem out front. I figured that it was a matter of minutes before the cops showed up, but I couldn't miss my chance. The fucking pear was beckoning me. I ran to the office door, locked it, and then I ran back and opened the safe and took two of the stacks. I even checked to see if there was dust around the area where the money had been, but there wasn't any. It was a very clean safe.

"Anyway, I didn't have the gym bag on me, so I went across the hall to the dressing room and shoved the money in the bag before the cops got there."

"Didn't anyone see you?"

"I dunno, the place was crazy. There were half-naked girls running around, and everyone was trying to get the hell out of there before the cops showed up. I decided to do what I'd have done under normal circumstances, and that was to stay put. So I stuck around and kept a cool head while everyone else was flipping out."

"That was a gamble."

She shrugged. "I didn't have a choice. If I'd left right then, they would have suspected me of something. I hung around and acted like I would have on any other night."

"So what happened to Jethro?"

"Well, it turns out that Romeo beat Jethro within an inch of his life. The cops arrived, then an ambulance showed up, and Jethro was taken to the hospital. I heard that he was in critical condition but was expected to live, and I had to make sure that he kept his fucking mouth shut."

"How were you going to do that?"

"I don't know, but it turns out I didn't have to worry about it."

"Why?"

"Because the next day we found out that Jethro left the hospital and skipped town."

"So you were off the hook? Vito blamed Jethro for the whole mess?"

"Yep. Jethro had evidently gotten smart for the only two seconds of his entire hick life and disappeared before Vito found him. Vito would have sliced him up."

"Wouldn't Vito have done the same to you?"

"Probably worse," Melanie replied. "He trusted me, and I betrayed him. Shit like that doesn't go down well in his world. That's why, once I made the decision to take the money, I knew I had to leave pretty quickly."

"How did you manage that?"

"I made up a story about a sick brother and said I needed to help my mom out with him." She smirked. "Wasn't that ironic? It turned out that I wasn't lying. I did have a sick brother—he was even *terminal*. And God, was I pissed when I found out about that!"

That struck me as odd. "Pissed? Why?"

Her eyes bulged. "Think about it, Meagan! I'd planned my entire life around killing these people, and then I found out that Bobby might die before I could get to him. Can you imagine? I would have been bullshit if he'd died before I could kill him!"

She was acting as if a department store coupon of hers had almost expired before she'd had the chance to use it. I was speechless, and she babbled on.

"But thankfully, I made my way to Bobby before he up and died on me."

"And Vito bought the story about your sick brother?"

"Of course. People are in and out of that business all the time. The dumb fuck even gave me a few bucks for bus fare. Of course, he thought I was going to Memphis. I certainly wasn't going to let him know where I was really going, in case he ever realized that he was missing some money."

"See, that puzzles me. Didn't Vito check his safe the minute that he found out about Jethro, Lover Boy, and the stripper?"

"Of course he did. I was even with him when he checked it."

"And?"

"And, like I've told you fifty times, he's a cokehead. He opened the safe, looked around, pulled out a few stacks of money, checked for his cheesy gold jewelry, poked around at his cell phones and guns and then shut the safe. He even said, 'It's all here.'"

"What a dumbass," I muttered.

"Exactly. The idiot probably didn't know if he had forty stacks in there or four hundred. He was always high. And quite frankly, if he ever did figure it out, what was he gonna do? Call the cops and say that some of his drug money was missing?"

"No, but he might have hunted down Jethro, and Jethro would have sung like a canary. Then Vito would have come after you."

"Well, Jethro isn't exactly going to be spilling the beans now."

"So you killed him too?"

She completely ignored the question. "You know, I'd never given Jethro a second thought until he showed up at my door."

I decided to roll with that. "How'd he find you?"

"I have no idea."

"What happened?"

She squinted at me. "He shoved his way inside my house and then beat the shit out of me. You didn't really think my arm was in that cast from a car accident, did you?"

I stared at her and remembered watching her try to stock the bar the first time I'd seen her. "I guess not." And then I thought for a second. "But your face was okay."

"Jesus, Meagan. Guys like Jethro don't want to raise suspicion. He just wanted to get my attention. And he certainly did."

"I guess that breaking your arm would do it."

"You think? He got me when I was alone and said he'd kill me the next time he stopped by if I didn't have the money I owed him. As if I owed him shit. We would have been home free if the moron hadn't come back to the office to check on me."

I didn't know what to say. This was not everyday conversation in my world.

"Don't look so perplexed, Meagan. It wasn't the first time I'd been beaten up. It was the first time that I'd had initials carved on me, though."

I was revolted. *"Carved on you?"*

"Yep," she said simply. "It turns out that Jethro really was a cowboy. After he busted my arm, he hogtied me like he used to do to cattle." She leaned back and pulled the left side of her jeans down a little bit. I saw what looked like a small tattoo on her left hip. I couldn't help but lean over to try to see it. It looked like there were a couple of letters there. Melanie obviously didn't like me moving in and put the gun squarely in my face, so I backed off.

"Take it easy, Melanie. I was just trying to see what you're obviously trying to show me."

"It's the letter 'U' and the letter 'O'."

"I don't get it. Why those two letters?"

"As in *YOU OWE* me. It's kind of hard to ignore a reminder like that. When he left, he said he'd be in town for a week and that I better have the fifteen grand before he left. He said he'd be back to collect it or to kill me."

"Fifteen? I thought you'd promised him ten?"

She looked at me as if I had three heads. "Call it interest, Meagan. How the fuck should I know?"

"Okay, so back up for a second. How did you get Jethro to go to Bobby's temporary place in Santa Barbara with you?"

"I told him that we were going to steal the money back from a guy who'd taken it from me. I also said that I'd need a gun that couldn't be traced. Jethro picked me up on a side road, and we drove with no lights up to the house. It wasn't easy seeing in the rain, but we made it. After taking care of Bobby, I shot Jethro up with drugs and wrote his supposed suicide note. It was as easy as that." She looked pleased.

I switched gears on her. "Did you kill Bobby's wife too?"

She looked startled for just a moment but recovered quickly. "Are you talking about Carol?"

"That's the only wife of his that I know of, yes. And I believe that her boyfriend, Glenn, turned up dead as well."

She chuckled softly. "Bobby's slut of a wife and her psycho hulk man? Another healthy relationship gone awry."

"Here's how I see it. I'm guessing that you must have met Carol when you were snooping around in Florida, right around the time you burned down Victoria's house. Obviously, Carol wouldn't have known who you were. When she came to Boston to visit Vic, looking for answers, you followed her. You somehow found out from her that Bobby was living in L.A. I'm curious as to how you did that?"

Melanie smiled slyly. "I told the greedy bitch the truth."

I cocked my head. "I'm sorry?"

"She did recognize me from Florida, and she asked what I was doing in Boston. I told her I was Bobby's long lost sister and that I wanted to help. She was so desperate to find him that we partnered up. She said she had a cop friend that might be of some use to us, but only as a last resort. That was the ape she'd been dating at the time, but she'd headed to Boston without telling him. Like I said, a real healthy relationship."

As if Melanie knew anything at all about healthy relationships. "So you got what you needed and then killed her?"

She sighed but continued. "Shortly after we arrived in L.A. last fall, Carol and I drove out into the desert one night and checked into a flea bag motel. The type where you pay cash and rent by the hour. She thought I'd contacted Bobby and that he was going to meet us there. She seemed a little leery when we pulled in, but I told her that he'd picked the spot because he was driving to Vegas and it was on the way. She was so damn gullible. We arrived well after dark, and I gave her three hundred cash to give to the clerk and told her not to use her real name. We got a room on the second floor towards the back of the motel, and no one saw me at all.

"When we got to the room, I chloroformed her, shot her up with all kinds of drugs, and she died. It's so much tidier than shooting someone, I gotta say. Then I took all of her identification and left. She was a Jane Doe lying in a morgue for a long time."

I shuddered. "And how did you get to Glenn?"

She smiled. "The ape? I also hooked him because of greed. Have you ever heard the phrase that the love of money is the root of all evil?"

"Yes, it's from the Bible."

Melanie rolled her eyes. "Figures you'd know that, you little goody-goody. There were so many assholes who wanted Bobby dead so they could get to the money. The viatical guy wanted him dead, Carol wanted him dead, and Glenn wanted him dead. And those fucking charities he gave money to probably wanted him dead, although they'd never admit it. They all gave me layers of alibis. I wasn't in it for the money because I didn't get a dime. I did it for revenge."

"So back to Glenn," I prompted.

"After Bobby's untimely death, his body was shipped back to Florida. From that, evidently Glenn got enough information to figure out where Bobby had been, so he headed out to L.A. He was trying to find Carol or the money, but he was striking out all over the place. The psycho was calling my home non-stop when Darrin started staying with me. I had to act all scardy-scared when, in reality, I was glad that Glenn had arrived."

"Really? Why?"

"Well, on the day I killed Carol, I found a long, sent text in her cell phone. It was a super-cheesy phone that you can buy at any convenience store. She'd probably bought it so that Glenn couldn't trace it to her. Anyway, her text was a bunch of crap to the ape about being sorry that she'd taken off and that she missed him. She'd written that she'd met up with Bobby's sister—me—and that she'd be seeing Bobby later that very night. She told him that Bobby was definitely dying and that she'd hopefully have the money soon." Melanie scoffed. "She actually was dumb enough to think that she was still the beneficiary. Anyway, she ended the text by saying that she'd be in touch."

"Did he write back?"

"Yeah, about a zillion times. And it really bothered me that she told him she'd met up with me. She hadn't given him my name, so I decided to keep an eye on her phone for a few months. Texts from Glenn showed up all the time, but I didn't respond. I didn't know how many minutes she'd purchased on her shitty phone, so I decided to just keep it until it died.

"And when the stupid ape did show up in Los Angeles, I decided that he was a little too close for comfort. So I sent him a final text from Carol's phone. I wrote '*Come Find Me*' and included the address to the morgue. He needed to understand that I wasn't to be fucked with."

"Did he go find her?" I asked quietly. He must have, which is why he hadn't asked me about Carol's whereabouts when he'd confronted me. He'd known she was dead.

"How the hell do I know what he did? I would think so," she said flippantly.

"So then what?"

"Well, I planned on killing him in L.A., but then you lured him across the fucking country, so I didn't get my chance. However, I knew he had to be dealt with because he was a loose end."

My head was spinning. "So in addition to getting to Vic, the other part of this trip to Boston was to kill Glenn?" I did some quick calculations in my head. "You must have been here for days before you did your entire arrival act at the airport."

"No shit, Meagan. Getting rid of that baboon was no easy task, but I managed. And none of it matters—I could tell you all of the sordid details about how I disposed of everyone, but you're never going to get the chance to prove it."

I didn't have a smart retort.

"You should have just left well enough alone, Meagan. You'd have probably lived to be an old woman. But do you know what I think? I think you needed to see it through because you couldn't do that for Tom."

She might as well have punched me squarely in the face and then kicked me repeatedly in the stomach and then run me over with a truck and then thrown me into a dumpster and then shoved me through a meat grinder. The car seemed to be swirling, and I couldn't breathe. I'd never had a panic attack, but I was well on my way.

I choked out the words. "Don't you say his name, you psychotic fucking bitch. You don't know anything about him."

She smiled coquettishly. "Oh, but I do, Meagan! You're not the only one who's done her homework. You don't have to save the world just because you couldn't save him."

I was again faced with the whole dilemma of hate. It was the second time this case had brought me face-to-face with that emotion. I hated her. I wanted to physically squeeze the life out of her.

Melanie waggled her finger at me and spoke in a condescending voice. "Tsk tsk, Meagan. I can see murder in your eyes. You shouldn't be thinking those thoughts when you're about to meet your maker."

I glared at her. "When I meet Him, He will welcome me with open arms. When you meet Him, He will send you straight to hell."

And then it came again, this time even quicker and stronger. The gun connected with the hairline above my temple, and the pain was instantaneous. I put my right hand over the gash, and it was full of blood when I pulled it away.

Melanie opened the glove box and fished around. She came up with a handful of napkins and shoved them at me. "Hold these to your empty head, Meagan. You're going to bleed everywhere. And pay attention to where the fuck you're going. You're turning in less than half a mile."

I turned my blinker on and inched over into the left lane, enduring several horns in the process. I had my left hand on the wheel as my right hand pressed the napkins to my bloody head.

Melanie and I seemed to have exhausted our conversation for the time being, and I tried to ignore the light-headedness I was feeling. I had to focus on finding Darrin, even though that might mean the end for both of us.

CHAPTER 49

After turning off the main thoroughfare, I missed the bright city lights. The GPS indicated that we were only ten minutes away, and I was trying to figure out if I'd ever been in this section of the city. I didn't think so, but with the darkness and snow, I wasn't sure. Street lanterns were few and far between, and the ones in existence seemed to be mostly of the non-working variety. It was evident that the tax base in this area didn't match Cambridge or Newton or the other surrounding suburbs.

Melanie and I arrived at our destination in silence, and I gaped at the house as I crawled to a stop in the street. Could this be the right address? From the little that I could see, the house looked to be totally abandoned, as did many of the surrounding dwellings. There were no lights coming from any of them, and it looked like we were in the middle of a mile or so of crack houses, likely filled with homeless people.

Melanie's singsong voice broke the silence. "Honey, we're home." I could just barely see her sardonic smile.

"What are you talking about?" With my woozy head, I wondered if I was hearing things.

She scolded me in a playful tone. "Why Meagan, mind your manners! It isn't everyday that I get to bring someone home, where it all began."

I shook my pounding head slowly and realized that this must have been where Vic, Victoria, and Bobby had lived. It's where Melanie would have resided if she hadn't been given up.

"Melanie, just looking at this place should make you realize that your mother was only trying to give you a better life than she could have provided. This is a shithole, and it probably wasn't much better twenty-some years ago. She tried to do the right thing."

"And that's exactly what I'm doing, too, Meagan. Right and wrong

315

are very subjective, don't you think? Now pull in the driveway and get the fuck out of the truck." Her face had turned hard, all playfulness gone, and her right leg was bouncing up and down in a nervous jitter.

"Is Darrin in there?" I asked as I parked the vehicle.

"Go in and find out for yourself."

"How did you get him here? He wouldn't have come willingly. Did you hold a gun on him, too?"

Her evil smile broadened. "I didn't have to, Meagan. I just told him that you were already here."

"*What?*"

"It was a gamble, but I guess he believed me. You evidently weren't answering your phone, so he concluded that I'd already gotten to you. He came without a peep. What a knight in shining armor," she said sarcastically.

A lump immediately formed in my throat. My lovely day at the spa had kept me from answering his call. And he came here hoping to save me.

Melanie barked at me. "Now *you* can try to be the hero, Meagan. So get out of the truck, but come out on this side," Melanie gestured towards her door. "I don't want you getting any smart ideas."

As I made my way over to the other side of the truck, I grabbed the keys with my left hand since my right hand was holding the napkins to my head. While still moving over towards the passenger side, I took a chance and reached up with my left hand and hit the little Red Cross button that was to the right of the OnStar button on the mirror. I'd thankfully never had to push the red button before, but I knew that it summoned emergency help, and I hoped that whoever came through the speaker would hear no reply and have the good sense to follow the satellite signal to the vehicle. I also prayed the storm wouldn't hold them up, because I didn't feel like time was on my side.

I quickly slammed the passenger door shut with my left hand so Melanie wouldn't hear the voice that would soon be booming through the truck. Then, taking total leave of my senses, I heaved the car keys underhanded as far as I could. It wasn't my throwing arm, but it was a pretty good toss, and the keys disappeared in the snow.

Melanie seemed nonplussed. "Really Meagan? Did you see that in a movie somewhere? And now I won't be able to get away because you've disabled the transportation? Ooohhhhhhhhh." She said it like she was pretend-frightened of a ghost. I wanted to choke the sarcasm out of her voice box.

Melanie and I trudged through the snow and walked up a couple of broken concrete steps through the opening where there'd once been a front door. I was afraid we might plummet right through the floorboards and hoped she'd fall first.

Suddenly there was a beam of light in front of me, and I realized that Melanie had a flashlight. We were inside and facing a staircase that led to the upper level. Several stairs were missing. To our left was a room that might have been a dining room at one time. It had a pathetic little gold chandelier that was hanging lopsided from a single wire. There were large holes in different parts of the walls, and the few remaining patches of yellowish wallpaper were ripped and faded. The windows were all broken out, and it was as cold inside the house as it was outside. The shadows cast across the floor added to the eerie feeling of the pathetic room, and I heard the scurrying of little animal feet as Melanie's flashlight perused the space.

"Victoria had quite a knack for decorating, don't you think?" Melanie's voice dripped with sarcasm.

"Where's Darrin?"

She ignored the question and shone her flashlight on a pile of what looked to be dirty clothes in the corner of the room. "Can you believe that people live here? It's disgusting."

"They're homeless, Melanie, and it's probably not disgusting to them. What did you do with them?"

I could see her smirk from the rays of the flashlight. "Let's just say I gave them a really good reason to leave."

I imagined those homeless people out in this storm and shivered. As if their lives weren't bad enough already. Then I refocused on the task at hand.

"Where's Darrin?"

"He's back making us supper, I would guess. Let's go find him."

She guided me towards the back of the house, and I felt the gun at my spine with every step. She directed me into an area that was at one time a working kitchen but now was as rundown as the previous room, and I saw a lump in the corner. It seemed to be moving.

Melanie turned her flashlight on the lump, and I could see Darrin's shivering form. His eyes were shut, and his face was bloody. He had ropes around his hands and ankles, and there was a gag in his mouth. Melanie seemed to have read straight from the how-to-tie-up-a-person-handbook because the bindings looked strong. I also noticed he didn't have shoes on and wondered about that. Maybe she thought he wouldn't escape out into the snow with no shoes. Yeah, right. He would have left if he'd been butt naked, I was sure of it.

"Go over in the corner by him, Meagan." Melanie's voice was menacing.

"No." My voice sounded much stronger than it felt.

I'd resisted the initial urge to rush over to Darrin. I knew that if I did, she'd have a clear shot at both of us and then be home free. She'd find the keys and ride off in his truck, and God knows when we'd be found. I wasn't going to make it easy for her, that was for damn sure.

She was a few feet away from me and put the gun directly in my face. She pointed the flashlight at me, and stars exploded in front of my already pounding head. I couldn't see her at all, but I felt her studying my expression. I hoped I wasn't showing any fear.

"Meagan, move the fuck over by him," she repeated, much more softly than before.

"No!" I repeated, my voice even louder than before.

She then swung her flashlight and gun towards Darrin. "Last chance, Meagan."

The lump moved, and I jumped when I heard Darrin trying to speak. Melanie reacted in an instant. She placed the flashlight on the semi-caved in countertop so that it was shining brightly in Darrin's face, and then she violently pulled the gag from his mouth.

His voice was hoarse as he choked the words out. "Take it easy, Melanie, just take it easy. What the hell is going on? What did Meagan do to deserve this?" He had one eye barely open and still seemed completely out of it.

I felt my eyes mist, and I willed myself not to cry. Despite the horrible situation and the blood oozing out of my head, hearing Darrin ask about my welfare made me realize that he was about as good and unselfish as a person could be. And I didn't know if I'd get the chance to tell him how sorry I was and how wrong I'd been for suspecting him. I wasn't as scared as I was sad. Sad that I'd missed so many opportunities to tell wonderful people how I felt about them. If I made it through this nightmare, I vowed to seize every opportunity to make my loved ones feel appreciated.

Melanie smirked and then pointed the gun at his head. With her free hand, she pulled something out of her pocket and jammed it into his neck.

"There you go, hero. I don't need you awake just yet. I'm going to get Meagan all snuggled up by you, and then you'll both go to sleep forever."

So she'd shot him up. She probably didn't want both of us coherent and working against her, even if she was the one holding the gun. He was drugged, I was bleeding from a head wound, and she had the weapon. Real fair fight. But I'd known for a long time that life wasn't fair.

With Melanie's attention momentarily on Darrin, I made a decision. If I stayed and joined him in the corner, we both died. My head was woozy from blood loss, and if I went for the gun in the dark, we again, both died. I thought my best chance would be to bolt for the front door and entice her to chase me. I knew where to find Darrin now, and I decided that he'd probably be better off if I lured Melanie away from him. I couldn't help but feel like I was abandoning him, but I didn't know what else to do. I thought I'd have an advantage over her for just the tiniest fraction of a second. She wouldn't be expecting me to run.

I charged like a horse from the starting gate and darted towards the front of the house. While running, I was also zigging and zagging and tensing up for the bullet that was sure to tear into me.

I raced out the rickety front door opening and was running like an Olympian when I heard it. The gunshot. But I didn't feel it. *How did I not feel it?* Because I wasn't hit. *Had she missed me in the dark?* She hadn't missed. *She hadn't chased me.*

The gunshot had come from inside the house. She wanted me to wonder if she'd shot Darrin so I'd have to go back. My God.

It took everything in me to go back through that broken down front door. I was crouched low, anticipating the flashlight beam or yet another gunshot. Instead of going to the left through the decrepit dining room, I went to the right and circled around to the kitchen from a different direction. I was hoping to catch Melanie off guard. Everything was quiet.

My eyes adjusted to the dark as I worked my way back to the kitchen. All I could see when I got there was that same lump in the corner. I still couldn't make myself go near him, as I thought that Melanie would spring out and kill us both.

Suddenly I heard another gunshot, but this time it was outside. What in the hell was going on? Who was Melanie shooting outside, and why would she leave without finishing me off? That's when I noticed the open back door off the kitchen.

I rushed over to Darrin and grabbed him by the shoulders. His head lopped over to the side like a rag doll. I prayed it was because of the drugs. I grabbed his torso and immediately felt the warm wetness from his chest. I'd miscalculated. Melanie hadn't chased me. She'd shot Darrin. And she was most definitely gone.

Bordering on hysteria, I ran outside and pulled at the doors of Darrin's truck in vain. I didn't have time to search for the keys, so I wound up my arm and used my elbow to pound on the driver's side window again and again. The window finally broke, along with my arm. With my good hand, I pushed both the OnStar and Red Cross buttons and frantically screamed for people to come help me.

While screaming, I saw a body lying a few feet from the truck. Was it Melanie? I jumped out to get a closer look and saw a woman in tattered clothes with a dark stain on her chest. She'd been shot, and I staggered to kneel down beside her. That's when the spinning began, the world started closing in, and everything went black.

CHAPTER 50
TUESDAY, MARCH 25TH-THURSDAY, MARCH 27TH

The following three days were a blur of police questioning, a brief hospital visit to fix my various ailments, and a whole lot of pampering-while-simultaneously-scolding from my family and Doob. By Thursday, it seemed fitting that it was pouring rain. I wouldn't have expected anything different for the night of Darrin's wake.

I arrived at the funeral home with an incredibly heavy heart. The receiving line was long, and I felt as if I stuck out like a sore thumb. My arm was in a cast, I had a fat lip, and I had fifteen stitches at my hairline. I noticed several people in line glance at me and then whisper to their companion. Despite the discomfort of the situation, I wanted to be in that line more than anywhere on earth. I simply had to pay my respects and say goodbye to this man who I'd let down so severely. I'd come by myself because I didn't want any comfort. I didn't want anyone telling me it was going to be okay, because it simply wasn't.

I dreaded the moment I would come face-to-face with Darrin's family. Once my turn arrived, I could barely make eye contact with David. His eyes were full of tears, and his pain was palpable. Words completely escaped me. I knew there was absolutely nothing I could say to ease his sorrow or feelings of guilt. I simply hugged him with my good arm, and he squeezed me back. It seemed like we held each other for an eternity, and I cried for his loss and for what might have been.

Darrin's mother was quietly sobbing beside David, and I knew I had to face her. It felt like there were a ton of bricks weighing my head down, but I forced myself to look at her. She grabbed my free hand as tears ran down her face.

"David told me who you are, Meagan. Are you all right?"

I barked out a huge sob. Here was this woman who'd gone through the worst agony anyone could endure, and she was asking about my well being. With my good arm, I hugged her hard and managed to whisper that I was so sorry. She then cupped my face with both hands and nodded sadly. Tears were streaming down both of our faces, and I thought I would physically explode with grief.

I don't remember going through the rest of the receiving line, and before I knew it, I'd rushed out of the funeral home and into the thunderstorm. I looked up to the sky and allowed the rain to pelt my face, hair, and clothes. I stood there for several minutes as the raindrops soaked me to the bone. If only it could somehow wash away my sorrow, my guilt, and grant me absolution.

As I stood there with my face lifted towards the heavens, getting wetter by the second, I felt a tap on my shoulder. The rain seemed to dissipate a little bit, and I lowered my head to see Gina Giovanni standing beside me with an umbrella over us.

I stared at her, not knowing what to do. I expected her to belt me with her purse, and I would have taken it without putting up a fight. Nothing could have made me feel any worse at that point.

She had to shout to be heard over the rain, and I braced myself for a verbal tirade. "Meagan, come on, I'll walk you to your car!"

I narrowed my eyes and briefly wondered if one of us had been struck by lightning. She smiled tightly. Then she put her arm through mine and turned me towards the parking lot.

I pointed towards the direction of my car, and we walked through puddles while she did a good job of keeping the umbrella over both of us. I opened my car door and slid in behind the steering wheel. She shut the door behind me and was gone before I had time to thank her.

My wet clothes soaked into the seat of my car, and I didn't care. I couldn't move and didn't trust myself to drive. I wasn't supposed to be driving with just one arm anyway. My chin fell down into my chest, and I sobbed. I made sounds that came from deep down in my gut, primal sounds like a wounded animal. My body shook, and my head ached. I wanted to crawl in a hole until the pain went away.

I finally rested my head on the steering wheel, and I couldn't help but revisit the pain of Tom's death. I would have given anything for a rewind button on life. I would have given anything to be with him that final night. And since that wasn't possible, I would have given anything for a fast-forward button for my life. I'd simply wanted to get past the ache. I'd tried bargaining with God, wanting to just feel nothing. It didn't work then, and it wasn't going to work now. Life didn't have rewind or fast-forward buttons. It simply was. I just wasn't sure if I could deal with it. With Tom, I wasn't there with him. With Darrin, I was there and it hadn't done a damn bit of good.

My purse vibrated, and I reached into it to retrieve the new cell phone that Moira had picked up for me. I was obviously acting on autopilot, because I wasn't in the mood to speak with anyone. Doob's number appeared on my screen, and I clicked the button to answer. But I couldn't speak.

"Meg? Meg, are you there?"

I sobbed loudly.

"Where are you, Meg?"

I still couldn't find my voice. Doob would have to telepathically figure out where I was.

"Are you at the funeral home? Press a button once if you are. Press a button twice if you're somewhere else."

I pressed the pound button once, and Doob responded immediately.

"Meg, I am on my way. Do NOT drive, and do not go anywhere. I will be there in about fifteen or twenty minutes."

I smiled sadly because Doobie was at least twenty-five minutes away, especially in this rain. I shut my eyes and must have dozed off. True to his word, Doob was knocking on the driver's side window twenty minutes later. As I got out of the car to go around to the passenger's side, I watched the cab that Doob had arrived in pull away. My little Iowa friend had come to take me home.

CHAPTER 51
JULY

Three and a half months later, Boston was in the midst of a record setting heat wave, and the Sox were three games up in the division going into the All Star game. Since I bury my head in work when I'm depressed, my business was picking up at a nice little pace, and I was learning new tricks of the trade every day. I'd had some interesting cases during the months of April, May, and June, and July was promising to have another interesting caper for me. Staying busy at work seemed to be a good way of keeping the guilt from burning a hole through my heart. I was doing my best to keep up the facade, but it wasn't very convincing. I'd lost weight, and not in the good way. Pop kept telling me that I'd lost even more sparkle in my eyes, which I hadn't known possible after Tom's death. Norman and I now had two open cases that I wasn't sure would ever be closed. The first was Tom's murder, and the second was finding Melanie. While there was no paying client in either case, Norman understood my need to keep both cases open. It had to be that way for my fragile psyche.

During the weeks following Darrin's murder, I'd worked closely with the police to follow Melanie's tracks from before, and immediately after, her stay in Boston, in attempt to determine her current whereabouts. After verifying with the rental company that Melanie had rented a car back in L.A., we confirmed that she'd driven to Boston. As she'd told me, she pretended to fly here and had parked the vehicle in the parking garage at Logan to complete the ruse. The timeframe confirmed that she could have easily been in Boston when Glenn was killed.

After speaking to several cab companies in the area, we found a cabbie who remembered picking Melanie up at a convenience store on the day of the storm and driving her to David and Darrin's building. The location of the convenience store was a little over a mile from the abandoned house where she'd killed Darrin, and it looked as if she'd parked her getaway/rental vehicle there after retrieving it from Central Parking. She had to have done all of that running around after tying Darrin up at the abandoned house. I'd recalled that she'd had a winter coat, hat, and boots on that day, things that she wouldn't have brought from Los Angeles. Looking back, that should have tipped me off that she had planned on doing some walking that night, but hindsight is always twenty-twenty.

She'd evidently walked to the convenience store after murdering Darrin and retrieved her car. She'd then gone back to Logan and turned in the vehicle at the rental agency. She hadn't rented another vehicle, and she hadn't booked a flight, either. Video cameras around the airport didn't identify anyone who looked like her, but she could have easily disguised herself. We considered a bus ticket, but no one recognized her picture at any of the bus terminals, and their video cameras hadn't helped, either. It seemed like we'd run into a dead end, and a couple of days went by with no communication from the police.

It was after those few days of silence that I woke up at about three o'clock in the morning and realized what she'd done. I called the detective on the case the minute that proper etiquette would allow for it the next morning, and I told him to check on rental cars or flights under the name of Melanie McBride, not Melanie Summers. He called me back within the hour to say that a Mel McBride had stayed at the airport Marriott the night of the snowstorm and had caught a flight to San Antonio, Texas, the following day. Evidently getting a credit card in the name of McBride had also been part of Melanie's master plan. Somehow no one had considered her traveling under her original family surname. Further complicating the issue was the name Mel, which could have been mistaken for a man. Once her escape route was discovered, authorities in San Antonio had tried to be of some assistance, but they'd come up empty handed.

Melanie was probably quite south of the border by this point, but I was certain that our paths would cross again someday. As unhinged as she was, the fact that Vic was still alive and well was probably eating at her twisted brain.

On the Los Angeles front, I'd also had several conversations with Officer Simonetta, and while they hadn't reopened the case, he'd agreed that Melanie was very likely the one who'd killed Bobby and then Jethro.

He said the drugging was what convinced him. Melanie wouldn't have shot Jethro in the car because it would have left too much stuff—brain matter, blood, all kinds of bodily fluid—on her. She'd simply injected him with enough cocaine to kill an elephant, made sure he was dead, and slipped away in the rain. Like she'd explained to me, she must have had a vehicle parked somewhere nearby, and Officer Simonetta said that it could have been almost anywhere, given the private location and the vegetation surrounding the home on the Santa Barbara coast. I remembered that Melanie had a rental car during that time. I'd even ridden in it on the trip to DiMicci's. Her vehicle had supposedly been in the shop because of the supposed car accident that also supposedly broke her arm. She'd fabricated everything, and I shook my head at all of her planning.

The one thing that continued to nag at me was the dead homeless woman. Given all of the attention to detail that had gone into Melanie's killing spree, why the homeless woman? The police concluded that Melanie had probably killed her to avoid being identified, but that made no sense. It was dark, Melanie was bundled up, and more importantly, I could certainly identify her, so why was I spared?

These were the things that held my attention over the summer, and I couldn't get beyond all the mistakes I'd made. Kayla had done everything from threatening me with violence to telling me to fuck off to actually attempting to be nice, but even that hadn't been able to get me out for margaritas during the past few months. I felt like I was operating under some type of sheet of ice that I couldn't quite break through, and work seemed to be the only thing that kept me trudging through each day. I have a friend who once told me that she doesn't "do guilt" but I would submit to her that she'd never been through an ordeal like mine. Plus, I was raised Catholic. Guilt's a requirement.

I hadn't been back to the coffee shop since Darrin's funeral. The thought of possibly running into David made me physically ill, and it overrode any addiction for caffeine I'd ever had. I'd discovered a little coffee house about two blocks farther than my original one, and their caramel latte concoction tasted like ass, but I somehow felt that was appropriate. I was in the midst of a self-imposed exile from fun, good coffee, good-but-bad-for-me-food, men, and even my family and friends, to some degree.

Doob had finally taken drastic measures. Last Friday, he'd told me that he needed to pick up his cousin at the Providence airport the following day, and he'd asked me to ride along. I'd never heard a word about a cousin before, but I agreed to go, more out of curiosity about Doob's family than anything else.

We left early that Saturday morning, and when we zipped past the Providence airport, I asked Doob what was up. He confessed that there was no cousin and that we were going to the beach in Narragansett, Rhode Island. He said I looked like a depressed albino and that he couldn't take me moping around anymore. This coming from Doob was a slap in the face.

I looked out the car window in a huff, not sure if I was mad or sad, but I had to admit that I was touched by Doob's concern. When I looked into the rearview mirror on the passenger side door, I spotted a sporty black Cadillac close on our tail.

"Doob?"

"Yeah?"

"Is that Moira behind us?"

"Yep." Doob turned up the radio, in a feeble attempt to block any further conversation. I reached over and turned the radio off, and Doob winced at the silence.

"And she's going to the beach with us?"

"Yep."

"Why didn't she just ride with us?"

"Because then you would have known that we weren't going to the airport, and you wouldn't have come."

Touché.

When we arrived at the beach I smiled when I saw that Moira had brought Sampson along. In addition to half of our apartment. She had blankets, a big umbrella, a huge cooler, a picnic basket, an obnoxiously out-of-date tune box, and a couple of backpacks piled high with lotions, sunscreens and what promised to be some cheesy paperbacks.

She was jumping up and down like a little kid as she approached our car. "I brought you a couple of swimsuits, Meg. You can change in the restrooms." She held out two colorful bikinis. I stared at them for a minute, and it felt like time stood still. Moira and Doob seemed to be holding their breath, wondering if I was going to go along with their ploy to cheer me up. I sighed as I grabbed the bikinis and then walked over to Moira's car to scoop up the big cooler. Then I trekked off to the ladies room in the pavilion.

After walking a little ways, I turned around and looked back at my sister and my friend. Poor Doobie was saddled down like a pack mule, and for the first time in a long time, I laughed out loud. Moira had plopped a sad little fishing hat on his head and then loaded him down. He was stumbling along with the umbrella tucked under his left arm, the tune box in his left hand, while the two overstuffed backpacks dragged him down. His right arm was stretched to maximum capacity, as Sampson was straining against the leash to take in every sight and smell of the parking lot. Moira had taken on the dire task of carrying the picnic basket, and she'd donned sunglasses that made her look like a blonde Jackie O. Moira would always look beautiful and effortless anywhere.

I found myself getting excited as I changed into my bathing suit, but then I chastised myself for feeling happy. There was simply something in me that thought I didn't deserve to have fun anymore. I promised myself that I wouldn't enjoy the day too much and then scampered out to the beach.

I panicked for a moment, not knowing which way Moira and Doob had headed, but then I saw a flash of black and white about two hundred feet to my right and watched Sampson charge into the surf. Moira clearly hadn't thought about the smell of wet dog in her Caddy for the ride home. She'd probably send Sampson home with us in the Doob-mobile.

There were about nine thousand colorful blankets surrounding the umbrella that Moira had perched in the sand, and it felt like I'd stumbled upon a Banana Republic commercial. That's when I heard a cackle of some sort and turned around.

Kayla was traipsing her way through the sand with a mini-keg disguised as a blanket under one arm, and she was getting appreciative looks from many of the men in her wake. A hot girl with a keg gets them every time. She had on a bright pink bikini, with a sheer sarong that left little to the imagination. She had a matching pink backpack on her back, and her hair was in a ponytail on top of her head. Her Ray-ban sunglasses perfectly framed her face, and she looked to be about sixteen years old. "Would someone take this fucking thing? I hate walking in sand, and my feet are ready to fall the fuck off!"

Doob jumped to her rescue and retrieved the keg. She walked over and grabbed me by the shoulders and stared at me. Then she gave me a huge hug and didn't say a word. That was about as much emotion as I'd ever get from Kayla. After that she got situated on the blanket and pulled four red plastic cups out of her backpack. "Let's get sauced!"

I smiled sadly, picturing Kayla and me on the train in our more carefree days. I missed those days but had to face the fact that they were long gone. "You're driving, Kayla, so be careful."

"None of us are driving, Miss-Stick-Up-Your-Bony-Ass," Kayla said, studying my backside. "I have my dad's timeshare for the week, and it's less than a mile walk from here. We'll stagger home or cab it, but we are *definitely* having cocktails today."

I looked accusingly at Doobie, who was looking down. I then looked at Moira who shrugged. "We're staying until tomorrow night, Meg. You can be miserable or you can allow yourself to have some fun. It's time you stop beating yourself up."

Then, in very un-Moira-like fashion, she grabbed a red cup and let Kayla fill it to the brim. She held it up high like a blonde Statue of Liberty and waited for all of us to follow suit.

"Let's everyone make a toast," Doob suggested.

"To all of these hot men!" Kayla squealed as she looked around appreciatively and made kissy faces at a few of our nearby beach mates.

"To Sampson," Doob said heartily and raised his cup high in the air. Moira looked at me and waited for me to say something.

"To family and friends," I said quietly, holding my sister's gaze.

"To living," Moira said and her expression was pleading. She had always read me like a book.

Kayla wrinkled her turned up nose and put a hand on her hip. "Living? Where the hell did that come from?"

Moira looked at her pointedly and said, "From three months of exile from life, that's where."

Kayla caught on to what Moira was getting at, and for once, she kept her mouth shut and just nodded her head in contemplation. Doob kicked around at the sand, knowing a chick moment when it presented itself.

The breeze picked up while I continued to hold Moira's gaze, and Kayla announced, "Here here! Commence cocktailing." Sampson barked in agreement, and we all took a swig of beer, each of us lost in different thoughts.

We enjoyed a great day at the beach, and everyone had a sunny glow by the end of the afternoon. Doob's color somewhat resembled a fire hydrant, and even the hat and sunscreen hadn't prevented several new freckles from sprouting on his forehead.

After a lazy walk to the timeshare, the four of us cooked lobsters that evening. We also grilled steamers, corn on the cob, and a big, juicy steak for Doobie. Ever the Midwestern boy, he would probably never acquire a taste for seafood. We did the whole beach thing again on Sunday, minus the alcohol, and headed back to Boston around six that night. For the umpteenth time in my life, I thanked God for Moira, Kayla, and my disheveled little neighbor. What I'd ever done to deserve them I'd never know.

CHAPTER 52

After the beach weekend, I hopped out of bed before six the next morning and made myself a promise to get back to normal, whatever the heck that meant. I brushed my teeth, got dressed in a tee shirt and shorts, and tied my hair into a knot on top of my head.

I tiptoed across the apartment to Moira's bedroom, a bacon-flavored doggy treat in hand. Moira was sound asleep, and Sampson was sacked out on his doggy bed, but he must have heard me because his ears perked up as he groggily looked my way. Then his nose kicked in, because he suddenly shot off his four-poster bed like a cannon, all signs of sleep vanished. He started sniffing wildly at my hand and spinning in circles. I put my finger to my lips, as if that would keep him quiet, and then lured him towards the kitchen with the bacon smell.

After giving him the treat, I filled a little canteen-dog-dish-gizmo with cold water—and okay, I threw in a few ice cubes—and strapped it on in a diagonal across my body. As Sampson and I spun our way to the front door, I grabbed his leash off the little hook, and away we went.

We hit the streets at a brisk pace and enjoyed the sights and smells of early-morning Boston. Sampson especially enjoyed the smells and was prancing around like a dog who had just won the lottery. I lost all track of time as we meandered through the brownstones with their art galleries, eclectic jewelry stores, upscale boutiques, mom and pop cafes, book stores, trendy furniture shops, and real estate offices. We stopped a few times so I could give Sampson some water out of the canteen-dog-dish-gizmo, and I marveled at how much joy I could derive from simply watching him lap up the water. He drank furiously but managed to get more on the sidewalk than in his mouth. Our walk was incredibly relaxing, and I couldn't believe that nearly two hours had passed when I finally glanced at my watch.

We got back to the apartment just before eight and found a note from Moira. She'd left for work and thanked me for taking care of Sampson. She'd written that she'd be home before six and that we should go out for dinner and watch the Sox game somewhere that evening. Sounded like a plan.

Beside her note was a stack of mail I hadn't gone through, so I started in on making some piles. One was for bills, one was for junk, one was for miscellaneous, and those were further broken down into recyclable and non-recyclable piles.

I was about halfway through the stack when I spotted the postcard. I knew who it was from even before I turned it over.

Meagan, nice play at the house that night. It was dark and snowy, and I thought the woman in the front yard was you. So I guess that you will have her __and__ Darrin on your conscience for the rest of your life. But maybe I can ease your pain by shortening that life span of yours, time will tell. I will be thinking of you and Vic nonstop until we meet again. Sleep well, Meagan, sleep well.

I read and reread the words until they blurred in my eyes. The shiny brown postcard hailed from Brownsville, Texas, but the postmark on it was from Lisbon, Portugal. I went online and pulled up a map of Texas and saw Brownsville at the very southern tip of the state, hovering just above Mexico. And Portugal was, well, far away. How she'd done it, I didn't know, but Melanie was long gone. However, I knew with certainty that our paths would cross again. Something primal in me even hoped for it.

I reached for my cell phone, scrolled down to the familiar number and pressed the send button. I smiled as the strong, familiar voice answered the phone.

"Hey Megs, how are you kiddo?" The idea of the geriatric frat house having caller ID was adorable to me for some inexplicable reason.

"I'm good Uncle Lare, how are you?"

"Doing well, the tables have been good to me lately." He then went on to tell me about his latest winning streak, and I grinned at his enthusiasm.

"Hey Lare, I need to speak with Vic if he's around."

Uncle Larry's voice became a little guarded. "Yeah, we figured you'd be calling. I'll go get him."

Figured I'd be calling? What did that mean?

While I waited, I thought again about the weird circumstances in life that bring different people together. Vic was not too keen about getting out of prison and having his insane daughter waiting to kill him, but the authorities weren't too keen on helping a cop-killer stay safe. When I told Larry the story, he said that one of the guys was having trouble making rent and that Vic could stay with them if he kept his nose clean and paid his share. I worried that the geriatric frat house would overrule Vic's arrival, given the circumstances, but the old guys rallied around him and seemed kind of excited that a whacked-out chick was trying to kill him. He was probably as safe there as he'd be anywhere.

"Hi Meagan. I got a postcard today." Ah ha, *that's* how they knew I'd be calling. Vic's voice was hoarse, and I pictured a tired man on the other end of the phone.

"I did too, Vic."

I heard him sigh. "I can't believe that something I did so long ago has hurt this many people. Talk about the sins of the fathers."

"You screwed up, Vic, but you didn't have anything to do with what Melanie's done. She's a grown woman."

There was a long pause. "Yeah, well tell that to the guy I see in the mirror every day, Meagan. I blame myself for all of it."

I didn't know how to assuage his guilt; I was lugging around enough of my own. "Vic, you're still here, and I'm still here, and as long as I have air in my lungs, I will do whatever I can to stop her. She's going to pay for all of this."

"I'm scared," he said simply. His brutal honesty tugged at my heartstrings.

"So am I, Vic."

"I don't want anyone else to get hurt."

"Larry and the guys know exactly what's up, Vic."

"So what do we do?"

"We continue living, we stay alert, and then we deal with it when she makes her move."

I heard him snicker. "We'll face our fears and all that shit?"

"Something like that," I replied, wondering if I could do it when the time came.

EPILOGUE

Today the time has come for something else entirely. It is Monday morning, and my mind is made up. But I'm basically shitting my pants because of it.

My cell phone rings, and I see Doob's number and smile.

"Hi Doob."

"I figured that you might be chickening out, and I just wanted to call and give you a pep talk."

I exhale loudly. "Well, you're absolutely right. My heart rate is about a billion beats per second right now. So I could definitely use that pep talk."

Silence.

"Doob?"

"Ummmmm. I don't actually *have* a pep talk prepared. I thought that calling would suffice."

I laugh. Ever the good-hearted Doob. "It means a lot that you called, Doob. And I won't chicken out. I need to do this."

"I know. Sampson and I are sending good vibes your way."

"Thanks."

I sigh again and look at my surroundings. I'm back at the coffee house on Boylston Street. There are a few new faces behind the counter, along with some familiar ones who welcomed me back like an old friend. It feels like it's been years since I've been here. I'm in the corner sipping my caramel concoction, and I am letting myself savor every drop. I revel in how much I've missed my addiction, and I think about how much my life has changed since last being here. However, the smells of the coffee shop and the comings and goings of busy Bostonians make me feel like I'm slowly breaking through the layer of ice that I've been under for the past few months.

I look up and feel my breath catch and my heart accelerate when a certain person with wavy black hair, deep brown eyes, and preppy, square, designer glasses with dark frames walks through the door. He looks a little tired and maybe a tad older than when I spotted him all those months ago. But he is still beautiful. David Fontana glances over at me and does a double-take. I gesture at the coffee across the table from me. He smiles slightly and heads my way. Here's hoping.

THE END

ACKNOWLEDGMENTS

I owe a debt of gratitude to the following people: Tracy Daniel, Sharon Summers, Ellen Hoctor, Mollie Maloney, Nancy Michelson, Elaine Bush, and The Shuber Family—Tony, Staci, Ali and Jack. Thanks for your friendship and encouragement throughout this process.

A heart-felt thank you goes to Long Ridge Writers Group, who introduced me to Tom Hyman, a successful novelist and wonderful mentor. Tom was the first person outside of my family to read this book, and his words of support meant the world to me.

To my other early readers, I appreciate the time you took out of your busy lives to give me your candid feedback and suggestions. The story became better because of all of you. In no particular order, I would like to thank: Deb Adams, JoAnna Hinsey, Claire Guadagno, Lee Smith, Dr. Edward Rielly, Michelle Kobayashi, and Nancy Luce. A special nod goes to Jennifer Levine, who taught me all about em dashes and who uses a green (rather than a red) pen.

Thank you to Carl Graves for a fabulous cover and professional service. Your ability to decipher my ramblings was spot-on. Along those lines, I'd like to tip my hat to Sarah Koletas for her suggestions and eye for detail. You artsy people never cease to amaze me.

Loretta, I am purposely leaving out your last name because I'm fairly certain you don't want people to know that you have actually used Febreze on your dog. Many thanks for lots of laughs and a great smelling canine.

Little Elvis does exist, although I haven't had the pleasure of meeting him yet. Kudos to Dean Chatfield for getting the kitty into a warm home.

Pleasant Valley Country Club in Sutton, Massachusetts, was the backdrop for the author picture. I appreciate John and Rachel Magill's generosity in allowing me to use such a beautiful setting.

It's incredible to have a family who's always believed in me far more than I've ever believed in myself. Anne, Mom, and Dad—I love you. And Mom, thanks for the picture of the moon that served as the corner background on the cover.

I am blessed to have my biggest fan, wonderful man, and most-vocal-marketer all-in-one in my husband, John. Thank you for your patience, sacrifice, and faith in me. You are truly an inspiration and the fastest golfer I know.

In closing, you "dog people" will completely understand this final thank you. While I'm pretty sure that he won't take the time to read this, I simply don't have the words to express my appreciation for my Springer Spaniel, and Sampson's inspiration, Phantom. He was by my side, or at my feet, for nearly every word and revision of this book, and I couldn't have done it without him.